The Final Edit

Also by Bret Kissinger

Forever Fleeting

Gone the Way of the Dodo Bird

The Final Edit
By
Bret Kissinger

This is a work of fiction. With the exception of historical figures, all names, characters, places, and incidents are either the products of the author's imagination or have been used fictitiously. Any resemblance to actual persons, living or dead, events or locales is entirely coincidental.

ISBN-13: 978-1-7361071-3-3
Book Cover Design by Damonza.com

Special Thanks

To each and every one who has read my books and provided positive feedback and encouragement.

To FBI Agent Jeffrey Heinze, for fielding many horrible and awkward questions.

To Dayna and Brandi, for providing feedback on word choice and phrasing.

To those of you who were privy to my "murder book" idea and told me I had to write it.

Madison had been chased before. But right now, she's not being chased, she's being hunted. The sharp wind pierces her skin like needles, draining her strength like a sedative. The bare branches claw at her face. The fresh snow numbs her feet as it sucks her deeper into its depths with each terrified step. Strong gusts rip the breath from her lungs and shove her backward. Even in her victory, there is defeat—the snow leaves immaculate footprints for her predator to track. Everything in this wooded labyrinth is his ally. Mother Nature has forsaken her.

Madison tries to catch her breath, but she is afforded only sips of air. Every swallow feels like shards of glass. The wind whistles a ghostly dirge. But a horrifying realization paralyzes her.

It's not the wind whistling.

It's him.

"London Bridge is falling down… falling down… falling down…"

Mingled with the violent wind, the sound becomes a cruel cacophonic keen. Her body understands the peril it is in—a gazelle being chased by a cheetah. One wrong move, one moment's hesitation, one slipup, and death follows. A myriad of chemicals spew inside her, all in the name of one thing: survival.

The whistling grows louder.

Louder.

And louder.

A whisper away.

She pleads to the black sky, hoping a bright, full moon will lead her to salvation. But the celestial goddess has abandoned her too.

"London Bridge is falling down… falling down… falling down…"

A long and winding road lies ahead, carrying with it the fragile hope of escape.

Escape.

The exhilarating prospect of utopia becomes so overwhelming that she nearly cries. It is now just ten feet away. Five. Three.

Human claws tear into her, wrenching her back into the cemetery of trees. Her screams are swallowed up by the wind's ghoulish moans.

"Madison?" A voice called out. "Madison?" Her name sounded warped as if it was coming from a speaker above her head.

Like a character in some science-fiction movie, Madison was transported instantly from the wintry Wisconsin woods to an opulent office in Chicago, sitting in a comfortable chair, being stared at like a zoo animal through the glass by an annoyed and unimpressed spectator. If there was glass to tap, he would have.

"Was it the same flashback?" Dr. Frett asked.

He knew the answer. It was one of those annoying rhetorical questions where an answer is still expected. Goosebumps crawled along her back. Coming here and reliving the utmost terrifying experience of her life was a weekly occurrence now. She spent most of the designated duration deflecting Dr. Frett's questions. Instead, she played *The Price is Right* by guessing the cost of the furniture, paintings, and upholstery in the office.

Silver-haired Dr. Frett sat across from her in a chocolate-colored Chesterfield chair. He looked normal in his chair; Madison looked like the eighth dwarf, Fidgety, in hers. Surely, making patients sit in a seat so obnoxiously large wouldn't help diminish any feelings of ineptitude a person might have. Madison didn't meet his gaze. Instead, she stared at the Newton's pendulum on his desk.

How cliché.

Dr. Frett often lectured her on finding balance. His office was designed for optimal Feng Shui. Her chair was, by far, the most comfortable chair she had ever sat in. It was like sitting on a cloud. She had googled them to see if she could afford one. Nope. Even after selling a kidney on the black market, she'd be short.

"Madison, would you care to join us?" Dr. Frett asked.

His voice—a pleasant blend of famed narrator Peter Coyote's clean diction and the gentles of Sir Ian McKellan—was one that could have captivated Madison had he been reading a phonebook. Yet, despite this, he still annoyed the shit out of her. And his therapist uniform—a sweater, slacks, and loafers—looked as though he had raided Mr. Rogers' closest.

"Sorry," Madison said with little conviction.

Speaking or silent, he got paid regardless.

"You're falling back into the same pattern," Dr. Frett said.

Another staple phrase from the psychology handbook. Pattern? He wanted to talk patterns? Plaid. Stripes. Now, *those* were patterns.

"Every time you relive the event, you struggle to communicate, and you disappear into your own thoughts. You've seen that painting enough times to have it memorized. Focus on me."

Madison brought her gaze from the watercolor painting to him. She hated the way his oval glasses displayed her reflection like a carnival mirror, drawing particular attention to the bags under her eyes, the constant redness from the fits of insomnia she was dealing with. It's not vain to wish to age gracefully. Every woman wants to look like Helen Mirren when they're 70 years old. But for Madison, that hope looked more foolish every passing year. With the straining stress, weathering worry, and avalanching anxiety, she was on pace to be one of those 40-year-olds who look 70.

"I know it's painful, but you have to confront it," Dr. Frett said. "You can't put the past behind you until you get out in front of it."

Words. Words are easy, but actions are exponentially more difficult. For Dr. Frett, these flashbacks lasted sixty minutes. When Madison left his office, Dr. Frett didn't have to think about the Man in the Mask for a whole week. But the Man in the Mask stayed with her, 24 hours a day. 7 days a week. 365 days a year. No respites. No reprieves, not even on Christmas. If she was lucky, she had dreamless nights where her mind floated in the sea of serenity. But they were few and far between.

She took a deep breath and tried to tell him about the attack with as much emotion as if she was reciting how to make unrisen bread for Passover. She pretended the words didn't hurt. It was a lie she sold, but one she never bought.

She then fell silent, studying that watercolor painting of a bowl of fruit for the umpteenth time. She could never decide on how much it cost. It was either $20 from some dollar store or over a grand and sold by a rare art dealer. Considering the cost of the chair, she was inclined to believe it was the latter.

"You're fleeing the cabin, sprinting through the woods. The road's ahead..." Dr. Frett said, feeding her lines like a theater director offstage.

She nodded. Worry manifests in physically destructive ways. Madison didn't bite her nails because she was overly aware of the billions of bacteria and germs swarming her fingers. Instead, she ground the inside of her gums until her mouth was filled with the taste of pennies.

"In these nightmares, do you make it to the road? Does the car stop? Are you saved?" Dr. Frett asked.

"No."

"What happens?"

"He takes me... again."

That memory, no matter how deep Madison had tried to bury it, never died. Its cadaverous hands broke through the fragile grave. In mediocre horror movies, characters made stupid decisions. Going to Dr. Frett was like unlocking all the doors or investigating a strange noise. She didn't feel relieved after going to him. She never left thinking *I'm glad I did that*. It was always *I'm glad that's over with*. That was part of the reason she didn't go the recommended twice a week. That and the cost. She would have a nice break from him as Dr. Frett and his husband were going on sabbatical for the next three months. He'd introduced her to a colleague, but Madison doubted she'd go. Facing the same old questions with someone new was not something she wanted to do. It took a long time for her and Dr. Frett to get on the same wavelength. Dr. Frett had prescribed an assortment of medications to help her relax and sleep. She had tried nearly every antianxiety and antidepressant drugs out there. Some didn't work at all; some worked but only for a while before she needed a higher dose. The first year after *it* had happened, she was on so many meds she sleepwalked through life—never fully awake, never fully in the moment. A pill or two shy of a chemically-induced lobotomy. She had weaned herself off them.

Madison left Dr. Frett's and picked up her groceries from Mariano's—her weekly soiree out. She tried to force herself to go for walks, though those were more prevalent in the hot summer months. Now that autumn had crept on the waves of Lake Michigan toward Chicago, and the days grew shorter, her walks lessened… to none. But odd as it was to some people—and they were sure to tell her so—the densely populated city of Chicago didn't give her anxiety. Quite the contrary, it soothed her. *It* hadn't happened in the middle of a major metropolis. No, *it* had happened on a secluded back road. Alone. With no one to hear her screams. Here, she was surrounded by thousands of people all the time.

Summer had held on longer than it had in recent years, something she was grateful for, but as September crept along, something in the depths of Lake Michigan had changed. The water temperature plummeted, and the winds along its coast turned arctic. As the dreaded date approached (Madison refused to call it "anniversary"—that word is for celebrations), the nightmares and day terrors grew more frequent. Our most disturbing and depressing memories breed in the dark and the cold, and winter is the perfect Petri dish for them.

Madison parked her white Chevy Impala on the first-level parking lot of her apartment building, Essex on the Park. The rent was criminal, but it did have its own fitness center, game room, swimming pool, spa, and yoga studio. They were all very nice or so she'd heard. But it was the location that was impossible to beat. Located on Michigan Avenue, it was within walking distance of the Shed Aquarium, Buckingham Fountain, Millennium Park, the Art Institute, and, depending on your definition of "walking distance," the John Hancock at two miles. Yet, what she loved most about Essex on the Park was her apartment on the 54th floor. At a height of 580 feet, she didn't have to worry about anyone crawling in through her window, and the chances of a break-in were next to none.

She grabbed her groceries and rushed inside the apartment complex, past the front desk, and into the elevator. It might not be her most admirable quality, but she enjoyed watching people on elevators. Most people couldn't wait to get off. They death-gripped the straps of their purse or the handle of their briefcase. They didn't blink as they watched the digital display count the floors. It was one of the few times normal people appreciated the possibility of the worst case scenario—that the power could go out, trapping them inside, or a cable could snap, plummeting them to their death. Selfish as it may be, Madison found it strangely enjoyable to see other people face that fear. But they could breathe that sigh of relief when the elevator reached its destination.

That fear never followed them when they stepped off. Madison never got off the elevator.

Never take your eyes off your surroundings.

The first rule she had learned in a self-defense class. Keys in hand, she stepped out, looking both ways as if she was about to cross an interstate on foot.

He was leaning against the wall near her apartment but straightened up when he saw her, his long fingers running through his dark wavy hair.

"5414, I have some of your mail again," he said, holding out a stack. A quick glance showed it was bills, junk credit card offers, an issue of *The Hollywood Reporter*, and a manila folder.

Madison took the stack, avoiding his eyes, concentrating instead on his black boots. "Thanks, 5114."

"I'm starting to feel like USPS should really be paying me for services rendered."

5114 was tall—not NBA tall but real-world tall. He had a laid-back manner, a constant smirk on his thin, long face, and a hairstyle that was a perfect blend of carefree yet styled. The resulting effect showed a man who didn't let a single thing bother him for more than a minute. He never struck her as someone who had been conventionally good looking. Perhaps being a tall, gangly kid with ski-sized feet and braces had led to awkward teenage years. He must have had braces. His teeth were great. But that's as far north as Madison's eyes would travel.

"I have some of yours too. Give me a minute?" she asked.

"I see how it is. I trek up here to deliver yours, but you wait for me to ask for my missing American Express bill. Classy, 5414. Classy."

Madison managed a nervous smirk, which was the extent of her physical flirting game now. She unlocked her door and stepped inside, swiftly closing it behind her before he could even take a tentative step inside. Madison locked the deadbolt, then drew a Glock from her purse like a sword from a sheath. It was a model G21 SF, matte black in color. Holding it with both hands, she checked her apartment—first, her washer and dryer to the left, then the kitchen and the living room. Next, she headed to her bedroom and the bathroom. She checked inside the closet, under her bed, and behind the shower curtain. If there was even the smallest space where a garden gnome could hide, Madison checked it.

All clear.

She breathed a sigh of relief, the kind of relief most people only experience when they wake from a bad dream or the doctor delivers great news. She set her purse down on the counter and opened the fridge, looking at it like a doctor would an x-ray. Then she noticed the stack of mail beside her purse. *Shit!* Cursing herself, she grabbed the stack addressed to 5114.

"Jeez, I thought you might have accidentally ended up in Narnia," he said.

Madison couldn't fully explain the delay, so instead muttered a generic apology.

"Don't sweat it," 5114 said.

Sweet sentiment, but "sweat it" is what she did.

He sifted through his mail. "Actually, some of these are bills. You can keep them." He held them out.

"I've got enough of my own," Madison said.

Rent and Dr. Frett was enough. Her mom often said, "Don't fret" when it came to most of life's problems—advice she was now considering in a different way.

5114 spent as much time as he could reading the envelopes addressed to him without actually opening them. He was obviously delaying.

"Name's Casper, by the way…" he said.

"I know. I get your mail."

There was rarely a day when their mail didn't get mixed up. They were both set up with auto pay, so the fear of missing a payment was non-existent. On most occasions, they could have tossed each other's mail in the garbage. She certainly could go without reading about credit card offers, insurance offers, and soul salvation.

Casper laughed. "Well, I thought if we didn't want to sound like machines, we could use our human names."

"I think you know mine. You get *my* mail," Madison said.

"Madison Monroe, yeah, but I would of preferred to learn it from you, rather than from your mail. It's less respectable, more creepy and stalkerish."

"Well, my name is still Madison Monroe."

"Alright, I'll let your sarcasm go. So, Madison. Monroe. Named after two presidents. Intentional?"

"Yeah, my mom was betrothed to a man named Hamilton, but since Hamilton was never a president, my mom left him."

He studied her face. His eyes lit up when he realized it had been a joke. "So, what's the middle name? Eisenhower?"

She laughed. A rare, genuine laugh. "No, it's Nicole. I don't really tell people that though."

"Why not?"

"Because of the initials."

Casper thought on it, then got it: M-N-M. M&M. She had been the butt of M&M jokes all her life—grade school had been particularly brutal. None of the jokes were clever and some didn't even make sense. Still, having the name Casper must have been awful in a world where ninety-five percent of people were amateur comedians. Casper and the friendly ghost were forever linked.

The conversation ended abruptly and awkwardly. She could tell he wanted to say more. Was he nervous?

"So, 5414, M&M, Madison, any plans tonight?"

Her first reaction was to laugh. Plans on a Friday night? Umm, no. The secondary and overwhelming response was fear. Going out to eat or to a movie on a Friday night were what normal people did. For people who could go outside in the dark and not be on the verge of an all-out panic attack.

"Sorry, tonight's not a good night," she said.

Please don't ask why… Please… But she expected that question, no matter how rude. But, thankfully, he didn't ask it. The rejection dimmed his jovial demeanor but only for a moment. His lips defaulted in a smirk.

"Hey, no worries. If you change your mind, I'm in apartment 5114." He cracked a wide smile.

She rolled her eyes and smirked. His smile was a home run; hers grounded out to short. "Okay, Casper Jackson."

He strutted away, then turned back toward her as he waited for the elevator. "Oh hey, I may have read your *Hollywood Reporter* while I waited for you. Great interview with Kate and Leo on page 14."

At that moment, Madison decided Casper was one of those people who didn't worry about being trapped in a metal box.

Madison stepped inside her apartment, contemplating which task to accomplish first. She wasn't overly hungry and certainly not enthralled at the idea of having to cook. Cooking required patience that she did not have. Plenty of chicken breasts had turned out black-charred crisp on the outside and lukewarm pink in the center because she cooked at too high a temperature. Knowing she would only spend thirty minutes alternately checking her fridge and cupboards, she poured a glass of Riesling and drew a bath.

She tested the water temperature with her toe, made a slight adjustment, and then stepped in. The bathroom door was left open so she could hear anything from the other rooms. Eyes closed, she let the bubbles and the hot water coax her into tranquility. This was her Friday routine—a bubble bath, a glass of wine in her right hand, and the Glock in her dominant left, resting on the tub ledge. Madison was fully aware of how psychotic it was. It was Joker territory, especially on those Fridays when she cried in the bath and the makeup ran down her face. There was a moment every Friday night when she rose from her bath, wrapped her towel around her body, wiped the mirror free from the fog, and stared at herself. A moment of clarity. *I'm not okay.* But, by the time the steam had dissipated and the water had run down the drain, she retreated back to living the lie.

She tossed a pint of Ben & Jerry's into the microwave for a few seconds to soften it up. It was already half-finished by the time she decided on which movie to watch. Madison had the benefit of being an over-thinker—*what a great trait*—so, though her eyes were trained on the screen, internally she was critiquing every word she had said to Casper. He had hinted at a desire to take her out on a date. It had been years since she had been on a date—long enough that her first thought when she heard the word date was a specific day on the calendar, and then the dry fruit. The social activity between two people was a distant third.

A movie in and a pint down, Madison had hoped to be drowsy by now. But her mind was too anxious, too crowded with thoughts. She read the time on her microwave: 10:03. However, it felt like two in the afternoon. She drank a glass of water and sorted through her mail, sending all the junk mail sliding across the counter and into the garbage bin. Then, she flipped through the magazine, reading the article about Kate and Leo that Casper had mentioned. Eventually, all that was left of her mail was the manila folder. She peeled it open and slid a sheet of paper out from within. The print was in Centaur font. Most of the books she edited were either in Garamond, Baskerville, or Century, though the few screenplays that came her way were exclusively in Courier New Font.

Ms. Monroe,

I understand you are a savant in your field. I am an unknown writer, yet to have had my words slashed and stabbed and stained in red. Would you be my first? I ask you to be honest yet gentle. Stern, yet forgiving. I shall send my sample at 9 p.m. I hope my writing ignites an emotional response in you. I hope you can see, hear, and feel the words as if you've lived them.

Humbly Yours,

August Wolfe.

The return address on the manila envelope belonged to a post office in Chicago. Interest piqued, she went to her work desk, situated right in front of a window. The view was worthy of being a screensaver. She had dual monitors—both 32" screens—so she didn't need to minimize and maximize and squeeze all the programs onto one screen. She loaded her Gmail, again sending all junk mail to the trash folder. Then, she opened August Wolfe's email. The body of the email was brief, simply stating, "Enjoy." Madison opened the Microsoft Word attachment titled "The One Who Got Away." A catchy title for sure but also commonplace. Her first recommendation to Mr. Wolfe was to consider a title change. If someone googled "The One Who Got Away," they'd most likely be directed to a YouTube link to Katy Perry's song of the same name, and once someone stumbled down the YouTube rabbit hole, it was game over. They'd emerge hours later with no memory of the time elapsed, looking at their recommended videos and wondering "How did it come to this?"

She tapped her thumb below the spacebar. Should she read the book now or leave it for next morning? The clock in the lower right-hand corner of the screen showed 10:07. Had it just turned 10:07? Or was it seconds away from 10:08? Apparently, 10:08 was too damn late. She muttered a non-committal "screw it" and started working, tracking her changes and adding comments. Free sample edits usually ranged between 250 and 350 words. Sometimes, she allowed for 1,000 words, but even that number was malleable. Edits were expensive, and she wanted prospective clients to feel confident in her skill. Just don't get greedy was her motto. She finished her glass of water, then set to reading. First time through was a straight read, no pauses to correct a misspelt word or a misplaced comma. Reading through helped gauge an author's voice and style. It was vital any changes she recommended retained the author's voice.

The secluded road is blanketed in darkness, the trees alongside it silhouettes, looking like gray ghosts as I ride by. It's an ominous place, but it's a route I've taken dozens of times—it's all bark and no bite. Still, I pedal faster. The darkness is split by an immaculate white light. I glance behind me. I squint and turn away from the blinding light. It's a truck; its driver doesn't give me the courtesy of shutting the brights off nor does he show decency by getting into the other lane when he drives by. It's so tempting to flip him off.

His fire-orange taillights fade into a dying ember and the darkness reunites into one mass. But the dying ember reignites into blazing red. Had he hit a deer? I slow my pedaling; I do not want to see a deer die. But then the realization hits. He hadn't slammed on his breaks. There was no squeal of rubber locking against asphalt. His stop hadn't been the result of some unforeseen event.

It was planned.

Fear swarms inside me like locusts. The truck does a Y-Turn; the brights blind me. It creeps forward with a soft rumble coming from the engine. It reminds me of a tiger stalking its prey. The engine roars like the aforementioned beast. I lose my balance. The truck races in my direction, crossing over the center line into my lane.

Is he drunk?

But I know the answer is no. It's too deliberate. This isn't caused by inebriation. It's caused by intention.

The lights burst brighter like two stars exploding. The engine is deafening, the roar of a tiger before it tackles its prey. He's seconds away from splattering me across his grill and windshield. I have no choice but to turn toward the ditch. I'm flung from my bike and crash into the hard snow.

The truck skids to a stop with an ear-splitting screech. On hands and knees, I crawl into the woods as the truck races in reverse. It spins wildly so that it's facing the woods, the headlights illuminating the darkness. The engine purrs and rumbles, letting out a gravelly cough.

I hide behind a tree, avoiding the two globed spotlights. A door creaks open. Boots grind against the cold asphalt. I ball the front of my shirt and bite down on it so I don't scream. I'm glad I do so because when the truck door slams shut, I jump, my mouthful of cotton muffling my scream.

I can't stay here. If I do, he'll find me. Of that I have no doubt. But the snow traps me. Every step I take, it will crunch like a cracker and scream out my location. The snow is deep, the ground uneven. It grabs at my legs like hands. My knees and wrists, having taken the blunt impact of my fall, throb, but my body knows there's no time for pain. It has released an overdosing amount of adrenaline. I scan my surroundings for anything I can use as a weapon. All of the broken branches and stones are buried beneath the snow.

I consider sprinting for his still-running truck. But I could be running right into his waiting arms. The wind howls, then whistles. My heart clatters against my ribs. Then the wind dies, leaving only terrifying silence.

But then the wind whispers, whistles, and wails. I make a dash for another tree, skidding to a stop beside it. The wind falls silent, allowing him to pinpoint where the sound of scrunching snow came from. I'm silent, listening for him as he listens for me. No sound. Not a damn ping. A vacuum of space. A shadow spreads from the darkness—Darkness shaped in the silhouette of a man.

The world goes black.

The relief of waking from the horrible nightmare is elating. But I don't even have to open my eyes to know this isn't my bed. My bed is memory foam, soothing every muscle, contouring around my body. This bed is old. The springs have poked through, screeching and squealing like restless pigs. I try to sit up, but my arms and legs are duct taped to the bed posts. My eyes snap open. I scream, but it's muffled by the duct tape wrapped around my mouth. However cliché it may sound, my heart truly stops. I've never been more startled, more terrified in my entire life. I opened my eyes to see a masked man inches from my face, watching me with upside-down half-moon eyes. The same thick black mesh covers the elongated smile. He can see me. I can't see him. The mask is hairless, flesh-colored, and made of latex. He's cloaked in black—black boots, black pants, black acrylic gloves, and a black sweatshirt. A demon from the spirit world.

I thrash wildly like the possessed when shown a crucifix. But this living, breathing nightmare only worsens. I'm not wearing my black pinafore dress with my gray shirt underneath nor my leggings... nor am I wearing my bra or underwear. I'm cloaked in a baggy, silk nightgown, pearl white in color. I cry, realizing he'd stripped me naked and dressed me. It's a violation that pulverizes the air in my lungs. Panic chokes me. I can't breathe, my heart drumming so violently I think my breastbone will break. I can't see his eyes or expression, but his lust is palpable. Horror doesn't dawn on me; it suffocates me. I am at his mercy. Victim to whatever fancies him. There's not a single thing I can do about it. I can't punch him. I can't kick him. I can't bite him. I can't even scream. I'm a fully aware anesthesia-induced patient on the operating table.

He extends his gloved hands, using his thumbs to wipe the tears from my eyes. The silence is broken by the sound of duct tape ripping away from itself. He presses a piece of tape over my eyes—the world abandons me, leaving me in total darkness. His breathing is loud and animalistic. His hand caresses my arm, traveling toward my shoulder. He slides the strap off.

Please God, let me pass out.

I try to think of my happiest memory, hoping I can disappear into the sanctity it can provide. I pray for something that has never crossed my mind even in my darkest days.

Please God, spare me. Take my life. End it. Please. Please! But there is no saving grace. I cannot wake from this nightmare.

Except for her finger controlling the mouse, Madison's body was paralyzed. She couldn't blink. Couldn't breathe. But then an explosive reaction followed. She pushed her chair away from the desk, knocking it over as she leapt to her feet. So much air blitzed her lungs that she started hyperventilating. The room morphed into a Hitchcockian dolly-zoomed scene. Her apartment shrunk; claustrophobia inflicted and afflicted her. Yet, at the same time, she was in a mansion with a thousand and one places for the Man in the Mask to hide.

Madison paced the length of her apartment, nervously clawing at her scalp, biting the inside of her cheek, and grinding away at it until she tasted blood. After a quick deliberation, she grabbed her Glock and her phone and got in the elevator.

The hallway felt haunted like the one in *The Shining*. Madison half-expected two dead twins to appear at the end of it. She pounded her knuckles on the door and waited. But she couldn't afford to wait, so she kept pounding until the door opened.

"Madison?" Casper asked, shocked to see her.

He took in her demeanor, then the Glock in her hand. His eyes widened, and out of instinct, he raised his hands to show his submission. His flabbergasted mind must surely be thinking, *"I asked a psycho to dinner!"*

Madison stuttered, unable to form the necessary words. "I... can you come with me?"

This was the part where he should have stepped back inside and slammed the door shut. She certainly would have. And eventually, Casper did shut his door—but behind him. He followed her into the elevator and to her apartment, and then, stood by in confused horror as Madison scanned the rooms with her Glock in both hands.

"Why don't you set the gun down and we'll talk, okay?" Casper suggested.

Sitting wasn't something she could do—it felt like it would be weeks before she could relax enough to do that—so she paced like a caged animal as Casper, seated on a kitchen chair, watched nervously. Madison rushed to the sink, filled a large glass with water, and downed it without pause, but it was as useful as watering sand. It felt like the computer watched her too, like a predator in a dark alley. But this predator didn't hide. The bright white screen waited ominously like a cursed artifact.

Why didn't she call the police? Simple—she was afraid. Of what had been written in the manuscript? Of course. But there was a deeper fear, one she'd had since *it* had happened. The fear that one day she would go insane. That her anxiety, the palpable paranoia, would weigh so heavily it would snap her tenuously tethered string of sanity. What if that Word document was something else entirely? What if she had made it all up? And what was truly written on it was a fantasy novel or a children's book. What if her past had tainted her present and created an alternate reality?

Casper spoke her name, patient yet pleading.

"I don't know how to start… " Madison said.

"Just start and you'll find your way," he said with a supportive smile.

Another glance at the computer. Maybe she didn't have to tell him; maybe she could *show* him.

"I need you to read something," she said.

Casper failed to hide his surprise at the request but followed her to her computer desk. She pointed to the screen.

"What's this?" he asked, lifting up the chair and sitting on it.

Madison explained it was a sample edit, that it was basically an audition. Casper refrained from asking any more questions and started reading. She retreated to the kitchen, not wanting to be anywhere near the computer as the cursed incantations inscribed on it were read. She switched from chewing the right side of her cheek to the left.

Balance. Right, Dr. Frett?

She studied Casper's hand, looking for the finger twitch that meant he was advancing through the document. He finished, spun around, and then faced her.

"You said this was a sample edit? For a book?" he asked.

Madison nodded.

Casper's eyebrows furrowed. "Madison, I don't understand... "

"It's me."

"What's you?"

"The person in that story."

Casper stayed silent. She knew he needed more answers. But she needed more courage. She summoned what supply she had and told Casper everything. The secluded road, *London Bridge,* the truck, the shack, her escape through the wintry Wisconsin woods—everything.

Casper processed what she'd said and then did what most people did when they found out what had happened—he apologized. A kind gesture. But what do you say? What *can* you say?

"They never caught him?" Casper asked, though he seemed to know the answer.

Closure was something Madison had never been afforded. The Man in the Mask could return to her life at any given moment.

"They couldn't get DNA?" Casper asked.

Madison shook her head. "He bleached me... after... every time..."

Casper's face filled with sadness at the mention of *every time.* Plural. More than once.

"Could this be someone messing with you?" he asked.

"No. What's written on there... it's a level of detail I could never put into words. Not to the police, not to Dr. Frett. I never told anyone else the full story, least of all my family. It would kill them if they knew."

Casper hesitated. Here's where the insanity pitch comes, certainly posed as a question, not an accusation.

"Do you think maybe because you've been through something so similar, your mind is merging your experience with the story?"

"There are details in there that only two people know. Me. And him."

The only explanation she could offer was a feeling in her gut, the part that warns us when something isn't right. She just knew she was the character in that chapter.

Casper nodded. "I believe you. Will you come with me? I have an idea."

They took the elevator two floors up, and she followed him to apartment 5664. Casper knocked on the door. Madison asked whose place this was, but before he could reply, the door whipped open. A man, roughly six feet tall with deep wrinkles, scowled at them. His face looked incapable of smiling, a scowl of scar tissue preventing his facial muscles from contorting in such an unfamiliar shape. His bushy eyebrows resembled two caterpillars squiggling across his forehead.

"What time is it?" the man asked in a deep, slightly gravelly voice.

Casper pulled his phone from his pocket, not realizing the man's question was of the aggressive rhetorical variety.

"It's, uh, 11:13."

"A.M.?"

"No... "

"Oh, so you mean it's 11:13 p.m., as in close to midnight?"

Catching on, Casper let out an annoyed, mute puff of air. "Yeah, I'm sorry about the time, but this is really important."

"I'm not interested in discussing old cases," the man said, hugging the door close.

"We're not here about any old case," Casper said, but catching the inaccuracy of that statement, he added, "not any of yours at least."

Casper fidgeted, leaving enough space for Madison to clearly see the man behind the nearly closed door. She had seen him hundreds of times around the building but only in passing. Both settled for unpolished and unfinished nods rather than verbal greetings. He stared at Madison, studying her. She was terrified, and it showed. His honey-brown eyes, which had initially appeared cold, turned warm, compassionate even. He sighed, frustrated with what he was about to do.

He followed Casper and Madison to her apartment. She had them wait outside so she could ensure the rooms were clear—behind the shower curtain, inside the closet, and under the bed. Then she let them in. The man's name was Atticus Wallace. He wore Wranglers and a flannel shirt, both appearing to be a decade old. Everything about him seemed small-town wholesome. He was the kind of man who would enjoy having his closest neighbor be two miles away.

Madison led Atticus to her work desk and asked him to read the sample chapter. Atticus read, and the way he used the mouse revealed computers were not a huge part of his life, if at all.

"This is you?" he asked after he had finished.

Madison nodded. "Do you think I'm crazy?"

"These details must be things only you and he would know?" he asked.

She nodded again.

"Then you're not crazy. There're two possibilities here. One, it's a hell of a coincidence. Or two…"

He didn't need to explain what the second was. She knew. It meant whoever wrote this piece of "fiction" was the same person who had run her off the road, abducted her, and… raped her.

"So, what do we do?" Casper asked.

Madison appreciated his use of "we."

Atticus pulled an old flip phone from his pocket. It looked similar to the ones Madison had played Snake on in the mid-2000s. Ending his call, he told Madison the police were on their way and they'd look into the email. Atticus pointed to the manila folder and told them to not touch it any more than they already had.

"Can I be honest with you?" Atticus asked.

Madison nodded, and though the question triggered a storm of anxiety, she appreciated his willingness to be blunt. She despised being tip-toed around.

"If this was written by the man who took you, there're two ways this plays out," Atticus said. "Either the police finds where that email was sent from without much issue. If so, he'll be arrested before the sun rises."

"Or?" Casper asked.

"Or, he has covered his tracks, taken precautions, and planned this out. Which would mean it'll be a lot harder to get him."

"He's too smart. They couldn't catch him the first time," Madison said.

"I agree. This is the first time you've received something like this? No phone calls? Letters? Emails or Facebook crap?" Atticus asked.

She shook her head. "Nothing."

Madison was grateful both Atticus and Casper waited for the police, and more so when Atticus explained to the police officers how the chapter mirrored her ordeal, preventing her from having to repeat it for a third time. Atticus also translated the police lingo into civilian speech. At quarter to one, Atticus left. Casper lingered but a moment longer. Madison muttered a generic thanks, unable to add any eloquence to it.

"You know when you said you couldn't go to dinner tonight, I thought you were just blowing me off. It's refreshing to know you actually had a reason," he joked.

His humor and his smile disarmed her. Somehow, she smirked. But then she realized any fanciful thoughts she'd ever had about taking him up on his offer to a night out were over. He knew her secret, and she didn't blame anyone for distancing themselves once they knew. A dark, ominous cloud hung over her, carrying with it the promise of storms.

"Listen, I understand if you want to keep distance. I can just leave your mail outside your door and knock, and if you want to do the same—"

He cut her off. "Shut it, 5414. Do you think I'd ghost you? Who do you think I am? Casper?"

A cheap dad joke, but it landed. Madison flashed a grin. She'd never seen somebody's jaw muscles in better shape than Casper's. It wouldn't have surprised her if he smiled all damn day. The endurance he must have! She strained a smile less than three times a day and had to ice her jaw with an Old Fashioned afterward.

Before leaving, Casper gently patted her shoulder and said everything would be okay. A mantra she often told herself. It held as much validity as saying Candyman in front of a mirror five times. But forget about urban legends. Madison didn't need any fictional or supernatural beasts or demons. She had her own.

The Man in the Mask had returned.

Nightmares were a nightly ordeal for Madison. Even though *it* had happened almost a decade ago, she hadn't forgotten any details. Her nightmares were so realistic there was nothing about them, even after she woke up, that gave away that she had been dreaming. Everything was how it had been—the smell of the musty cabin; the feel of the old mattress and its springs poking into her back; the constricting grip of the duct tape around her wrists, ankles, and mouth; and the Man in the Mask's delicate touch. But what made her flesh tremble as if an invisible army of insects was crawling across it was the fact that he hadn't forgotten any of it either. But unlike her memory, which had been painfully engraved through trauma, his came from a sickening joy. Hers was an undesired scar, his a chosen tattoo. He had spent as much time thinking about her as she had him.

If all the minutes of sleep that night of the email were added together, Madison would have had roughly three hours. But a new day filled with her routines did dawn eventually. Routines were comforting. Calming. They gave her day purpose and a sense of order and normalcy. And boy did she need that. She showered before breakfast. Madison was not a lounger, even on weekends. Her restless mind didn't allow her the gift of relaxation. She stood in the shower, letting the hot water therapy relax her until she felt guilty about how much water she was using. Afterward, she scanned her cupboards and the fridge for something enticing. But she didn't have to scour long. There was a knock on the door. Casper was behind it, holding a box of cheese kringle.

Simon and Garfunkel. Frodo and Sam. Thelma and Louise. Forget them all. Fat and sugar were the greatest duo. Casper had taken the liberty of eating nearly a foot-long's worth of the pastry on his walk from Lauer's Bakery. He asked how she was doing. "Okay," she answered. "Okay" had been her answer for a long time, a permanent gray area between "Good" and "Bad." He left shortly after.

Madison had time to kill but lacked any weapon to do so. She had hoped the police would have called early and declare they had arrested the email sender, found at his apartment or his local library. The more time passed, the more worried she became they wouldn't catch him so easily. Atticus had warned her that because there had been no threat of violence, this case wouldn't take precedence over other, more urgent ones.

After glancing at her computer a dozen times over the course of an hour, she summoned her courage and checked her emails. She made her living on the computer. She had enough phobias and could not afford to add technophobia to the list. Spam littered her inbox, making her envious of Atticus. Based on his unique over-pronunciation of the word email, the only spam Atticus knew of was the gelatinous meat in a can. The email clearing took all of seven minutes.

Just before 12:30, Atticus stopped over. He was dressed in a dark pair of Wranglers and a green plaid flannel that looked fuzzy and cozy, smelling of leather. Something about the way he dressed comforted Madison, like the corny Hallmark movies she watched around Christmas.

He too asked how she was doing. She shrugged in response. He looked around the apartment. It appeared innocent, but Madison knew the old policeman was taking inventory, making connections, and coming up with assumptions about her.

"I wanted to say I'm sorry for being an asshole last night," Atticus said. "I get a lot of young people who do those podcasts or the YouTube asking about old cases. True crime has become very popular. Damn morbid if you ask me. I assumed you and the lanky guy were there for that reason."

She shook her head at his unnecessary apology. "You were a police officer? Here in Chicago?"

Atticus nodded. "Homicide detective."

She wanted to ask more, but he'd made it clear he didn't want to speak about his time as a police officer. Madison wasn't going to be one of those people who asked anyway. He attempted small talk for a few minutes, but it wasn't something either of them was fluent in. Like Casper, he promised to check in later. If only the police had made a similar promise. With the amount of nervous energy that was traveling through her body she could have powered her toaster. She had to get rid of it somehow, so she harnessed it into a workout. Working out cleared her head, one of the few times the thousand thoughts running rampant in her mind shut down and shut up. She knew Essex on the Park had a great gym facility—based on the pictures she had seen. But she chose to work out in a small area set up in the back corner of her living room, equipped with a few dumbbells, a barbell, bench and rack, and a Century Bob punching dummy. YouTube had taught her how to strike, but for the last three years on Tuesdays and Thursdays, a friend named Lana Sanchez had been coming over and training her in jujitsu.

After working out, she re-read *Harry Potter*. There was something supremely comforting about going back to Hogwarts. But then, finally, her phone rang. It was Officer Jones, an officer she'd spoken with the previous night. He confirmed that the email had indeed come from a man named August Wolfe. Wolfe lived in Fountain Hills, Arizona. But Officer Jones said he thought they were barking up the wrong tree. She asked why.

"'Cuz he's 86," he answered.

Wolfe had sent three emails since the address was created in 2011. He had lived in Arizona since 1973 and lived at Spring City, a nursing home facility, since 2016. The IP address showed the email had come from Fountain Hills, so the sender was half the country away. He told her to rest easy. Madison didn't rest, and if she did, it certainly wouldn't have been easy. Were they still living in an age where the wagon was the main mode of transportation, she could've rested easy. But half the country away in this age? That distance could be conquered in a measly couple of hours. Madison asked for clarification on IP addresses, but Officer Jones used too much jargon for her to understand.

What she did understand was that an IP address wasn't like a social security number. IP addresses change. Simply resetting your router changes your IP address. Go on vacation, and you'll get a new IP address because you're connected to a different network. As for the hope any prints had been found on the folder, there had been. Unfortunately, they belonged to Madison, Casper, and an older postal worker at the post office.

She told Atticus what Officer Jones had said. He, like her, was not overly enthusiastic at the result, and he understood IP addresses even less than she had, reacting as if she had switched to Swahili mid-conversation.

Casper stopped by at around five, dressed in a nice pair of jeans and a green sweater. He must have a date with some girl who wasn't in the middle of a crisis and had stopped on his way down. Madison was greatly relieved yet insanely jealous. But after she told him what the police had found out, he hesitated by the door. His silence increased her anxiety. Her brain tried to convert his body language into thoughts she could read.

"What is it?" Madison asked.

"Let me take you to dinner. You need something to take your mind off... this."

She bit her lower lip, giving the inside of her cheeks time to heal. "I can't guarantee I'll be good company."

"That's fine. I can't either."

"I may not even talk... public places sometimes..."

"Then I'll order for you." Another homerun smirk.

She considered it. Her mind was still debating when her mouth agreed to go. Casper was right. Madison needed something to take her mind off of *this*. Though going out brought on its own wide array of worries and anxieties, at least they'd be different and fresh. She grabbed her black double-breasted faux-wool peacoat and a plaid green scarf, and they headed to the elevator. When they stepped outside, the cold didn't attack her. Instead, it reinvigorated and relaxed her with each deep breath. It seemed a cheat code of which she tried to take full advantage.

"I'm going to ask you ten questions," Casper said.

"Okay…"

"It helps reduce the 'get to know you' stage."

"Oh, really? Is this a proven method?"

"Still in the clinical trials, but it's looking promising."

She laughed and not because she was nervous or didn't know what else to do.

"So, you ready?" he asked.

"I don't know. I'll probably fail," Madison said.

"Fail? Jeez, I'm not giving out grades here."

She conceded with a nod. Her brain tried to guess what his first question would be.

"Favorite color?"

Madison laughed again, not expecting that question in the slightest. "This helps you get to know me quicker?"

"It's an accelerant, yes. Believe in the process."

"Cerulean."

Casper looked at her as if he was trying to figure out if she had given a genuine answer in a different language or given the name of a pharmaceutical company. "That's, uh, that's oddly specific. And, umm, what family would cerulean belong to?"

"The blue family."

Casper nodded and then recited lyrics from the famous 90s song by Eiffel 65 as if they were poetry. Madison laughed yet again, loving that reference from a halcyon time when life was so much simpler. A time before the Man in the Mask.

"So, do you know me so much better now?" she asked.

Casper stood tall and nodded. "I do."

"Care to enlighten me?"

"Sure, 5414. Your answer reveals a lot. You're well read, as evidenced by your vocabulary. Words are important to you. You don't rush to speak. You're not a fan of texting lingo. I imagine you enjoy reading letters soldiers wrote home during the world wars, a time when people wrote like poets."

Madison gazed at him, waiting for him to reveal his magic trick. So much of what he had said was true. In fact, it was *all* true.

"That or you had the Crayola 64 pack with the built-in sharpener," he joked.

Again, she laughed. Her cheeks cramped. The jaw muscles, like any muscle, were use 'em or lose 'em. Hers were practically atrophied by now.

"Both are true," she said.

Casper shrugged arrogantly: *I told you so.*

She asked him what his favorite color was.

"Black. But for you Crayola folk, it's called Black Stars."

Conversations with Casper were effortless. When any words would have felt forced, he let silence fill the spaces instead. However he shifted from one topic to another so organically—whether it be a street performer or a historical landmark they passed—that there was rarely a lull in their conversations. The two miles from Essex on the Park to The Cheesecake Factory below the John Hancock building had indeed taken her mind off of the chapter, and it seemed every time it threatened to become the dominant thought again, Casper intervened.

When they arrived, the hostess told them to expect a twenty-minute wait. They sat on the steps leading up to street level. People were scattered about, couples and groups filling their wait with cocktails and conversations. Casper and Madison talked about their apartment's most famous residents. There was a man who had been busted for hiring prostitutes... nine times. A coke dealer who had jumped from his window to the ground three stories below, shattering his legs but continuing to crawl to avoid capture. Then there was the person who rivaled Al Capone as the most notorious person to ever call Chicago home—the chunky, Jell-O-filled eleven-year-old boy who had completed the unholy trifecta in the apartment's swimming pool: puke, poop, and piss.

Soon it was their turn, and they headed inside. Casper scouted the cheesecakes on the tables as they passed by. Madison ordered a pineapple ginger daiquiri, and after hearing the name, Casper switched his order of a dark beer to the same.

"How am I faring on the questions?" she asked.

"You're doing good... Excuse me, you're doing *well*. And that's y-o-u-apostrophe-r-e. Me don't want no editor thinking I no good with words," Casper teased.

The questions were light. What was her favorite movie? *Ghost*. What was a typical day—working, going to the gym, catching a bite to eat, reading, watching a movie, shopping, etc. It was technically true, but they all occurred in her apartment. Favorite guilty pleasure band—ABBA. Favorite smell—Pine. And the random question if Madison considered crocs shoes or sandals. The answer proved more thought provoking than it had any right to be.

"If you had access to Doc Brown's DeLorean, and given you have enough road to get up to 88 miles per hour, what event do you go back and stop or change?" he asked.

It was a light-hearted question with a dark answer. Madison had thought about this question or a variation of it all the time. She'd stop herself from going to that Halloween party. But she didn't say that. Instead, she said she would stop the Titanic from sinking. Then she asked him the same.

"I would give Kevin McAllister the necessary time to eat his macaroni."

She laughed, but Casper genuinely looked serious.

"Kevin comes up with this grand scheme, blueprints and all, but he doesn't leave himself time enough to eat the macaroni," he continued. He had obviously given it a tremendous amount of thought. "I watch that movie a dozen times every December, and it still gets me. Every kid deserves macaroni on Christmas."

Madison smiled, feeling another jaw cramp setting in.

"You're really making me search my soul with these questions," she teased.

"Question eight. Are you having a good time?"

Her joking smile vanished. He was looking for an honest answer. No playing. His dark yet warm eyes were locked on her cobalt blue ones. She could have used a menu to hide behind right about now.

"I am," she said, even though her demeanor didn't show that the way she wanted it to. "It's not easy for me to relax."

"In public?" he asked before taking as manly a sip of his daiquiri as he could manage.

"Anywhere. But I am as comfortable now as I can be… if that makes any sense."

"I'd like to take credit, but it's the cheesecake. They put this chemical in it. Yet to be approved by the FDA."

"Thanks for telling me," Madison said with mock intrigue. "Any side effects I should look out for?"

He shook his head as if he were reassuring a child the monster in their nightmare was just their imagination. "Nothing major. Dizziness, nausea, excessive drooling, speaking in unknown tongues."

She laughed, fighting through the cramping sensation in her cheeks. When they finished their cheesecakes, Madison was in jeopardy of looking like the inflated Violet from *Willy Wonka*. Casper insisted on paying, stating he was old-fashioned that way.

After the bill had been paid, Casper rose and pulled her chair out for her. A quaint gesture from a bygone era. His hand rested on the small of her back as they meandered past the tables. His touch was soft, not forceful but firm enough to let her know he wanted to be more than a friend. Madison had become so desensitized to having a nervous stomach she'd forgotten how it felt when it wasn't caused by fear or apprehension but from excitement.

The air outside was brisk, colder than it had been on their walk here. The city had fully come alive. Golden headlights brushed the city in sepia tints. It was city quiet—just the sounds of occasional traffic, the homeless asking for change, and the drunk chatter of college-aged people. Madison spent the final block in inner turmoil, wondering if Casper would try to kiss her. Thoughts multiplied. Did she want him to? Did she not want him to? Would he? Would he not? If he did, what type of kiss would it be? Would he expect more? If he didn't kiss her, how come? Before *it* happened, Madison was a social butterfly, her jaw muscles Olympian-fit. She used to love this moment. The will-he-won't-he moment. Now it terrified her. Not because it was Casper. He had instilled a feeling of security and, equally important, normalcy. Even if it was fake, it wasn't the magician's fault the illusion wasn't real.

The answer to the hypothetical question—if she wanted him to kiss her—was more complicated than yes or no. She thought her verbal answer would have been yes. But she didn't know how she would react physically. She hadn't kissed anybody since *it* happened. A psychological fear had clawed its way deep into her psyche, entwining itself within the cerebral fibers.

London Bridge is falling down.

She tried to get the whistling out of her head as they stepped into the elevator. She trembled, but she pretended it was the cold that caused it. Casper raised his hand to the panel. Would it be the 51st or the 54th floor he chose? He hit the latter, and her stomach plummeted as if the elevator had gone down in a freefall. When the doors opened, they stepped off. Her nerves were now radioactive. Madison wanted the hallway to be three miles long. She squeezed her keys to stop her hands from shaking. They arrived at her door. Casper looked into her eyes; she looked at his boots. He gently lifted her chin. But he didn't go for the kiss she feared yet desired. He simply thanked her for coming and wished her a good night.

When Friday dawned, it marked a week since August Wolfe's email. There had been no further updates or new email. Madison celebrated that day of significance (not an anniversary) with a pint of Ben & Jerry's. Casper was out of town—not that she had expected they would have had plans. Or would they have? She spent the next five exhausting minutes going through a hundred hypothetical conversations. Falling back into her Friday routine felt like covering up with a warm, thick blanket on a cold January night.

After showering and dressing in her Walmart best—lounge pants and a baggy shirt—she had a few emails to send before she could indulge in cinema and cuisine. At her desk, she loaded the necessary programs, adjusted the settings, and got to work. She had finished a sample edit for a novel titled *A Tango in Tijuana*—a forbidden romance between two married co-workers who begin a passionate love affair while traveling on business. The author, Michelle Wilde, had used *was* and *had been* incorrectly and either obsessively used commas or neglected them entirely. She had done a great job detailing the two characters' meet-cute moment but had spent a bit too much establishing the scene at the cost of greatly hindering the flow of narrative. Madison hoped she was selected to be her editor because she saw great potential in the novel, and she wrote as much in her email to Michelle.

The second submission she had edited was written by T. F. Hamels and titled *Saturn's Moon*. She had expected it to be science fiction and was correct. The plot was a worn-out trope of the genre—A.I. decides mankind has to go. He had ignorantly used "there" for "their" and "they're" throughout the text. *There house. There coming.* His writing read more like a synopsis, and he was on pace for a 90-page book. This was not the kind of work she wanted. In a 542-word chapter, he had 112 grammar and spelling errors as well as word placement issues, and she couldn't even keep count of the number of -ly adverbs—a writer's mortal enemy. Madison decided to not send the edited document back and simply wrote to Hamels that she was currently unavailable. Finished with her tasks, she was about to put her computer to sleep when an email notification popped up in the lower right-hand corner. She clicked it, unaware she was holding her breath, waiting for the name August Wolfe to show. She breathed a sigh of relief, one she felt in her entire body—the email was from somebody named Lorraine Lyon. The subject line read:

Sample Edit Request – The Night the Lights Went Out Forever.

Intrigued by the title, she read the chapter.

Every single rising day and falling night, upon every passing hour and each fleeting second, the lights go out for someone. For some, the light fades in gradual gradient. For others, the light vanishes in a flash. A bright cosmic explosion followed by the nothingness of space. For Andrea Collins, it was both.

An impressive opening hook that had sunk into her and dragged her in. One that left the reader no choice but to continue.

I've always thought of cooking as juggling. Watching a pot to make sure it didn't boil over while simultaneously stirring a pan to make sure the contents didn't stick and burn while glancing at a recipe on your phone, tapping it before the screen went black. I don't know how to juggle, and I certainly don't know how to cook. My train of thought has been derailed. I look about trying to salvage the wreckage. The noodles are drained. I have a stick of butter melting, an unopened white pouch of powder cheese on the counter.

Milk.

I open the fridge, shifting the items on the top shelf. No milk. I let out a PG-13 curse. I consider using coffee creamer, but as soon as I lift it, I know there's about an eighth of a teaspoon left. This warrants a Rated R curse.

I give credit to my cooking prowess when I contemplate using water. I groan. I hate late-night trips to the store. The local Piggly Wiggly in Turkey Creek, luckily, isn't far. Walmart is cheaper, but the Pig is closer. I'll pretend my reasoning is to support local business and not the giant chain. But let's be honest, if I wasn't feeling lazy, it'd be good old 24/7 Walmart. Instead, I'll be the asshole who barrels through the doors at 8:56. I smile apologetically at the cashier at the service desk. She tells me to f— off with her eyes. My guilt expands when I have to walk across the freshly mopped floor to get to the dairy cooler. I walk on my tippy toes like that helps at all. This high schooler holding the mop looks at me like I pushed him out of a locker room naked in front of his crush. I'm partial to 2% milk, but the spot's empty, and I won't commit an egregious tertiary sin and ask him to check the back. I take a ½ gallon of skim instead. I hurry to check out. The cashier says nothing except my total. Get used to minimum wage.

The doors are locked the moment my ass clears them. Nothing like good old passive aggression. The lone light in the parking lot is out. The wind swirls debris around my feet. I rush to my car. I have the strange, uncomfortable feeling I'm being watched. I look around. The employees' cars are parked at the back of the lot, and apart from them, there's only my car. I put my hand on the sensor, and I hear the beep as it unlocks.

A figure is cast in the faint reflection of the window. Before I can react, a cloth is pressed over my mouth. The weight in my legs disappears as if I'm descending on a swing as I'm drugged into a catatonic stupor.

I awake to the sound of traffic zipping by and the occasional mechanical shifting of semi-trucks. The crisp wind swarms me, pecking at my flesh. I'm naked; my wrists, ankles, and mouth are duct-taped.

A shimmer of silver slashes through the darkness. I squirm—bait on a hook. The knife rips through my rib cage and into my lung. Every nerve ending in my body converges there. A second stab pierces the other side. My lungs can no longer inflate. I'm losing breath, and once that pocket of air leaves, I'll die. I gasp before it can fizzle out.

He watches me, studying my death with intrigue, maybe even arousal. Salvation is on that interstate, hundreds of cars passing by every few minutes. Dear God, please let one stop! But a small line of trees blocks me from their view. I motion for a deep breath, but my lungs do not fill with air. I gasp, my eyes grow wide, and the light dies.

Intense. A story about murder was near the bottom of the list of genres Madison wanted to read, and the idea of having to spend hours editing such a subject gave her anxiety. But it was the best submission she'd received in a long while and certainly the most polished. She had noticed few errors, and those too were preferential, like an errant comma here and there and longer sentences that could be broken apart. Killing off what Madison assumed was the main character in the first chapter was shocking, reminiscent of Drew Barrymore's quick demise in *Scream*. Would a new heroine—the final girl—be introduced in chapter two? Or would the antagonist be the main character? Both possibilities intrigued her.

She saved her work, then prepped her station for movie viewing. The soda and snacks kept her awake, but once they were gone, she was defenseless against the overwhelming drowsiness. She closed Netflix—the ten o'clock news taking its place—rinsed her dishes, and loaded them into the dishwasher.

"Tragic news out of Turkey Creek, Tennessee, as the search for—"

She switched off the TV, fighting a yawn as she stumbled to the bathroom to brush her teeth. Then Madison wrapped herself in her covers, hoping the Man in the Mask wouldn't find her in her dreams.

Madison slept great. Too great. When her 5:46 alarm chirped—she was one of those who never liked to set repeat alarms at the standard fifteen-minute intervals—she only got as far as whipping the covers off. A half hour later, she awoke in a panic, feeling like half her day had been wasted.

After a shower, Madison got dressed and turned on the TV for background noise. She poured a cup of cold brew coffee. Cold brew allowed her to drink her coffee quickly—she was not a sipper. Plus, the caffeine is so much stronger.

"… We go to Turkey Creek where Jeanette Weaver is covering. Jeanette…"

"Good morning. Andrea Collins has been missing for three days." Madison jerked her head to the TV at the mention of that name. *"Her family and friends have been holding onto hope; the community has been praying, but last night, police found an unidentified female body in a wooded area off Interstate 129 near the Tennessee River. This morning, that body has been confirmed to be that of Andrea Collins."*

Madison froze.

"Collins's car was left at a local Piggly Wiggly on September 17th. Employees at the grocery store recall seeing Andrea Collins just minutes before closing. Employees thought it odd her Honda Civic was still in the parking lot when they left for the night. There are no security cameras in the store's parking lot. Police are asking anybody with knowledge of Andrea's disappearance to come forward. Andrea Collins, murdered. She was just 28 years old."

Madison must have been in a cyclonic nightmare. The night terrors always seem logical and coherent when trapped in them, just as they did right then. But soon, something would tip her off. She'd jump locations or timelines or she'd hear her alarm blaring like a loud speaker. But no tell-tale signs came. This wasn't a nightmare. She hurried to her work desk and logged in.

Was she forcing pieces of a puzzle to fit? She reread *The Night the Lights Went Out Forever.* Neither Andrea nor Collins was a unique name. But Andrea Collins together? Andrea Collins from Turkey Creek, Tennessee? Andrea Collins from Turkey Creek, Tennessee who stopped at a Piggly Wiggly shortly before 9 p.m.?

Madison hadn't eaten in almost ten hours, and yet, she felt sick like she had eaten past the point of being full. So full, she had the urge to vomit. Once again, the easiest explanation was that she was losing her mind. Since Casper was away, Madison called Atticus over. He cared very little that it wasn't even seven o'clock. Besides, he looked like he'd been awake for hours.

"There's an email," Madison said, gesturing Atticus to her kitchen table where she handed him a printed copy of *The Night the Lights Went Out Forever.*

He sat at the table, rubbing his forehead as he read. Then he looked at Madison.

"Okay…" he said when he was done. "This obviously isn't you."

"No, it's not," she agreed. "Have you seen the news today?"

"I don't watch the news. It's either depressing or bullshit. And they sure as hell suck at forecasting the weather."

Madison strode to her computer and brought up an article. Atticus followed and sat. Rubbing his forehead, he read the article detailing the murder of Andrea Collins—two stab wounds into and through her rib cage, wrists and ankles duct taped together. With each sentence, the massaging of his forehead grew more aggressive like he was kneading dough.

"Still think I'm not losing my mind?" she asked.

"I sure wish you were. Tell anyone about this?" he asked.

When she shook her head, Atticus took out his flip phone and called the police, repeating the same process from the previous Friday, stating the email sender's name and email address.

"Have any whiskey?" Atticus asked afterward.

Madison always kept a bottle of Jack Daniels, and while her taste for fine wine had yet to fully develop, she had an affinity for whiskey. It soothed her, and she had to be careful to keep it to a drink or two.

Atticus took his whiskey with a splash of water. Madison added a bit of Pepsi Zero Sugar to hers. She couldn't help but take note of the time. She hadn't drunk this early since college. Atticus took a sip and let out a relaxing sigh. His reddened nose told her he'd gone to the drink more than he should have.

They were both quiet until an idea came to Madison. She went to her desk and opened the email from "Lorraine Lyon." She clicked reply.

Lorraine,

I thoroughly enjoyed your opening chapter to The Night the Lights Went Out Forever. I would be pleased to edit your entire manuscript. Before I do, can you please confirm the information on the attached Word document? I look forward to working with you,

Madison.

"What's on the document?" Atticus asked.

She said it was standard contact information: name, address, email, and payment details.

"I know it's a long shot," Madison said.

"So are Hail Marys," Atticus replied. "But you still chuck 'em up at the end of the half. What's the worst that can happen?"

"The other team intercepts it and returns it for a touchdown," she said with a deadpan expression.

Atticus nodded in defeat. Madison hit send, and that nervous feeling when you've sent an important email started setting in. Seconds later, an email appeared in her inbox. It was too quick for her to experience any sort of promising excitement. The email came from Mail Delivery Subsystems. Its subject read Delivery Status Notification (Failure). Address not found. Your message wasn't delivered because the address couldn't be found, or is unable to receive mail.

"It's gone?" Atticus asked.

Madison could only nod. She hadn't expected an answer, but she didn't expect the email address to be vanished from the digital world. They returned to the table and to the whiskey.

"Both manuscripts were sent by the same person," Madison said.

Atticus looked at her, nodding.

"So, twice the chance to catch him, right?" she asked, trying to keep the desperation out of her voice.

Atticus shrugged. "You can ascertain a lot from a letter. Do you remember the two snipers in D.C. in the early 2000s?"

Madison thought on it and nodded, remembering the terror that took hold of the people in the area, not knowing if at any given second a bullet would rip through them.

"Police found a letter. 'This is for you Mr. Police. Call me God. Do not release to the press.' From that, the FBI determined there were actually two snipers."

"From just that? How?"

"They figured one was young, based on the use of 'Mr. Police.' Mister meaning a figure above him—authority most likely. But the word 'press'—"

"—is an older person's word." Madison finished for him. "Young people call it media."

"Exactly."

"But this is fiction," she said, trying to refrain from digging into the cuticles of her nails until they bled. "He can write in the voice of anyone he wants to. Man. Woman. Old. Young."

"Exactly. Which is why deciphering what is fact and what is fiction will be difficult," Atticus said. He took a satisfying sip of whiskey.

"But all this..." Madison said, nodding at the news article on the computer screen and at the printed chapter on her kitchen table. "It's all true. Not fiction—not the major facts at least. Why?"

"To show us he's for real and that we need to take him seriously. It also establishes him as the one in control. Makes you feel helpless and scared."

"Well, it worked."

Atticus gestured to the pot of popcorn left over from the night before. She told him to go ahead. He grabbed the pot and tossed a few pieces into his mouth, watching Madison as she struggled to mask her fear. She shook her leg, grinded her cheek, and picked at her nails. Her worry was self-destructive. And those were only the physical manifestations. Inside, that worry ate away like a ravenous cancer.

"Doctor says salt'll kill me," he said casually. "I hope it does. Wouldn't be a bad way to go."

Madison's confusion at such a comment showed on her face.

"In 1988, my partner and I responded to a call on the South Side. A gang shooting. Darnell Wicker was a member of the Black Disciples. Had a history of selling heroin and beating women. You know what a teardrop tattoo signifies?"

She nodded. "That he has killed."

"He had a face full of tears. Anyway, we show up to talk to him. We're fairly confident he's our guy. He knows that. Pulls out a Beretta 92. He shoots me. Bullet hits above my collarbone."

He lowered the neck of his shirt, revealing a raised scar.

"I don't know if I'm lucky or unlucky," Atticus continued. "But my partner... he got hit in the throat. Wicker takes off, but the stupid son of a bitch trips when his pants fall to his ankles. Gets hit by a cab. High on some drug, he didn't feel a thing. Backup arrived. He got life."

"And your partner?"

"He died. Bled out right next to me. Wicker bragged about being a cop killer. He's in his fifties now. Probably'll outlive me. When I die, I want Darnell Wicker sat down, and I want him told that the biggest, baddest motherfucker on the South Side wasn't even as deadly as table salt." He leaned toward Madison. "Whoever is doing this... he's just a man."

There was a lot packed into that story, and it all played out on his face. A pain that hadn't been there before filled the wrinkles of his face and glossed

40

over his honey-brown eyes. There was an extra pause when he raised his glass to drink. Though he didn't say it aloud, Madison knew he was toasting his fallen partner.

Casper stopped by later that evening. Madison told him about Andrea Collins, and the topic dominated the conversation so greatly she didn't even remember to ask how his trip had been. *If* it had been a trip. He hadn't said. Was he offended she hadn't asked? Did he think she was cold and indifferent? Or would he have thought it weird if she did ask? Lying in bed, she scripted everything she should have said.

The next Tuesday, he stopped back over, dressed in his work "uniform"— khakis and a pine-green sweater. Far nicer than the sweats and hoodie Madison worked in.

"Any updates?" he asked.

"Email came from an IP address in Knoxville," Madison told him. She had received that information earlier that day.

"I figure it would have," Casper said.

"You think he actually sent it from there?"

Casper shrugged. "I don't know. It took the police a while to find out for sure. He has to be using a VPN."

Madison told Casper the police had said the same thing. She considered herself fairly tech savvy, but her knowledge was mostly limited to Word, Excel, Photoshop, and internet browsing. She did not know *how* they worked. When she lost connection, her I.T. skills were limited to unplugging the router and plugging it back in. To her credit, that usually did the trick.

The police had explained IPs and VPNs, but it was a crash course weighed down with too much jargon. Casper started by explaining that IP stood for internet protocol.

"Think of it as a street address," he said.

An IP address is how a computer knows where to send the results of what you're looking up. They contain four numbers, ranging from 0 to 255. VPNs—i.e., virtual private networks—encrypt your connection to the internet and hide your IP address. Casper said his company had enforced VPNs on employees working remotely. He also said he's able to access different shows and movies on Netflix that are not available in the U.S.—but in, let's say, Germany—through the use of VPN.

"Apart from unlocking Netflix, what are the pros of a VPN?" Madison asked.

"Well, with a VPN, your IP address is hidden because your traffic—" he paused, recognizing he had used jargon. "By traffic I mean websites you've visited, anything you've downloaded, and apps you've used—it all goes through the VPN. It makes hacking you much harder. The VPN is the only one who can see your real IP. Think of it as having your own house removed from Google Maps."

Like everything, the more a person is willing to pay, the more advanced and secure a VPN you could get. There were illegal ones too.

"So, he could have sent this email from downstairs but make it look like it was from Knoxville," Madison said.

"Exactly," Casper answered, knowing it wasn't what she wanted to hear.

"That's comforting."

"Yeah, but the FBI's got ways of finding the true IP. Don't worry."

Madison expected they did, but in the same way, they had techniques and tools to catch serial killers. But they didn't always catch them. And some of them were caught only decades after their first murder, sometimes because they get arrested for some other minor crime.

For now, according to many outlets, there were currently no leads in the murder of Andrea Collins.

Don't worry.

A phrase that has the exact opposite effect than intended. Her personal dictionary defined it as, "to cause a limitless amount of worry."

Her week, however, was productive. Madison had learned to live and work in a constant state of paranoia. Only now, her paranoia had been vindicated. She had finished the final edit for *Living in the Gray in a Black and White World*. And she had completed a round-one edit for the first 250 pages of a new historical fiction novel. The author had channeled his inner Stephen King and submitted a heavy 929-page manuscript. At such a weight, it could be used to bludgeon someone to death. Though the edit would be time consuming, it would be well worth it.

Friday came with its comforting routine—early morning workout, work from six thirty to three, her Friday night bath (weapon and wine in each hand), and a movie with Ben & Jerry's. After reading a book until the words on the page started to blur, Madison lumbered to bed. Uncharacteristically, maybe even supernaturally, she fell asleep within minutes. Her drapes kept the city's unending light from drifting in. Her cell phone illuminated, defeating the darkness. A Gmail notification popped onto the screen.

Madison woke twenty minutes before her alarm would ring—her body's way of telling her it had received enough sleep. She listened to it, knowing too much sleep resulted in her feeling worse than if she had too little. After showering and eating breakfast, Madison checked the notifications on her phone. Seven emails, a text from her mom, and a few YouTube notifications. She didn't have Facebook, Instagram, Twitter, or TikTok. She'd always feared that the Man in the Mask could come for her again, and she certainly wasn't going to make it easier for him by posting her every move. Besides, social media was a world of fictitious characters posting illusive images of a grand, problem-free life that she had no interest in. Dr. Frett had told her that, and for all her criticisms of him, that was great advice. She sent her mom and dad a group text, not telling them about any of the emails. They'd hadn't gotten over what had happened to her any more than she had. They felt responsible as if they had failed her by not giving her karate lessons or buying her a pistol. Madison knew they would want to know, but they couldn't help. So, why burden them with the same worry?

Her day was lazy busy, spent with online shopping, reading, laundry, and more reading. Early in the afternoon, she checked emails on her computer to get a look at any new submission before Monday morning. Sometimes, a quick response on the weekend was enough to gain the business. She clicked on one which read:

> From: Madeline Hawk
> Subject: The Vanishing - Request for Sample Edit
> Ms. Monroe,

Your silence last week made me realize the character of Andrea Collins had to be killed off. I hope you enjoy our new heroine much more. I feel she has potential, but I'll leave it up to you if she gets a second chapter or not.

Happy Reading,

Yours Truly

Atticus came as soon as she called. Her self-mutilation was in full swing by then, and her breathing was rushed like she had just finished a race.

Madison had always revered the power of words. She knew they could mend wounds or inflict them. Commend or criticize. Inspire or demoralize. But she had never respected the power words hold more than she did now as the black High Tower Text print contrasted menacingly against the 92 brightness white paper.

They sat by her kitchen table, reading. Both of them fell victim to their nerves—she, biting the inside of her cheeks and shaking her leg, and Atticus, rubbing his forehead.

I sees her before she has any idea theres someone else there. Her heels clacking against the wet concrete. A street whore this one. I won't even have to lift her skirt, there's not enough fabric to cover nuthin. Her fishnet leggings'll be torn. She deceives with a push up bra, lying to men like all women does. Just like my mama did. Just like my sister done, leaving with that Jimmy to pop out 2 kids. Sense I's got let go from Turnwell Meat Packaging I can't afford these street treats no more. Sluts are nuthin but items on a mini-mart shelf. And those get robbed all the time. Like the one I just robbed for some Coke and Jack. And this peach is ripe for the pickin to.

Her dark hair is pulled into a tight ponytail, I'll pull that shit even tighter like I'm tryin to strangle her with it. Her eyeliner is blue, her eyes a shade lighter. She go by Shawna. Another lie. That white hoe most definitely has one of those white hoe names. Hoe first. Hoe last. She gotten busted befo fo whorin round. Bet she sucked and fucked her way thru the police to get out early. They got her fingerprints, she got their dick.

The hoe stops to lite a cigarette, but judgin by her skin and eyes, cigarettes are the least of the poisons she be puttin in that body. I get horny stalkin her, she ain't havin no clue. To busy suckin on cancer and tryin to get her next client. One block down is the pharmacy, besides the back of the car, she spends most her time there. She never said no to puttin nuthin in her mouth.

I flip my hood up. She turns away from the busy streets, leaving the roar of the birds further in the distance. Dumb slut is leavin the safety of the herd. I squeeze the wrench in my hand, once she turn down by the river, I'm gonna knock her bitch ass out. A song gets in my head, it's a catchy fuckin tune that white hick sing. When she wake up, she'll be naked, and once she know what up, I'm gonna bang that bitch. And once she's been used, I'm gonna let that bitch suffer, be humiliated. I'll let her suffer for 2 days, duct taped to a bed in that river shack. In 2 days, I'm gonna drown that bitch in her sorrow and muddy water and then send her skank ass downstream, blood drippin out her like a spigot.

"We have to alert the police," Atticus said after they had finished reading.

A few minutes later, someone knocked on the door. It was too soon to be the police. Madison gasped. Even Atticus looked unnerved. She went to the door and looked through the peep hole. Casper waved. Relieved, she opened the door, and before he could even speak, he read her nervous face and saw Atticus at the kitchen table over her shoulder. Madison let him inside and asked him to read the chapter.

"Have you checked the news to see if it's real?" Casper asked when he finished reading.

"I don't know how to. He doesn't give us a city," Madison said.

"He hasn't killed her yet," Atticus added.

"So, this chapter is what? A warning?" Casper asked.

"He said it's up to me if she gets a second chapter," Madison answered, then paused. "He wants me to try to save her."

Atticus nodded.

"How though?" Casper asked.

"There must be clues within this chapter that gives us a location," Madison suggested.

"She's right," Atticus said.

After speaking with the police, Casper had little hope they would find the true IP address in time. Atticus, a man with no faith in nor affinity for technology, was certain they wouldn't.

"Then *we* find out where. We find the answers in this," Atticus said, holding a copy of the chapter.

They reread together. Madison studied Casper to see if he had any nervous ticks like she and Atticus did. But he was annoyingly stoic save for the fact that he ran his hands through his hair when he reached the end of a page.

"I don't want to sound racist—" Casper started.

"But you're going to say something racist?" Atticus cut in.

Casper glared at him, his eyes two middle fingers. "He sounds black."

"He wants to sound that way," Madison said. "But look at the body of the email. Two very different people. Different education level, different word choices, maybe different class background. But I don't think there are two people."

She looked at Atticus, remembering what he had said about the D.C. snipers. He nodded, looking impressed.

"He references Turnwell Meat Packaging. Use google on that," Atticus said.

Madison used her phone. Nothing jumped out in the results, and after checking the first seven pages, she abandoned the search, judging it futile.

"Okay, so what else is a clue? He's got issues with women. Says his mama and sister left him," Casper said.

Madison had no qualms contradicting the written word. However, doing so in person had always given her pause. But she couldn't be timid now; there wasn't time. "That's all character. It could be entirely fictional. But dialogue and voice may help tell us where he lives…" she paused, realizing the alternative. "Or he could be misleading us."

"This is a game," Atticus said, shaking his head. "For it to excite him, there has to be something at stake. If he gave us an unsolvable puzzle, I don't think he'd enjoy it."

"How exactly do we use dialogue to solve this?" Casper asked.

"People in different regions speak differently," Madison explained. "They may even use different words for the same thing. I'm from Wisconsin, we say 'bubbler.'"

"Bubbler? What's that?" Casper asked.

"Her point exactly. We call it a 'drinking fountain' or 'water fountain.' Most states do," Atticus said. He scanned the document. "Here." He pointed to the final line on the page. "Spigot. In the Midwest, we call it a faucet."

"So, spigot is used in…" Casper asked.

"The South," Atticus answered.

"And he says he stole some coke," Madison pointed out.

"Coke as in cola or coke as in cocaine?" Atticus asked.

"It says he took it from a mini-mart," Madison pointed out. "I think the question is if it's being used in the Southern way in that all soda is referred to as coke."

Atticus nodded, looking impressed with her reasoning. Then the silence returned as they read through the printed chapter once more.

Casper sat up. "This part about a river. 'A song gets in my head. It's a catchy fuckin tune that white hick sing.' It must be a song about a river."

"Bruce Springsteen has a song called 'The River,'" Madison said.

"If this bastard's calling The Boss a white hick, I'll kill him," Atticus said. He didn't sound like he was joking.

Madison rose from the table and googled songs about rivers on her computer.

"Here we go. Top results. 'River' by Joni Mitchell, 'River of Dreams'—Billy Joel, ummm…" she scrolled. "'Proud Mary'—CCR, 'Green River'—CCR, 'Big River'—Willie Nelson." She turned back to Atticus and Casper. "Nelson could be called a white hick."

"Could be," Atticus said. "I don't know if it matters but that was a cover. Johnny Cash wrote the original."

"Cash is white," Casper said. "And an argument could be made he's a hick. Not my argument though."

Madison turned back to face her dual monitors. She searched the lyrics. "The song references so many cities. St. Paul, Davenport, St. Louis, Memphis, Baton Rouge… He's toying with us."

"We can eliminate the cities where 'spigot' isn't used: St. Paul, St. Louis, Davenport," Atticus said.

"So then, it's either Baton Rouge or Memphis. Andrea Collins was killed in Tennessee. Logistically, it makes sense," Casper said.

Madison searched for Memphis, Tennessee, on Google Maps. She zoomed out. A river stretched along the western portion of the state—the Mississippi River.

"We have to tell the Chicago PD," Casper said.

Atticus shook his head, frustrated. "They can't do anything but alert the Memphis PD—not sure they'll even do that. There's not a lot of definites to go on." He held his breath and then painfully exhaled. "I know someone in the FBI. Here in Chicago."

The radio was off, the groaning rumbling of the truck's engine the only sound. It was a clear sign the late-nineties Chevy had passed its prime. It was just Madison and Atticus. Casper had offered to come, but Madison had assured him he didn't have to. She would keep him posted. Atticus's demeanor had transformed since he mentioned his contact in the FBI. He stopped at every red light and slowed for every pedestrian crossing, but it was obvious his mind was elsewhere. He looked pained like he was in the midst of an on-setting migraine. Madison asked him if something was wrong, but he only shook his head. He entered the lobby of the FBI field office with the manner of someone who wanted to get their colonoscopy over and done with. He told the middle-aged man at the front desk they were there to see Agent Vasquez. The man asked if they were expected—to which Atticus emitted a sound that was part grunt and part chuckle. The man looked unsure of his next move, but Atticus told him to give her a call. The man asked for his name.

"Clayton Jones," Atticus said.

He shot Madison a warning look. She stayed quiet, but why had he given a fake name? Surely someone had a computer with facial recognition software that identified every single person who walked in. They probably knew Madison's ACT score and every game of Monopoly she had cheated on. The man made a call and told them it would be a few minutes, so they took a seat. A few minutes turned out to be fifteen but felt a lot longer. Madison didn't feel comfortable having her phone out, fearing someone would think she was arming a bomb, so she stared at the wall. Atticus was part of the last generation who knew how to wait in line for something without a cell phone in hand. At last, a middle-aged woman greeted them, asked if Atticus was Clayton Jones, and—after he said yes—escorted them to the elevators. However, this wasn't Agent Vasquez but one of the secretaries. They stepped off on the sixth floor, and the woman led them to an office. She knocked on the door, alerted the agent inside that Clayton Jones was here, and then left.

Atticus gestured for Madison to enter first. A tsunami of anxiety crashed over her. She was the sort of person who snuck in with the herd. One deep, powering breath later, she called her nerves enough to step into the office. Atticus followed. Agent Vasquez rose from her desk. She was a naturally gorgeous woman. Knowing Atticus must have known her when he was a detective, she had to be over fifty. But it seemed impossible. She had a figure reminiscent of Jane Russell, and Madison couldn't help but think of what Howard Hughes would have done to discover such a woman. Her skin was the color of creamed coffee, her hair a vibrant golden brown, and her eyes olive green. She had a welcoming smile, not intimidating in the slightest, but that smile vanished when she saw "Clayton Jones." What that smile was replaced with Madison couldn't pinpoint.

"Atticus…" she managed to say.

"Allie," Atticus replied, not meeting her gaze.

Madison could feel the force between them. Powerful. Painful. Palpable. Poignant. And for her, extremely awkward.

Atticus introduced her, and Agent Vasquez and Madison shook hands.

"So, how can I help you, Ms. Monroe and *Mr. Jones*?" Vasquez asked.

Atticus and Madison took turns explaining why they were there. Had it gotten any easier to talk about? Not one damn word. Vasquez barely reacted, but this didn't surprise Madison. Law enforcement needed world-class poker faces.

"Do you have this chapter?" Vasquez asked.

Madison handed her a printed copy.

"Has the FBI gotten stringent or will coffee be provided?" Atticus asked.

Vasquez didn't look up from the page. "This is the Federal Bureau of Investigation, not the lobby of a Days Inn." She leaned back in her chair when she finished reading. "There's not much to go on here."

"There are clues as to where this Shawna could be," Atticus said.

Vasquez nodded. "Spigot. Coke. You think somewhere in the South?"

"Yes, and there's a reference to a song."

"A catchy tune by a white hick."

"We think it's a Johnny Cash song," Madison said, then recited the lyrics of the song they had found (neither of them were going to sing it).

"Memphis?" Vasquez asked.

"Geographically, it makes sense based on where Andrea Collins was murdered," Atticus said.

Vasquez was silent, clearly going over what she had read and heard. She took a deep breath, chewing her gum like it was a piece of steak.

"So, you want me to find a woman named Shawna, which most likely is a fake name, in Memphis, a city of over half a million?"

"Well, we know she's a woman. And she has dark hair, blue eyes, and she's white," Atticus said.

"If he's telling the truth about that," Vasquez pointed out.

"He's telling the truth," Atticus said more firmly.

"How do you know?"

Atticus nodded at Madison. "Because she's white, has dark hair and blue eyes."

Vasquez studied his face. He didn't meet her eyes. Throughout the meeting, whenever Atticus looked at Vasquez, she looked away. And when she looked at him, he wouldn't meet her gaze.

"I just eliminated millions of possibilities without any of your fancy little gadgets," Atticus said.

Vasquez scoffed. "Fancy gadgets? I see you're still as open as ever to learning new technology."

"You know they won't be able to track that email in time. A search and a phone call is all I'm asking," Atticus said.

"Okay."

Vasquez got to work, typing with a form and posture that revealed she had taken a class to learn. Her typing was flawless, and she used her keyboard to shift between search fields rather than using her mouse.

"He doesn't tell us when she was arrested, but if we take Madison's age into consideration and her age at the time of the incident, let's use an age range of 18–36."

Madison appreciated Vasquez saying "incident" rather than "abduction" or "rape."

The search results narrowed after the age range had been applied. Vasquez filtered them further—dark hair, blue eyes, Caucasian.

"Eight results… one is dead, two are incarcerated," Vasquez reported.

"We need to find these five women," Atticus said.

Vasquez bit her lip. "You're sure about this?"

"I am."

For the first time, they met each other's gaze. It was a powerful force. Both had been heavily shielded, but that gaze destroyed their armor. When it broke, it was as if a spell had been lifted.

Vasquez slowly nodded. "Let me make a call."

Madison didn't ask Atticus about his enigmatic relationship with Vasquez, but man was she curious! In the forty-five minutes they were in Vasquez's office, they had conveyed a dozen emotions. Atticus was silent on the drive back, a different silence than the one on the drive there. This silence was somber. Reflective. His face showed no quiet optimism of possibly having saved an innocent life. Madison suspected he was like her, unable to feel pleased about any achievement, always moving on to the next worry.

When they reached Essex on the Park, Atticus returned to his apartment with only a wave. Casper stopped by shortly after Madison reached her apartment, and she told him about their visit to the FBI.

"You like Italian?" Casper asked after.

"Ice?" she asked facetiously.

Casper chortled. "Food."

In her apartment, they cooked the simplest yet delicious staple of Italian cuisine—buttered noodles. Casper helped clean up, something limited to washing the kettle and sauce pan. Everything else fit in the dishwasher.

He stayed for a movie, enjoying the Old Fashioned Madison had made. The movie was action packed, riding the edge between believable and asinine. But her mind drifted to "Shawna," whoever she really was. Had the police found her? Was she safe? Or was she in her own cabin, duct taped to a rickety bed, punctured by the mattress springs? When the movie ended, it was only 7:15. Casper turned to her and asked if she wanted to go get ice cream.

"Maybe live on the edge and make it a double? You're not driving," he said.

Madison put on a hooded sweatshirt, and together, they set out into the crisp Chicago air.

Atticus had fallen asleep in his recliner. A little over ten years ago, he had bought a new mattress, one guaranteed to give him the best sleep of his life. He hadn't believed the bullshit when the salesman spewed it back then, and time had certainly debunked it now. His recliner was fifteen years old, the leather cracked, the color faded. But damn if he didn't sleep on it like he'd been anesthetized. It was when he laid on that thousand-dollar mattress that he struggled to sleep. But no matter how often he fell asleep in that recliner, he was never in a deep sleep, so he woke on the first knock. Instinct shaped over a forty-year career was impossible to break, and his first reaction was to reach for his .357 Magnum Revolver. He had initially set it on the end table but then kept it in his hand. If these were podcasters or true crime fanatics, a loaded gun would send the right message. He opened the door.

"What time is it?"

"Check your watch."

One of the last people he had ever expected at his door. Alejandra Vasquez. Allie. She looked at the gun in his hand.

"Expecting a fight?" she asked.

"Something like that. What are you doing here? How do you know where I live?" he asked.

"Please, I work for the FBI."

"Seems like an invasion of privacy."

"Because it is."

Atticus opened the door and allowed her inside. Vasquez took a few steps in but stayed close to the door like it was a buoy. "I can't stay. I just wanted to tell you Memphis police looked into your 'Shawna.' They sent officers to the addresses of those five women."

"And?"

"And they're all safe and accounted for. Well, safe is arbitrary. Two will more than likely die from a heroin overdose in the near future."

"That's great news... well, not the heroin part."

Vasquez laughed to mask her nerves. "So... why the fake name?"

"I wasn't sure if you'd agree to meet me."

Vasquez didn't know what to say, so she moved on. "So, when did you move from Glenbrook?"

"After Mary died."

Vasquez bit her lip, mulling over what to say and how to say it. "I'm sorry to hear that. I know she and I... anyway, I'm sorry."

Atticus nodded dismissively, and she knew he didn't want to talk about it.

"I always pictured you in a small town. One church, one restaurant, one bar."

"Yeah, so did I..."

A dangerous silence descended. Their gazes met, perilously powerful.

"Anyway, I appreciate you doing this," Atticus said.

"When Atticus Wallace has a hunch, it's always right."

"Not always."

Another silence.

"So, how do you know the Monroe girl?" Vasquez asked.

"Hardly know her. Lives in the building. But she's a strong girl. A quiet strength, you know? One she's not even aware she has. Got your instincts too."

Vasquez smiled nostalgically. "There he is, always trying to find the next great protégé."

"I was right about you."

Nostalgia lurked around every corner and behind every door. If Vasquez wasn't careful, nostalgia would attack her, overpower her, and consume her.

"Take care of yourself, Atticus," Vasquez said.

Both could have said more but neither would. Vasquez turned and headed toward the elevator.

Chicago never failed to mesmerize Madison, and though she loved summer with its blue skies and bright, hot sun synonymous with happiness, there was something indescribably alluring about fall. Back home in Wisconsin, it had been the crimson and Tuscany-yellow leaves, campfires, and s'mores. But in the city, it was the sensation of the crisp breeze filling her lungs and the way the lights of the skyscrapers looked so much sharper in the cold that enticed her.

She and Casper had finished their Baskin-Robbins ice cream when Atticus called to tell them the five possible "Shawnas" were all safe. Riding that celebratory high, they stopped at Dunkin' Donuts. Madison took a break from cold brew and ordered hot so she could use it as a hand warmer. Coffee in hand, they strolled to Grant Park, the South Rose Garden, and then sat on a bench overlooking the Buckingham Fountain spraying water into the night sky, illuminated by the myriad colored lights.

Casper had nearly finished his coffee before Madison had even taken her second sip. She had used the coffee to warm her hands, but now, since she couldn't feel its heat anymore, she took three large gulps.

"I wanted to ask you about *it*, but if you don't want to answer, you don't have to," Casper said.

Madison took a sip, nodding tentatively

"Is there anyone you think could've done this?"

She shook her head. "I think about that every day, but no."

He asked if anybody at any party had gotten a bit too handsy. There were plenty.

"A guy named Shane Benson, but I don't think he could have done something like that. He didn't like hearing no, but he never forced himself on me. He just tugged me toward him, not letting go of my hand right away."

A brief hesitation.

"What is it?" Casper asked.

"My English professor made a pass at me once."

"Sexually? How?"

"I had gone to his office to go over a paper, and he sat at the chair beside me, not the one behind his desk. I found it odd but harmless. But then, he put his hand on my thigh. Initially, I gave him the benefit of doubt that it was an innocent show of support. But then, his hand traveled further up my leg. I pushed his hand off and jumped to my feet and stormed out. That was the only time. I never allowed a chance for it to happen again. I don't think my experience was unique though. There was a saying about him, 'You can get a D or you can take the D.'"

Casper scoffed. "What a stellar sculptor of young minds."

Madison forced a laugh, then took another sip of coffee. Casper squeezed her hand and then polished off the remainder of his coffee. He rose from the bench to throw his empty cup away, granting her a reprieve from the uncomfortable memory. They enjoyed watching the fountain until the warmth of the coffee inside their bellies faded. Then they walked back to Essex on the Park.

"There's something I've been meaning to ask, and maybe it's too soon…" Casper said.

Nerves flared up throughout her body. Her mind raced to anticipate what he would ask. In seconds, Madison had mapped out a dozen hypothetical situations. Casper looked at her—no smile at the plate, on deck, or even in the batter's box. Instead, he looked like he was in line at a wake to pay his respects.

"Malts or shakes?"

Madison laughed from the relief the question brought. This was not one of the two-hundred twelve possible questions she had considered.

"I would have to go with malts," she said.

"Made me nervous for a second. I thought we would have to go our separate ways."

The light turned, granting the two of them the right to cross the intersection.

"What about snow cones or Icees?" Casper asked.

"Icees. You?"

"Uh, please," he said, acting offended at such a foolish question. "Icees by a landslide."

"Could have said avalanche," Madison remarked.

"Well played, 5414, well played."

Though her stomach was filled with coffee and ice cream, the snow cones that Casper mentioned stayed on her mind. It was like a brain freeze she couldn't get rid of. It wasn't because she craved one; it was something else. But what, Madison couldn't say. And still, it stayed on her mind like frost on a windshield.

When they got back to Essex on the Park, Casper stopped at his apartment, giving her time to clear hers, Glock in hand. When he returned, they played a few games of cribbage. Casper, as it turned out, came from a long line of players and counted the points like it was a language with its own cadence. No matter how hard Madison tried concentrating on potential pegging points, she couldn't get the thought of snow cones out of her head.

"We don't have to play if you don't want to," Casper said.

"Sorry, I do. I just can't get something out of my head."

"What can't you get out of your head?"

"Snow cones."

She knew how psychotic that sounded.

"Snow cones..." Casper repeated.

"I know, crazy. But it's like they're important."

"We've already established they are not."

He smiled, trying to ease her mind. But it wasn't one of his home run smiles, it was a fly out. One forced for her benefit.

"It's like I know something, but I can't remember what."

They finished the game, and then Casper said good night. Madison got ready for bed, all the while trying to discover what sort of significance damn snow cones had. She laid in bed, her eyelids growing heavy. The poem, *A Visit from St. Nicholas,* came to mind. Why? She had no clue. Every night before bed or in the middle of the night after she had gotten up to get a glass of water or go to the bathroom, a random thought would enter her head. An event, a conversation, or a movie or book from years, even decades, ago. Her mind was a faulty jukebox, randomly grabbing memories, thoughts, and worries to play for her.

While visions of sugar plums danced in their heads.

The only creature stirring in her apartment was her tireless mind. *In her head arose such a clatter.*

Sugar plums... no, not sugar plums... snow cones...

Plum snow cones? No, not plum... grape!

"Grape snow cone?" Casper repeated. Madison had called him back to her apartment. "Madison, I have no idea what you're talking about."

He was dressed in a Save Ferris t-shirt and pajama pants tucked into his shoes in his rush to get there.

"It's a song," Madison said.

The beat of the song had come to her, and it played on a loop. But the only words she could think of was "grape snow cone." She had recalled nothing but the instrumental theme, which was entirely maddening. Madison paced from door to window, grinding away at the inside of her cheeks. The taste of a piggy bank's worth of pennies filled her mouth.

In the movie adaptation of *The Shining*, Jack Nicholson's character had typed "all work and no play makes Jack a dull boy" over and over and over and over. Madison was having her own such moment, but her mind instead typed out in Courier New Font: `Grape Snow Cone. Grape Snow Cone. Grape Snow Cone.`

Her thoughts veered on a Jack Nicholson tangent, going over his filmography. *One Flew Over the Cuckoo's Nest, Batman, As Good as It Gets,* and *A Few Good Men,* which also starred Demi Moore, who was in *Ghost,* her favorite movie.

Stop! I need to focus. Think. Think, dammit!

And then, more words came in a flash. She sang them out.

Casper did his best to hide his confusion and worry, but, suffice it to say, he wasn't a theatre major but more likely the guy who got stuck playing a tree in his school play. Madison rushed to her computer. There must be a code in every operating system that makes a computer run twice as slow when the user is in a mad rush. Madison cursed. She typed in the lyrics and waited for the results to load. It took so long that it felt like she was waiting for dial-up in 1998. The search result sent an arctic chill through her.

"What? What is it?" Casper asked.

"Chattahoochee."

Casper tilted his head. "Chattahoochee? What is that?"

"It's a river…"

"I think we made a mistake."

Those were the words that woke Atticus from his second slumber. A late-night college football game played on the TV. He stumbled to his kitchen and splashed water on his face and neck. Then he grabbed an ice cube and rubbed it on his lower back. It was a secret of his and one he swore by. How do you go from dead tired to fully awake in seconds? Rub ice on your lower back, one of the body's most sensitive areas to cold. He finished the half cup of now day-old coffee, then headed to apartment 5414.

"I think we got the city wrong," Madison said, skipping any polite greeting.

"Why do you say that?" Atticus asked.

"Casper and I were talking, and the topic of snow cones was brought up," she said.

"As it tends to," Atticus said acerbically.

"It made me think of a song. A country song."

"You think it's the one mentioned in the chapter?"

Madison wanted to say yes, and she wanted to say no. If she said no, then the five possible Shawnas were safe and accounted for in Memphis, Tennessee. Cowardly as it was, she wanted to shake her head violently and scream no! Because yes was terrifying, fatal. It meant "Shawna" was in danger. But yes was necessary. So she forced herself to nod—the result looked like an uncontrolled muscle spasm.

"The song's by Allan Jackson," she said.

The name meant nothing to Atticus.

"Wears a cowboy hat, cowboy boots, an offensive amount of denim," Casper added.

"A white hick," Atticus surmised. "And what's this song called?"

"Chattahoochee," Madison answered.

She displayed the Chattahoochee River on Google Maps on one of the computer screens. Atticus studied the long, winding river.

"That covers three states," he said.

"I know, but if we reread the chapter and focus on clues for someplace in Alabama, Georgia, or Florida…"

Madison hurried back to her kitchen table, Casper and Atticus following in her wake. She slid a copy of the chapter toward them. It looked like one of her edits—filled with red slashes and circles, highlighted words, and notes written in the margins.

Atticus picked it up and read the highlighted sentence she pointed to. "*And this peach is ripe for the pickin to.* That's a pretty common idiom."

"I agree, but the use isn't consistent," she said.

Both men waited for further explanation.

"Everything up to this point is vile and derogatory. Slut, whore, hoe… then peach? It doesn't make sense. Peach is a term of endearment. It makes me think its use is intentional."

Atticus nodded, hopping on to her train of thought.

"So, what if peach is in reference to the location? And what state is most commonly associated with peaches?" Madison asked.

"Georgia," Atticus replied.

"Right. So he uses peach to reference Georgia," Casper said, "But we still need to narrow it down more."

"I know," Madison said, scanning through the page. "Listen to this line. It was something I initially overlooked. '*I flip my hood up. She turns away from the busy streets, leaving the roar of the birds further in the distance.*' Roar of the birds? Birds don't roar."

"No, they don't," Atticus agreed.

"So, either roar or birds can't be taken at face value," Casper said.

Madison nodded. Atticus rubbed his forehead as he reread, looking for more clues. Then he paced to the computer and stared at the map on the screen, studying it. She hoped he'd come to the same conclusion.

"Atlanta," he said.

The same answer she had come to. She nodded, emphatically and excitedly.

"How do you know that?" Casper asked.

"The Atlanta Falcons. He's talking about their stadium. Roar of the crowd," Atticus said.

He flipped his phone open and then grabbed the business card Vasquez had given him.

"It's Atticus. We need you."

Alejandra Vasquez believed in God and routines. Her career was chaotic, the only constant being change. She needed some consistency in her life. She woke at 3:50 every weekday, 5:15 every Saturday, and 5:45 on Sundays. Because of her job, she didn't need to worry about choosing a wardrobe. She wore the same style of blouse and skirt, either black or navy blue. Wearing a skirt and blouse of different color gave criminals an easier target to shoot at. She drank her coffee with a splash of half and half. She had dozens and dozens of routines for different days of the week, but what hadn't been routine for decades was getting a call from Atticus Wallace.

"We need you."

Extremely brief. Frustratingly vague. Highly urgent. She'd been in bed for a little over two hours. But Vasquez had three decades of experience in getting called out of bed in the middle of the night. She splashed warm water on her eyes—cold water didn't help with the rheum—and then grabbed an ice cube and rubbed it across her lower back. Though she'd been doing this routine for over thirty years, she still gasped when the frozen cube touched her flesh.

When she turned into the FBI parking lot, Atticus, Casper, and Madison were waiting for her. On the walk inside and the elevator ride up, Madison explained her Chattahoochee theory.

Vasquez sat at her computer and logged in. She applied the same filters as she'd done earlier, only replacing Memphis with Atlanta. A dozen women remained as possibilities. She turned her monitor so the others could see. She clicked through profiles—each woman eliminated because of either weight or height (if they didn't fit Madison's svelte figure and stand within an inch or two of her height, they were out).

The last mugshot showed a woman strung out on drugs, her beauty withering in the early stages of an unnatural erosion. Her dark hair was unwashed and disheveled. Her sky-blue eyes bloodshot, and the mascara smeared by tears. A tight tank top, deliberately a size smaller than she should have worn, revealed a busty cleavage and her navel and torso.

"That's our Shawna," Atticus said.

Vasquez read the bio. "Kimberly Johnson. 26 years old. Lives in Atlanta, Georgia. Arrested for prostitution and felony drug possession."

Madison swallowed a rock of spit as her head swirled and made her queasy. She had been right. There was no doubt about it. Kimberly Johnson had been chosen by the Man in the Mask because she shared physiological traits with her. The dark hair. The blue eyes. The same figure.

Vasquez picked up her desk phone and called the Bureau headquarters in Atlanta, explaining the chapter and Kimberly Johnson. To add to the gravity of the situation, she mentioned Andrea Collins' murder. At the end of her call, her final words caused a frozen blade to pierce Madison's worried stomach.

"She is believed to be in danger."

Waiting is Hell. Madison truly believed that. Sometimes, it's unfathomable how cruel time can be. Understandably, Vasquez couldn't have three civilians in her office all night, so they had to return to Essex on the Park. The first update had come before they even entered the elegant apartment building. The police had stopped at Kimberly Johnson's apartment, but she wasn't home. Casper tried to make Madison feel better by reasoning that a prostitute wouldn't be home before sunrise. As true as that may be, it did little to assuage her nerves.

Hours passed without another update. It felt like a loved one was in surgery and Madison waited for information from the doctor. She made the mistake of having Casper look up Kimberly Johnson on Facebook. They were able to view Kimberly's current and previous profile pictures. The pictures revealed the progressive degradation of a young, jovial, cute girl into an overtly sexualized woman with an increasing dependency on drugs. What had driven her to self-destruction? Some event in her past? Perhaps one similar to Madison's? Victims of sexual assault often turned to prostitution, sadly believing their violated bodies to be unworthy of respect and love. And Madison felt that. At times, it seemed as if she was battling an opponent who toyed with her, shoved her face into the mud, and took pleasure in laughing at her pain.

She called Atticus three times throughout the following day for updates, but he had none to give. She tried reading a book, but it was too passive an activity. Her mind raced when idle. Worrying is the most exhaustive activity—both physically and mentally. And when it came to eating when worried, there are two camps: You either binge eat in gluttonous excess or you didn't eat. There is no healthy area in between. Madison fell into the latter camp. Over the years, she had learned to force herself to eat, but when her anxieties became extreme, eating seemed as impossible a task as sprouting wings.

The sun had set and the clock on her microwave showed 5:43 when someone rapped on the door. Madison looked through the peephole before letting Atticus and Vasquez inside. The special agent gave her a polite nod.

"Did you find her?" Madison finally asked.

But she knew the answer. Had Kimberly Johnson been found alive and safe, they would have said so right away. Their demeanors demonstrated the depressing news they had to share.

"She's dead," Madison said, not waiting for them to come out and say it.

"She is," Atticus confirmed.

He showed as much shock and sadness as a person who had received news like this for forty years could. Madison knew a certain level of detachment was needed in order to survive in that world, but it was still hard to view such a reaction as anything but cruel, cold, and callous.

"She was found in Proctor Creek," Vasquez said. "Stems off the Chattahoochee."

Madison sat on a kitchen chair, feeling dejected and defeated. Vasquez and Atticus sat across from her. His knees cracked, and he sighed from both the relief and the pain.

"How'd she die? Was it the same as in the chapter?" Madison asked.

Vasquez looked at Atticus, unsure of what she should say. He gave her a permissive nod.

"Preliminary examination shows she was bludgeoned on the back of the head, but the cause of death is believed to be drowning," Vasquez said.

"It's my fault…" Madison said. "I gave you the wrong city."

"We agreed on Memphis," Atticus said. "If it wasn't for you figuring out it was a game—"

"She'd be dead?" Madison couldn't help but sound like a sarcastic bitch.

"You're not the only one who has felt that way. We," a quick nod at Vasquez, "have felt that way a hell of a lot. It's not your fault. Other people—

professionals—read these emails too. They didn't find the answer either. It's not their fault, and it sure as hell isn't yours."

She wasn't looking for a pick-me-up talk. They didn't work on her.

"So, now what?" she asked.

Vasquez tapped her thumb on the table, deciding how to respond. "He's killed two women in two weeks. We have to believe it'll continue. The same pattern. Emails on Friday nights. Victims matching your appearance."

"Can I just delete my email?" Madison asked.

"You could. But it won't stop the killing," Atticus said.

Vasquez told her she didn't have to check any email; someone on Vasquez's team would.

"What about legitimate edit requests that come through?"

"Once they've been checked, examined, and verified, we'll alert you."

A tinge of selfishness colored Madison's reaction. Her career was made by editing, by sitting before a computer. The quicker she responded to requests, the better her chances of getting the author's business. What if it took the FBI a week—or two weeks—to verify a sample chapter as a legitimate piece of fiction? What if they contacted the author? It would surely freak out the writer to have the FBI reach out to them. But beyond her self-interests, there was something else worrying her.

"What if he knows I'm not reading them?" Madison asked.

Both Vasquez and Atticus looked for her to elaborate.

"He's obviously knowledgeable in cyber security," she continued. "What if he can tell by the IP address or something that I'm not opening the emails, that I'm not playing his game? What if he stops sending them and just... kills them."

"... It's a possibility," Vasquez admitted.

But the way Vasquez had delivered that sentence told Madison she was right. Hiding from her problems was tempting. Oh, so tempting. Disappear into the realm of fiction. Stay locked up in her apartment. But Dr. Fret had reminded her that our problems aren't some predator that'll grow sick of the hunt. They'll wait. They don't need to sleep. They don't need to eat. They'll sit there and wait until we face them or they have conquered us.

"I'll read them," Madison said, regretting that decision the moment it left her lips.

Vasquez had a look of approval, showing her respect with a subtle nod. Then she and Atticus left.

The discovery of Kimberly Johnson's body was already circulating on Atlanta news stations by the time Madison had the courage to google it. All the results stated "the body of Kimberly Johnson" and that didn't sit well with Madison. It wasn't the body of Kimberly Johnson found drifting face down in Proctor Creek. It *was* Kimberly Johnson. It was a flawed woman battling her demons and losing. A woman only 26 years old. A woman who could have turned her life around but now would never have the opportunity to.

Madison spent over an hour in her bathtub, staying until her fingers pruned. Then, after she had gotten dressed, she briefly debated on whether to go right to bed. But she ultimately ended up scrolling Netflix.

Halfway through a comedy, her phone chimed. A Gmail notification from Madeline Hawk. Surprising herself, she felt no inner turmoil on whether to open it or leave it to the FBI. She was too curious. Her mind would come up with things far worse than whatever was written in the email.

Silly Sheep,

I have written another pathetic, unlikeable character. Why would anyone care about a twenty-something drug-addicted street whore? The fault is my own. At a great distance she resembled you. But like some art, beauty is in the detail. Meant to be seen up close. She could never be you. But how do I write a character like you? Would anyone be able to suspend their disbelief that someone like you truly exists outside the world of fiction? An elegant woman with dazzling intellect, alabaster skin, cobalt-blue eyes, watermelon lips, space-black hair? A woman of remarkable resplendency. A woman with a subtle, salacious smile. A woman of wit. Kimberly Johnson could never be you. She was a single-celled organism, a strand of bacteria on her best day.

I'll continue to look for inspiration. But when they fall short, I can't help but hack away at them until I can see what they're really made of.

You'll hear from me soon,

Your Big Bad Wolf

Too many simultaneous emotions flooded her body for it to know how to react. Madison sat there like a dumb robot waiting for an update. Fear loomed large and ever present, a shadow encompassing everything. Yes, there was sadness for Kimberly Johnson and her family. But then came anger. And of all human emotions, anger is the juggernaut. It is a high-speed train. It burned within like a supernova. The Man in the Mask saw Madison as a sheep. The quintessential prey. He was too arrogant to think he could be caught. And now, there was a deep-seated yearning brewing inside Madison to prove him wrong.

And in that moment, she vowed to do so.

The calendar may have revealed the true month and year, but the hands of time had traveled back decades. Atticus placed a bottle of Miller High Life in front of Vasquez. She sat at his kitchen table while he leaned against the wall near the tall window, his gaze fixed upon the city. Neither spoke, each instead hiding behind sips of their beer. Then Vasquez's phone vibrated, breaking the uncomfortable silence. She answered, then pocketed it when the conversation was over.

"More details on Johnson's body," she said. "Two fishermen had pulled her from the water. By the time the police and coroner showed up, the body had been out for over twenty minutes."

Atticus knew how those conditions can affect the human body. In water, a body decomposes slower due to cooler temperature and the anaerobic environment. This results in the secretion of a wax-like substance known as adipocere. The moment the body is taken out into the oxygen-heavy open air, it accelerates decomposition. And of course, most DNA evidence, if not all, would have been washed away. Atticus had been called to the shores of Lake Michigan over a hundred times throughout his career to examine bodies that had washed ashore. There are certain areas in police work where you develop calluses to help protect you. The most common practice was to accept a body as just a body. The soul of the person who inhabited that body had already ascended to Heaven or descended to Hell as merited. But seeing a human body at that stage of decomposition never got easy. Atticus had been a practicing Catholic his whole life. His faith favored burial because Jesus had been buried and had risen. But after seeing a body a month into decay for the first time, he'd told Mary to "burn me twice."

"Think she'll be okay?" Vasquez asked. "Madison, that is."

"She's resilient. It wasn't her mistake," Atticus said.

"Nor is it yours."

Atticus lifted his eyebrows and forced himself to say, "I know."

"I'm not talking about Kimberly Johnson."

Atticus paused, the bottle inches from his lips. Then he took a swig.

"You're still carrying that, aren't you?" Vasquez asked.

Atticus had his back to her, his gazed fixed on the Magnificent Mile. "What would you think of me if I didn't?"

Vasquez rose and walked around the table, stopping three feet from him.

"There were hundreds of people in that mall, Atticus. We interviewed every last one of them. Not one of them saw a thing."

"It was my job to find him."

"It was *our* job."

"The answers are always there. I just couldn't find 'em."

"No, sometimes, there are no answers. It wasn't right for her to blame you. You need to let it go. Evil things happen because evil people commit evil acts, not because good people fail to stop them."

Atticus took a mouth-filling gulp of his beer, then stared in silence out at the city. Vasquez reclaimed her beer and took an annoyed sip followed by a deep breath to calm herself. Her eyes caught an old family photo of Atticus, Mary, and their two children.

"How are Carter and Jeanette?" she asked.

"They don't come around often."

"Just holidays?"

"By often I mean ever."

Vasquez's face filled with sadness. The few photos he had in and around the living room and kitchen were mostly old ones that Vasquez had seen all those years ago. She hoped more current ones were somewhere in his bedroom, but it seemed unlikely.

"Where are they now?"

Atticus laughed, not with humor but a pain deep within his chest. "Last Christmas card I got, Vicky sent without Carter knowing."

"Vicky's his wife?"

Atticus nodded. "That was 2012. They were in St. Paul then. I sent a Christmas card a few years ago that came back 'return to sender.' Jeanette…" he shrugged. "I saw one of her friends from high school a year or two ago. Asked me if I was happy Jeanette was back in the area."

"… You didn't know…"

"Nope," Atticus replied shortly.

Vasquez couldn't hide her sorrow. Atticus was not someone who conveyed emotion through facial expressions, but at this moment, every line in his face pulsated with a pained moroseness, his eyes a pool of reflection. It was a pain that, in all the years she'd known him, she'd seen only a handful of times.

Was this the pain he'd worn that day all those years ago?

"I'm sorry, Atticus. I really am."

He dismissed her apology with a shake of the head. "I don't blame them. It's my fault. I made my choice, and they never forgave me for it."

The following morning, Atticus couldn't decide if the previous night had been a fortuitous dream or a tormenting nightmare. Time doesn't fly, it soars. Atticus had always been an "out of sight, out of mind"–type person. But now, the past was neither out of sight nor out of mind.

A knock on the door broke his pensive. Casper was at the door, nervously scratching at the back of his head. He asked if they could talk. Atticus invited him inside.

"Coffee?" Atticus offered.

"Sure," Casper accepted.

Atticus poured a cup and slid it over. Casper stared warily at the black liquid, clearly someone who was used to Starbucks with creamers and syrups.

"What's on your mind?" Atticus asked.

Casper took a sip, then winced at the bitter taste. "I asked Madison if she could think of anyone from her past that could do something like what happened to her."

"And?"

Casper exhaled a deep breath, a gesture of guilt. "I feel like a piece of shit for telling you."

"If it helps end this, you're helping her."

Casper thought on it and nodded. He told Atticus about Shane Benson and the English professor at Marquette.

"I think they're both married. Professor has kids," Casper said.

"That only means they file their taxes differently," Atticus remarked.

Serial killers are masters of disguise. They look like us. Talk like us. They're husbands, fathers, volunteers, teachers, and church-goers. Wolves who have assimilated into the flock of sheep.

Casper chugged as much of the lukewarm coffee as he could, then left. Atticus called Vasquez.

"I'm going to pay the professor a visit," Atticus said.

"If he isn't willing to talk, let me know. I'll stop by and cause a scene," Vasquez said.

Atticus poured the remaining coffee into his thermos.

"I'm going to stop by Madison and ask her to tell me everything she remembers about the day she was taken. I've read the file, Atticus. Her interview... it's not..." Vasquez trailed off.

She didn't like to openly criticize another badge, but there was a considerable amount of missed questions and wrong follow-ups to the few right questions asked. A special skill is required to extract information from a person in distress. Shock and trauma overwhelm victims. Times, locations, and faces get jumbled up. You, as the investigator, needed to be supportive yet indifferent, patient but pushy. But, when interviewing suspects, you needed to sort through fact and fiction without alerting the person to which pile you were sorting their statements into. The perp needed to think you were not only chewing their bullshit but swallowing it too.

Two officers had interviewed Madison after her abduction. One had been too compassionate, pausing whenever emotion consumed her. At one point, he had even said, "You can tell us later," which made Vasquez cringe. The other officer had come off as a complete asshole. For as blunt as Atticus could be, he had a deft touch when it came to interviewing and interrogating, and Vasquez had learned how to walk that tightrope too. But with the incident almost a decade ago now, Vasquez knew she might not be able to get any new, definitive information. In her experience, victims of violence or trauma reacted in one of two ways. They either suppressed it all, bleaching it clean. Or, the memories became a stain that never faded.

The Century Bob dummy still wobbled like a bobble head from her last punch. Madison had just finished her workout when Vasquez knocked on her door. Vasquez held up a medium-size coffee for her. Madison thanked her and asked for a few minutes to wash up and change. She grabbed her MMA gloves off the kitchen table on her way to her bedroom.

"You fight?" Vasquez asked when Madison returned.

"I train. I don't ever intend on being a victim again," Madison said.

Vasquez smirked, respecting Madison's resolve. "No, I can see that."

Madison thanked her again for the coffee and wrapped her hands around the hot cup. But she didn't even take a sip to test the temperature.

"Do you not like coffee?" Vasquez asked.

"I do. I can't drink things hot. I always wait for it to cool," Madison said.

Vasquez sat at the gestured spot at the kitchen table.

"So, what can I do for you?" Madison asked.

"I'd like you to tell me about the night you were taken," Vasquez said.

A rock plummeted in Madison's stomach. "Okay…"

Vasquez removed a pocket-sized notepad and pen.

"Do you mind if I record?" Vasquez asked.

"This won't… get out, will it?" Madison asked.

"No, no. It's just for me to remember what you said."

Madison nodded her permission. Vasquez used her iPhone to record.

"I know there are things that happened to you that are extremely painful to talk about. But I need you to continue to be brave and tell me all of it. Everything. Even if you think it's inconsequential. What someone in your field would refer to as 'useless exposition' I call possible case breakers. There's no limit on word count either."

Vasquez smiled. She had an effortless ability to make Madison feel safe, the same way Atticus did. Her strength was damn near radioactive, and Madison hoped she absorbed its radiation.

"I'll try," Madison said.

It was a word Dr. Frett wanted her to remove from her vocabulary. She paid him a ridiculous amount for the advice. Yoda had given it to Luke for free. Vasquez hit the record button. Madison took a deep breath, preparing to relive the horror.

"It was Halloween… I rode my bike to a house party. I met my best friend and roommate Jade there," she started.

"What made you ride your bike?" Vasquez asked.

"I almost always did. It gave me an excuse to not get super drunk. It was exercise, and Ubers and Lyfts add up when you're drinking every weekend. Our apartment had cheap rent but at the cost of being outside campus. Fifty-minute bike rides weren't uncommon."

"Tell me about this party."

Madison told Vasquez what she could remember. It had been a standard college Halloween party—loud music, kegs filled with cheap Busch light, bottom-shelf liquors, the stench of weed and warm beer, and people dancing. Most people had come in costumes, an excuse for girls to wear skimpy outfits and guys to dress up as a superhero or movie character. Jade and Madison had dressed up as Sam Wheat and Molly Jensen, characters played by Patrick Swayze and Demi Moore in the movie *Ghost*.

"What were those costumes like?" Vasquez asked.

"Umm, Jade was Sam, so she wore black jeans and a maroon shirt," Madison answered.

"And you? Was it a costume that revealed cleavage? A short skirt?"

Madison shook her head. "No. It was a black pinafore dress with a gray undershirt."

Then Vasquez asked Madison if she had drunk much alcohol. Madison initially shook her head but realized her stupidity. A recording does not pick up physical gestures.

"No, I can remember not feeling great," she said.

"How so?" Vasquez looked up from the notebook.

"Tired. Groggy. Just... off."

"Was that a feeling you had all day or something that came on at the party?"

"No, not all day. A little bit on my way to the party maybe. But as time went by, it got worse."

"Did you get your own drink or did someone get it for you?"

"Either I got it or Jade did."

Then Vasquez asked if anyone had tried to get her to drink more, or made a move on or a pass at her. The answer was yes for any girl who attended a college party. But on that specific night, it had been a friend named Vince Propelli who offered her drink after drink and kept trying to hold her hand. But she told Vasquez it wasn't malicious.

"Did he give you a drink?"

"I think he handed me something. I didn't drink it though. At that point, I was ready to go. You know how your body aches before you get a real bad cold? That's what I felt. I told Jade I was leaving."

"So, would you say this crappy feeling got worse rapidly?"

"Definitely. Had I felt that shitty before I left, I wouldn't have gone at all. I even finished a large coffee on the way over. I'm not overly sensitive to caffeine, but to drink nearly 16 ounces of coffee and then be barely able to stay awake..."

Vasquez set her pen down. Madison knew the question she was about to ask.

"Madison, do you think you were drugged?"

Her memories weren't clear; she seemed to have viewed them through the eyes of someone who badly needed contacts.

"I don't think so…"

"It could have been added to your cup. You take your attention away from your drink for a mere moment, and it's all someone needs."

"I can't say for certain, but that crappy feeling set in when I got to the party. But I… I don't know for sure."

Vasquez nodded and picked her pen up. "So, you tell Jade you're leaving. You walk out. Did you interact with anybody from that moment to when you got on your bike and rode home?"

"Vince tried to drag me to dance. He kept trying to pull me back, but it wasn't aggressive, more of a drunken playfulness."

"Did you and he have a physical relationship?"

Madison blushed. She'd never been one to kiss and tell. It was different for girls. Guys could brag and talk freely of their exploits, but girls got called a slut.

"Yes…"

"I know it's awkward," Vasquez said, "but it's not like this will be posted anywhere." She gave a reassuring smile.

"We had sex…"

"Once?"

"Three times spaced out over the year. Each time involved alcohol. But it was consensual," she added.

She didn't want Vince to come across as shady or creepy because he truly wasn't. And in this day and age, one sentence taken out of context or misinterpreted could destroy someone's life.

"But he accepted your decision to leave?" Vasquez asked.

"Yes. He was pretty drunk, so I don't think he even knew one way or the other."

"Anyone else?"

"Shane Benson. He was outside smoking."

"What was that interaction like?"

Madison scoffed. "Him trying to get my clothes off."

Vasquez asked if they had had sex.

"Almost, but no. He tried a lot."

"Not a fan of the answer no?"

"No, not at all. He offered me a ride, but he wasn't sober. I would have said no regardless." Madison leaned forward. "I'm painting him in a poor light, but Shane was like most college guys. They want their Friday and Saturday nights to end with sex."

Vasquez asked if he was a violent person. Madison didn't know how to answer. Violent sounded so... serious. Shane had gotten in bar fights, often seeking them out. But getting in a bar fight was drastically different than what had been done to her. Some men were simply irascible and pugnacious, barely evolved past throwing their own shit like howler monkeys.

Madison glanced at the notes filling the page. Vasquez had to write quick, concise notes so she didn't have to ask the interviewee to repeat answer after answer. She also didn't look at the notebook as she wrote. Her eyes stayed trained on Madison.

"So, that brings us to the ride home. You were tired. Do you think you were drunk?" Vasquez asked.

"Legally? I don't know. I didn't drink a lot. I had hoped the cold would wake me up."

"Do you know if Propelli or Benson stayed at the party? Or did they leave?"

"Jade said Vince was there all night, until like two or three in the morning."

"And Benson?"

"I'm not sure..."

"You want to say something, but you're not sure if you should."

"I don't want to get him in trouble for certain nocturnal activities of his."

"Drugs? I'm not interested in that."

Madison nodded. She had no doubt about the validity of Vasquez's statement. "He usually ended up doing coke someplace downtown. I have no idea if he did that night though."

Then she described her stop at a Kwik Trip for a Gatorade and a Reese's Big Cup. The cashier was a man she'd seen every Friday and Saturday night (technically Saturday and Sunday mornings). She couldn't remember the man's name but could offer the description Vasquez asked for. He was black; his hair kept in a small afro. Madison guessed his age at the time to be roughly thirty—no younger than that. He was of average build, the same physique most men who didn't take care of their bodies had—skinny arms, folded-in shoulders, and, because of the absence of any pecs, a gut appearing larger than it actually was.

"He'd give me crap for getting the same thing. He was always nice," Madison said.

"Did you get the impression he wanted the conversation to continue?" Vasquez asked.

"That night? Or any night?"

"Both."

Madison hesitated on the answer. "Yes, no. He was quiet, but he didn't mind conversation. I imagine it was a boring shift to work. But once I said good night, he never tried to keep talking or anything."

"Was there anybody else there that night?"

Madison recalled there'd been a group of guys buying beer. Most of the guys in the group had tried their one-liners on her. Vasquez said the police file stated the security cameras at the Kwik Trip hadn't been working, so it was on Madison to remember every detail she could. Vasquez asked if there had been any vehicles at the pumps. From what Madison remembered, there was just the black pickup the beer-buying guys had stepped out of.

After her Gatorade and Reese's, Madison had left the Kwik Trip. Roughly half a mile ahead, she had then come to the long, winding secluded road. Dark. Desolate. Dangerous.

"It was just me... until..."

Vasquez stopped writing and flipped through the journal toward the beginning of the notes she'd taken from the police file she'd read.

"You described the truck as a Dodge Ram, white in color, five to ten years old at the time of the interview," Vasquez read.

"Right. And it had a 'coexist' decal. You know, the one where the T is a cross, the O is a peace sign, the Star of David the X."

Vasquez knew the decal. She stopped the recording on her iPhone. "I know this next part is difficult to relive. If you need to stop and take a break at any moment, feel free to, okay? What we're going to go over are memories you've tried to bury and forget. If you need to think on something, do so. There's no shot clock."

Madison nodded, taking the opportunity to drink a few sips of the coffee, delaying until she could delay no longer.

"Do you think his pleasure came from the act itself or the power he had over you?" Vasquez asked.

"I can't say what he felt…"

"Try to think back. I know this seems impossible, but don't view what happened through your eyes, view it through his."

Madison closed her eyes, her mind erecting the layout of the cabin and everything within. Instantly, it all came rushing back. The descent into darkness was all too easy. She was back in that dilapidated, wooden shack. The scent of mildew and the faint, lingering smell of smoke. The tight, constricting grip of the duct tape around her wrists and ankles, the bed springs poking into her back. The hot breath on her neck, the way his hands caressed her skin, cupped her breasts. For the first time, Madison relived the experience not as the victim but as the Man in the Mask. His excitement. His overwhelming lust.

"… He thought he was making love to me…"

Uttering that sentence brought on the nasty side-effects of a bad pharmaceutical drug. Bile churned in her gut and rose up her throat. What had been the most God-awful, harrowing, life-altering experience of her life had been a moment of euphoric love for him—a steamy romance. She could taste the vomit in her mouth—she took a swig of coffee to mask the taste.

Vasquez reached over and squeezed Madison's hand to show silent support.

Madison detailed what those days in the cabin had been like. How, on a stool beside the bed, he kept a bucket in which she went to the bathroom. How she had slurped water through a straw from a jug, and how he had fed her and wiped food and dribble off her lips with his fingertips.

"How did you free yourself from the tape?" Vasquez asked.

"One of the bed springs near my left wrist had poked through. I used it to tear into the tape." Madison held up her left wrist to show Vasquez the faint scars where the spring had cut into.

"Then you freed your right hand and your legs. Correct? Then what?" Vasquez asked.

"My clothes had been neatly folded against the back wall, near the soot-ridden fireplace. I dressed back into my Molly Jensen costume and tied my shoes."

"Can I ask why you took the time to change? To put on your shoes?" Vasquez cut in.

"I knew once I made it outside, shoes greatly improved my chances of escaping. The snow, the cold... and all it'd take is for me to cut my foot on something sharp and I'd be done."

Vasquez nodded thoughtfully. "I'm always curious about what people do in that sort of situation. I've heard both answers given—get the hell out of there or think ahead."

"Which is correct?"

Vasquez tilted her head, lifting her eyebrows to show the right answer did not exist. "Both have been proven to be correct... and both have been proven to be a fatal mistake."

Survival hinges on so many actions taken or not taken. Vasquez ended her tangent and asked Madison to continue. All dressed, Madison had pried a few 2x4 boards off the window above the bed. She had enough room to squeeze through and land onto the cold, crunchy snow outside the wooden shack.

"I got on my feet and ran."

"And he gave chase?"

Madison nodded, and he had continued to give chase every night in her dreams. And in each nightmare, he grows faster, more feral, more mythical, like a lycanthrope empowered by a full moon. And in those vivid nightmares, Madison never made it to the road.

Vasquez was well aware of what would have happened had the Man in the Mask caught her.

"I reached a road. A car stopped. A man and a woman," Madison said.

The man and the woman who had picked Madison up had given conflicting stories on time and place.

"They were having an affair," Madison explained. "On their way to a hotel. They were trying to save face, but once they realized what had happened, they came clean."

"By which time he was gone and the cabin burned down," Vasquez concluded.

She thanked Madison for reliving the memory and then packed up her things. She promised to be candid whenever any developments arose.

Madison was relatively useless the rest of the day. Dr. Frett often compared reliving what had happened as competing in back-to-back Ironman races. However well-intentioned, Dr. Frett had no idea. No freaking idea. It's impossible to truly fathom the mutilation of rape unless it has happened to you. To feel his hot breath on your neck, to have his hands grope you, to endure the pain as he forces himself inside you. But rape isn't a solely physical act. The damage to psyche outlasts the physical wounds. They never truly heal. They'd scab over, but there was always something that ripped that scab off. Ironman had a finish line—the horror of rape had none.

Milwaukee. It was a city Atticus held a strong affinity for. He appreciated the people's ability to work hard and enjoy life by drinking beer and eating bratwurst. And though he was a Cubs fan (for far longer than it was cool to be), he admired the small-market Brewers' ability to compete at a fraction of the payroll of the Dodgers and the Yankees.

He'd driven I-90 to Milwaukee and back to Chicago hundreds of times and knew what time to leave and how fast to drive to avoid morning and evening rush-hour traffic. The city of Brookfield was about fifteen miles west of Milwaukee and where Madison's former English professor now lived. Atticus's visit was unannounced. Calling ahead was a good way to get told no or give time for the person—suspect or witness—to prepare for the interview.

Professor Grey Moore's house was evidence for why college tuition was so damn high. Three stories with a window directly beneath the middle of the roof that reminded Atticus of horror movies where the ghost of a murdered child stood to watch the living people outside. Hired help, all appearing to be of Mexican descent, raked leaves into piles, revealing luscious, vibrant green grass entirely unnatural for this time of year in Wisconsin. Atticus had golfed on worse. He couldn't respect a man who didn't do his own yard work. Atticus had no doubt that, while Moore supported equal pay for all genders and races, he paid the caretakers shit—a nickel above minimum wage, and even less if they were illegal.

Atticus stepped to the front door, eggshell white in color with a rustic copper knocker in the shape of a full-maned lion's head. He whispered a curse under his breath before knocking with his bare knuckles. A woman answered. She had tarnished her good looks by trying to hold on to them. She had tanned so much her skin had an orange-bronze tint, her teeth had been bleached so white they'd glow in the dark, and her hair was so caked in hairspray that God help her should anyone light a match within ten feet. But worst of all was the Botox shots to her lips and cheeks. Atticus had seen deer mounts with more facial dexterity. The saddest part was that she wasn't even forty.

"Good morning, I was hoping to speak with Grey Moore," Atticus said politely.

"Sure. You an old friend?" she asked with an accent Atticus could only pinpoint as south of the Mason-Dixon Line.

"Friend? No. Old? Yes."

The woman tried to smile; her taxidermy prevented it. She told Atticus to wait a moment and closed the door. Several seconds later, the door opened once more.

"Can I help you?" the man asked.

He was in his mid-fifties, at least twenty years older than the woman who had answered the door, though Atticus suspected she wasn't his daughter. The man's hair was greying on the sides, but the unnatural shade of black hair told Atticus the man used *Just For Men*.

"Professor Grey Moore?" Atticus asked.

"Speaking…"

Atticus introduced himself. "Mind if we talk inside? Bit breezy out here."

It was clear Moore wanted to say no, but before he said so, Atticus had pushed the door open and stepped inside. Atticus complimented Moore on his home as he strolled about, gazing at the photos lined across the fireplace mantel. The wedding photo proved the woman was not his daughter. The photographs of his family—two sons and two daughters—were all professionally shot. No candid photos at Christmas, at a beach, or other family vacations. There were no photos of Moore and his children when they were young, telling Atticus those photos must have had the mother/ex-wife in them.

"Is there something I can help you with, Mr. Wallace?" Moore asked.

"Been teaching at Marquette long?"

"Since 2007… If we could get down to why you're—"

"English professor, right?"

Moore sighed. "That's right."

"A friend of mine went to Marquette. Took your class. She remembers you very well."

"Oh, wonderful!" Spoken with as much sincerity as when you tell the Salvation Army bell ringer you don't have any change. "Who is she?"

"Madison Monroe."

Atticus studied Moore, waiting for a subtle reaction upon hearing her name, but there was none. He seemed to have no idea who she was, but he faked a response, lighting up with an inauthentic remembrance through a sham of a smile. He asked how she was doing. Atticus bit the inside of his lower lip to prevent himself from gritting his teeth. He hated the man more with each passing second.

"You don't remember her," Atticus accused.

A smug smile curled on Moore's lips. "I'm sorry. I've taught a lot of students over the years, and I'm afraid my memory isn't what it once was."

"I understand, but maybe this'll help you remember. You tried getting in her pants."

"Excuse me, sir!" Moore said indignantly with the dramatic air of a Shakespearean actor.

"Though, from what I hear, that doesn't exactly narrow down the field," Atticus continued.

"I have never!"

Moore's theatrical outrage wasn't worthy of community theatre. He opened his mouth to say more, but Atticus cut him off.

"You're a professor of English, not drama, so cut the bullshit. It'll save us both time."

Moore shut up. Atticus gazed at the wedding photo on the mantel. "She was a student, wasn't she?"

A rhetorical question, but Moore answered regardless.

"How I met my wife is none of your business. It's time for you to go."

But Atticus plopped down on the leather sofa with an exaggerated sigh. "We can ask her to join us."

Moore glanced nervously about the house in an attempt to ascertain where his wife was. Atticus possessed no sympathy for Moore, but he did have some for his wife. She probably thought true love—some indescribable, indelible force—had brought them together when in reality, it was nothing but lust.

"Madison's a smart girl, very smart," Atticus said. "She's an editor now, for novels and such. It's her job to find a person's mistakes and help 'em fix 'em. Sort of similar to what I did when I was a Chicago homicide detective, except I'd find a person's screw-ups and put 'em away for 'em."

Moore leaned toward Atticus, his hands folded together, pleading for forgiveness. "Listen, if I've wronged her, I am sorry. But this philippic conversation is at an end. If you don't leave—"

"You'll what? Call the police?" Atticus laughed derisively at him. "I don't think so. Because if you did, you'd have to explain this whole conversation to your student—excuse me—wife."

Atticus draped his arms over the back of the sofa. He nodded toward the pictures. "Give a lot of speeches?"

Moore diverted his gaze from his unwelcome guest to the photos. An annoyed sigh followed. "On occasion. Why?"

"Lucky. Travel wasn't part of my job. And it seemed like every time I had plans to, a body'd be found or someone would go missing."

Moore's wife stepped into the room. Moore looked as if he would implode. Pools of sweat were visible in his armpits, darkening his sky-blue dress shirt.

That's right. Sweat, you bastard.

Atticus had a keen awareness and ability to read people. The moment Mrs. Moore stepped into the living room, Atticus knew Moore cheated on her. The nervous wreck he'd been disappeared. He had an ability to seamlessly hide his thoughts, manipulate his expressions. A goddamn chameleon adapting to its environment. Poor Mrs. Moore hadn't a clue.

"Ya'll need somethin' to drank?" she asked.

"No, we're fine, sweetheart—" but Moore was cut off by his unwelcome guest.

"Well, that'd make me as happy as a dead pig in the sunshine." Atticus used the Southern idiom to gauge her reaction. Grey Moore had no clue what the hell Atticus had just said, but his wife smiled fondly at the phrase. He'd been right. She was definitely from the South.

"How's lemonade?"

"Divine."

Moore, the predatory chameleon, licked his lips. "Mmm, that sounds good. I'll take a glass too, sugar bear."

She sauntered to the kitchen, the fabric of her yoga pants hugging her backside. Atticus made another assumption—Moore had pressured his wife into getting work done. Not bluntly, but a planted seed. Phrases like, "Did you see so 'n so? What happened to her? She used to be so good looking." Or, "She looks good for her age." Mrs. Moore could have aged gracefully like Allie had, but instead she had pumped her body full of synthetics to the point that she now had the shelf life of a Twinkie. All because she wanted to please an unpleasable man.

Moore scooted to the edge of his wingback chair and leaned toward Atticus. "Listen, I've made my fair share of mistakes. If I made a pass at this girl, I apologize. I was a different man. Don't ruin my marriage."

Before Atticus could respond, Mrs. Moore was back with the lemonade.

"There you go, darling," she said.

Atticus thanked her. "Love your accent."

She flicked her wrist at him. "Oh, please, I don't have an accent. It's y'all that do."

"Where are you from?"

"Knoxville."

"Beautiful. The Smoky Mountains are incredible. My wife and I took our kids there. Pigeon Forge. That was years ago… decades actually."

They small-talked about the city for a few moments.

"Your family still there?" Atticus asked.

"Yes, sir. The whole family. I came here for grad school and was convinced to stay." She cast a comically dramatic look at her husband.

Atticus smiled. "He must have convinced you in June. I imagine if he had asked in January, you'd have told him to piss off."

Pleasant laughter from all three. Atticus gave Moore a warning look. These pleasantries were not for him.

"So whatcha y'all talkin' 'bout?" Moore's wife asked.

Moore tried to answer first, but Atticus was quicker to the gun and louder.

"Oh, we've had some complaints about professors engaging in inappropriate activity, coercing students, giving better grades in exchange for sexual favors."

Moore froze like a lizard sunning on a rock.

"I'm here asking if Grey's heard any rumors of pervert professors. Cryin' shame when people in power prey on those without it. Ought'a castrate 'em, you ask me."

Atticus downed his lemonade. It was damn good too, the perfect blend of sweet and sour. He rose and sighed—the Midwestern way to say, "Well, I ought'a get going."

"I hope you get to visit Tennessee again soon," Atticus said to Mrs. Moore.

"Oh, me too," she said. "We just got back a couple weeks ago, and I'm already fixin' to get back."

Atticus called Vasquez on his way back to Chicago and told her about his visit with Moore, including the fact they'd been in Tennessee in the last few weeks.

"Can you look into where they stayed, where they ate, plane tickets, movie tickets, museum tickets, credit card charges, anything that puts them in Turkey Creek on and around September 17th and 18th?" Atticus said. "And if they flew back out of—"

"Atlanta," Vasquez finished. "Nice work, detective."

A moment of silence. Vasquez was thankful she didn't have to worry about meeting his gaze.

"How'd your sit-down with Madison go?" Atticus asked.

Vasquez told him.

"You think she was drugged?" Atticus then asked.

"I don't know. She started feeling tired on her ride to the party. It got worse there, but... I don't know."

By the time Madison had been found, there were no traces of drugs in her system, but that was four days after the party.

"Did you dig into this Benson guy?" Atticus asked.

"Yes. Let's say he has spent more time adding to his record than his resume. Four OWIs."

"Four?"

"Yup."

"Shouldn't be allowed to drive a riding lawn mower. What else?"

"Public intoxication, disorderly conduct, assault, assault and battery, assault, the last one involving his ex-wife. Definitely a person of interest."

"I'd say. Sounds like a first-class piece of shit. And Propelli?"

"Nothing serious. Underage drinking, speeding ticket. Separate incidents."

"But he had a relationship with Madison. Madison's friend said he stayed all night?"

Even though it was posed as a question, Atticus knew Propelli had. Vasquez recognized it as something Atticus did when he didn't yet accept known details as facts.

"You're skeptical," Vasquez said.

"Big house party. Drinking. People in costumes. I would have expected 'I'm not sure' more than a definite yes."

"Could be more to that."

The scariest words for a detective are *I don't know*. They rarely spoke them out loud, but those words could play on a frustrating loop in the back of their mind. The list of suspects was small but growing. Did Madison know the Man in the Mask? Did he know her? Had this been planned, fantasized about? Or had sheer happenstance put Madison on that road the same time as that early-2000s Dodge Ram? Had it been a crime of opportunity? Wrong time, wrong place for Madison? Right time, right place for her abductor?

All questions. No answers. And time was ticking away.

Special Agent Alejandra Vasquez massaged her temples, taking deep meditative breaths in an attempt to fight the suffocating, overwhelming feeling that had crept upon her. Her eyes burned, forcing her to squint. Staring at the blue-light–heavy computer screen for the last twenty years had taken its toll. She wore blue-light–blocking glasses, something Atticus would have scoffed at and claim it was all a gimmick to charge extra. And right now, she'd agree with him.

Someone knocked on her open door. She looked up. Fellow agent Maurice Gold filled the door frame. He was built like a linebacker and had been one until a broken leg in his junior year at Notre Dame had ended his football career. Unlucky for him, lucky for the FBI.

"I found the man who worked at the Kwik Trip," he said in a deep voice, setting down a manila folder on her desk. She thanked him. He nodded and stepped out. The file contained job history, arrest records, contact information, and a copy of the man's license. Vasquez checked the time on her computer screen: 2:37. She tapped her pen, trying to make a decision. A few seconds later, she made it. She rose from her chair and grabbed her khaki–colored wool coat. Her Dodge Challenger managed to cut the drive by twenty minutes. Like Atticus, she was familiar with and attached to Milwaukee. It was home to many memories, both personal and professional. Some of the most poignant included visiting Atticus's friend John Majeskie, a fellow detective. When the Brewers played the Cubs, the two detectives stayed on the phone drinking beer as if they were at the ballpark. Sometimes, they reviewed each other's cases, looking for a fresh perspective. And when files needed to be shared in those pre-email, pre-FaceTime days, they'd meet at the overhead oasis near the Wisconsin-Illinois border. Majeskie had been at the Dahmer apartment after that famous arrest. He'd gazed in horror at what lay hidden in the fridge and freezer, at the shrine of skulls and male genitalia. Atticus had seen the Polaroid prints of hearts, heads, hands, and organs. In 1992, Atticus had gone inside the then-empty apartment. Later, Atticus had told Vasquez that he could feel the evil in there. But as Vasquez drove by where the apartment had been, there was nothing but overgrown grass. A group of Milwaukee businessmen had bought the building and had it destroyed. Even though it was just an empty plot now, Vasquez still shuddered as she drove by.

Her destination was located in the undesirable, crime-ridden part of the city. She passed three police cars, lights flashing and spinning, outside one house. This part of Milwaukee reminded her of the 4th District in Chicago, where she had started as a beat cop. It was the type of neighborhood where crime was rampant, and everyone could be a potential victim of senseless violence.

Vasquez parked a few houses away. Before exiting, she checked her Glock and surveyed the surrounding houses. She had about an hour until the sun set, and her goal was to be back on I-90 when it did. She approached the rundown house. With a quick glance, she noted the repairs needed: the flayed siding, a broken porch step, and the lopsided screen door. Vasquez dreaded the thought of the slovenly house in summer and how many bugs would be festering inside. A heavyset black woman swayed in her rocking chair, the wood groaning under the weight. It was far too chilly for the average person to sit short-sleeved, but the woman's size came with a built-in furnace.

"Canna 'elp a miss?" the woman asked.

"Yes, I need to speak with Lawrence Floyd."

Vasquez used declarative verbs, such as *need* and *have*, in a way that suggested saying no was not an option.

"Whatcha ya need my boy fo'?"

Vasquez introduced herself and showed her badge. "I need to ask him a few questions."

"Bureau of what? You talkin' 'bout da 'BI?"

"Yes, mam."

"My boy ain't no snitch, honey."

"I'm not asking him to be."

Mrs. Floyd stared at Vasquez as if simply by staring she could ascertain whether Vasquez was telling the truth. Vasquez met her gaze, unintimidated. Mrs. Floyd grabbed the handle of the dented screen door and yanked it open. The springs screeched. She yelled inside. Lawrence Floyd was at the door with a sprinter's speed—Mrs. Floyd didn't like waiting.

Floyd could have had a sinewy build had he not fueled his body with Mountain Dew and Doritos for the last fifteen years. His broad shoulders lacked the muscle for good posture, and he'd lost most of his hair.

"Yes, mamma?" he asked.

"This woman wanna speak witchya."

"Thanks, mamma." Then to Vasquez: "What can I do for you, mam?"

Vasquez introduced herself and asked if they could speak inside. Almost forty, Floyd still looked to his mother for permission.

"Go on," his mother said, shooing him in.

They stepped inside. An invisible cloud of effluvium hit her smack in the face—a rancid concoction of body odor, cat piss, mildew, and garlic. It was what Vasquez had expected. Housecleaning appeared to be an extraneous activity for Mrs. Floyd. The wallpaper had been peeled off in sections, giving the impression that they had planned to remove it but found out how much of a pain in the ass peeling wallpaper was and abandoned it. The coffee table had two nearly empty bowls of macaroni and cheese, the remaining noodles hard, a crust of dried cheese lining the sides—they'd been there for hours. Piles of newspapers and magazines were stacked about the living room like skyscrapers. A pile of books also stood nearby—books with no dust covers, just dust. However, the TV was monstrous. A 65" screen with 4K resolution. TV watching was probably a 50+ hours a week job for Mrs. Floyd, and she required the best.

Floyd grabbed a stack of newspapers and magazines from the couch in an attempt to tidy up. A nice gesture, but if he wanted to clean before they spoke, Vasquez would be there a month. But it was far from the most disgusting home she'd been in. Years ago, in the sweltering heat of summer, she and Atticus had gone into a meth house. The tenants were so high they hadn't realized one of them had died two weeks earlier.

Vasquez took a seat in the chair directly in front of the TV. Judging by the look of horror on Floyd's face, it was Mrs. Floyd's chair. Floyd sat on the couch, leaning forward, elbows on his legs—body language that told Vasquez he didn't expect to talk long.

"So, what can I do for you, mam?" he asked.

"You used to work at a Kwik Trip on Dawson Street, did you not?"

"Uh, yes, mam." It was clear he hadn't expected the question.

"When did you leave?"

Floyd arched his back, letting out a dramatic sigh as if Vasquez had asked him the amount of propulsion needed to send a NASA spaceship into orbit.

"Sometime in 2015, 2016 maybe. I can't remember exactly. I can, uh, find out."

"Did you quit?"

"No, mam. I was let go. Told I wasn't needed no mo'. Didn't break my heart too bad though. I walked to work. That sure sucked in winter."

"Do you remember a young woman named Madison Monroe?"

A common yet detrimental mistake novice interrogators make is jotting notes face down. Tongues lie. The interrogator's responsibility is to gauge the physical responses. Do their hands clench? Are they shaking their leg(s)? Do they meet your eyes or look away? Vasquez kept an ear out for trigger words like "I think," "for the most part," and "that sounds about right." And, the king of them all, the ubiquitous "umm," a placeholder allowing a person time to think of an answer, honest or otherwise.

Floyd's face contorted as he thought. A strong whiff of cat piss hit Vasquez's nostrils. She followed the smell, glancing behind to the kitchen, where a big puffy-haired cat pawed the litter, sending bits of it onto the kitchen floor. Floyd scratched his head; the white tank top he wore did nothing to stop the fetid smell of spoiled onions wafting about. Given Mrs. Floyd's massive size, bathing must have been a spatial-limitation problem and therefore probably as frequent as bank holidays, meaning Lawrence had likely never been taught proper hygiene.

Floyd said the name didn't sound familiar.

"You may remember her as the young brunette who came in to buy a Gatorade and a Reese's Big Cup. Always rode a bicycle."

Floyd's eyes lit up. "Oh, man. I remember. Man, she sure loved those Reese's."

"Are you aware that on October 31st, 2013, Ms. Monroe was abducted?"

Floyd's hand, which had been flat on his leg, tensed, his fingers curled.

"I think I heard that, but, umm, you know that sadly happens a lot here. Terrible though."

"You saw Ms. Monroe often. She said the two of you would talk… You'd tease her about her Reese's…"

"Yeah, I tried to be friendly with all the customers, you know what I'm sayin'?"

Vasquez showed Floyd a picture of Madison on her phone. "This refresh your memory?"

"Yeah, I guess I remember her."

"Pretty girl, huh?"

Floyd hesitated. "Yeah, she's uhh… cute."

Vasquez didn't think "cute" was the first word that came to his mind. He had wanted to say hot or sexy, but she understood why he hadn't. Cute was a safe word. One that didn't get you in trouble.

Vasquez asked Floyd if he remembered any other routine customers who came in around the same time as Madison—roughly 10 p.m. to 3 a.m. He said it was mostly college kids who would come in to buy beer and snacks. On occasion, they'd use pick-up lines on Madison.

Then, Floyd stood. "Do you mind if I get some water?"

Vasquez shook her head. She moved her hand closer to her Glock, her eyes trained on Floyd. But Floyd returned with nothing but a glass of water. Vasquez asked where Floyd had been living in 2013. He said he had been living here with his mamma. His two boys visit. Floyd hadn't been married—both his sons had been the result of one-night stands. Floyd had later found employment at Miller, a stable paycheck that kept his mamma off his back. At least about having a job.

The front door opened, and the large and in-charge Mrs. Floyd wobbled inside. "I gotta date with Pat Sajak in fo'teen minutes," Mrs. Floyd said.

"I promise you I'll be done by then," Vasquez assured her.

"Lawrence, go get the clothes from the dryer," Mrs. Floyd ordered.

Lawrence frowned apologetically at Vasquez before obeying his mother, evidently fearing her more than the FBI. It appeared Mamma Floyd was somewhat of a Svengali toward her son; whether it was intentional or not, Vasquez couldn't decide.

"Is Mr. Floyd around?" Vasquez asked.

Mrs. Floyd laughed. "He went to get milk."

"When was that?"

"1983."

"I'm sorry."

Mrs. Floyd shrugged. "He was a lazy bastard. Good lookin' tho'. Boy, he sure cunnit keep his hands off me, but once I had Lawrence and held onto a bit of weight… You have kids?"

"I do."

Mrs. Floyd looked Vasquez over with overt judgement. "Well, I decided to not purge my food."

Vasquez ignored Mrs. Floyd's ignorant comment. Mr. Floyd, according to Mrs. Floyd, stopped coming home right after work, coming home later and later until he never came home at all. He didn't pay child support after he left either.

"So, whatcha ya want wit' my Lawrence?" Mrs. Floyd asked. "He's been clean as a whistle for the last ten years."

Vasquez had let Mrs. Floyd ramble on without interruption, but the last sentence piqued her interest. "And before then?"

Mrs. Floyd crossed her arms, a maternal display of protection. "Theys worse things than stealin' cars from folks who have three or fo' of 'em. He made sure we didn't starve."

Given her size, Mrs. Floyd had never been in jeopardy of missing a meal in her life, let alone starving.

"He stole cars?" Vasquez asked.

"Pas' tense."

"There's no record of that."

"Cause he didn't get caught by no police. He got caught by his mamma, and I whooped his ass. He know better 'n to go an' do somethin' stupid like that again."

Lawrence returned, struggling to carry the laundry basket. He dropped the basket on the floor near the coffee table. Mrs. Floyd reached down and folded the clothes, unabashedly setting her massive bra and underwear on the coffee table.

"Damn it, Lawrence!" Mrs. Floyd yelled, slamming a pair of dark denim jeans on the coffee table.

"How many times I gotta tell you to check them pockets, boy!"

"I did, mamma," Lawrence said with all the embarrassment a forty-year-old scolded by his mother should have.

Mrs. Floyd pointed a threatening finger at him. "You lyin' boy! If you done check these, there wouldn't be no Kleenex in 'em. Lucky it's a snot rag and not no bus tickets again!"

Vasquez had been waiting to make her exit but brought her attention back to Mrs. Floyd.

"Had to buy 'em twice 'cause he washed the first pair," Mrs. Floyd said. "Praise be to Jesus he didn't have to wash his pants down there or he'd still be at that bus station!"

With Mrs. Floyd, yelling was more intense than Navy Seal training. She sucked the oxygen from the room. But Mrs. Floyd calmed down when the theme to *Wheel of Fortune* started playing. TV was her crack.

Dusk turned the sky a blazing orange, with darkness creeping behind it. Vasquez needed to leave now. She rose and handed Floyd a business card. Floyd took it with a nod and then set it on the coffee table. Vasquez thanked them both and then stepped out into the crisp air. She hadn't been fully aware how smelly the house had been until she took her first breath of fresh air.

It was moments like these when she wished she didn't have such a detailed knowledge in forensics. Even though she had dusted herself off and brushed the cat hair off her skirt and blouse, trace elements of cat hair, litter, dust, fabric from the chair she sat in, even the DNA—sweat and saliva—of Lawrence and Mrs. Floyd were all over her. It was hard to get over that feeling of disgust. Shortly after becoming a detective, Vasquez had had a period of obsessive compulsive disorder when she would shower over five times a day. And that number would get even higher if she had been at an especially gruesome crime scene. Bits of blood, bone, and even brain clung to her like parasites.

Once she had left Milwaukee, she called Atticus.

"Fits the profile. Absent father, domineering mother," Vasquez said, after detailing the sit-down.

"Big leap from stealing cars to rape and murder. What's the motive?" Atticus asked.

"When I showed him Madison's picture, it was obvious he remembered her a lot more than he led on. And his choice of the word 'cute' was not natural. It was what he thought he should say."

"So, a gradual buildup of lust? He sees Madison a lot. They talk. He takes it as flirting. The lust finally boils over."

"Floyd's relationships with women are terrible. He has two sons from two different women. Both of whom have custody."

"So, mama bear has given the cub an unhealthy view on women. They're either beneath him—"

"Or far superior," Vasquez finished. "Been controlled by women his whole life. Abducting Madison puts him in a situation he's never been in before."

"In control. Impressive, Agent Vasquez."

Vasquez smirked but didn't let it last.

"I drove by the Dahmer apartment… Where it was, I mean," Vasquez said. Silence from Atticus.

"Do you still talk to John?" she asked.

"He passed a few years back."

"I'm sorry to hear that. He was a great man."

"Yeah, he was. That's life, I guess…"

Vasquez stared at her phone mounted on the dashboard. Hesitating.

"He had a hell of a cabin," she said.

"… Hell of a cabin…"

Atticus opened the door on the first knock but disappeared back inside without uttering a word. Greetings had never been Atticus's strong suit, but this was a new low. Vasquez stepped inside. A shroud of smoke swarmed her. Atticus attacked it with a towel.

"What in God's name happened?" Vasquez asked, loud enough to be heard over the smoke detector.

"I made a pie yesterday. Some of it must have dripped."

"You baked a pie?" she asked skeptically.

Atticus cast her a stern now-is-not-the-time look, then removed his pizza from the oven. The result seemed to defy logic. The crust was burned to a black crisp yet the cheese hadn't even melted.

"Good thing you're near the top floor, gives everyone else the chance to get out of here when you burn the place down," Vasquez teased.

Atticus glared at her again.

"Frozen pizza? Kind of a depressing supper, isn't it? Still buying the six for ten, I see."

"Can't beat the bargain."

"But you certainly can beat the taste."

Vasquez shed her wool coat and draped it over the back of a kitchen chair.

"Sit down before we both die of asphyxiation. I'll cook," she said.

Vasquez searched his cupboards and refrigerator, taking a mental inventory of what was available to her. Then she piled the ingredients onto the counter.

"What are you making?" Atticus asked.

"Just go do a Sudoku or something."

"I'm fine."

"No, if you watch, you'll micromanage."

"Nice scrabble word. That an FBI term?"

Vasquez flipped him off and then pointed to his chair. "Go."

"I take a vested interest in what I put in my body."

"Really? Hard to believe, coming from a guy who's smoked cigars for forty years."

"Cigars were celebratory… and I haven't smoked one in years."

"You quit? How?"

"Nothing to celebrate."

His words were meant to cause a smile and they did, but there was a painful truth in them as well. Atticus grabbed his Sudoku book but gazed up from the pocket-sized book every few seconds. Nearly an hour later, Vasquez set two plates on the table. A fried tortilla, a bed of lime cilantro rice, seasoned beef, sautéed peppers, and a fried egg cooked over-easy. The smell transported him back in time. He was overcome by memories that seemed to belong to someone else.

"This was always my favorite," he said.

"I know."

It was as if no time had elapsed. When their plates were empty, they washed and dried by hand. Both were of a generation when dishwashers were reserved for holiday dinners with extended family. Atticus smiled to himself, a faint chuckle barely escaping his lips.

"What is it?" Vasquez asked.

He shook his head, then dried his hands and draped the towel over the oven door handle.

"Seriously, what's with the shit-eating grin?" Vasquez asked.

"What does the next five, ten, twenty years look like? Remember that?"

He didn't mean to deliver the words as a weapon, but their impact was like an anvil slamming on Vasquez's chest. Of course she remembered. She could only nod in return.

"I think we just got a glimpse," Atticus said.

His stare was mighty and magnetic. It always had been. Atticus had his own gravity that drew you into his orbit. And once you fell into it, breaking it required a Big-Bang–level event. Her olive-green eyes met his honey-brown ones. She blinked, keeping her eyes closed a moment longer.

"I have to ask. Is David okay with us working together?" Atticus asked.

"David and I aren't together anymore..."

"Oh... I'm sorry."

Vasquez shrugged. "Fate can be cruelly ironic."

"How so?"

Vasquez paused briefly. "He had an affair. A woman he met while traveling for business."

Atticus's second apology was unspoken, expressed by a sympathetic frown.

"Yeah, well, I can hardly judge," she said. "I'm sure it was easier for him after... Anyway, uh, he lives in Los Angeles with her now. She's half my age and twice as good looking."

"Half that's true."

Vasquez laughed. Atticus did not.

"When'd this happen?" he asked.

"11 years ago."

The all-consuming, all-powerful silence enveloped the apartment once more. Atticus broke the tension, sighing as he rubbed his head.

"Listen, I don't want you doing these interviews alone. Sooner or later—or maybe you already have—you're going to sit down and talk with the guy we're after, and I don't want you to be alone when you do."

Vasquez fought a smirk. "Bring the 90's back?"

"I never let 'em go."

Vasquez shook her head, amused. "Alright, Mr. Clayton Jones."

Atticus sighed. "Never gonna let that go, huh?"

"Nope... I got list of Madison's classes she took the semester of her abduction. The student teacher of Moore's class was a guy named Rigel Rose.

He's a professor now at Chicago State. I'm going there tomorrow to talk to him. You want in?"

"I want in."

Vasquez told him she'd pick him up tomorrow morning at eight. He escorted her to the door. She said good night.

"Allie," he called. She stopped and turned to him. "He chose wrong."

She turned away from him, waiting for the sanctuary the elevator would provide. The doors opened, and she rushed inside.

... I think we just got a glimpse...

Did those words hold the same power over him as they did over her? Did he feel their venom too? Tormenting thoughts filled her whole drive home to Lake Forest. That impromptu dinner had been a glimpse, a mirage. The ghosts of Christmas Past, Present, and Future had sat at that table beside them. And if the ghost of days gone by chose to visit her that night as she lay in bed, she'd welcome it.

But in the end, Vasquez would have settled for the mercy of a dreamless sleep. Years peel away, and years can be wasted, lived in fear and lived in regret. A person's life story is a map, ending with the same final destination as all living things. Forks in the road present themselves. Sometimes, we have no say in which direction we must take. But often times, we carry the mighty burden of choice. Do you continue on the known road, one with miles of clear visibility? Or, do you venture into the unknown and hope your journey through the unforeseeable darkness leads to a better life? The choice is ours. But once you choose, you could never turn back. The same fork in the road never presented itself twice.

Vasquez had chosen to continue on the known road. The safe road.

... You can never turn back...

Ugh! This God damn cold! My throat's a desert, and it feels like I'm swallowing glass shards. My nose runs a marathon, and my eyes are red and itchy. I look like I'm clinging to my last precious seconds of life before I turn into a full-fledged zombie. Fantastic. I have been examining every last bag of cough drops at this Walgreens. I'm so tempted to go for the ones that taste like candy, but I know I'm at the stage where I need something that will actually help. I grab a bag of Halls, the blue bag, the ones that make drinking water painful for the next hour. Like the water might actually freeze half-way down your throat.

When I step outside, the air is disgustingly hot, making it seem downright impossible that I have a cold in this heat. That's what I get for traveling to the shitty northwest and their pestilential rain. And then volunteering to travel to conduct another plant audit. I don't complain—aloud at least—out of hope that they'll eventually send me to one of the world's grandest cities like Paris, Rome, Vienna, or New York. But I'm disappointed every time. Instead, I have traveled to Wichita four times, Kansas City three times, Tulsa twice, and one to St. Louis. God, what an awful trip that was. I thought I'd never leave. But then fate offered a generous hand. My coworker, Preston, couldn't make the trip. I finally get to go to a good city, hopes of a steamy love affair pulsing through my body. But here I am sucking on cough drops, sniffling back my runny nose, my mouth drooping like I was shot with a tranquilizer. In addition to the Halls, I've taken enough cough medicine that I should probably put the Poison Control Center on speed dial. But I've got a fantasy to live out. The only problem is none of the men seem to know that.

Why couldn't someone come up to me and ask me in French to dance? This is a city for saints and sinners; is it too much to ask for a saint who wants to sin? And please, Lord Jesus, don't let me sneeze in his face.

My hotel has a bar, and though I hate to fall to stereotype, I sit there. Since I'm sick already, I eat the bowl of mixed nuts, not caring whose hands had dug in there before me. They're all peanuts at this point, some other shameless patron had picked out the higher-quality nuts. I laugh. What a metaphor for *the situation I'm in. All the good nuts taken, me scrounging for anything I can get. I'm about to admit defeat when a man sits beside me.*

"There are hundreds of restaurants in this city, and you're eating peanut dust?" he asks.

I turn toward him, forcing my drooping, half-paralyzed face to form a smile. He's handsome. I can feel my blouse begging to be undone.

"Well, maybe I'm waiting for a guide. Big cities can be dangerous."

"Oh, you must be a small-town girl."

"And you're a city boy?"

He laughs. It's a great laugh. From his attire, I take him to be a salesman. A good one——I'm sold already.

"I am. East Los Angeles actually."

We exchange names. His name sounds made-up, like something from a steamy romance novel. He insists he take me out for a proper meal. We leave that sad, disgusting bowl of peanuts behind. He's an effortless conversationalist. He takes me to an outdoor restaurant.

"We can't have you leave without trying this city's famous dish," he says.

He surprises me with what he orders for us. It's definitely outside my comfort zone, but there are enough appetizers I can fill up on if need be. And it may not be "okay" in today's world, but I find him ordering for me incredibly attractive. I am willing to eat anything if it helps lead us to a bedroom.

"You come here often?" I ask.

I hope the strong smell of Vicks is mitigated by a half dozen squirts of Chanel, and the strong smell of medicinal cough drops masked by my third glass of wine.

"Oh, yes. I love it here. I love the music, the night life, the food, the accents."

I smile. He is simply enchanting. When the food is set before us, I hope my cold has destroyed my sense of taste.

"Well, the food's a bit better than a little bacon and a little beans, right?" he asks after a few bites.

"It's delicious." I lie. You would too if you saw the way his eyes sparkle when he smiles.

Does he know how easy it would be to have me? How everything in this city is literally screaming it?

We stroll the city, then leave it behind. He has the knowledge of a tour guide but with a storyteller's flair. As much as I'm enjoying myself, it's getting late. I have an eight a.m. audit and a twelve-thirty flight. Because of my cold, this won't be an instance where I can get by on four hours of sleep. I'll need at least six, and I expect an hour of fooling around.

His history lessons don't appear to be coming to an end. He's just mentioned the year 1788. If I have to wait for him to get to the 21st century, we won't even have enough time to get naked.

I stop him. Turn him toward me and kiss him. For an agonizing, humiliating moment, he doesn't react.

Is he gay? I don't know. I'm from one of those towns where the only gay person you know is one of your friend's uncles who have been excommunicated from the family. Gay men know all about culture and customs, right? Please don't fall to stereotype. Handsome. Well-spoken. Well-dressed. Please don't swing from the other side of the plate. At least be a switch hitter.

Or worse than being gay, was he straight and simply didn't find me attractive? Oh, God!

But then he presses his lips against mine, penetrating my mouth with his tongue. I don't waste any time. I cup his crotch with a firm grip. If he wants to take me in one of these with the eyes of the unseeing watching us, go ahead. He spins me around. Underneath this gentlemanly façade is a freak. My arousal defeats my cold.

He tears my dress skirt. I would find that incredibly hot had it not cost me seventy dollars, and I didn't have to walk or hail a cab back to my hotel. He shoves me forward against the hard, unforgiving stone and wrenches my head down.

It's like one of those romance novels I used to sneak-read in the back of the library growing up. I pull down my underwear. He tears it off and balls it up and shoves it in my mouth.

"Can't have you screaming," he whispers into my ear. His voice is different, less suave, more maniacal.

I gag. I try to pull it out, but he won't let me. When I keep attempting to, he slaps me. I'm no longer turned on, but repulsed. Salacious lust replaced by skin-crawling fear. I try to push him off, but he's too strong. He forces himself inside me. I mumble to stop.

My face is against the rough stone, grinding against it. The more I resist the more it hurts, and the more he enjoys it. He climaxes inside me. Then he spins me around. My makeup is smeared, tears streaking my face in mascara and eyeliner. He rips my underwear from my mouth, wipes my face with it.

From his jacket pocket, he grabs a roll of duct tape. I realize none of this night has been random. He planned to lure me to this very spot. The realization makes me sob. I scream out of fear and the necessity of survival. Somebody hear me! I breathe deep to unleash a powerful, guttural scream that could wake the dead, but he punches me in the stomach before I can release it. I fall to the ground, gasping for breath. I'm now entirely unaware of my sore throat, runny nose, or itchy eyes. There's too much else going on. I hear the sound of the duct tape unleashed. He wraps it around my hands, then my legs and then my mouth. Three wraps. No way will I be able to break it. He stares at me for a while, examining what he's done to me. There are hundreds of people around us. Please, God, let someone stroll through. He keeps staring at me, breathing heavily. I tremble, absolutely terrified, waiting for what he will do next. In one sudden charge, he drags me inside. I see the Virgin Mary through those windows. I beg for her to help me. To come down from heaven and save me. He continues to watch me. For how long, I don't know.

He leans forward. His breath tickles my ear. He breathes in my scent like a predator sniffing the wind to locate his next prey. But he's found his. As it is in the animal kingdom, so it is in Man's. He's gone after the sickly woman.

"You have until midnight, Ryla. Then I'm going to come back and kill you."

Silly Sheep, will poor Ryla make chapter 2? Or will you fail again? Either way, there's gonna be a lot of red.

Special Agent Vasquez and retired Homicide Detective Atticus Wallace strolled the small campus of Chicago State University. Crimson and gold leaves littered the ground, dancing in the breeze. The student body was divided into two demographics: those who were ready for Autumn, wearing hooded sweatshirts or scarves, and those holding onto the remnants of summer—wearing shorts or jeans and a t-shirt.

Vasquez and Atticus approached an irregularly shaped building with two protruding rectangles of different size on the left-hand side. The windows appeared turquoise in color. Atticus commented how stupid the design was. Inside, Vasquez followed the signs leading to a staircase, down a hall, and up another stairwell.

"No wonder kids go to school for five years. It takes three days to get to class," Atticus said.

The nameplate outside the door confirmed they were at the right office. But office seemed a poor choice of word. It was triple the size of Vasquez's own office, almost like a small, private movie theatre.

"You can dig deeper, Simone," a voice from inside said. "Even if you can't see it, I can."

Vasquez and Atticus observed a cute blonde sway nervously. "Thanks, Professor Rose. Can I do anything else for you?"

"You can grab that shovel and start digging. You are capable of beautiful prose. If you've read it on Twitter, it doesn't belong on this page," Rose said, brandishing her paper in the air. Simone smiled and blushed once she realized there had been an audience. She rushed out.

"Excuse me, Rigel Rose?" Vasquez asked.

Rose looked up from his computer monitor. "Yes?"

He was in his mid-thirties with dark hair styled in a quiff. He wore black browline glasses that accentuated his gray eyes and fit his lean, defined face. He was handsome in a 1950's way. Vasquez introduced herself and Atticus.

"Rigel. There's a unique name," Vasquez said.

Rose laughed in a charming manner. "My mother's been an avid stargazer since she was a young girl. Rigel is the brightest star in the Orion constellation."

"What makes it so much brighter?" Vasquez asked.

"Stars burn brighter before a supernova," Rose explained. "It's a good reminder to never waste time. We never know when we'll burn out."

"Your mom put all that thought into the name?" Atticus asked.

Rose smiled in an if-you-only-knew-my-mother way. "It was just her and me growing up. My parents were divorced." He said his father had lived out west. But he kept it short, knowing neither had come to hear about his childhood.

"Well, it's a good name. Lot better than the shit they're naming kids today," Atticus said, putting his own end to it.

"Well, we all can't be named after one of the greatest literary characters ever put to page," Rose said.

Atticus nearly tore his facial muscles forcing a smile. He had heard a variation of that comment almost every time he stated his name. He loathed it. Thankfully, it had died down. *To Kill a Mockingbird's* popularity had diminished considerably.

"I came before the book," Atticus said.

Rose smiled cordially before asking how he could help.

"You were a student teacher for Grey Moore at Marquette University, were you not?" Atticus asked.

"Yes, I was."

"Can you confirm the year?" Vasquez asked.

"Certainly. 2013... well, 2012–2013. I taught the whole year. To be even more precise, I taught a bit the previous year as well, though nothing official."

Atticus was old school, jotting down notes in a pocket-sized notebook.

"So, what can I do for you?" Rose asked.

"Do you remember a woman named Madison Monroe? She was a student in one of Moore's classes," Vasquez asked.

"Absolutely."

"Were you close?"

"I certainly considered us friends."

"Are you aware that Moore made a pass at her?" Atticus asked.

Rose frowned and leaned back in his chair with a disappointed sigh. "I thought the conversation would go here. I was not aware he made a pass at Madison, but I know there were others."

Vasquez and Atticus gave nothing away during interviews, never giving the appearance of being surprised or rattled. They acted as if everything they heard was what they had expected to hear.

"You know or you heard?" Vasquez asked.

"I'm ashamed to say I witnessed."

"Did you notify anyone?"

"I'm even more ashamed to say no."

"Why didn't you?" Atticus asked.

"Professor Moore had the power to get you a job or make sure you never got one. When I started student teaching, the person I replaced told me that. It was relayed to him by the person he replaced and I relayed that to my successor. Moore's got the reputation of being the Hoover of the English Department."

"Can you explain?" Atticus asked.

"If you did your work—and by your work, I mean *his* work—and you kept your mouth shut, Moore would fly to the ends of the world to help get you a teaching position. But conversely, if you did something to wrong him or anger him, he'd burn your name and reputation to the ground. It needs to be noted that I have no proof to confirm or deny that, but I certainly didn't want to find out firsthand."

"These witnessed accounts of inappropriate behavior..." Vasquez said. "Can you elaborate?"

"Well, one time I had something urgent to tell Professor Moore, so I opened his office door without knocking. Usually, he would be playing a match of chess on his computer... Well, I opened the door to find him receiving oral pleasure from a student. Now, I believe this was consensual—I mean he wasn't forcing her—but it certainly was an abuse of power."

"You said there were other times?" Atticus asked.

"Nothing to that extent—a hand on a young woman's back, a thigh squeeze of support. There was... uh..."

"What?" Atticus asked.

"There was a student whose paper I had graded. I had given it a C minus. When I checked her grades some days later, her score was changed to an A. I had a suspicion Professor Moore changed it in exchange for, shall we call it, services rendered."

"But you did not witness Moore's advance on Ms. Monroe personally?" Vasquez asked.

"No," Rose answered. "That I did not."

"Do you think she could be lying?" Atticus asked.

Rose shook his head adamantly. "No, Madison wouldn't lie about something like that. I don't think she'd lie about anything."

Atticus had zero trepidation that she would either.

"So, Moore targeting Ms. Monroe makes sense?" Vasquez asked.

"I wouldn't use those words, but for him to be attracted to Madison... Yes, that makes complete sense. Madison's a beautiful girl."

Vasquez appreciated his use of present tense. "Moore ever mentioned her? Changed grades as punishment?"

Rose shook his head. "No, he wouldn't have gotten away with that. Madison's smart. Her papers were always well-written. Concise. Provocative. I never gave her anything less than an A. If Professor Moore had given her a D, or even a C, and Madison had gone to another professor or the dean, they'd know there was something else going on."

Rose removed his glasses and wiped them using a lint-free cloth. Without his glasses, he squinted to the point where his eyes were barely open.

"That was the same semester Madison was taken. I think Moore tried to distance himself. The police didn't have many clues. Quite frankly, I think they were in over their heads. But as far as any interaction between Professor Moore and Madison, she actually never came back to class at all after she escaped."

"Why do you say the police were in over their heads?" Atticus asked.

Rose shrugged to show he meant no offense. But Atticus had taken it.

"I think they were used to open and shut cases. Gang killings, murder-suicides. There was a strong demand for answers, but there just weren't any."

Civilians critiquing police had and always would annoy the everlasting shit out of Atticus. Life happens in real time. It did not happen in Zapruder-like film rates. And true crime wasn't a Netflix series wrapped up conveniently in ten episodes.

"Looks like Moore followed through for you," Atticus said. "Got you a job."

"I earned this job, but it's true I didn't do anything to make Moore stop me from getting it." He took a deep breath. "I'm not proud of my silence. So, if you're here because Professor Moore has inappropriately touched or assaulted a woman, I will be a character witness for the prosecution."

"He has," Atticus said. "Madison Monroe. What we're trying to find out is if this inappropriate touch turned into kidnapping, rape, and what would have been murder."

"What do you remember about that day and the days that followed her attack?" Vasquez asked.

"I was at an airport in Wyoming, waiting for my flight back to Milwaukee, when a friend called and told me what had happened. Mostly rumors and guesses. But once I got back to campus, it was everywhere. The details that came out... just horrible."

Vasquez and Atticus gave his comment a reverent silence.

"What was in Wyoming?" Atticus asked.

"Yellowstone."

"Never been."

"You strike me as an outdoorsman. You owe it to yourself to go. It won't disappoint."

Atticus smiled derisively. Vasquez handed a card to Rose. Given the organization of his desk, the likelihood of him finding it was astronomically higher than that for Lawrence Floyd.

While Vasquez wrapped up, Atticus examined the bookshelf behind Rose's desk. All the staple American authors were present—Hemingway, Steinbeck, Orwell, and Atticus's favorite, Stephen King. He didn't read his books but enjoyed the movie adaptations.

Vasquez and Atticus left, the latter again cursing how long it took to get outside. The surprisingly mild day had transformed into a chilly, cloudy afternoon. The leaves no longer danced around their feet; they blew violently in their own twisters.

"What'd you think?" Vasquez asked.

"I think he's arrogant. Wouldn't doubt if he spends an hour staring in the mirror. I don't like him."

"Well, you don't like anybody."

Atticus conceded her point.

"I'll admit I didn't care for his comment about the Milwaukee police, but it doesn't mean he's wrong," Vasquez said.

Atticus shrugged, unwilling to yield. Vasquez grabbed his arm, stopping him.

"It's you and me, no cameras, so you can't look me in the eye and tell me you wouldn't have noticed that the man and woman who picked Madison up wore wedding rings but had different last names, that you wouldn't have been suspicious about where they were going at 1:30 in the morning? That they'd have something to lose if the truth came out?"

"… Maybe…"

"You're full of shit."

"Did you try talking to the badges who did the interrogation? See what they remember?"

She shook her head. "Can't. Cancer got them both."

On the car ride back, they discussed what Rose had said about Moore. It all fell in line with the image of Moore they'd had. Then their conversation steered toward the murders of Andrea Collins and Kimberly Johnson. No DNA had been found. With serial killers, there are two types of offenders—organized and disorganized. Disorganized killers left crime scenes in a hurry. They were victims to impulse and left evidence like candies at a parade. On the other hand, organized killers were thinkers and schemers. They stalked. They planned. They stayed calm before and after, fully aware of incriminating evidence they may leave behind.

"Andrea Collins wasn't his first kill," Vasquez theorized.

Atticus agreed. Psychopaths fantasize about murder. What starts as passing thought becomes an all-consuming obsession. They lie in bed thinking about it, the arousal overwhelming, until they act out and kill. But after fulfilling their ultimate fantasy, worry consumes them. It's not remorse, just the nagging fear they would get caught. A period of dormancy would begin. It would sometimes be years before they killed again. Jeffrey Dahmer had committed his first murder in 1978. His second wasn't until 1987. By the time he was arrested in 1991, Dahmer was averaging a murder per week. The cooling-off period decreased; the length of satiation lasted less and less. Soon, what once satisfied no longer would. The murders would become more gruesome. It was an addiction, an ever-evolving dopamine response. The question here was if Madison would have been his first victim. Had he killed someone years before he abducted Madison? Or for the first time shortly after? There are never rules with serial killers, only guidelines. Most killed out of that uncontrollable urge, but the Man in the Mask also killed because it was a game.

"Did you look to see if there are any unsolved murders of women matching Madison's looks around Milwaukee? Going back a decade or so?" Atticus asked.

"Maurice is running it through VICAP," Vasquez replied.

The Violent Crime Apprehension Program contained information on crime scenes including photographs, victims and offenders, court records, and statements. Had it been around in the 70's, it would have helped state law enforcement in Washington, Oregon, Utah, Colorado, and Idaho realize they were all looking for the same man responsible for the brutal killings of over twenty women: Ted Bundy.

"Two murders in two weeks," Atticus said, rubbing his forehead in thought.

"You know what this means."

Atticus did, but he wish he didn't. "It means we're due for an email."

It couldn't have been what Casper had expected or hoped for. He probably wanted the night to involve cheesecake or ice cream or, God willing, both. Instead he sat at Madison's kitchen table reading a chapter detailing the rape and impending murder of a young woman. When Atticus and Vasquez arrived, it became a library study table. Except it wasn't rocks, oceanic life, or the Middle Ages studied. Madison's apartment was silent apart from the sound of ballpoint pens scratching and highlighters squealing against the printed copies.

"Well, the Walgreens clue does shit for us. There's only like a thousand in Chicago alone," Casper said.

"She flew out of the Northwest," Atticus commented a few moments later.

"That could be a misdirect," Vasquez warned.

Madison circled a word. "*Volunteering* isn't in italics, but the rest of the chapter is. It must mean the exact opposite. Forced... No, that's too aggressive... commanded... no... told."

"*The air is disgustingly hot,*" Vasquez read.

"So, somewhere south. Texas? Arizona?" Casper suggested.

If they could trust that that declarative sentence was true, they could eliminate half the country. But that temporary victory was usurped by an army of possibilities. What if these "characters" were standing next to a campfire in Alaska?

"*Why couldn't someone come up to me and ask me in French to dance?*" Atticus read.

"... You don't think he kidnapped someone in the South of France, do you?" Vasquez asked, breaking the silence the line had brought.

Madison reread her copy, looking for something to refute that possibility. "Here, it says that she wishes she had been sent to Paris. I think if she was in

France, an international flight more than likely would have landed in Paris. *I finally get to go to a good city.* She referred to Paris as one of the grandest cities in the world. The adjective doesn't fit."

Vasquez and Atticus exchanged discreet glances. Atticus smirked.

"*A city for saints and sinners...*" Casper read. "Las Vegas? That place is disgustingly hot."

"True. And maybe *disgustingly* is used as an antonym for 'clean' and 'pure.' Gambling, prostitution, vice, they're all impure," Madison said.

More reading, more underlining and highlighting words and phrases ensued.

"He says he's from Los Angeles. What if that's the city?" Vasquez asked.

"He wouldn't be staying at a hotel then, would he?" Casper answered.

"Hotels hold work conferences, and it doesn't state he's *staying* at the hotel. Just that he's there. He may want us to make that connection," Atticus said.

Debate was critical, but it wasn't hard to get annoyed when someone thought they found a legitimate clue only to have someone else, or everyone, pick it apart and find holes.

Vasquez read in the form of a question a line she had previously highlighted. "*His name sounds made-up, like something from a steamy romance novel.*"

"So, like Harry Johnson or Rod Steel?" Casper said.

"Have you edited any romance novels? Could it be a character from a book?" Atticus asked Madison.

"I have edited one. The protagonist's name was Richard S. Hugh," she said.

Madison remembered only because of how the character had introduced himself—the worst knockoff of "Bond, James Bond" she'd ever read.

"Richard S. Hugh? That doesn't sound like a corny porn name," Casper said.

"Dick S. Hugh," she explained, cringing. The character had introduced himself an obnoxious amount of times, each time causing Madison to recoil more than the last.

"Oh... Nice. Very classy," Casper said.

She arched her eyebrows in reply. After a brief detour into James Bond sexual innuendo names, they moved on from the possible clue.

"Famous dish? Which cities have famous dishes?" Vasquez asked.

"We got the deep dish; New York has pizza; Philly's got the cheesesteak; Texas has barbecue," Casper rattled off.

"Loves the night life, the music, the accents," Madison said.

"Miami? It's known for its night life, and the people have accents," Vasquez suggested.

"What about a famous food?" Madison asked.

"Probably something Cuban," Vasquez answered.

"Or, if you go further south, key lime pie," Casper added.

He explained that he watched a lot of Food Network and Travel Channel. Madison couldn't help but think of their dinner at The Cheesecake Factory. What if someone had used that as the subject of the chapter? The thought made her shiver.

"Okay, this line makes no sense," Casper said, pausing to find it. "Here. *Eyes of the unseeing watching us...* unseeing and watching? Those contradict each other."

"Right, which means their use is deliberate, and they can't be taken literally," Madison said.

Another spell of silence. More rereading.

"Her face was against rough stone. Arizona? Disgustingly hot, Mexican accent. Phoenix or Flagstaff," Vasquez said.

Atticus shook his head. "Mountains are too far of a walk."

Vasquez let out a frustrated sigh, not because Atticus had contradicted her or because he was right but because the clock continued to move, minute by minute, second by second. They skipped over the rape section—it didn't need to be read aloud.

"How can he rape her with hundreds of people around?" Vasquez asked, frustration thick in her voice. The thought angered her, sickened her.

Madison read, "*I see the Virgin Mary through these windows.*"

"Is she hallucinating? Maybe he drugged her? Some drugs take longer to set in than others," Casper suggested.

They were in jeopardy of becoming conspiracy theorists. The only thing missing were tinfoil hats. The clock on the microwave continued to snip away at the time. It had been nothing but a vicious cycle. They eliminated one possibility and two more sprouted in its place. Now Madison knew what Hercules felt like fighting Hydra.

"What if this is all bullshit?" Casper asked.

The thought had crossed all their minds. Madison couldn't lie and say it hadn't crossed hers.

"We can't think that. We can't believe that," she said. "From what you," a look at Vasquez and Atticus, "have told me, he's a narcissist. He's supremely confident. He thinks he's smarter than us. He doesn't have to create an unanswerable riddle. The whole thing is a big F You. Here's her name, here are the clues, go find her."

After reading through it once more, Madison opened a spreadsheet, listing cities vertically on the left-hand side with the criteria listed on top, left to right. If a city met any of the listed criteria, she wrote an X in the corresponding cell. In ways, it was a messed up game of Bingo, but no free space was given.

Boston had met all the criteria—accents, nightlife, water, famous food (cream pies, clam chowder, baked beans)—but it was not a "disgustingly hot" city. The frustration increased with each passing minute. They had to be missing something.

Madison had read through the chapter ten times, trying to stay calm, but she had reached the point where she was too frustrated to even process what she read.

"Alright, since we're at a dead end, I keep going back to this line," Casper said. Then he read, "*Well, the food's a bit better than a little bacon and a little beans, right?*"

"What about it?" Atticus asked.

"It's a weird combo. I mean bacon and eggs, burger and fries, yes. But bacon and beans? And the wording, *a little bacon* and *a little beans*. Why not a little bacon and beans?"

Vasquez, Atticus, and Madison stared at him as if waiting for the punchline to a joke they didn't know had already been said.

"Okay, maybe it's nothing," Casper conceded, retreating to the pages.

"All we have is nothing. So, if you think you have something, follow it," Madison said.

Vasquez agreed with an encouraging nod; Atticus stared blankly at Casper.

"Eggs and bacon, right? The separating of bacon and beans... has to be intentional," Casper said.

Another pause. No one could help him out, and Casper struggled to explain it any clearer. They had no choice but to move on.

"Last time, lyrics were incorporated. Anybody see any?" Vasquez asked.

"Saints and sinners sounds like a band name," Atticus said.

Madison's concentration on finding lyrics broke when Casper started humming. He nodded to the rhythm. Then filled in the missing lyrics with the ubiquitous lyrical fill-in—*la la la la*.

It reminded Madison of a person singing along to a song in their car and not letting the minor fact they didn't know the words stop them from belting it out.

Casper continued with the same melody, singing the same words, until his eyes lit up.

"I think I got it!" he nearly screamed.

They granted him their attention, but Atticus's face showed he didn't have it for long. But if it stopped Casper from humming, it was worth it.

Casper cleared his throat and sang Johnny Horton's famous song about Colonel Jackson and the War of 1812. He paused for dramatic effect when he got to the end. "New Orleans."

"What is that?" Vasquez asked.

"It's a song!" Casper said.

Vasquez had never heard the song. Atticus had, but those lyrics weren't in the letter at all. But nonetheless they spot checked the chapter for clues that fit New Orleans.

Madison read the criteria on her spreadsheet. She typed an X, then another, and another, marking each box she scrutinized.

"Casper's right," Madison said. "It's hot; people there have accents, a distinct cuisine, raucous nightlife, and there's even more if we read this with New Orleans in mind."

They waited for her to continue. She scanned the chapter, looking for examples.

"New Orleans Saints. Sinners. That could be a reference to Mardi Gras. And here," She slid her paper toward the middle of the table and tapped on a line. *"Does he know how easy it would be? How everything in this city is literally screaming it?* The Big Easy."

"Famous dish that'll lead us to bed. Oysters," Atticus said.

"Eyes of the unseeing watching us," Madison read. "I think it's a cemetery."

"New Orleans has tons of them," Vasquez said.

"Right. Then the line about seeing the Virgin Mary through the window… it's a mausoleum. Probably stained glass," Atticus added.

"Which makes the line about there being hundreds around them make sense. Vasquez was right; she's not getting raped out in public. But when the said hundreds aren't living people, it makes sense," Madison said.

They all looked among each other, waiting for someone to say "but wait" and demolish the house of cards they had just built. But no one did. The foundation was strong.

Vasquez rose from the table and made a call.

"… Woman is in her twenties or early thirties. Dark hair, blue eyes. Five feet three to five feet ten, slender, athletic build. First name, Ryla. R-Y-L-A…"

Less than a minute later, Vasquez pocketed her phone.

"I'm going to New Orleans," she declared.

"I'm coming with," Atticus said, rising from the table, his arthritic knees cracking and popping.

"I'll go."

Madison looked to see who had spoken. It wasn't Casper; the voice had been feminine. Then the horrific realization hit her. *She* had said those words. A strange sensation of self-betrayal swarmed her. It seemed somebody else had spoken those words from her lips. It was that alpha she-wolf who came and went as she pleased. The rest of the pack, a mix of cowardice, worry, and fear, wouldn't challenge her. And because of it, Madison was going to New Orleans.

The small aircraft shuddered. The armrests vibrated. The flashing runway lights shrunk as the plane rose higher into the Chicago night. Atticus clamped his eyes shut, a death grip on his armrests. The plane shook violently; he cursed under his breath.

"Haven't you ever flown before?" Vasquez asked with a wry smirk.

"Yes, but never on Buddy Holly's plane," he answered.

Vasquez smiled. "I can put some music on to help you relax. Maybe some Skynyrd? Otis Redding?"

"Ha. Ha. Ha."

Once the plane reached its cruising altitude, the turbulence ceased. Vasquez checked up on Madison, promising she'd be surrounded by the FBI and the NOLA police. Madison forced an appreciative nod. However well-intentioned, no one could ensure her safety.

The flight was a stretch over two hours, a time she spent nervously drinking bottle after bottle of water. As expected, Madison needed to go to the bathroom every five minutes. But the plane had no bathroom, making for a terribly uncomfortable flight. Madison and Casper attempted to calm the tumultuous, roiling ball of nerves by listening to the swooning voice of Frank Sinatra. Vasquez spent most of the flight on her satellite phone, receiving updates or seeking updates. The NOLA police had searched every hotel in the city and surrounding cities for a guest with the name of Ryla. But if the room she had stayed in wasn't under her name, they wouldn't find her. Atticus sat in silence—no music, no sleep. Vasquez pocketed her phone. It would be the last update before they descended for landing. Vasquez glanced at Madison and Casper, both were lost in music.

"What?" Atticus asked.

Vasquez looked into his honey-brown eyes. "We finally made it onto that plane."

Pain reflected from his eyes. Hers mirrored his. It was a pain she'd caused, a pain she could never take back.

The pilot's voice boomed out over the speakers, notifying them to buckle up and prepare for landing. Vasquez motioned for Madison and Casper to take their headphones off. What Madison had initially taken to be only runway lights were actually police lights, illuminating the ground like a Vegas slot machine.

Unlike the few flights Madison had been on, where exiting the plane took over twenty minutes, they were off the plane before the engines even stopped. Two people rushed to meet them. The first was a woman roughly Madison's age with blonde hair. She wore a navy blue jacket with FBI sprawled on the back. She introduced herself as Ellen Connor. The second person was the NOLA chief of police Marcus Bazelmore, a black man well into retirement age. His face showed the same weathering as Atticus's.

"Chief Bazelmore's running the show, but he knows we're here to do all we can," Agent Connor said.

"Uniforms are searching the cemeteries, but now's a good time for that needle in a haystack phrase 'cause we have over forty cemeteries in the city alone, not to mention a lot more outside city limits," Chief Bazelmore said in a deep, Louisiana-accented voice.

He then passed the invisible baton back to Agent Connor.

"Hotel guest lists came back. We have seven Rylas. We crossed off two. They're in their rooms. We're contacting the numbers listed when they checked in, and we're also asking guests if they're traveling with someone by the name of Ryla," Agent Connor reported.

However, these calls would appear as unknown or a random ten-digit number. If the guests were anything like Madison, they'd ignore every last call.

"We need to cross-reference any debit or credit card transactions at Walgreens," Atticus said.

"And have security monitors looked at for a woman matching our description. I know it's a long shot, but I want every option exhausted," Vasquez said.

"We're on it," Agent Connor answered, then rushed off to delegate responsibilities.

Vasquez turned her attention back to Chief Bazelmore. "Chief, is there somewhere these two can stay?" She nodded at Casper and Madison.

Chief Bazelmore waved over two officers and ordered them to drive Madison and Casper to the Hyatt on Bourbon Street. Vasquez gave Madison a police radio and showed her how to use it. Knowing the horrible news she could potentially hear from it, the radio weighed as much as a ninety-pound kettlebell. Casper was transfixed by the spectacle, the look of being overwhelmed warping his face. He must regret coming. Madison had the same feeling. That alpha she-wolf who had boldly volunteered to go better not abandon her now. But Madison could already feel that she-wolf trying to slip away from the pack.

Atticus put a supportive hand on her shoulder and asked if she was alright. Her nod had zero conviction. Two officers led Casper and her to their police car. Then, lights flashing and spinning, the car sped off at a speed worthy of the runway on which it drove.

"Now what?" Agent Connor asked.

Vasquez strapped her bulletproof vest and loaded her clip into her Glock and pulled the slide. "We grab flashlights and go find this girl."

Bourbon Street was overrun with people in various stages of inebriation—some with beads drooping from their necks, others in rhinestone masquerade masks. Their ride had slowed to neutral. The people in front were either too drunk or the music belting from the bars too loud for them to notice the police car behind them. With a steady hand on the horn, they made it to the Hyatt. The lobby floors were immaculate, a glass-like painting reflecting the ceiling and its extravagant lights that hung like diamond-encrusted stalactites. Law enforcement and hotel staff crowded the lobby, scurrying about like ants running in and out of an anthill. Concerned guests looked on and asked the same questions. Since 9/11, the worst is always assumed. There must be a bomb somewhere in the hotel or a gunman planning to shoot up Bourbon Street. And speaking of bombs, Madison's bladder was ready to explode.

"I'll wait outside," Casper said when Madison told him she had to use the restroom.

But before waiting, he pushed the bathroom door open and asked if anyone was inside. When no answer came, he checked the stalls to ensure they were actually empty. Then he stepped outside, granting Madison her own multi-stall and multi-faucet private bathroom.

After, they asked each guest, entering or exiting, if they knew a woman named Ryla. Most responded as if they'd been asked if they had any heroin for sale. Having obtained no result, they sat on a couch and searched the chapter for more clues. The first two rounds of an edit usually required a hacksaw, but the more you edited, the more precise the instrument needed. Trying to mirror the precision of a surgeon's scalpel, Madison sought out the tiny tumor hidden among the benign expositional tissue. Somewhere, there were more clues that would help find Ryla. The alpha wolf in her hungered to hunt them down.

Agent Connor led Atticus and Vasquez through the sweaty heart of New Orleans. A voice broke through the radio, nearly impossible to hear over the boisterous music and cacophonic conversation. The radioed drawl belonged to Chief Bazelmore. Vasquez asked him to repeat.

"… 13 cemeteries. I repeat, we've eliminated 13 cemeteries…"

All three looked at each other with grave expressions. Atticus checked his watch. 10:27. They had until midnight. It wasn't just unlikely or improbable to search the remaining thirty-plus cemeteries in 93 minutes, it was mathematically impossible.

"We have to be thorough," Chief Bazelmore said, intuition telling him what their silence signified. "Last thing we want is to declare a cemetery clear and find out later we missed her."

Vasquez thanked him, trying to remove the frustration from her tone, a frustration certainly not caused by him or the NOLA police.

"We're running out of time," Vasquez said to Atticus and Agent Connor. She brought the radio to her lips. "Madison, do you copy?"

"I'm here."

"We need to make a choice on where to concentrate our efforts. Can you find anything that can help us narrow down our search?"

Madison stared at the radio, mortified at the words that came out of it. "I… I can't make that choice…"

"It won't be your choice, Madison. We're taking theories from everybody."

"Okay… I'm looking."

Madison changed the chapter's font on her phone.

"What are you doing?" Casper asked.

"It's an editing trick. When you've read the same thing over and over, your mind fills in the sentences. It becomes hard for you to notice any mistake because you know what it's supposed to say. By switching font, it's like you're reading it for the first time."

"Any reason for Comic Sans?"

"It's light, non-threatening, and makes me think I'm not trying to find the location of a soon-to-be-murdered woman."

"Well, uh, good call then."

Atticus and Vasquez stood frozen in place. Agent Connor was a few feet away, phone pressed to one ear and a finger in the other in an effort to block out the deafening noise. With time being limited, they had to stay centralized: an equal distance from most cemeteries. The brave men and women of the New Orleans police were scattered about the city looking for a single woman. When Vasquez first became a detective, she had found it unbelievable how a person could seemingly disappear without a trace. Atticus had a simple explanation: People don't worry about other people. It wasn't malice. It was just the busyness of everyone's day—stresses, worries, excitements, thinking back, thinking ahead. And in this digital age, people have been unhealthily engrossed in their phones, unable to describe a single person who shared the same bus or subway.

"These just came through," Agent Connor said, hurrying back to them.

She held out her phone, showing copies of licenses belonging to the missing Rylas. The first belonged to a woman named Ryla Geneckie. She was 42, 5'2" tall, and 157 pounds. Vasquez opened the second attachment. She had hoped it'd be another quick no. Ryla Billingsley was a 26-year-old organ donor. Vasquez had the morbid thought of her organs being harvested this very night. She had blue eyes but blonde hair, at least in this photo. But her weight and height were within range of Madison's.

"Not blonde, right?" Agent Connor asked.

"She could have dyed it," Vasquez said.

She swiped right for the time being, hoping the third Ryla resembled Ryla Geneckie more than Ryla Billingsley. Instead, it was a combination. Ryla Lively, 37, 5'10", 126 pounds. Her beauty was more mature than Madison's, and though she had the same dark hair as Madison, her license listed her eye color as brown. Vasquez knew colored contacts were a possibility but swiped again. Ryla Schmitz, 17, blue eyes, dark hair, 5'7", and 110 pounds.

"Too young," Atticus said.

Hopefully, being only seventeen, she was traveling with her family and not alone. If the Man in the Mask was honest in writing Ryla was traveling for work, Ryla Schmitz was not their Ryla.

The fourth Ryla gave her chills, but she quickly swiped to the right to see what number five looked like. 38, 4'11", 130 pounds. Not their Ryla. She swiped back left to Ryla #4. Ryla Abrams. 30 years old from Kokomo, Indiana. 5'8", 138 pounds, blue eyes, dark hair. She was a beautiful girl with a beaming smile not even the normally crappy license photo could diminish.

"Her," Vasquez said.

Agent Connor took the phone and made the call. In less than a minute, Ryla Abrams' photo would circulate the city.

"Let me see your phone, Allie," Atticus said.

Vasquez handed it over and continued talking with Agent Connor. A few minutes later, Atticus tapped her on the shoulder and held her phone out to her.

"Ryla Abrams is employed at Charlton Hughes as an auditor. She checked into Portland International Airport last week and, two days ago, flew into Louis Armstrong New Orleans International Airport and checked into Hyatt Centric. She's wearing a blue dress skirt," Atticus rattled off, sounding like a savant.

Both FBI agents were familiar with profiling, but this wasn't profiling—this was clairvoyance.

"That's a hell of a profile," Agent Connor commented.

"Not my profile. Hers." Atticus said.

Vasquez shot a quizzical look.

"The Facebook," Atticus explained.

"You were on Facebook?"

"Exactly. And if I could trace her steps this easily, that means..."

Vasquez scanned through Ryla Abram's profile, seeing all her check-ins, random quizzes she had taken and shared when she was bored, and memes she had found funny. People post their exact whereabouts all over social media. Announcing to hundreds, even thousands, of people how their homes were left unattended, what their political beliefs were, and—thanks to those seemingly harmless quizzes—the answers to password security questions. People knew where you were and—even scarier—where you *would* be. Stalking used to be a physical, laborious process; it involved sitting in a parked car for hours, digging through trash. Now it only required a quick scroll of a person's Facebook. And if that didn't make you shudder, you weren't appreciating the inherent danger.

"Atticus," Vasquez said. "That's the hotel Madison's at."

Madison had read the chapter enough times she could recite it verbatim. Casper had shown the chapter to the local police to see if anything jumped out at them or if there was some New Orleans slang they hadn't picked up on. Madison resorted to googling "New Orleans" plus a random word from the chapter. But Google came back with millions of results. Were there even any more clues to find? Even if there weren't, she had to keep looking. When locked in that cabin, Madison had prayed that everyone was looking for her, doing everything they could. Right now, Ryla Abrams recited that same prayer. Ryla Abrams, who had stayed in this very hotel, had walked in this lobby. Had the Man in the Mask been in here too? The thought made her shudder. But she couldn't dwell on that. She needed to keep searching, to find another clue.

I don't complain, aloud at least, out of hope that they'll send me to one of the world's grandest cities like Paris, Rome, Vienna, or New York. But I'm disappointed every time. Instead, I have traveled to Wichita four times, Kansas City three times, Tulsa twice, and one to St. Louis. God, what an awful trip that was. I thought I'd never leave.

I don't complain, aloud at least, out of hope that they'll send me to one of the world's grandest cities like Paris, Rome, Vienna, or New York. But I'm disappointed every time. ~~I traveled often in hopes they would send me to the grandest cities of the world—Paris, Milan, New York, Vienna. Instead, I have traveled to Wichita four times, Kansas City three times, Tulsa twice, and one to St. Louis.~~ God, what an awful trip that was. I thought I'd never leave.

Madison called Casper over with a Midwestern "Hey." "This line... *and one to St. Louis. God, what an awful trip that was. I thought I'd never leave.*"

"What about it?" Casper asked.

And without warning, but with great annoyance, Madison couldn't remember why the line was of any importance.

"I'm gonna run to the bathroom. You gonna be okay?" Casper asked after close to a minute of Madison sitting there thinking.

Madison nodded, staring at the floor as if the reason the line was important was a scurrying beam of light, and that if she lost track of it, it'd be gone forever.

… And one to St. Louis…

One. Not once, but one. Was that natural? Or intentional? An honest mistake?

The lobby's constant chatter, amplified by its acoustics that would make any Greek amphitheater architect proud, subjected her to every last word spoken.

… One to St. Louis…

She would have said *once to St. Louis*. But was that a Midwest thing? Was *One to St. Louis* normal for other parts of the country?

Suddenly, a fire alarm started wailing like a World War II bombing siren, wiping every thought from her mind. She leapt to her feet, the air evacuating from her lungs. Everyone in the crowded lobby looked around for smoke. A mass exodus ensued. People spilled out of the stairwells. Guests who had been in the elevator when the alarm sounded rushed out of them in a wave. Police asked for everyone to remain calm and exit the hotel. Madison looked for Casper, but the lobby was as crowded as the floor of a rock concert. Too many people blocked her view of the bathrooms. Casper was tall, but she wasn't tall enough to see over most of the men around her. Was Casper still in the bathroom? Or had he been forced outside by the herd of people?

Madison didn't have a choice in staying put. A police woman grabbed her arm and prompted her out. Once outside, she tried to find a place where she could focus on the chapter once more. Where had her train of thought been heading before the fire alarm derailed it? Where was Casper? She dialed his number, but it went to voicemail. She could barely hear the ringing even with her ear pressed against it. There was no way he'd be able to hear his phone if it was in his pocket.

There were too many thoughts bouncing around in her head. Madison closed her eyes and exhaled deeply. She needed to focus. Hotel guests filled the street, arching their necks in an attempt to see smoke billowing out of the upper floor windows. She had to force herself to reopen the chapter and ignore the excitement. The city was loud, a mix of music, fire alarms, and conversation.

… And one to St. Louis…

The thought came back suddenly, and the fog was lifted, granting clear visibility. She used the police radio and called Vasquez. When Vasquez answered, Madison read the paragraph she had been staring at for the better part of ten minutes.

"*One to St. Louis*. St. Louis is a cemetery," Madison explained.

"*I thought I'd never leave…*" Atticus remarked.

"There are three cemeteries named St. Louis. Which one?" Agent Connor asked.

Vasquez repeated the question to Madison.

"One. One trip to St. Louis. One St. Louis," Madison answered.

"Great work," Vasquez said.

Three-quarters of a mile to the cemetery in question, Vasquez and Atticus loaded into a police SUV. Vasquez called and informed Chief Bazelmore. A police escort cleared the congested street. The police lights reflected off the buildings—a warning to get out of the way or risk getting run over. They sped through red lights, a steady orchestra of car horns and squealing breaks adding to the music. Oncoming traffic screeched and slid. The police vehicles came to an aggressive stop outside the hallowed cemetery. Headlights were left on to light the night. Together with NOLA police and FBI, Vasquez and Atticus rushed into the labyrinth of the dead. And if the dead had their way, one more would join them tonight. Overhead, a police chopper circled, shining its spotlight on the graves below. The mist crept along the ground like formless ghosts. The Catholic Church owned the cemetery, but God would forgive the breaking of a few tombs and mausoleums to save one of his children.

"We have to find one with a stained glass window of Mary," Atticus said.

They aimed their flashlights, hoping to see Mother Mary staring back at them. The cemetery was only one square block but the final resting place of thousands. It was past midnight, but it didn't matter now. Ryla Abrams was here. They would find her—alive or dead.

Police shouted Ryla's name repeatedly. The arthritis in Atticus's knees tightened and throbbed. He cursed to help soothe the grueling pain; he wouldn't let it stop him. He needed to find Ryla. Vasquez, on the other hand, showed no signs of her age. She hadn't only kept herself looking good, she kept herself fit. She swept her flashlight beam left to right, then right to left. Then she whipped it back.

"Atticus!" she shouted.

Atticus limped toward her. Vasquez nodded ahead. Atticus followed the beam of light to a chipped, faded white-stone mausoleum. It had a stained glass window of a woman in billowing steel-blue and ivory-white robes, her hands folded in prayer—The Virgin Mary, Mother of God.

Casper may as well have been the ghost who shared his name. Madison's call went to voicemail yet again, and this time, it didn't even ring. The fire department parted the sea of people, their painfully loud sirens and horns wailing like mandrakes. People clapped their hands over their ears to escape the shrieking. The street wreaked of booze and sweat. Firemen rushed inside. Confident there were no more clues to be found, Madison moved through the crowd in an effort to find Casper. In front of the hotel was a raised flower bed lined with terracotta brick. She stepped onto it and scanned the crowd.

A group of partying people wandered past. What was revealed in their wake paralyzed her. Less than fifty feet away, standing wide, head tilted to the side, studying her, was the Man in the Mask, wearing the same mask he'd worn all those years ago—black, half-moon eyes and a black empty smile. Venom raced through her blood, a dizzying sensation flooding over her. There was no mistake. It was not a stranger who happened to be wearing the same mask. Those hidden eyes were fixed on Madison. His head slowly tilted left, then right, like a dog's. Even from that distance, his hot breath was on her neck, the sound of his panting tickling her ear.

In movies, when a character thinks they are hallucinating, they close their eyes.

Fuck. That.

She didn't blink. She needed to know where he was. He was dressed all in black, no logo or brand name visible. His hands were covered in black cloth gloves. He draped his hood over his head. Then, as if he had written the screenplay himself, a second wave of people created an obstructing river between them. Her breath left her. If this was a movie, he'd emerge right in front of her. She wanted to run, but her body was rooted in place. The alpha wolf had abandoned her.

Was the Man in the Mask even real?

A lone tear clung to the corner of her eye. Fear she hadn't experienced in nearly a decade, completely and utterly debilitating, engulfed her. The wave neared its end. Her heart beat violently.

The crowd passed.

The Man in the Mask was gone.

The Immaculate Mother seemed to be pleading with Atticus and Vasquez to save Ryla. The entrance was sealed with a padlock. Based on its sheen and the absence of rust on it, it was new. Atticus avoided touching the lock in case prints could be extracted, but he tugged on the chain in an effort to break it. Then he tried prying the stone door open to no avail.

Vasquez looked through the stained glass window. With the flashlight aimed just right, it revealed the silhouette of a woman.

"She's in here!" Vasquez shouted.

Atticus limped toward her. He said a quick preemptive prayer for what he was about to do then used his flashlight as a club and broke the stained glass. Then he ran the flashlight along the windowsill to break any remaining jagged shards. He helped Vasquez up, then climbed in after her.

Ryla Abrams stood with her head hunched over, arms above her head with cable tied around her wrists. Atticus followed the cable from Ryla's wrists to a crypt handle to which it was fashioned. Both spoke Ryla's name, hoping for any reaction. A strong smell of bleach attacked their senses.

Atticus stepped toward her and nearly slipped. The liquid beneath his feet was too thick for it to be water. His next suspicion was oil, but even with the tomb smelling like an over-chlorinated pool, he would have been able to pick up its smell. He aimed his flashlight at his feet. The liquid was blood. It covered the whole floor.

Vasquez slipped a latex glove onto her left hand, then checked Ryla for a pulse. In the unbearable heat and humidity as sticky as glue, Ryla Abrams was ice cold. This once-beautiful blue-eyed, dark-haired woman who laughed, smiled, and cried had become "the body."

A loud grinding of stone on stone echoed as the mausoleum door opened.

"She's gone," Vasquez told the officers trying to enter. "The scene needs to be examined. Nobody comes in."

There are truly remarkable tools at the disposal of law enforcement to find fingerprints, electrostacking being one of them. It uses sheets of plastic to lift prints and high intensity polilights to see them. Vasquez hoped the crime scene examiner would be able to find at least one usable print.

No matter what any detective or police officer says to the contrary, you took pieces of the crime scene with you—not only physically, like at the Floyd house, but emotionally as well. Some you dragged around with you like chains. In 1994, Vasquez and Atticus had investigated the murder and rape of nine-year-old DaVante Smith. Murder, then rape. In that order. If that wasn't horrible enough, the killer had taken trophies—the boy's genitals, nipples, and his head. Vasquez had gazed upon the boy's mutilated, headless body. And less than an hour later, Vasquez had been at her son Julian's Christmas pageant, watching fifty grade-schoolers perform Christmas songs. She'd made it through one verse of "Oh, Holy Night" before she ran out of the auditorium. She had cried for twenty minutes. She wouldn't wish anyone to see what she'd seen. But how grateful she was that Atticus had been beside her. That poor boy had been laid to rest in someone else's mind too.

Sympathizing with the victim was easy, heartbreaking but easy. However, to be a great detective, you had to put yourself in the mind of the murderer. You had to feel their anticipation, their excitement, and whatever twisted pleasure they experienced from their atrocity. You had to if you wanted to solve the tried-and-true formula: Why + How = Who.

The Man in the Mask preyed off women who resembled Madison, the one who literally got away. Ryla Abrams had been raped, tied up, and then stabbed enough times that nearly all her blood had poured out of her body. Atticus and Vasquez knew how, and they knew why. But who?

Nothing came over the radio, not even the crackle of static, since Madison had last spoken to Vasquez and Atticus. The fire department had cleared the hotel, not finding a single puff of smoke. Madison was close enough to overhear a firefighter speaking with a police officer. The firefighter guessed that someone had pulled the fire alarm as a drunken dare. The policeman reacted as if this was a common occurrence. She imagined it was. People do stupid things when they're drunk.

Somebody grabbed her shoulder. She flung it off and almost fell over. Paralyzed by fear, she couldn't even scream, only gasp. But then her training with Lana took over, and she cocked her fist, ready to smash someone's nose or crush their windpipe.

"Woah!" Casper said, flinging his hands up in surrender.

Madison exhaled in relief, her trembling fist falling to her side.

"Where were you?" she managed to say when her breath returned.

She didn't know if she was more upset, concerned, or relieved, and her tone was as indecisive.

"I'm sorry. When I got out of the bathroom, there was like a thousand people in the lobby. I tried finding you, but a cop forced me to leave. I figured you'd gone out the front, but she wouldn't let me follow you. I was forced out back. And out there, they wouldn't let me go around the hotel because of the fire trucks."

"I called you."

Casper took out his phone. Madison knew it was dead before he even said anything. Dead cell phones seemed to actually look dead.

"It was dying since we landed. As soon as I tried calling you back, it croaked," he said.

She couldn't stop herself shivering from the remnants of shock and fear of having seen the Man in the Mask again.

"What's wrong?" Casper asked.

"I saw him…"

"Him? The Man in the Mask?"

There was no skepticism in his voice, just a look of abject horror.

Madison nodded. "Same mask… same stance… And the way he looked at me…"

Goosebumps rose across her body when she thought about the way he had stared at her—a disgusting mix of intrigue, curiosity, and animalistic lust, all so palpable they even permeated through the mask.

The police radio crackled.

"… Madison…" Atticus's voice came through the distortion.

"I'm here. Did you find her?"

"We did."

A pause. She knew what it meant.

"She's dead…" Madison said.

"Yes. She's gone."

Madison squeezed her eyes shut, wanting to throw the radio like it was a piece of graphite from Chernobyl. Casper ran his hand through his hair and whispered a curse word to himself.

"You were right, Madison," Atticus said.

"It doesn't matter. She's dead either way."

There wasn't anything Vasquez, Atticus, or Casper could say to make Madison feel better. Casper tried often, Vasquez once, but Atticus, in his wisdom, didn't try at all. Madison wanted to get home, shower, and collapse onto her bed. But she wasn't even on the plane yet. They were still inside the lobby of the Hyatt.

Casper handed a plastic cup of coffee to her. "Good news, bad news. Good news, it's lukewarm, so you'll be able to drink it right away. Bad news, it tastes like shit," he said, trying to draw a smile from her.

She couldn't give him one. The coffee was black, cheap, and stale, but it had caffeine, and that's all that mattered. Atticus and Vasquez were spritzed with sweat and caked in dust. Even though his knees felt like there were shards of glass in them, Atticus refused to sit—he knew that once he did so, there he would stay. Vasquez rolled her neck, resulting in a series of cracks. A staff member handed them two bottles of water that were quickly downed. Madison had spent most of the night in the air-conditioned lobby, but the thirty minutes or so she had been outside was enough for her to know how damn hot and humid it was. Atticus and Vasquez had been out all night. They would have to peel their clothes off.

But there was something Madison needed to know or her restless mind would create a thousand answers.

"How did she die?" she asked.

Madison wanted to know, not just for Ryla but for the morbid curiosity of knowing how the Man in the Mask would have killed her had she not escaped that cabin all those years ago.

"A stab wound to the heart," Atticus said.

Silence took hold. A stab to the heart. A Shakespearean death. Madison imagined it must have been some intricate dagger he had used.

"Lobby's pretty full for 1:30 in the morning," Vasquez remarked.

It wasn't only police, hotel staff, and guests stumbling in from the bars. There were children too, clinging to their parents' arms, half asleep and powering through yawns.

"Fire Department left a bit ago," Casper said.

"Fire Department? There was a fire?" Atticus asked.

Casper grimaced at the taste of the stale, watered-down coffee. "No, they think some drunk pulled the alarm."

Madison hadn't told them about her stare-down with the Man in the Mask yet. She was building up to it, but at an evolutionary pace. Madison took a deep breath, then detailed her paralyzing rendezvous with the Man in the Mask. Vasquez told the local police to examine traffic cams around the hotel.

The Hyatt offered complimentary rooms, but Madison was elated when the others said no before she had to chime in. The Man in the Mask had been here. There was no way she'd sleep knowing he was in the same city. On the same street. At the same hotel. Agent Connor drove them to the airport. Madison collapsed into her seat, the takeoff time seemingly interminable. Casper, exhausted, fell asleep shortly after takeoff. Atticus sighed when he sat, a grimace on his face. Vasquez removed her sweat-laden body armor that had practically been a space heater and breathed deeply as if for the first time in hours.

Madison let the beautiful voices of the Righteous Brothers fill her ears. A million thoughts crashed around in her head, and she prayed she'd be granted the mercy of sleep. Halfway to Chicago, Agent Connor called Vasquez. The Man in the Mask had been seen near the Hyatt, but with the congested streets and chaos from the police and fire trucks, he had disappeared.

After the plane landed in Chicago slightly before 4 a.m., a local policewoman drove Casper, Atticus, and Madison back to Essex on the Park. Vasquez drove her Challenger home to Lake Forest. A new day had arrived, sunrise on the horizon. What should have been a feeling of infinite possibilities, a blank page, now merely signaled a day closer to another email and another victim.

Vasquez never accepted defeat as permanent. She believed the war was never over as long as you were willing to fight. And she was willing to fight. Of all the skills and mindsets Atticus had taught her, he never had to instill a strong work ethic. Neither of them were wired for idleness. She slept short of three hours before the desire to catch the bastard trumped any of her body's pleas for more sleep. Tenacity fueled her body. Once at her office, she sipped her coffee as she waited for her computer to boot. Agent Connor had sent over the street-cam footage with a note marking the timestamp to fast-forward to. Vasquez hit play and leaned forward. Even in the grainy film, the Man in the Mask was terrifying. She recalled what Madison had told her—the way his head tilted, his hot breath, his dog-like panting. Vasquez tried to gauge his height based on his surroundings and the people moving past. There wasn't a piece of skin showing. For all she knew, he could be a damn xenomorph underneath. The crowd moved forward like a swarm of mayflies. Vasquez lost sight of the Man in the Mask instantly. She rewound and rewound again and again, only to lose him again and again. Could he have taken the mask off? The sweatshirt too?

Maurice knocked on her door, leaning into her office.

"Good morning. I have an update on murders in Milwaukee within the last fifteen years for women matching the physical profile of Monroe," he said.

He handed a stack too thick for Vasquez's liking. She scanned the documents.

"Any cases involving notes or letters to the family or left at the scene?"

"Three ransom cases, but nothing like what we're getting now."

"Any unsolved murders around Milwaukee?"

Maurice shook his head. "Not for women matching Monroe's looks. But I have Westin Pierce's contact info for you."

Vasquez tilted her head, confused. "Who is that?"

"He worked with Lawrence Floyd at the Kwik Trip in Milwaukee."

Vasquez pinched the bridge of her nose, apparently more tired than she thought. "Did I ask for that?"

"No, I looked into it on my own."

Vasquez nodded, impressed. "Calling your own blitz."

"Let me know if you get a sack."

"Could use a fumble."

Maurice hesitated.

"What is it?" Vasquez asked.

"I know this is a hell of a lot more serious than football, but we have to treat it the same way. I know that sounds stupid, insensitive even, but my junior year, we played USC. Ranked number two in the nation. Had a Heisman-winner quarterback by the name of Colton McKnight. We knew we had to stick to our assignments. McKnight was going to make a mistake. We needed to capitalize on it when he did. This guy's no different. He will make a mistake. And you will capitalize on it."

Vasquez smiled and thanked him. It wasn't hard to see why he had been team captain. "Win the game?"

Maurice smiled. "McKnight threw a pick late in the fourth... Oh, forgot to mention, there's info in there on Moore's flight to Atlanta too."

She thanked him again, reviewed the information, and then called Atticus.

"Moore flew from Mitchell Airport to Tyson, non-stop," Vasquez said.

"And the return flight?" Atticus asked.

"Tyson to Mitchell."

"Damn. No stops in Atlanta?"

"None, but get this. The day after he arrived in Knoxville, he rented a car from Enterprise at the airport."

"The day after?"

"Exactly."

"Well, that makes no sense. If you were able to leave the airport and get to where you were going without needing to rent a car, why do you need one the day after?"

"Returned the car two days later."

"So, the question is where did Moore go? Interesting." His go-to word when a potential breakthrough developed.

"I was thinking about going to Milwaukee to visit Lawrence Floyd's old co-worker from the Kwik Trip. You up for it?"

"Sure. Can't promise I won't sleep the whole way though."

Vasquez picked Atticus up. In the confined space of the car, she got a strong whiff of his aftershave. Brut. What a smell. A smell loaded with memories.

"Westin Pierce?" Atticus asked as he read the info Maurice had gathered. "What does this guy do? Millionaire playboy by day, crime fighter by night?"

"Close," Vasquez said. "He works at Buffalo Wild Wings."

Pierce had only one prior—drug possession of a single joint. Most weed smokers were passive, eating too much food as they binged episodes of *Golden Girls*. People on heroin or meth, on the other hand, turned violent when the hellish hallucinations started. It had been their experience that people using weed ran *from* the police. People on heroin or meth ran *at* the police. After he finished reading the file, Atticus dozed off.

"Great copilot," Vasquez muttered.

"I have this condition that when I sit down, I sleep," Atticus responded without opening his eyes. "Had it for forty years. No cure."

Sleep certainly enticed. The heat from the vents, the sunlight magnified through the windows, and the comfort of her seat were like PEDs for sleep. Vasquez took a swig of her sugar-free Red Bull. Coffee wouldn't cut it. Westin Pierce had agreed to meet them in Glendale at The Cheesecake Factory, located at an unconnected mall of department stores and other restaurants including Buffalo Wild Wings.

"Cheesecake considered a business expense?" Atticus asked.

Vasquez ignored him and accepted water for the table from their waitress. Ten minutes later, blond-haired Westin Pierce, wearing his Buffalo Wild Wings uniform, hurried to their table. His "homemade" cologne—a mixture of beer, wings, and deep-fried appetizers—was overpowering.

"Sorry I'm late. Lunch hour was rushier today," Pierce said.

Atticus looked at Vasquez, mouthing "rushier." Vasquez kicked his leg.

"Sorry, we could have met there," Vasquez said.

"Truth be told, I picked here so my tables didn't see me talk to the FBI. Makes people a bit... not comfortable." He flashed a grin of crooked teeth that didn't compliment him.

"We'll get started so we don't take up too much of your time," Vasquez said.

She took out her yellow legal pad and hit record on her iPhone. She first had Pierce verify the dates he had worked at the Kwik Trip.

"How well do you know Lawrence Floyd?" Vasquez then asked.

He scrunched his lips. "Not really. I haven't talked to him since I quit."

"How would you describe him?"

"Didn't talk much. Said about four words total the first week I worked there. But he opened up."

"What did you talk about? Apart from work?"

"Girls. Lotta talk about that. Talk about weed—"

He caught his comment, his face flushing as red as the hot sauce he tossed his chicken wings in.

"We're not concerned about your cannabis usage."

Pierce exhaled like a deflating balloon.

"Did Floyd have a temper?" Vasquez asked.

"Every time he looked at his paycheck, but who doesn't? Uncle Sam's a greedy bitch."

"Anything else?"

"One of his kid's mom. Always asking for more money and shit."

Atticus showed Pierce a photo of Madison. "Recognize her?"

"Oh, shit yeah! Reese's girl."

"Floyd ever talk about her?" Vasquez asked.

"Just how sizzling she was."

"Ever mention wanting to ask her out? Had he asked her out?"

"No, not that I recall. His dick was scarred from his last piece… woman. Sorry, I don't know how to word that."

Atticus shook his head in mock defense and fought the urge to pick up the menu and select the cheesecake he'd take home. A wasted trip. Judging by Vasquez's tone, she was approaching the point of pulling the plug.

She asked Pierce if he had ever hung out with Floyd outside of work.

"Nope." But then he shrugged. "Well, no unless you'd count riding to work together."

Vasquez stopped jotting. "Ride to work?"

Pierce nodded.

"You two drove to work together?" she repeated.

"Yeah…"

Vasquez's demeanor had shifted, and Atticus acted accordingly. She'd found something—a drop of blood in the water.

"You drove?" she asked.

Pierce shook his head. "Nope. Didn't have a car. Smoked a deer a couple of weeks before. Kept the insurance money."

"Did the two of you ever walk?"

"Fuc—I mean, heck no. Lawrence lived about a dollar and some change away. I was about a fifty-cent away. I dunno what he did before or after I was there, but he drove."

"What type of vehicle?"

"Truck."

"Do you happen to remember the license plate number?" Vasquez asked.

Certainly a long shot, but she hoped for a break.

"No, didn't have one. I told 'im he'd get pulled over for it," Pierce said.

"Do you remember the make?"

"Make?"

"Brand," Atticus clarified.

"Oh, yeah. Dodge. Had one of them sheep with horns, you know what I mean?"

Vasquez's skin tingled. Atticus refrained from slapping Pierce across the face and telling him it was a ram, because he too, had the same sensation as Vasquez.

"Tell me everything you remember about this truck," Vasquez said.

Pierce thought on it for a moment. "White. Wasn't new, but I wouldn't of kicked her out of bed. Bit rusty 'round the tires. No idea how the hell he afforded it. I knew what he made and what he paid in child support. Sold it before winter. Dumbass. Part of the reason I quit. Sure as fu—heck wasn't gonna walk in minus twenty for glorified minimum wage. I had to do that once before. Never again."

Atticus leaned forward. "This truck, did it have any decals or bumper stickers?"

"Yeah, one of 'em coexist bumper stickers."

Once Westin Pierce was out the door, Vasquez turned to Atticus.

"That's the exact truck Madison described. That makes Floyd one of the last, if not *the* last, person to see Madison before her attack and somebody who drove a similar truck or *the* truck."

Atticus refused to leave without indulging in a slice of cheesecake, comparing it to going to church and declining the Eucharist. It didn't take much coercing for Vasquez to get a slice too. Then they got back in her car, played Springsteen, and hit the road.

"You missed the exit," Atticus said.

"We're going to pay Lawrence a visit," Vasquez replied.

"Do you have any info on him?"

"Yeah, in my attaché."

He scowled at her use of the word *attaché*. It was a damn briefcase. He opened it and grabbed the folder Maurice had put together. The moment he saw Floyd's picture, he closed it.

"He didn't do it."

Vasquez glanced at him, equally annoyed and confused. "What?"

"He's not the man who's killing these women. Therefore, he's not the one who abducted Madison."

"Floyd drove a truck of the exact make and model, with the same color and the same decal, for Christ's sake."

"I know."

She glared at him.

"Watch the road," Atticus said.

"I'll worry about the damn road," she said.

He fell silent, looking out at Miller Park, now called American Family Field.

Vasquez exhaled, aggressively enough to put out a candle. "Do you care to elaborate, Wallace?"

"If these killings hadn't started, I'd tell you to cuff Floyd right now."

"But the killings did start."

"Yes, exactly."

Vasquez sighed, horribly annoyed, partially because she understood his reasoning. "Because he's black."

"Because he's black."

"Well, maybe serial murder has desegregated."

"Maybe."

Statistics showed serial killers rarely killed outside their race. As if on cue, they drove by the empty plot of land where Dahmer had lived; he was an exception to the rule as he predominantly killed men outside his race. Atticus was silent, and Vasquez respected it. A few minutes later, they arrived at the Floyd house. Vasquez grabbed a tub of Vicks Vapor Rub from the center console and applied a small layer beneath her nose. She held the tub out for Atticus to do the same.

"What do I want that for?" he asked.

"Trust me."

He took the Vicks and applied a generous amount. It was an old trick, something to help block the atrocious odors. Then they walked up the steps. Vasquez knocked.

"Who there?" Mrs. Floyd barked from inside.

Vasquez announced herself. Mrs. Floyd told her to step inside. Given her less-than-welcoming tone, Vasquez withheld any words seeking permission. The putrid smell of cat piss, body odor, garlic, and mildew attacked them.

"You gonna disrup' my game shows again?" Mrs. Floyd asked. Then her eyes found Atticus. "Who this white man you be bringin' into my house?"

Vasquez introduced Atticus, listing his credentials and calling him a special consultant.

"From Chicago? We ain't in Chicago, we ain't from Chicago, and we don't go to Chicago."

"Is Lawrence home?" Vasquez asked, completely ignoring Mrs. Floyd's last comment.

Mrs. Floyd sucked in air like a tsunami pulling back from the shore and then released it like a tidal wave. "Lawrence! That 'BI woman wanna talk witch you again!"

Lawrence jogged down the steps, bringing with him a cloud of new smells—weed and whiskey—to add to the lethal mix.

"I'm gonna go take a bath. I expect this gonna be done when I come back down," Mrs. Floyd said.

With thunderous, labored steps that made her resemble a T-Rex, she made her way to the stairs. People had climbed mountains with less strenuous exertion.

"So, what can I do for you, mam?" Lawrence asked.

"We had an interesting sit-down with an old co-worker of yours," Vasquez said.

"Really? Who?"

"Westin Pierce."

"Oh, haven't seen him in a minute. How is he?"

"We asked him the same questions I asked you. Interestingly though, his answers were different."

"Answers that should have been the same as yours," Atticus added.

Floyd looked at Atticus who stood a mere foot from him. "He wanna sit?" he asked Vasquez.

"He's fine. He's got a condition," Vasquez replied. "How did you get to the Kwik Trip?"

"Walked." His eyes followed Atticus as he strolled around the living room, hands behind his back as if he was viewing priceless paintings at the Louvre.

"You walked…" Vasquez repeated. She would give him one more chance to come clean.

160

"For the most part."

Here came those trigger words.

"Pierce said you drove. Picked him up."

"So one of you is either forgetful or lying," Atticus said, examining an *EW* magazine from 1998 amidst a titanic heap.

"Well, it's not Lawrence who's forgetting. I mean, he just reconfirmed," Vasquez said to Atticus.

"Pierce remembered a lot of details though," Atticus replied, now glancing at Mrs. Floyd's newest romance novel. He arched his eyebrows and then tossed it back down.

"So, that means one of them is lying," Vasquez said.

"Right. So, the question is who has something to gain by lying, something to hide."

Vasquez turned away from Floyd and gave her undivided attention to Atticus, acting as if Floyd wasn't even in the room.

"It doesn't seem like Pierce has any reason to lie," she said.

"Exactly. I don't think someone would lie about not wanting to walk to work in the winter. So that means Larry here lied."

"Interesting," Vasquez said with a showman's theatrics.

"What kind of vehicle did Pierce say Larry drove?"

"A white Dodge Ram."

"From the early aughts."

"Said it was a bit rusted around the tires. Had a decal too."

Atticus snapped his fingers. "That's right. One of those coexist ones… Why does this make, model, year range, color, and decal sound familiar?"

Vasquez tapped her cheek—the clichéd gesture for thinking. "Ms. Monroe, A.K.A. Reese's girl, was forced off the road by a man driving—"

"An early-2000s white Dodge Ram with a coexist decal," Atticus finished.

The back and forth banter, that had come so naturally to them, brought on a rush of nostalgia.

Sweat streamed down Floyd's forehead. His eyes darted upstairs as if looking at the ceiling would help him hear the running bathwater better. Atticus sat across from Floyd, leaning forward. Doing so forced Lawrence to lean back, as Atticus knew it would. This simple gesture, and Floyd's response, gave Atticus the power and control over the conversation.

"Larry..." Another power play. Atticus knew full well Floyd went by Lawrence. Floyd hadn't corrected him—more power gained. "I'm going to list a few things. You will answer with yes, or you will answer with no. Not but, maybe, umm, or I'm not sure. Understood?"

Floyd nodded. His receding hairline looked like it had been polished. His funyuns-weed-whiskey body odor radiated off his armpits like two spraying skunks.

"You worked at the Kwik Trip on Dawson Street," Atticus said.

"Yes."

"You worked late night to early morning."

"Yes."

"A woman named Madison Monroe came into the station often."

A slight hesitation. "Yes."

"You didn't walk to work."

An even longer hesitation. "... No..."

"You drove an early-2000s white Dodge Ram with a coexist bumper sticker."

Decades of experience had given Atticus and Vasquez a level of intuition akin to clairvoyance. Floyd's feet turned toward the door, his weight transferring from his ass to his feet.

He was going to run.

He shot up from the couch, stepping onto the coffee table. He slipped on the stack of glossy magazines. Atticus grabbed him by the back of the shirt collar and shoved him toward the wall. Floyd landed on a heap of old *Milwaukee Journal Sentinel* newspapers. Before he could get back to his feet, Vasquez aimed her Glock at his chest.

"Okay! Okay!" Floyd yelled, his hands up in surrender.

"You better start talking real fast," Vasquez told him.

"Better listen, Larry. Her finger twitches," Atticus warned.

"Let me tell y'all outside. Away from my mamma."

Atticus deferred to Vasquez.

"Fine. But I promise you if you try running again, you'll be check-marking a different gender from here on out."

Atticus offered his hand to Floyd and yanked him to his feet. He and Vasquez blocked the porch steps. The only place Floyd could go was back inside. Floyd reached into his pocket, but Vasquez gave him a warning look and told him to stop.

"Just gettin' a cig," he said.

Vasquez allowed it. Floyd pulled from his dark denim jeans his pack of Marlboro Reds, lit one, and took a long puff.

"More talking, less puffing," Vasquez ordered.

Floyd cursed, not at Vasquez or Atticus but at the situation he found himself in.

"I did drive to work in a truck."

"In a truck or *the* truck Pierce and Monroe described?" Vasquez asked.

"The one described. Even had that fuckin' bumper sticker."

"Why'd you lie?" Atticus asked.

"Why you think? I don't wanna go to prison for no auto theft."

A slight pause. It wasn't what they were expecting.

"You stole the truck?" Vasquez asked.

Floyd exhaled a cloud of smoke away from Vasquez and Atticus. "Yeah. I thought you knew… Oh, shit…"

"Keep talking," Vasquez ordered.

"I'd done told my mamma I was done stealin'. But shit man, you ever walk a mile in minus twenty-five? I did that whole winter, man. As soon as it started getting cold again, I stole that truck. Got rid of the plates. Tried peelin' that bumper sticker off too, but that sucker was on there for good."

Vasquez fought the urge to look over at Atticus.

"That's why you're here, right? Reason for all them questions?" Floyd asked.

"When did you get rid of the truck?" Vasquez questioned.

"I didn't. It was jacked the same day Reese's girl was taken."

"Somebody stole the truck you had stolen?"

Floyd nodded, enjoying the last few puffs of his cigarette.

"That's highly convenient," Atticus said, his arms crossed.

"What'd you want me to do? Call the police and report it stolen?"

A valid point.

Floyd shifted his weight, then leaned forward. "Can I get trouble for what I say?"

"Yes. That's what we call a confession," Atticus said.

Vasquez had to bite her lip to stop a smirk.

"Any ideas on who stole it?" Atticus asked.

Floyd vehemently shook his head. "Drove it to work. Went outside later for a smoke break, and it was gone."

Vasquez asked what time he had taken his smoke break. He said he couldn't remember, only that it was after Reese's girl had been in. Atticus asked if he'd stolen any other cars. Vasquez knew the answer but wanted to see if Floyd would be honest about it.

"Yeah, I did before then. But I ain't stole another car since. Swear to God. Mamma don't know about that truck. I parked it a few blocks away in case the police were lookin' for it."

Floyd was trying to save face, and even though parking the stolen vehicle away from his house was smart, the main reason for doing so wasn't from fear of the police. It was fear of his mamma's wrath.

"What was in Baton Rouge?" Atticus asked.

The curveball took Floyd by complete surprise. "Nothin'."

Vasquez exhaled in frustration. "Lawrence, we know you purchased bus tickets. Two sets because you washed the first. Both were from Union Station to Baton Rouge, Louisiana. There's an open investigation in New Orleans for a woman's murder. We believe the person who abducted Madison is the same person who killed this woman."

"Jesus, I didn't kill nobody!" Floyd exclaimed.

Atticus put his hand on Lawrence's shoulder in a fatherly way. "Nobody likes a long, drawn-out trial. Costs taxpayers' money. Juries, they want to be home before supper. Here are a few key words that'll be used at the trial. *Motive. Means. Opportunity.* You check all those boxes. Now, you're poor, so you'll be forced to accept the attorney the state provides. It'll be someone who squeaked past the bar exam after his father called in a favor. He's going to tell you to take the plea deal. What would you say, Allie? Thirty years?"

Vasquez shrugged. "I was thinking thirty-five or forty, but he may get a kind judge."

Atticus turned back to Floyd, his hand still on the poor guy's bony shoulder.

"You'll want to plead innocent. You will lose, and you will spend the rest of your life in prison, praying some cancer takes you. But prisons aren't what they used to be. They're not Shawshank. Decent food, exercise time, excellent medical care—you may live to be ninety. That's fifty years in prison."

"Jesus Christ, man! I told ya I didn't kill no one!"

"Then why won't you tell us what was in Baton Rouge?" Vasquez pressed.

"'Cause it's gonna get me arrested, that's why."

"Looking like a foregone conclusion," Vasquez said.

Another curse from Floyd. "I was in Baton Rouge. I got picked up, and we gone to New Orleans."

Vasquez wasn't going to prod him along any further. He'd keep talking or she'd cuff him. Lawrence clawed at his bald spot as if hoeing dirt to promote growth.

"I was picking up product," he said.

"Drugs?" Atticus asked.

Floyd nodded, exhaling a deep breath. "Cocaine. Listen, it come up from Mexico, but instead of going over the border, it goes across the gulf. I pick it up. One duffel bag goes to Chicago, and one comes back here to Milwaukee. I swear I don't do nothin' violent."

Painful silence prevailed as Atticus and Vasquez studied Floyd. Atticus never lost a staring contest. Vasquez removed her hand from her holstered Glock.

"You leave Milwaukee and I swear I'll have you arrested. Understand?" she said.

"Yes, yes, I do," Floyd replied with accompanying bobble-head nods. "That mean you ain't arrestin' me now?"

"If I find out you lied or left any detail out, you're going to have a new mamma in prison."

They left Floyd on his porch, where he sucked down another cigarette.

"I see you agree with me," Atticus said once they were in the car.

"He does check certain boxes—domineering mother, for one. But he's not a writer. There's a difference between writing badly and being a bad writer. Plus…"

"He's black," Atticus finished for her.

Vasquez gave him a death stare. He may have been right, but he could still go screw off.

Instead of continuing on I-94 back toward Chicago, Vasquez took an exit.

"Now where are we going?" Atticus asked.

"Waukesha."

The city of Waukesha had masterfully blended idyllic suburbia and modern metropolitan with a pleasant balance of small businesses and national chains. Near Maple Way North, Vasquez turned onto a driveway. A Yukon, a Chevy Tahoe, and three child-sized electronic Hummers were parked in front of the two-stall garage. The front yard was covered in disheveled piles of leaves, evidence that children had been playing in them. The house had strong bones with a bit of modern plastic surgery. The husband's toys—a boat, a motorcycle, and a four-wheeler—were parked inside the garage.

"What the hell does she do for a living?" Atticus asked.

"Daycare. Makes you wish you had gone into daycare, huh?"

Atticus scoffed painfully. "I failed with two."

Vasquez had knocked before he had spoken. She wished she hadn't. His comment deserved to be refuted, but the door opened before she could. The woman who answered the door had shorter hair than in the photographs Vasquez had seen of her. But it was still as vibrantly dark. She too had blue eyes, though a shade darker than Madison's. She was attractive, but Vasquez's initial impression of her had been as "a poor man's Madison." She had gained a bit of weight, but the smile on her face radiated a love of life, and sometimes, that love of life meant love of food.

"Jade Allen?" Vasquez asked.

"It's Stockem now. But Allen is my maiden name," she answered, slightly out of breath. She was dressed in sweat pants and a hooded sweatshirt.

Behind her at the kitchen table, her husband, two sons, and a daughter carved pumpkins. Vasquez and Atticus introduced themselves, and Vasquez disclosed why they were there.

"Do you mind if we speak in the backyard?" Jade asked.

Neither objected, and they followed Jade around the house on a stone walkway. The backyard was a homeowner's dream. There was a twenty-five–foot pool with a wooden deck, pitched tents for impromptu backyard camping, a fireplace, a granite countertop with a built-in oven and grill, and a mini-fridge. Jade opened the fridge and offered them their choice. It was stacked full of beer, hard seltzers, sodas, bottled water, and rows of juice boxes.

"Anything non-alcoholic," Vasquez said.

"Anything alcoholic," Atticus chimed.

"Sorry for my appearance. I just got back from a run," Jade said.

Atticus and Vasquez both dismissed the unneeded apology.

After a few sips and a couple of compliments about her family and home, Vasquez got down to business.

"I'd like you to tell us what you remember about the night Madison was abducted."

Jade's smile vanished. Her face was a Jackson Pollock painting of emotions—regret, sadness, pain.

"Maddie didn't want to go to that party. She was out earlier for coffee. When she got back, she was tired. Just wanted to stay home. I talked her into going. I mean, we went as Demi Moore and Patrick Swayze from *Ghost*. My costume wouldn't have made much sense without her." She hesitated, blushing ever so slightly. "And Maddie was what our friends called a dick magnet. Guys were drawn to her, and being her best friend, you caught shrapnel, if you know what I mean."

Atticus smirked, appreciating her phrasing.

"God, I begged her to go to that party," Jade said. "I never... I don't think I will ever forgive myself for that."

"Madison mentioned Vince Propelli and Shane Benson," Vasquez stated.

"Yeah, I remember the police interviewing both of them."

"Did either strike you as off-putting?"

Jade shook her head. "Maddie and Vince had hooked up a few times. Shane... Shane was your stereotypical drunk sorority guy. Was he a gentleman? Absolutely not. He always made passes at Maddie and me—really, anything that walked on two feet and had a vagina. And depending on how much he drank, the two feet thing wasn't a deal breaker."

Atticus laughed. He appreciated wit. It was easy to see why she and Madison had been such great friends.

"Did you try contacting her after she left the party?" Vasquez asked.

"I had tried convincing her to stay. I thought once she got a bit buzzed, she'd feel better. But I could see she wasn't going to. She looked... off."

"How do you mean?"

"She normally had this glow, always smiling, laughing. I sent her a text right after she left. Feel better, see you later—that sort of thing. Asked her to let me know when she got home. She took her bike. I expected it to be a while before she responded. After an hour and a half, I called her."

"And obviously, there was no answer," Atticus said.

Jade nodded with a shiver. The memory still haunted her. "Just rang and rang, then went to voicemail."

"What time did you get home?" Vasquez asked.

Jade peeked toward the patio door, making sure her husband and children were still occupied carving pumpkins. Her cheeks reddened once more. She rubbed her fingers on the necklace around her neck. Gold with three birth stones—Ruby, Opal, and Blue Topaz. Something both Vasquez and Atticus understood as a gesture meant to comfort, something Jade did when she was stressed.

"... I didn't go home. I never told Maddie this, but I don't want to lie to you... I stayed with Vince."

"Stayed with..." Vasquez hung onto the last word.

She wasn't stupid. She knew what "stayed with" meant, but in her line of work, you had to verify assumptions.

"We had sex. They were never serious, but I felt guilty, and then, with what happened to her…"

She shook her head and looked away, too ashamed to see her own reflection in the glass patio door.

"What time did you get home the following day?" Atticus asked.

"Ten-ish. I thought it was strange her bike wasn't out in front of the apartment building, but Maddie was an early riser, and she had left the party relatively early. So I thought she was out and about already. I was hung over, so I went back to bed. Woke up, and she was still gone. Called her phone. No answer. At that point, I became pretty worried. I had chalked up her not answering the night before to her phone having died. But when I examined the apartment, there were no signs she had ever made it home."

Jade shuddered, nearly choking on those last few words.

"Then you alerted Campus Security?" Vasquez asked.

"Yes, and after she wasn't found on campus, the Milwaukee police were informed."

"Madison was well-liked, was she not?" Atticus asked.

"Yes. Everybody loved her. She was nice to everyone. She had that ability to make everyone feel important."

"She attract a lot of guys wanting more than friendship?" Atticus asked.

"For sure. She was asked out all the time," Jade said.

"Do you remember any such… incident with Professor Moore?"

Jade's brow furrowed. Her mouth formed into a slight scowl. "Yes. That's not uncommon for him. But yeah, she said she was super creeped out. I forget his name, but the student teacher was awesome with her. I don't think he knew there was a specific instance, but he knew enough to act as the mediator between Maddie and Professor Moore, making sure she never had to be alone with him again."

"Would this be Rigel Rose?" Vasquez asked.

Jade nodded emphatically. "That's it! We used to crack jokes about his name all the time. Like, 'Will you accept this rose', you know, from *The Bachelor*? He asked Maddie out, but she turned him down."

Atticus leaned forward. "He asked her out?"

"I believe so. I mean, at least I remember it that way."

"And she said no?"

Jade nodded, unsure why it had been brought up.

"Do you know how he reacted when she said no?" Vasquez asked.

"He was great about it. It was more of a 'Would you like to get a drink?' She said it may not be a good idea. He understood, and as far as I know, it was never mentioned again. It's a shame. I think they really would have hit it off. Maddie could be the most outgoing person one day, needing to be surrounded by fifty people crammed in a basement belting out karaoke, but the next day, she'd need to be alone, wrapped in a blanket with a good book. The conversations the two would have about books and authors... They were blind, that's for sure."

A moment's pause ensued as each took a sip of their beverage.

"The day of the abduction, do you remember what that day entailed for Madison?" Vasquez asked. "There may be clues Madison doesn't remember because of what she'd been through."

Jade took a moment to gather her thoughts. "She was up early. Was already done with a run by the time I woke up. We had breakfast at a place downtown. We watched a couple of horror movies. She got coffee; I think she was gone for maybe an hour or two. She came back to the apartment, and I talked her into going to the party."

"Nobody at breakfast stood out to you? A man staring? Somebody she interacted with? Friend? Stranger?" Atticus asked.

Jade shook her head. "Not that I recall."

"And the two of you drifted apart afterward?" Atticus asked.

Jade squeezed her eyes shut and nodded, her face again contorting with regret and sadness.

"Any particular reason?"

"We're both at fault. After... it happened, I think she needed to leave Milwaukee and everybody in it for a new life in Chicago. I was a reminder of what had happened. I accepted that she needed space. But a month turned into a year. A year turned into five."

The older you got, the more unnatural time appeared to you. Months turned to weeks, weeks to days, and days to minutes. Vasquez finished her Pepsi Zero. Atticus took the unintentional hint to finish his Miller High Life. Jade walked them to their car.

"Please tell Maddie 'ditto.' She'll know what it means," Jade said.

The ride back to Chicago was silent apart from the nineties hits playing softly on the radio. Both Vasquez and Atticus replayed the interview in their heads before commenting on it.

"Sweet girl," Vasquez said.

"Yeah, good bones."

"She seemed heartbroken at what happened."

"Not her fault. Life can be stripped down to hours or minutes that ultimately define our lives. Madison deciding to go to that party is one of her moments."

How different her life could have been. Or maybe not. Maybe Madison had been destined to go through that horrible ordeal. If not that October night, then maybe the next week or in the following month. She could drive herself mad going over every minute of that day and wondering if something had taken one minute longer or one minute shorter, could it have changed everything?

"Why didn't Rose tell us he had asked her out?" Atticus questioned.

Vasquez shrugged at what she perceived as an innocent oversight. "Do you remember every girl you asked out?"

"Yeah, I do. All two of 'em."

Vasquez glanced at him, an invisible hundred-pound weight dragging her face into a frown. But she wouldn't let that almighty stare take hold once more.

"Jade said there were no hard feelings on being turned down," she remarked.

"Yeah, so he said," Atticus muttered, turning his attention to the world speeding by his window.

"Was it really only two women?" Vasquez asked. "There wasn't any after…?"

Atticus shook his head, keeping his eyes on the world outside his window. "After dining at the Ritz, dumpster diving never appealed to me."

Vasquez bit her lip and scrunched her toes, focusing on the road. "I never thanked you for your letter of recommendation."

Atticus nodded in a way that dismissed its significance.

"Even after… everything… you still wrote it."

"You've always been a great cop. Everyone knew that."

"No one else put their neck on the line for me."

Atticus brought his gaze from the speeding black and gray blurs outside his window to Vasquez's vibrant caramel face and her olive-green eyes.

"I put more than my neck on the line for you."

Rarely did Madison have trouble forcing herself out of bed, but she did the first few days after New Orleans. She didn't even shower. She spent her days in a zombie-like haze, mindlessly scrolling through her TV. When there was a knock on the door, her first thought was an irrational one: The Man in the Mask was behind it. She called herself an idiot. As if the Man in the Mask would knock. She looked through the peephole, then opened the door.

"Fo'got, dintcha?"

Lana Sanchez, her MMA trainer, stepped inside, sporting a new tattoo on her forearm—a tribal rose surrounded by barbed wire and the Spanish word *amor*. She was running out of canvas for her art. Lana had that naturally beautiful bronze skin tone Latinas had, but not only did she conceal it with ink, drugs and alcohol had depleted its glow, and a career of getting punched and kicked had resulted in bruises and scars.

"Shit, give me a sec," Madison said.

She rushed into her bedroom and changed into her workout attire, stopping by the bathroom to splash cold water on her face. Lana stripped down to her sports bra and spandex shorts, revealing more ink, including the word *victory* across her ripped abdomen. Lana was trained in Brazilian jujitsu and had fought amateur since she was 17. She had hopes to make it to the UFC, but fighting had never taken priority. It hadn't even taken the bronze. Women, alcohol, and drugs had taken gold, silver, and bronze.

They practiced self-defense, blocks, and strikes using Muay Thai. Then Madison pummeled Century Bob. Each punch more anger-driven than the last.

"Hey, hey, hey, calm down, girl. You'll break your hand," Lana said.

Madison stopped, her chest heaving in rhythm with the wobbling Century Bob.

"Look how exhausted you are. You've lost," Lana said.

"I'm fine," Madison replied, trying to sip air instead of gasping as if she had nearly drowned.

"Yeah? Come at me then."

Madison would lose whether she was winded or not, but she was too proud to admit she had lied. She threw a punch, which Lana lazily blocked and then tossed Madison to the ground. Madison groaned from the impact. Lana yanked her to her feet.

"You're out of control. That's exactly what he wants. Control. And if he's got it, you dead. You ain't gonna be stronger than most men. Fo'get the bullshit they be pushin'. And if you accept that fact as truth, it won't make no difference. You gotta be smarter. He gonna come at'chu with wild, reckless force. He think you a damsel in distress. A sheep. Hell with that. You a bloodthirsty warrior."

They then worked on transitions, grapples, takedowns, and full and half guard. Lana called out when Madison should lock her legs, squeeze her hips, or go for a submission.

She forced Madison onto her back and mounted her. She wrapped her hands around her throat, squeezing harder and harder. Madison tried prying Lana's fingers loose but couldn't. She reached for Lana's face; Lana simply leaned her head back. When it was clear Madison had no exit, Lana released her grip.

"Your body's response is wrong. If you listen to it, you dead. Squirming, scratching, clawing—that's how prey respond. You know what a wolf does when it gets bit? It bites back. You need to learn to ignore the prey in you. React like a predator."

It was exactly how Madison had reacted in New Orleans on seeing the Man in the Mask. Like a silly sheep.

They resumed positions—Madison flat on her back, Lana on her knees between Madison's legs. Lana enveloped Madison's throat with her long fingers, but this time, she didn't squeeze.

"Wrap your legs around me in a closed guard. Cross your feet," Lana instructed.

Madison did.

"Now you got me trapped. I can't get away," Lana said.

She proved it by trying to push free. Madison kept her legs crossed and wouldn't let Lana break away. But why would she want to trap him as he choked her to death? She trusted Lana had a reason.

"Now cross your arms and put your hands on my elbows," Lana said.

Madison followed her instruction.

"Now press down while lifting your legs onto my shoulders."

Even at a walkthrough speed, Lana grunted from the pressure put on her elbows.

"Now you blast your hips up, and you break his fuckin' elbows."

They swapped positions. Now Madison was the attacker, and Lana the victim. Madison wrapped her hands around Lana's throat and then watched as Lana slowly but fluidly executed the steps, stopping short of the final step that would have broken her elbows. A stinging pain exploded in Madison's elbows even at the slow walkthrough pace. They ran through it a dozen times until Madison could do the first few steps in a continuous motion without having to think about it. When the workout was completed, Madison's recently acquired laziness could no longer ignore her need of a shower. The workout was exactly what she needed. It never failed to clear her head.

They leaned against her kitchen countertop, gulping down water by the glassful. Casper announced himself with a knock on the door. Madison let him inside. As Lana put on her pants and shirt, Casper stuttered and looked away. Madison made the introductions and explained why Lana was there. The intimidating instructor acknowledged him with a lazy nod. She finished her water and wiped her mouth on her sleeve.

"Remember, stay in control. Imagine Bobby wearing that mask when you punch him. Learn to harness your fear. Don't react like a prey. It's not fight or flight," Lana said.

… Or fright…

"It's fight and fight and fucking fight."

She gave Madison a fist bump, then left.

"Well, she seems extremely intimidating," Casper joked.

Madison was un-showered and sweaty and extremely self-conscious because of it.

"I have come to ask you to dinner," he said. "Do I remember you telling me it's hard for you to say no in person? Yes. Did I use this information to my advantage?" A guilty shrug.

"That's quite the manipulative scheme, 5114," Madison said.

"I know."

It was always incredibly difficult for her to say no when asked face to face—she would even say impossible. So, she agreed to dinner. There was a small part of her excited for the feeling of normalcy it offered. After he left, she showered. He said he'd stop by at six o'clock. She had expected another dinner at The Cheesecake Factory, but he surprised her by taking her to a steakhouse, the kind that had four $ signs next to it when you googled it.

Madison was incredibly underdressed in jeans and a sweater. People were more dressed up for steaks than she had been for weddings. She examined the menu. Pumpkin was a seasonal addition currently available—pumpkin ale, pumpkin cider, pumpkin pie, pumpkin cheesecake.

"Do you carve pumpkins?" she asked, but immediately realized that Casper, who probably had not taken notice of the many pumpkin-flavored items on the menu, must have considered the question random and awkward. Madison bit her cheek and scrunched her toes to cause herself some deserved pain for her awkwardness.

"No, not in years… decades actually," Casper said. "My pumpkins always turned out looking like people that came from a long line of inbreeding. You know, like two teeth, one eye drooping lower than the other…"

Madison laughed.

"Why? Do you want to?" he asked.

"No, not really."

"Well, okay…" he chuckled.

"Sorry."

He dismissed the apology with a wave. "No, this keeps me on my toes. You bring up a subject you have no interest in. I respond. And you kill the conversation."

"I just noticed how many pumpkin-flavored food and drinks were on the menu."

"Oh, you like pumpkin?"

"… No…"

They both laughed.

The food was good. Had the price been cheaper, Madison would have called it great. She ate her steak well-done, something Casper condemned as a culinary sin. His steak was medium, and each time he cut a piece, blood oozed from its reddish-pink center. She swore she could hear the meat moo.

"Parents got it all wrong. You're not a ghost—you're Dracula," she teased.

"Hey, was that your first Casper joke?" he said, mockingly clutching his heart.

"I guess Halloween's got to be a busy time for you?"

Casper was mid-chew, so he couldn't speak, but he motioned for Madison to bring it on.

"With so many walls to pass through, so many bathtubs to pop up in."

"Wow. Back to back. I didn't see that coming."

"Ironic coming from a ghost."

"Damn girl, slow down. We got all night."

Casper handled the bill, and they left the restaurant and began their walk back to Essex on the Park. The winds off the lake were exceptionally violent, a warning that winter was closer than expected. Hundreds of people were on the streets, and not a single one appeared to give Madison any attention. And yet, she couldn't help but suspect one of them was the Man in the Mask. The chill that followed that thought was something the icy winds could never produce. They rode the elevator and got off on Madison's floor. Their timing was fortuitous. Vasquez was at Madison's door.

"I was hoping we could talk," Vasquez said.

Casper squeezed Madison's hand before leaving. Would he have tried to kiss her had Vasquez not been there? The thought both terrified and tantalized her. Madison invited Vasquez inside and offered her a spot at the kitchen table. Under the guise of needing to go to the bathroom, Madison cleared her closets, under her bed, and behind the shower curtain. Then she offered Vasquez something to drink. Since this was a personal visit, she asked for whiskey served the way Frank Sinatra drank it. It was alternatively referred to as "the 3-2-1". Three ice cubes, two fingers of whiskey, and a splash of water.

"How are you holding up?" Vasquez asked.

"Feel like I've been put in a paper shredder and taped back together," Madison said.

"Well, they did a good job."

Madison smiled feebly.

"Atticus and I just got back from talking with your friend Jade," Vasquez said.

The sound of Jade's name brought with it hundreds of memories and a wide smile to Madison's face. But the smile left as fast as it had come. It'd been over five years since she'd last seen Jade.

"She told me to tell you 'ditto,'" Vasquez said.

Madison laughed through a smile as tears welled up in her eyes.

"It's from the movie *Ghost*. It means I love you," she explained.

Vasquez's smile was a heavy one.

Life pulls people apart. Like two rafts in an ocean. Sometimes, people fail to react because the drifting is so gradual, but by the time they realize, the current is too strong.

"So, why'd you talk with Jade?" Madison asked between sips of her old fashioned.

"To hear what she remembers about that day," Vasquez answered. "She said you could be the life of the party."

Madison scoffed. "That was a different woman. One who's been gone long enough to be declared legally dead."

"Dead? No. In a coma? Perhaps."

Vasquez took a sip of her whiskey. The world may know it as the Sinatra special, but she knew it as Atticus's drink. The one he had imbibed to the point of blacking out that night. That horrible night. She forced the memory away from her mind.

"Jade mentioned you had been asked out by the student teacher," Vasquez said.

Madison thought on it, then shook her head, finding no such memory. "Student teacher?"

"Rose."

"Oh, yeah! Such a nice guy... Gosh, I haven't thought about him in years. I never told him what Moore did, but I think he knew. Either way, I never had to go to Moore for anything again."

"Did you two have any relationship outside of school?"

Madison nodded, as the memory of him flooded back. "We'd meet for coffee and discuss books we'd read and recommend new ones to each other. It was like our own little book club."

"Jade thought you two were blind, that you were perfect for each other."

"Rigel was sweet, but I never thought of him as anything but a friend."

Vasquez nodded, enjoying another sip of her Sinatra special.

"What about you?" Madison asked.

"What do you mean?"

"You and Atticus. There's history there. I can feel it."

Madison couldn't believe what she just asked outright. She had certainly been curious about it. But it was incredibly insolent of her to have actually asked.

"There most certainly is," Vasquez replied as she raised her glass to her lips. She let the whiskey burn her throat and chest.

Madison apologized, feeling like a complete idiot, and a rude one at that.

"No, it's fine. You had to tell me your deepest secrets." She took another sip.

Was she looking for liquid courage the same way Madison was?

"In 1988, Atticus and his partner responded to a homicide. Gangbanger. Shot and killed. He'd stolen ten grand worth of cocaine. They went to arrest the shooter. He resisted. A gun fight broke out. Atticus was hit in the collarbone, his partner in the neck. He died in Atticus's arms."

Madison had heard Atticus tell this story, but he hadn't given it the gravitas it deserved. It also felt like Vasquez was building up her courage and needed to start with a preamble.

"Atticus needed a new partner. I was a beat cop at the time. I worked my ass off, but no one would take a chance on me. Talent, hard work... they only take you so far. You need luck, a break, someone to give you a shot. It wasn't happening for me. One day, I'd just had it. I was sick of all the bullshit, all the woman jokes and the Latina jokes. I stormed into the captain's office and went berserk. I didn't even realize Atticus was there. I laid my badge and my gun on the captain's desk and left, absolutely certain my career in law enforcement was over. Atticus asked for my file, and after reading it, demanded I be his partner. Now, this is 1989. There were no minority or women quotas in the workplace to help you get noticed. Give you a shot. He picked me because of *me*. Handed me my badge and gun and told me I was his partner."

Vasquez paused to finish her drink. She nodded to the bottle, asking for more. Madison nodded for her to go ahead. The ice had melted enough to cover the splash of water Vasquez desired.

"Atticus... he taught me everything. Not just the job but tricks like how to go from dead asleep at 1:40 in the morning to wide awake at a crime scene at 1:55. Taught me how to handle the awful things you see... We solved a lot of cases."

Vasquez took another drink, this one not a sip but a swig.

It was selfish of Madison to feel good about hearing the conflict Vasquez experienced. But it was a reflection of the pain she lived with. To see a woman as strong as Vasquez feel the same pain she did meant that maybe she wasn't as weak as she thought.

There was an even ruder question Madison wanted to ask, and she didn't know if it was the whiskey or the fact that everything seemed so inconsequential in comparison to Ryla Abrams' death—or maybe both—but she asked it.

"When did it become more than being partners?"

Vasquez looked at Madison, then retreated her gaze back to the caramel-colored whiskey in her glass. Madison immediately apologized and rose from the table. Vasquez put her hand on Madison's to stop her. She sat back down. Vasquez gathered her breath.

"You develop a bond... a trust. You see things you don't dare bring home to your family, things only the two of you've experienced. In 1991, a young boy named Gabriel Peterson disappeared. He was at a mall with his mother. She stopped to look in her purse, looked up, and he was gone. We interviewed every person who said they were at the mall, examined every store for clues, drove around day and night looking for him, looked into every registered sex offender in the city... We did everything we could to find that boy."

"But you didn't..."

Vasquez shook her head, fighting to keep her emotions in check. Even after all those years, the memory still cut deep and festered with salt.

"His body was found in black trash bags in a drainage canal outside Glenbrook. Chopped up and discarded like trash... His mother... She was inconsolable. To this day, I've never heard someone in so much pain. When

Atticus told her, she punched his chest, blaming him for what had happened. When I tried to pull her off, he shook his head. He let her punch him until she collapsed. Later that night, Atticus headed to The Moonlight—it was this hotel-slash-bar. It's been torn down..." She shook her head to stop her tangent. "... He drowned his sorrow in liquor. I couldn't get him to leave. Only when he was a drink shy of blacking out could I finally pull him away. On the ride home, he broke down. It was the only time I've seen him cry. I pulled over and held him.

"I think, at that moment, we both realized how much we needed each other. I was never more vulnerable than when I was with Atticus, but never was I stronger. Respect. Admiration. Trust. Love. It was all there. An attraction to who we were. We tried to deny it, but it was hopeless. He was married. I was married. It didn't stop us. Nothing could..."

But Madison knew the ending. Something *had* stopped it. Vasquez held up a strong front. She was a proud woman, but beneath the surface, she was in ruins. Emotions can be unfathomably destructive. The FBI agent had her flash of pain and sadness, but then, she collected herself. Vasquez thanked Madison for the drink and her time and left.

Tears from a reservoir Vasquez thought had long dried clung from the lids of her eyes. She stepped inside the elevator but didn't take it down. She instead went up. On her way to his apartment, she reached into her purse. She knocked. The door opened. Vasquez held the item out in her hand for Atticus to take. His eyes shifted from hers to what she held. He took it. A plane ticket—O'Hare, Chicago, Illinois to Orly, Paris, France—dated December 14th, 1996.

The emotions were cataclysmic. Vasquez summoned her courage and looked Atticus directly in the eye.

"I couldn't get rid of it. I've carried it every day... I couldn't let it go."

Freedom looks good on me. *Listen, Burke's a great guy for sure. He's an even better father. But I settled. I took the easy choice in marrying him. I was 22 when I tied that knot and 32 when I cut it. I won't fight for custody, and after all, like I said, he's a great dad. I wouldn't punish our kids like that. Burke asked if I had cheated. I told him no, and that was the truth. But the truth was I thought about it. I thought about those steamy affairs, taking the great risk. I had thought about talking to my mother about all of it. After all, she married when she was only 20. Surely, these thoughts must have gone through her head. But did I really want to know if my mother wanted to have random, passionate sex with complete strangers? Even if I wanted her opinion, I already knew she would consider my thoughts to be nothing short of treason. She was old fashioned. A compliment and a criticism. My brother Chris would understand. He simply dated. Nothing serious, always casual. Always easier for a man to do such a thing than it is for a woman. But he would show support, show love. But in the same way I don't want to know about my mom's hidden sexual desires, I'm sure he doesn't want to know about his sister's.*

I have to stop thinking of this, or it'll show on my face. While my still single or recently divorced friends told me I needed to try Tinder, I prefer to find my spark the old-fashioned way.

I order a few cocktails, sipping away, acting like I'm waiting for a friend. It feels like ages since I was out in the city, and centuries since I barhopped during my college days. How did I survive those years? The days of a college budget. Old-fashioned oatmeal and ramen noodles were diet staples and enough to cure any minor hangover.

So what if it took 32 years to find out what I wanted? Most people told me I was foolish to leave my husband and quit my job—without a plan or place. It was Common Sense they said. But that was part of the riveting nature of it all. It made me feel alive.

"Seat taken?"

God, I was so consumed in my thoughts I was completely unaware of the handsome guy right beside me.

"It's a free city."

He smiled. Wow. But before I focus on his fantastic facial features, I need to examine that left ring finger. Naked. I hope the rest of his body follows that finger's lead before the night is up. I bite my lip to stop from smiling at my lascivious thoughts.

He orders me a new drink, not asking what I want. I like that. He is confident.

"I have to ask what a beautiful woman like you is doing out on a school night?" he said.

"I have to ask what a handsome man like you is doing out on a school night?"

I cross my legs, the heel of my foot ever so slightly caressing his leg.

"I just got out of a meeting with fifty-five others going through every monotonous detail of every word on a business contract before everyone signed. I am in need of a drink. And by drink, I mean one long, continuous drink."

We chat for an hour, enough time for both of us to get a buzz off the strong booze. He asks if I want to go for a walk.

"Ever married?" I ask stupidly.

Why bring up an ex-wife? What good could come from that? Or what if he is married?

"No. Sadly, she got away before I could show her how I feel."

"I'm sorry... I'm an ex-wife."

"I know."

"How did you know that?"

Do I know him? Is he a friend of Burke I've forgotten?

"You have a tan line on your finger."

"I'm a bit disappointed you're checking out my finger," I say.

"Oh, believe me. I've gazed upon you enough to sketch you. Your marble blue eyes, your raven black hair."

"Oh, you're an artist."

"It's a passion, though I never could sketch clothing."

I can't believe in college all it took for me to hook up with a guy was for him to show some interest and tell me I was "fricking hot." The man before me is an old-fashioned, authentic man. God...I'm using the same word I had used to describe my mother.

I shiver from the wind. He puts his scarf around my neck. It smells of cologne—a perfect mixture of leather, vanilla, cedar and citrus, all aphrodisiacs apparently.

"Tell me about yourself, Jasmine," he asks me.

"I don't know what to say except I feel like I'm finding my life for the first time. A path I choose."

"Freedom."

I nod. "Freedom."

"Did he sign?"

I look at him for clarification.

"The papers... divorce papers."

"He did."

"Free indeed."

We stroll in silence, only the wind whistling past our ears. The saying the wind nips doesn't do the wind justice. It bites. We're heading to the seclusion of a trail disappearing into the trees. I'm hesitant. It's pitch black in there. And since when did hiking trails ever work out for women my age? The man hadn't committed an error since he first sat down. But if there was something he could do or say to make me not want to sleep with him, it was this—taking me into the woods through a trail at night.

"We can turn back," he says.

The idea of a mile hike or however long it is certainly doesn't appeal to me. He seems excited. If I say no, will it hinder this thing between us? New journeys begin with a single step, right? This one just happens to be a literal one. Am I dressed for a hike? Heavens, no. Hopefully we come to some sort of clearing where I can stop him, kiss him and get down to why we're both here. Then, we can turn around. Well I can turn around. If he's still up for a hike, bless his heart.

"No, let's go," I say.

He smiles. "I love a bit of history, but I love the hidden paths nature has for us. All we have to do is follow the yellow brick road."

I state how chilly it is. He tells me it's the winds coming off some Indian-named river I'm not even going to ask to have it pronounced again. He's well-educated—I can tell by his pronunciation of that river's name. Not like some of the men I had gone to school with who pronounced Rio Grande as Rhy-O, not Ree-oh. Or my personal favorite, Ree-Oh Grandey.

We pass a few other people, exchanging polite smiles and nods. One couple even gives us a "we know what you're going to do" look. Judging by her flushed cheeks, they had just done it themselves. I feel better about where we are. It seems those from the city knew the place where adventurous couples went to have sex.

The trees are thick, blocking the moon and stars but also providing a barrier against those crisp winds. It doesn't stop them entirely, but it's enough that I stop shivering... from the cold at least. I ask him if he's been here before. He says yes, and that it isn't much further. When we get to it, I look around for whatever it is I'm supposed to be seeing. But there's nothing but rocks and trees.

"What am I looking for?" I ask.

He throws his hands up in frustration. "This is a piece of history here."

One woman's trash is another man's treasure.

"Care to venture forward?" he asks.

He puts his arms around me, his hands traveling south. A revelation of his true intention.

I look around to see if anyone else is nearby. It's just us. I nod. He smiles again. We continue. Okay, I lied. It wasn't pitch black before. Now it's pitch black. I take out my phone and turn on the flashlight. I scan ahead.

"Are you coming?"

No answer.

I turn around. My flashlight illuminates his face. A face that is foreign, no longer feigned with a smile. There is rage there. He has a stone in his hand. I push past him, trying to free myself. But a sharp pain erupts in my head, and I fall to the ground, head throbbing like a beat drum.

When I come to, I can feel the cold wind stabbing my exposed flesh. It's like an animal that waited at the tree line until it saw I was injured, then attacked. My clothes have been stripped, my mouth duct taped. My hands and legs are restrained and spread wide like I'm frozen in the middle of a jumping jack. There's a shadow by the entrance, a face hidden behind a terrifying mask. Two black half-moons for eyes and a warped smile. I mumble, then cry when I realize I can't speak. He stands there, watching me. His head turns right and then left as if surveying me. He walks toward me, unbuckling his belt and yanking down his pants. Panic and fear consume me. I struggle against my restraints. I close my eyes, trying to let some happy memory take hold and get me through the next few minutes.

His grunt tells me it's over. He pushes himself off me, then runs his fingers through my hair.

"You're never going to see anyone again. You're never going to leave here," he whispers into my ear.

The printer hummed as it laid the black text onto the white pages. Madison took the pages in her hand the same way she'd hold a dismembered body part. She set the copies on the kitchen table, and there it rested like a corpse on a mortuary table, waiting for them to perform an autopsy. Only three this time—Casper wasn't home.

It was hardly the time for it, but knowing the deep, complicated history between Atticus and Vasquez made the energy between them seem so much more palpable, and for Madison, so much more awkward. But she forced the thought from her head and focused on the overwhelming task at hand.

"There's a mention of a river with an Indian name," Vasquez said.

Though it narrowed the infinite possibilities, there had to be a thousand creeks, rivers, and lakes with Native American names. Then there was also the possibility that the name was just an attempt to mislead.

However trivial, and it most certainly was, Madison felt a certain power every time she found improper wording or missed commas. But then she couldn't help but wonder if these were legitimate mistakes, or did he plant those to slow her down, knowing she would find them? That her brain would be drawn to correct them?

Madison circled words and highlighted lines as she read, trying to remember she needed to solve a puzzle and not scan for spelling and grammatical errors. It was like rewriting software.

"He uses the word *free* or a variation of it often," Madison observed.

"Maybe a misdirect? Could be a city in a state that was part of the Confederacy," Atticus said.

She tried to ignore the clock on the microwave, but its neon-green glow was impossible to ignore. *Control.* Lana's advice replayed in her mind. He set the time. His hands may not be physically wrapped around her throat, but that suffocating panic was there. He knew the chaos a ticking clock created. The life of an innocent woman was at stake. Each minute that passed brought them closer to damning her to a cruel fate. Madison kept her eyes fixed on the pages in front of her.

Don't react like prey.

"55 people in a meeting. That's a lot of people…" Atticus said.

"Conference? Maybe a workshop?" Vasquez suggested.

"56," Madison corrected. "55 people plus him. *Going over every word before everyone would sign.*"

As to why 56 was important, none of them could say, so they moved on.

"What about the yellow brick road? Do we know where *The Wizard of Oz* was filmed?" Atticus asked.

Madison googled the question on her phone. "Culver City, California. But there's an actual yellow brick road in Banner Elk, North Carolina."

"Every murder's been in the South, so Carolina would fit," Atticus said.

Madison didn't think the clue could be taken at face value. She knew she should say something, but right now, she could only shrug.

"You don't think so?" Vasquez asked, picking up on the gesture Madison's body had betrayed her with.

"I think it's simply used as an idiom," Madison said.

"Okay, so that brings us back to the liberal—no pun intended—use of the word *free*," Atticus said.

"So, what cities are linked with freedom?" Madison asked.

"New York, D.C., Philly, Boston…" Vasquez listed off.

"Maybe San Francisco. Freedom for gays," Atticus said.

Madison continued reading, letting the two of them discuss. *56… 56 signatures… going over every word before everyone would sign… sign… 56 signatures…* She picked out certain key words. *Great risk. Treason. Common Sense. Common Sense* was capitalized, meaning it was a proper noun. Was it a movie? Or a book? Her mind searched the impressive list of books and movies she'd read and seen. Flashing back to her high school days in American History. *Common Sense* was a book written by Thomas Paine, who had championed America's independence from Great Britain.

Treason. The great risk. 56 signees. She googled once more for verification. The document did have 56 signatures.

"… The Declaration of Independence…" Madison uttered.

Vasquez and Atticus looked at her. She explained the clues she'd found.

Atticus nodded. "Very good. D.C. then? It's kept at the National Archives."

"Not where it is now. Where it was signed," Madison said.

"Philadelphia."

Madison found the excerpt she was looking for and slid the page toward the center of the table so Atticus and Vasquez could see as well.

"*Old-fashioned oatmeal.* What's the first image that comes to mind when you think of old-fashioned oats?" Madison asked.

"The Quaker," Atticus answered.

"And they're most commonly associated with what state?"

"Pennsylvania."

"The conversation on art… It's the Art Museum," Vasquez added.

"Right. And then this line…" she tapped it with her pen. "*My brother Chris would understand… But he would show support, show love.* Brotherly Love."

Atticus speed-read through the chapter. "Son of a bitch…"

Vasquez rose from the table and made a call. "Plane will be ready in twenty minutes," she announced after she hung up.

So much of Madison didn't want to go. She wanted to stay behind and enjoy her Friday routines—her bath, her Ben & Jerry's, her newest read, and her Netflix. But she couldn't do that. Madison couldn't forsake another woman to her own cabin. She also couldn't shake the way the Man in the Mask had stared at her. He knew the power he had over her.

Control. Fear. Two separate entities the Man in the Mask possessed and imposed. Control fear. The single mantra Madison kept repeating on the drive to O'Hare.

Madison was ready to vomit. Sitting still was torture. When her mind was this anxious, she needed to be moving. Needed to pace, to stand. This whole plane was a straightjacket.

The plane flew at an altitude of 41,000 feet—roughly 10,000 feet lower than where her anxiety currently soared. The Rat Pack, contrastingly confident and cool, played on her phone.

A quick glance showed that Atticus hated the flight even more. Every time the plane shook, he squeezed his eyes shut. Vasquez, in contrast, was a seasoned pro. She sat scrolling through her phone, looking like she was on a slow moving carousel.

As the plane started landing, Vasquez handed a bulletproof vest to Madison, stating it was merely a precaution. Odd as it may seem, it didn't create any additional worry or fear. The Man in the Mask wouldn't shoot her. It was too impersonal. He'd kill her close, using a knife like it was a penetrating phallus.

Red and blue lights reflected off the runway. Madison had never been to Philadelphia, but she always wanted to; however, trying to find a missing woman and stopping her murder had never been part of her imaginary itinerary. The plane engines shuddered their last breath. A short and stocky black man in his late-fifties hurried toward them. He introduced himself as Agent Jefferson.

"We searched for women based on the age and the physical description you gave us. That yielded four Jasmine's. We then searched divorce records going back six months. That narrowed it down to one."

Agent Jefferson unlocked his tablet, revealing a photo of a woman with a heart-shaped face, deep-seated sapphire-blue eyes and long, luscious, soft black hair. Jasmine Sanders. 32 years old. Mother of two.

"She recently moved into an apartment in the city. No cell phone pings in the last 27 hours. Last one came from the Museum of Art."

"Museum being searched?" Atticus asked.

"It is, but if she were pinned to the wall like a piece of art, someone would notice."

"Social media?" Vasquez asked.

"Has it, but no recent posts or tweets."

"The river with the Indian-sounding name, any guess?" Atticus asked.

"Most obvious is the Delaware. The Schuylkill River too. That's a long, winding son of a bitch," Agent Jefferson said.

"We need a car, Allie," Atticus said.

A young local cop stepped forward. "I'll drive you."

"You know the city?" Vasquez asked.

"I may be a rookie, but I lived here my whole life," he answered.

He said his name was Sam Hunt, but he stated his nickname was Ketchup. Not only because of his last name but also because of his speed on the track. He had run anchor in the 4x100 and 4x200 meters relays, and it was his job to catch the competition. It was the untimeliest dive into etymology. Ketchup was destined to be a cab driver in another life. Every moment of silence was for him an opportunity for small talk, for random facts and stats.

"Do you know of any trails by an Indian-named river?" Madison asked.

Ketchup exhaled in a way that told her her question wasn't necessarily foolish but naïve. "Whew... yeah, too many. Wissahickon has a bunch of trails. It's in the northern part of the city. Used to fish there as a kid when Gramma didn't feel like chasing me and my cousins—"

"Head that way," Vasquez said, cutting him off.

The glow of city light faded. Darkness gathered, encompassing all. The Man in the Mask, concealed in black, could blend in like a chameleon.

Control. Fear.

Control fear.

Ketchup turned on his police light, speeding through every red light. The speedometer rose and rose, reaching 80 miles per hour when he drove onto Kelly Drive. Prone to car sickness, Madison kept her window down. The rushing wind helped offset the nausea from staring at Google Maps in a speeding vehicle. She zoomed in and back out on the city of Philadelphia, switching in and out of satellite view.

… Follow the yellow brick road…

"I found it! The yellow brick road! It's the Yellow Trail," she said.

Ketchup responded by pressing harder on the gas pedal.

"Any popular sights around there?" Atticus asked.

"Yeah, Hermit's Cave and Lover's Leap," Ketchup answered.

A sickening sensation roiled in Madison's stomach. Lover's Leap. It was too easy to imagine Jasmine Sanders thrown to her death, her broken body surrounded by a moat of blood. Lover's Leap was the sort of overly dramatic location that belonged in the realm of fiction.

"What's Hermit's Cave?" Atticus asked.

"Just as it sounds. A cave. Also called the Cave of Kelpius—German guy who was a doomsday prepper. If you didn't know it was there, you'd never find it," Ketchup said.

Vasquez studied her watch. "There's no time to check both."

Atticus reluctantly nodded. "You three go to Lover's Leap. I'll go to Hermit's Cave."

"Alone?" Vasquez asked, her tone making it clear she didn't like the idea.

"Allie, there's no time."

"I'll go with him," Madison said.

Vasquez gave her the chance to change her mind. But she wouldn't. "You're right; there's no time to check both. Not unless we split up."

"You and Ketchup search Lover's Leap. Madison and me will search Hermit's Cave," Atticus said.

Soon, the car could take them no further. Ketchup kept his brights on, giving them a beacon. Atticus asked to borrow the Remington shotgun mounted between the driver and passenger seats. Hunt deferred to Vasquez. She nodded—repercussions about the ethics and legality of her decision could be worried about later.

"Alright then," Ketchup said. "She's yours. Be warned. She's got Old Testament wrath."

Atticus took the Remington 870 Express in his hands. It weighed less than ten pounds, but it could stop a bear in its tracks. He turned the mounted light on. Ketchup pointed in the direction Atticus and Madison needed to go.

Vasquez and Atticus looked apprehensive. Their worry was not self-directed but instead focused outwardly on each other. They wanted to say much more, but both settled on telling the other to be careful. Then Vasquez and Ketchup, with flashlights on, ventured into the black labyrinth.

"You ready?" Atticus asked Madison.

"No, but let's go," she replied, drawing a smirk from Atticus.

They crept among the trees, their branches spread out like bared claws. Atticus swept the path ahead of them with the mounted light. The canopy was so dense not a single star could be seen. It seemed civilization was a thousand miles away. Madison kept a hand on Atticus's back, fearing they'd get separated. Apart from the telescope-shaped beam of light, all around was only shades of black. A bone-chilling breeze had snuck through the trees, whistling eerily. The leaves rustled. Branches creaked.

… London Bridge is falling down…

The whole forest whistled that song.

Fight, flight, or fright. Every nerve ending in Madison's body demanded one of the three. Currently leading was the desire to pull a Superman and fly the hell out of there.

Ketchup had left the brights of his cruiser on, but it might as well be parked back in Chicago. Not a single beam of light could be seen. The further they advanced, the darker it became. A different planet. Her phone beeped. Madison jumped, grabbing a handful of Atticus's shirt. She apologized, then answered Vasquez's phone call.

"Did you find her?" Madison asked.

"No, nothing here. But we have to make our way down to the bottom to search. There're too many leaves to rule it out from up here," Vasquez explained. "Are you at the cave?"

"Not yet. It's pitch black. I don't know how close we are."

"Keep me posted."

Madison hung up and, with a trembling hand, slid the phone back into her pocket.

"You have your Glock?" he asked.

"Yeah," she answered, though she wasn't holding it yet. But she knew Atticus meant she should take it out.

"I don't want to make a mistake," she said.

Though having the Glock in her hand instilled a feeling of security, there was also an inherent nervousness. She had fired the Glock, and she respected its power, but facing a life-or-death, shoot-or-don't-shoot decision was nerve-racking. The fact that this decision would have to be made in a split second was enough to make her tremble.

After close to half a mile, they emerged onto a clearing. A rectangular stone monument inscribed with an epitaph lay directly ahead. It was too dark to read it. To the left was the fabled cave. They called out Jasmine's name. The only answer was the faint whistling breeze. Atticus scanned the edge of the woods. When no eyes reflected back at him, he aimed the light into the cave. Madison's scream curdled in her throat, and only a horrified gasp made it out into the chilly night. Jasmine Sanders hung against the back wall, legs and arms spread like da Vinci's Vitruvian Man. She was naked, her arms and legs fastened with electrical wire to keep her upright. Her head drooped forward, her long dark hair concealing her cold face. Blood stained her pubic area. Atticus left the light on her long enough for them to see that Jasmine had been stabbed repeatedly. The Man in the Mask had raped her with a knife. Even though she was clearly dead, Atticus still checked her pulse. The horror of seeing Jasmine's mutilated body gave way to a different feeling. Less horror, more terror. The feeling of being watched. Madison gazed at the tree line. The wind whistled.

… London Bridge is falling down…

She whispered to Atticus and repeated herself when he didn't acknowledge.

"Turn the light off," she said.

He did. "What is it?" he whispered back.

"He's here."

Somewhere inside the woods, the Man in the Mask was watching them. He wasn't a manifestation in a haunted forest. Madison knew he was there. She drew her Glock. Atticus pumped the Remington.

Silence.

Their eyes played tricks, turning the shadows and silhouettes into shapes.

Silence.

Bang!

A shot rang, hitting the wood around the cave entrance and blasting wooden shrapnel through the air. Atticus wrenched Madison to the ground. He kneeled and fired at where he thought the shot had come from. Madison's eyes adjusted to the dark; she was now able to make out individual tree trunks and the distance and depth between them. Her eyes fixated on one. While the other trees had almost perfectly straight trunks, this one had an abnormal protrusion. A faint gasp escaped her lips. The Man in the Mask stared at her from behind the tree. His arm lifted.

"Get down!" she yelled, tackling Atticus to the ground.

Bits of dirt shot into the air mere feet ahead of them. In the tumble, Atticus dropped the shotgun. Madison scrambled to it and turned the flashlight on, aiming it directly at the Man in the Mask. He stared straight into what for him was a stage light. He stepped out into the light with the flair of an actor strutting to center stage to accept his applause. If roaring applause was what he wanted, then roaring applause he would get. She dropped the shotgun and raised her Glock. As someone who had fired the weapon, she knew it wasn't like it was in movies. From this distance, the likelihood of her hitting him was slim. She fired once. The bullet was way off mark. She adjusted and fired twice more. These two struck the tree above his head. She was getting closer. The next bullet was a mere foot and half above his head. The Man in the Mask retreated to cover.

Atticus pumped the shotgun and fired two shots. The blasts were so powerfully loud that they rattled Madison's bones. His experience with the weapon resulted in shots that struck the tree the Man in the Mask hid behind.

"Stay here! Call Vasquez!" Atticus shouted as he gave chase.

The thought of staying there alone horrified her. New Orleans had been frightening enough, even with hundreds of people that included dozens of policemen surrounding her. Fear. Control. He had both. The Man in the Mask had crafted a scheme in which, somehow, in a city of millions, Madison was alone.

Ketchup cautiously descended the steep hill to the pit of Lover's Leap, the leaves crumpling under his feet like tin foil. He aimed his flashlight ahead, hoping he didn't suddenly see a protruding hand or foot. He gently kicked at the ground around him, fully aware there could be a body hidden amid the leaves.

Vasquez watched from up high, her head on a swivel. Gunshots echoed. She jerked her head toward the sound. The two shotgun blasts that followed made her jump. Her phone buzzed.

"Madison? What's going on?" Vasquez asked. Madison rambled an answer but too fast for Vasquez to make anything out. "Slow down."

"He was here! She's dead… Atticus… he took off after him!"

Vasquez clenched her eyes shut, biting her tongue and the curse word it formed. "We're on our way! Stay hidden."

"What's going on?" Ketchup shouted from below.

"He was at the cave! We have to move!"

Ketchup used his hands to help climb the hill. This was exactly the kind of moment Vasquez thought of to power her through her grueling morning cardio sessions. She ran faster than she had in decades. The ground was unforgiving, pounding the soles of her feet with hammer-like force. Her lungs felt as if they would pop, and her throbbing side ache threatened to bring her to her knees. Her hamstrings tightened, feeling like stretched rubber bands ready to snap. But her heart was up to the task. It beat faster and faster, doing all it could to pump oxygen-rich blood through her body.

True to his nickname, Ketchup caught up.

"Suspect's near Hermit's Cave! Send backup and seal off any possible exits!" he shouted into his radio.

Faint gunfire rang in the distance. Hope and dread tormented Vasquez. Who had fired the shot? Who was it fired at? And what had the bullet hit? She was mindful of the ground ahead of her, knowing the slightest divot or root could trip her up. If she sprained an ankle now, she would be powerless to help Atticus. The boughs protruded out like arms, and the twigs, like razor blades, clawed at her. But if these woods wanted to stop her, they would have to make her bleed a hell of a lot more.

Atticus ignored the shooting pain in his sides from running. His surgically repaired knees were brittle as glass. But he didn't need to run faster than the Man in the Mask. He needed to be fast enough to get a clear shot. He didn't care that in today's world criminals won. The media would twist the story to fit its desired narrative. Atticus wasn't a resident of the state, nor was the weapon he was firing registered to him. They'd track down some criminal he had forcefully arrested decades ago to give testament to his volatile violent streak. He didn't give a shit. Let them send him to prison. The way his body ached, he had a mere handful of years left anyway. It'd all be worth it to put a baseball-size hole in this bastard's chest.

The Man in the Mask sprinted through the tree line and across the road separating the two patches of forest. Atticus hesitated, debating whether to shoot now or not. But too many cars zipped past. He couldn't risk it. The Man in the Mask had the advantage of speed, agility, and endurance. If Atticus continued to simply chase after him, his body would fail and their unsub would get away. So, instead of following him across the street and back into the woods, Atticus veered left toward Barnes Street then sprinted toward Henry Avenue. Enough adrenaline pumped through his blood to bring a dead elephant back to life. His goal was to cut off the Man in the Mask. Atticus ran on flat, even pavement. The Man in the Mask ran on uneven ground, weaving around trees and avoiding being clotheslined by low-hanging branches.

Atticus got to Henry Avenue first. He readied the shotgun, his feet firmly planted. He steadied his breathing. It was time to end this sadistic game. The Man in the Mask stumbled through the brush, limping, and frantically looking behind him to see where his pursuer was, oblivious to the fact that he had just entered his own Dealey Plaza, and Atticus didn't need a magic bullet.

The Man in the Mask broke through the brush. He jerked his head toward Atticus, instinctively diving toward the street as Atticus fired. The shot that would have ripped through his flesh and splintered his ribs had he stayed upright a second longer went errant. Atticus pumped another round, but the Man in the Mask crawled desperately onto the road on his hands and knees. Cars honked, swerved, and skidded to a stop. Rain fell. A light tap at first, but now hard and fast. The drops hitting the cars sounded like machine-gun fire. The Man in the Mask got to his feet and limped forward, narrowly avoiding becoming a bug stain on a windshield. A hatchback fishtailed out of control. Atticus wiped the rain from his eyes in time to see the Man in the Mask pointing something at him. By the time he realized he was staring at the barrel of a gun, there was nothing he could do.

Bang. Bang. Bang.

Three shots ripped through the rain and cut through the cold air. The force of the bullets blasted Atticus backward. He landed on the passing hatchback, smashing the windshield and flipping over the hood, before his body smacked against the unforgiving asphalt. The rain pelted his open mouth as he gasped for breath.

Vasquez pushed through to Henry Avenue, breaking branches, refusing to slow down. Police sirens rang in the distance as they raced toward the scene. The Man in the Mask was nowhere to be found. Atticus was sprawled on the road. She dropped to a knee beside him. He had a gash on his forehead. She tore open his jacket. His bulletproof vest had stopped two bullets, but the third had made it through, above the vest strap and below his collarbone. Blood poured out at a rate not even the rain could wash clean.

"Stay with me, Atticus!" she shouted, squeezing his hand.

An ambulance wailed. Atticus's strength could be gauged in his eyes. They drifted, then found Vasquez and then the star flashing behind her. He focused his gaze on her as long as he could, and then his eyes closed.

Police and SWAT swarmed the area around Hermit's Cave. A police helicopter circled above, scanning the forest below. Police dogs sniffed the area and followed the scents they picked up. Across from Henry Avenue was an 18-hole golf course, and unless the Man in the Mask was hiding in one of the holes, he was nowhere to be found. Beyond the golf course was nothing but woods.

Ketchup drove Vasquez and Madison to Roxborough Memorial Hospital where they waited in the ER lobby for a doctor to provide an update. Every time the doors opened and a nurse or doctor came through only to walk past them, Vasquez cursed under her breath. Neither could sit. Madison wanted to pace, but Vasquez already was, so she had to settle for leaning against a wall and grinding away at the inside of her cheeks.

A young doctor approached. He asked if they were there for Atticus Wallace; Vasquez nodded.

"He's resting now. The bullet was lodged below his clavicle. He has pretty significant scar tissue there that actually prevented this from being much worse. The cut on his forehead required stitches, and he ruptured the bursa sac in his right knee. It's very swollen. But that should go down in a couple of days. He definitely needs to take it easy for a while," the doctor said.

Vasquez thanked the young doctor, and then she and Madison rushed to see Atticus. His left arm was in a sling, his forehead covered in mesh and bandage, his right knee wrapped in an icepack.

"How're you feeling?" Vasquez asked.

Atticus ignored the question. "He got away, didn't he?"

"The area's still being searched."

But her tone had said it all. Atticus slammed the back of his head against his pillow and uttered a sentence in which the F word was noun, verb, adverb, and adjective.

"I had him, Allie. I cut him off, and he ran right into my sight…" Atticus said.

"He got lucky."

"Yeah, he's been lucky, and it doesn't appear that's going to change."

"They need to get lucky every time. We only need to get lucky once. You know who said that?"

"The IRA."

Vasquez rolled her eyes. "You, you pain the ass."

Atticus wasn't in the mood for words of wisdom, especially when they were his own.

"Did you see anything that could be used to help identify him?" Vasquez asked.

Atticus shook his head and let out a frustrated sigh. "No. Just like Madison described—a man in black, a damn Johnny Cash wannabe."

Vasquez mentioned that the police had run ballistics. 9mm casings had been found near Hermit's Cave and Henry Avenue. Atticus rolled his eyes, as if to say "go figure." 9mm was the most common bullet in the world. As for fingerprints on any of the trees or bullet casings, it too was fruitless. Just like in New Orleans. Not only had he been gloved, he had worn cotton. Leather gloves were individually unique and therefore easier to pinpoint, often even leaving latent fingerprints. Cotton gloves were anonymous. Many a criminal wore gloves for a crime and tossed them out. Forensics could simply turn the glove inside out and find fingerprints. But of course, no gloves had been found. The Man in the Mask was too smart for that.

Atticus asked Madison how she was.

She shrugged. "I didn't get shot or hit by a car."

"It was a hatchback." Atticus smirked, then frowned. "Sorry, I left you."

Madison dismissed his apology with a shake of her head. She stepped out to grant the privacy Vasquez's voice couldn't ask but her body language screamed for.

Vasquez stayed silent, worried a nurse would come in at any moment. The coward in her hoped one would.

"When I saw you lying there…" she paused, staring out of the window at the indecipherable blackness outside. "I… I—"

A knock on the door. A plump nurse entered, mercifully stopping Vasquez from finishing a sentence that would have destroyed her.

Atticus was cleared to leave the following afternoon. He took two Vicodin pills before takeoff and slept every minute of the flight home. A couple of days later, Vasquez dropped off a taco casserole, granting Atticus a reprieve from Stouffer's.

"How's our suspect board?" he asked as he ate.

"Worry about not choking."

He ate the two pieces in under two minutes, wiped his face, and stood.

"Where are we going, and who are we going to see?" he asked.

Vasquez knew better than to even attempt talking him into staying put and watching TV. The swelling in his knee had subsided, but his legs were sore. Once inside the car, Vasquez leaned over to buckle him in.

"Jesus, Allie, I'm not a baby."

"Such a shame. I'd love to put a pacifier in your mouth."

Once again, they drove north into Milwaukee. Vasquez pulled into a driveway only far enough that the back end of her Challenger wouldn't get clipped. The house was a fixer-upper that had never been fixed up. It belonged to Shane Benson. His police file proved his life had gone south since college. He was married twice, divorced twice, and his job history consisted of stints at various production factories—Miller, Usinger's, and Milwaukee Electric Tool among others.

Opportunistic weeds sprouted in the cracks of the concrete driveway, the faded gray color accentuated by black skid marks from when Benson had squealed out.

The garage was open, and a lone swinging light bulb lit the space. A dead deer hung upside down. Shane Benson—Newport cigarette in his mouth, a can of Pabst Blue Ribbon in one hand, and a skinning knife in the other—worked equally hard at smoking, swigging, and skinning.

"Shane Benson?" Vasquez called out.

Benson turned toward them, squinting in a way that showed he was drunk.

"The fuck you want?" he asked, cigarette dangling from his lips.

His heavy smoking had prematurely aged him. He was within a year or two of Madison's age, but he looked a decade older. Vasquez flashed her badge and announced who she and Atticus were. Benson nodded. Translation: "Woopdee-doo, get to the point."

"We need to talk about the night Madison Monroe was taken," Vasquez said.

Benson sniffed back his runny nose, and when that didn't solve the problem, he wiped it on his wrist. His right hand was covered in blood. His "clean" left hand was stained with oil, grease, gas, and a dusting of Cheetos powder. He took a final puff and tossed his cigarette.

"Ask away."

"What do you remember about that night?" Vasquez asked.

Benson laughed as he lit a new cigarette. "Not much. Not too many Friday or Saturday nights I remember from college."

Judging by his appearance and the heap of beer cans in his garbage, he wasn't remembering Friday or Saturday nights now either.

"You made a pass at her," Atticus said.

Benson shrugged, then belched. "If you say so."

"You disagree?" Vasquez asked.

"I don't agree. I don't disagree. I did hit on her before. But that night? I can't say."

"You got a bit handsy during those times?" Atticus asked.

"This was before the MeToo bullshit."

Vasquez fought the desire to pistol-whip him. "Did the two of you have sexual relations?"

Benson laughed derisively. "Jesus, who are ya, Bill Clinton? You askin' if we fucked?"

Vasquez sighed. "In a less crude way."

"Then, no. Her legs locked at the knees for me."

He continued to multitask—conversing while he skinned the carcass.

"Did that anger you?" Atticus asked.

Another mock laugh from Benson. "Anger me 'nuff to kidnap and rape her? No. You'd have to be retarded to answer yes to that."

"You have a history of violence. Cost you a couple of wives and a few tours in a cell. It needs to be asked," Vasquez said.

Another cocky shrug. "You say cost; I say freed."

"Are you bragging about beating your wife?"

Benson took a puff of his cigarette, then stepped toward Vasquez and yanked down the neck of his shirt. Four vertical scars ran down from his neck to his collarbone.

"That's a goddamn stab wound from a fork. Just as much a victim as she is. I can show you my groin. Gotta matchin' scar."

"I don't think there's enough light for us to see anything on your groin," Vasquez said.

Atticus smirked but also sensed her frustration, so he stepped in. "Anyone else you know of wanted to be with her?"

"Is that another less crude way of asking did anyone else want to bang her?"

No elaboration from Atticus. He wouldn't play this game.

"The answer was who di'nt?" Benson said.

"Specifically?"

"Vince. I knew they screwed a few times. Dude was a sad puppy dog anytime Madison talked to another guy."

"Vince Propelli?" Vasquez asked.

"Yeah, Italian-looking dude. Greasy black hair. Jew nose."

"I'm sure you were upset Madison chose him over you. Each and every time."

"Yeah, of course. But you really want to know if it made me so upset that I kidnapped and raped her. Which I already answered. No. Come on, guys."

"You think we're wasting your time?" Vasquez asked. "You waste another second of our time being a prick, I'll have you watched 24/7, and the next time you drink and drive—I don't care if it's after communion—you will be arrested."

"It was a Halloween party, okay? Costumes, booze, beer, weed. I don't remember much. Just that she left early. Somethin' about her not feeling good, but I thought it was somethin' else."

Vasquez's threat had evidently been well received.

"What did you think?" Atticus asked.

"Another guy."

"Who?"

"Well, if it wasn't me or Vince, I thought maybe it was that T.A."

"Teacher's assistant?"

Benson nodded and cracked open another PBR. "Yeah, they spent time readin' and shit."

"That make you jealous?" Atticus asked.

"No, 'cause I thought he was gay. Wore a bit too many scarves," Benson said.

"What's his name?" Atticus asked.

Benson sucked in a deep breath to help him think. "Ummm… Rose. That's it. Straight outta gay porn."

"Anything else you can tell us?" Vasquez asked.

Benson shook his head. "You really expect to catch him after all this time?"

"Absolutely," Vasquez said.

Benson lifted his eyebrows: "Good luck."

Atticus limped forward and pointed at the deer. "I see you like to hunt."

"Yup. Relaxes me. You hunt?"

"I do."

"Deer?"

"No, criminals—murderers, rapists, pedophiles. It's a shame I can't mount them on the wall."

Vasquez smirked, then handed her card to Benson.

"Well, that psycho checks all the boxes," she said on their drive back to Chicago.

"Yeah, too many boxes. Arrogant," Atticus concluded.

"An asshole. If he hits another woman, I'll string him up next to that deer."

Atticus spun the radio dial, scanning through the stations. "And then we have Rose mentioned yet again."

"Do we know if he's gay?" Vasquez asked.

"You know, it never came up," Atticus said, heavy on the sarcasm.

Vasquez lifted her hand to deliver a back-handed slap but stopped when she remembered his left arm was in a sling.

"Rose seems... He's—"

"Careful, Allie. Your career could be over in one sentence," Atticus teased.

Vasquez rolled her eyes. "He's well dressed and has a certain flair that would make one think... oh, whatever. You know what I mean."

"So, if he's gay, you're ruling him out?" Atticus asked.

"Our unsub is raping women."

"True, but it's the violence that arouses him. Maybe he is gay and trying to 'fix' that."

"And when these women can't, he kills them... He is an English professor, so he knows how to put words to the page."

"And has a propensity for scarves."

Vasquez chuckled, then tapped her steering wheel, her face scrunched in concentration.

Atticus studied her. "You want to go shake the tree and see what falls down."

"I want to cut the goddamn thing down with a chainsaw."

Rigel Rose sat behind a desk inside an auditorium-style lecture hall in Chicago State University. Atticus grimaced on the descent down the stairs. The fluid in his knee may be gone, but the pain certainly wasn't. Rose had a pen in his hand, with which he tarnished black texts with red ink as he circled, crossed out, and wrote in the margins. Vasquez announced their presence. Rose looked up, then flashed a charming smile.

"Agent Vasquez, retired Detective Wallace, a pleasure to see you both." Then he noticed Atticus's condition—arm in a sling, stitched forehead, and a pronounced limp. "Oh my God! You look like you got hit by a bus. Are you alright?"

"It was a hatchback, actually."

Rose laughed but then realized Atticus wasn't fibbing. "You're serious?"

"I was out of the hospital before the hatchback was out of the repair shop, so there's that."

"I'm sorry for saying what I just said. I've heard and used that phrase a thousand times, but the person had never actually been hit by a car."

"Hatchback. Don't shortchange me like that."

Rose mockingly put his hands up in surrender, with a smile on his face that Atticus couldn't decide was genuine or fake, polite or derisive, armed or disarming. Did he use his jovial disposition as a tool to make friends, empower students, and get promotions and dates, or did he use it as a weapon?

"We've been interviewing a lot of Ms. Monroe's former friends to talk about what happened to her," Vasquez began.

"Okay…" Rose said, holding the second syllable unnaturally long.

"There seems to have been more to your relationship with her than student and T.A.," Vasquez said.

Rose tilted his head, confused. "More to our relationship? How do you mean?"

Vasquez mentioned their two-member book club, sipping coffee, reading, and dissecting character motives and plots.

"You asked her out," Atticus then said.

"Why didn't you mention that?" Vasquez asked.

Rose's eyes ping-ponged from Vasquez to Atticus. "We never called it a book club, but yes, we'd meet to discuss books. Madison was, and I assume still is, a voracious reader. So am I. She could find the essence of a character, what made them tick. We'd debate the benefits of a first-person narrative and third-person. We had great conversations about books."

"And the date..." Atticus prompted, not giving a single shit about the essence of a character. He'd heard plenty of that bullshit from defense lawyers in courtrooms.

"I did ask her to dinner once, but it was obvious she was uncomfortable with the idea, so I rescinded the offer."

"That must have been upsetting," Vasquez said.

"Of course. I was pretty bummed. Never easy getting turned down. Madison's beautiful, but it was her mind I was most drawn to."

Atticus examined the spines of the books on his desk. He picked one up and fanned through the pages, mostly for the quick breeze it produced. It was titled *The Death of Antebellum*, and judging by its cover, a story of forbidden love between a white Southern belle and a black slave before the start of the Civil War.

"Ever think of writing your own?" Atticus asked.

"Every day. I have a hard drive full of unfinished manuscripts. Writing is easy. Rewriting is hell. There is no creation without destruction."

"That's deep. How do you mean?"

"Imagine you build a house. It has everything you want—double-stall garage, fireplace, swimming pool, walk-in closet. Everything. Then imagine being told it's too large or too bland or unlikeable, and now, you have to set fire to your own creation and rebuild it from the ashes. That, my friend, is rewriting."

"I'd tell them to get the hell out of my house."

Rose laughed.

"What genre do you write?" Atticus asked, setting the book back on the pile.

"Until I've written something worthy of print, let's call it a mystery."

"Madison's an editor. Did you know that?"

Rose's face lit up. "No, I did not. That's truly wonderful. It certainly fits her."

"Maybe she can prevent you from having to set fire to your creation."

Rose laughed cordially. "I doubt even the great Madison Monroe could stop that."

Atticus smiled, but the whole while, he was intently observing Rose, looking for any inauthentic reaction or tentative pause.

"Have you done any traveling recently?" Vasquez asked.

Rose hesitated. "That depends on your definition of the word. Travel out of the city?"

"Anywhere outside Chicago," Vasquez clarified.

"Then, yes."

"Philadelphia?"

"Are you asking if I've been there recently or ever been?"

"Sure."

"I've been to Philadelphia. I gave guest lectures there a few times, most recently last month."

"But not a few days ago?" Atticus asked.

"No..."

"University said you were on vacation last Thursday and Friday," Vasquez remarked.

"That's correct..." Rose answered.

"Staycation or vacation?" Atticus asked.

Rose forced a disingenuous smile. "I'll play along, though I'm sure you already know. I was in Aspen, Colorado."

"What was there?" Vasquez asked.

"Skiing."

"You and a girlfriend?"

"No, I don't have a girlfriend. Skiing with friends."

"Guys weekend?" Atticus asked but actually wondering if it was *a guy*.

"There were women too."

"Ah, any you had your eye on?"

Rose shook his head, laughing weakly as if in disbelief. "I think I know what you're trying to get at—and excuse me for saying so—rather ineptly. You want to know if I'm gay," Rose said.

Atticus mockingly pointed at himself. "Me? No, none of my business. But since you brought it up..."

Rose shook his head in good fun. "No, I'm not gay."

"No judgement if you are."

"That's kind of you. I'm not gay, but if that changes, it sounds like you'd like to be the first to know. You'll forgive me if I let my mother know first?"

Atticus played along. "Of course."

"So, apart from confirming my sexual orientation, is there anything else? I have nothing to hide. I'm not gay. I did ask Madison out. I did find her incredibly attractive."

Atticus was silent, studying Rose like a microbe under a microscope, then his demeanor softened. "Any parting quote for us?"

Rose thought on it. "Life is a puzzle. Pity those who figure it out too early, and pity those who never do. Pity those who try and those who don't."

"Shit, that's good."

Rose smirked. "It's mine."

Atticus asked Vasquez if she was all set. She nodded.

"Say, could you walk us out of here?" Atticus asked Rose. "Had a hell of a time finding this room."

"That's by design. We want people to stay a minimum of five years before they leave," Rose said.

He slid his chair back and, with a struggle unbefitting a man in his thirties, stood up. From beneath his desk, he drew out two crutches. He hobbled around the desk, revealing his right foot covered in a black walking boot.

"You get hit by a hatchback too?" Atticus asked.

"No, something significantly less cool and certainly more embarrassing. Got my ski stuck in the snow."

"Sounds painful," Vasquez said.

"Not as painful as paying for a doctor's visit only for him to tell you to ice and rest."

The stairs proved a challenge for Rose, but he made it up them. He instructed Vasquez and Atticus how to find their way to fresh air before he returned back to his desk. Vasquez stayed quiet until she and Atticus were outside.

"You've never forgotten a street in your life, and you certainly don't get turned around. Why have Rose walk us out?"

"Our unsub was limping in Philly. Must have injured himself running through those woods."

Vasquez smiled. "So, did he really get that injury skiing?"

"Exactamento."

"Great. You're still trying to speak Spanish by adding an O to everything."

A moment of silence passed as they got into her car and drove off-campus.

"So, Rose? What are you thinking?" Atticus asked.

"We know he can write. He certainly had a crush on Madison. And I'll admit his quote at the end rubbed me the wrong way," Vasquez said.

"It's a different time, Allie. No one has the courtesy to tell you to just go fuck yourself anymore."

Vasquez and Atticus stopped at his apartment. Atticus popped open two Miller High Life's while Vasquez spoke with Maurice on speaker phone. Maurice stated that the casings taken in Philadelphia were from a Beretta. Vasquez asked if they had been run under a comparison microscope which would've scrutinized the casings to a potential match by studying them simultaneously. Every gun barrel has grooves within it that twist left or right. When a bullet is fired, these markings are imparted on the bullet. Maurice confirmed they had been tested, but no match had been found. It was expected but disappointing nonetheless. Adding to the disappointment was the fact that none of the men they had interviewed owned a Beretta. Legally, at least.

Vasquez rubbed her temples in frustration. Were they even on the right path? Wandering around the woods thinking that the clearing was just ahead, but in reality, they wandered deeper and deeper into the woods? Atticus believed the answers were always there. Vasquez started to doubt. Would this be another Peterson case?

"What about Rose?" Vasquez asked, waiting for news that could only further add to her creeping doubt.

"Rigel Rose boarded Flight AA198, Milwaukee to Chicago on October 31st, 2013," Maurice said.

"What about recently? Did he fly to Colorado?" Atticus asked.

Maurice was silent as he sifted through his notes. "Yes. Rose did fly out of O'Hare to Aspen/Pitkin airport. Checked into Aspen Snowmass Resort. A few debit card uses at restaurants as well."

"What about the doctor visit?" Atticus asked.

"Checked into Aspen Valley Hospital last Sunday."

Both were frustrated. Every person they had interviewed and suspected had means or motive, yet none seemed to fit.

"Bit too far to jog on over to Philadelphia, huh?" Atticus asked.

"Maybe if he was Kenyan. It's 1900 miles from Aspen to Philadelphia," Maurice said.

"Well, it was nice of our unsub to clean the bullet he shot me with. I'd have hated to get an infection," Atticus said acerbically.

Vasquez thanked Maurice and hung up. They finished their beers and went to Madison's apartment. They briefed her on what Maurice had told them about the ballistics test.

"Have you been able to find out where the emails are being sent from?" Madison asked.

"Yes, they've all come from the cities where the murders occurred. But we can't find out quickly enough," Vasquez said.

She elaborated on what Maurice had told her about the complexity of the most sophisticated VPNs. It was largely a more convoluted version of Casper's explanation.

"He doesn't care if we find out where they're being sent from, only that we can't find out in time to stop him," Madison said.

Atticus confirmed with a nod. After a drink, Vasquez left, and a few minutes after that, Atticus started his goodbyes. He took note of the unhealthy number of empty sugar free Red Bull and Bang energy drink cans in Madison's recycle bin.

"Trying not to sleep?" he asked.

She shook her head. "I've been dreaming a lot these last couple of weeks... dreaming about him."

"Medication doesn't help with that?"

"No. To numb that, I'd have to be practically brain-dead from the dose I'd need."

"I hear you there."

"Can I ask you something?"

He nodded.

"Vasquez told me about the Peterson boy… Do you ever dream about that day?"

He paused. His whole demeanor changed. It was like he had been hit by another hatchback. A searing sense of shame reddened Madison's skin, and her stomach churned from guilt at the obvious pain she'd caused him. She didn't expect an answer—wasn't sure she deserved one—but he gave one nonetheless.

"I do. Used to be almost every night. I did what you're doing now— consuming reckless amounts of caffeine, sleeping 4 or 5 hours a night. When the caffeine failed, I went to the bottle."

An exact synopsis of what her life was like and where it was heading. She'd been having an affair with Jack Daniels, but affairs are temporary. They end. One way or another. You either go your separate ways or the affair becomes permanent, taking on a different meaning and needing a different word.

"How'd you get over it?" Madison asked.

"I didn't. I get *through* it."

Wise words from a kindred spirit. Advice Dr. Frett had struggled to get her to understand. Maybe it only stuck now because Atticus had lived it. Madison wasn't ever going to get over what had happened and what was happening. It was crazy to think she would. She had to get through it every day. The verb *get* would never become past tense for her. Madison never said it out loud but part of the reason she could never truly be happy was guilt. The guilt that somewhere, someone was having the worst day of their life. They might have just said goodbye to a loved one, or received an unexpected call that there'd been an accident or that the cancer had finally taken someone dear to them. People being raped or murdered somewhere right now. Madison understood their pain because she had been that person. Jade and many of her friends had been dancing to *Thriller* while Madison was being raped. Maybe the peace Madison sought could never be because she was still at war with the idea of reaching some metaphorical mountaintop where she would forget all about what had happened. Maybe peace would finally come when she accept that such Elysian Fields existed only in the realm of fanciful fiction from writers who couldn't comprehend unrelenting pain. But Dr. Frett had given her the wise adage, "You can't put the past behind you until you get out in front of it." She'd always been running, and she had to keep running, not away from the Man in the Mask but *ahead* of him. From there, she could make her final stand. Control. Fear. Control fear. The Man in the Mask was a real, tangible person. Madison couldn't stop him from manifesting in her mind. He'd always be there. But she could stop him from running rampant. Cage him in a dark cellar, tethered and bound like a titan in Tartarus. In the real world, he ran rampant in the open. But his time doing that was coming to an end. She was going to find him.

The following morning, shortly before nine, Atticus stopped by, a cold brew coffee in hand. His topic of conversation was Madison's old T.A. and unofficial book club co-founder, Rigel Rose.

"There was never a time where he made a move? Tried to hold your hand, caress your thigh?" Atticus asked.

Madison shook her head right away. There was no need to think on it.

"Do you think Rose is gay?" Atticus asked.

"No. I mean… without knowing him, I guess I can see why you'd think that. He was well-dressed and well-spoken. When we started talking, the comments he made… they told me he was straight. Shane told you he was gay, didn't he?"

"He thought that, yes."

She shook her head, upset at Shane's brashness. Apparently, he was still an asshole. "Rigel's from a different era. He treated women with respect—opened doors, pulled out chairs, stood when you entered a room. People probably think he's gay because he never said things like, 'I'd bang her.' The way he talked about female characters… I felt like I had to remind him they weren't real."

Atticus asked how often they'd meet. She told him usually once a week for coffee at a local café to discuss all things books. Or they'd go to various bookstores—small and large—to mine them for their next read.

A memory came to her, bringing with it a smile. "I remember him giving me a hard time for having bought a bookmark. He said I should have used the five dollars as a bookmark, and when I finished the book, I'd still have the five dollars."

"Gotta agree with him on that one."

"So, he took my five-dollar bill and folded it into an M. I made him an R."

Atticus listened as she detailed forgotten memories from her past. So many people from a past life—Rigel, Vince, Shane, and, most importantly, Jade. Would the shorthand Jade and Madison had had still exist? Or would it have been forgotten like the Spanish she had learned in high school?

Atticus steered the conversation to movies. Though his movie knowledge extended only up to the turn of the century, there were plenty of great films to talk about. Madison appreciated his attempt at normalcy. It certainly was a nice break from having to talk about her abduction and rape or piecing together clues to stop another woman's murder. When his ability to contribute to the conversation was exhausted, he left.

Madison forced herself to work and was grateful the novel she had to edit was a coming-of-age dramedy, reminding her of Stephen King's books before bodies were found and children disappeared. She fell back into her comforting routines. At seven o'clock, there came an unexpected knock on the door. She checked the peephole and saw a man's svelte torso. It had to be Casper. He backed up so she could see him, knowing she'd be looking through the peephole.

"I thought you ghosted me," she said when letting him inside.

Casper frowned, shamefully dropping his head like a defendant waiting for the jury's verdict. "I know. Sorry. I'm also fully aware of the irony of that statement."

"You missed a lot of stuff."

A lot of stuff was a nondescript phrase she'd tell authors to elaborate on. She was annoyed for using it, but she was upset, maybe even angry with Casper, and she desperately wanted to avoid having to talk about what had happened in Philadelphia.

Casper nodded, unable to meet her eyes. "I know. I'm sorry. But I know you did everything you could to save Jasmine."

"Do I get to know where you went?"

"… I had to travel for work. Company's putting a new system in."

"You could have said that before you left."

She couldn't hide her frustration. Madison didn't need someone who checked in and out of her life on a whim. But then embarrassment flooded her face. She was acting like a jealous girlfriend, and she had no right to.

"I didn't tell you because I was embarrassed… ashamed even. I mean, you're getting psycho emails and murder maps, and what do I say? Sorry, I have to install software?" Casper said.

An awkward moment fell between them. It was unbearable. Madison told him she didn't want to talk about Philadelphia. They went out for street tacos and ate them on their stroll back to Essex on the Park. She was surrounded by normal people. Couples embraced for a quick peck. When would Casper try? Why hadn't he? Or would he never? Maybe he was one of those unbelievably nice people who helped others when they needed it, feeling an overwhelming sense of responsibility. She was nothing more than a flat tire that needed to be changed. But those relatively normal, harmless thoughts were again trumped by the uneasy notion that the Man in the Mask was watching her from somewhere. She scanned the crowd for masks. Her heart jumped when she saw a man ahead wearing black pants and a black sweatshirt. When he stopped at the intersection, he looked both ways before crossing, granting her an unimpeded look at him. He was in his early twenties, had shaggy blond hair, wore over-the-ear Bose headphones, and took puffs of his vape pen.

"You okay?" Casper asked.

She nodded, dismissing his question with a muttered "Yeah."

Casper's shoulders slouched. His walk usually looked like he had springs in his feet, but now, his feet dragged along. He acted like he had failed Madison. She tried assuring him he hadn't. He cared and stayed when most men would have pulled a Forrest Gump and charged out the front door and just start runnin'. He'd planted his feet and braced the whirlwind of chaos that was her life. Madison had slept with men who hadn't cared about her at all. Some treated her like a motel—a night's stay and then sent on her way like used room service dishware. Many men would have left once they found out what had happened to her. Most would have ghosted her once the chapters started coming. How ironic the man sharing the name of a famous ghost was among the few who wouldn't ghost her? Casper stayed. Stayed around for nothing. Not even a kiss. He had never pressured her for it.

Madison hadn't been with a man since the Man in the Mask. The last person to kiss her neck, run his hands across her body, and be inside her had been the Man in the Mask. Some people think rape is cold and un-intimate. But they're wrong. Intimate is defined as private and personal. And in that regard, rape was intimate. Did the Man in the Mask know she hadn't been with anyone since? It was yet another form of power and control over her. Did he take pride in that, carrying it like a trophy? The feeling of impurity was overwhelming, and it wasn't just emotional. It was the sudden feeling of utter disgust that made her want to shower and scrub and scrub and scrub until she bled.

Control. Fear.

Madison had once read an article about spontaneous human combustion. Some woman sitting in her chair had burst into flame, or so the article claimed. It seemed farfetched, something Stephen King's version of Harry Potter would have included. But in the elevator ride up to Casper's apartment, she legitimately considered spontaneous human combustion a possibility. She was scared, worried, anxious, nervous, excited, maybe even aroused. It was like her mind was a warehouse full of emotions that spilled out of their containers, and her brain was trying to straighten up the mess, one emotion at a time.

When they were inside, she knew the words she wanted to say. Knew what she wanted to do, but there was also the fear of how her body would react. She called Casper's name. It came out as if she cleared her throat. Madison called his name again. He turned toward her. She staggered to him, the bones in her legs replaced with bungee cords. The nervousness and excitement in her stomach felt like a firework show, but the fear and lasting pain hardened in her constricted chest. She reached up to his face and guided it down to hers. She kissed him. An internal mantra kept repeating over and over in her head.

He's not the Man in the Mask. He's not the Man in the Mask. He's not the Man in the Mask.

He looked shocked, and at first, Madison thought she had overstepped, but then a coy boyish smirk formed. He returned her kiss, cradling her face in his palms. She took his hand and led him to his bedroom. At the foot of the bed, he gently resisted.

"Are you sure?" he asked. "… We… don't have to."

It was all Madison needed to affirm her decision. His king-size bed was haphazardly made, but the sheets smelt freshly washed, the liquid soap he used—a pleasant aroma of fig, blood orange, cardamom, and lemon zest—telling her he showered before bed.

She held his hands, kneading them, her eyes lost in a daze.

Casper gently lifted her chin. "What is it?"

"I haven't… I haven't been with anyone since…"

The peace she sought needed to be won on the battlefield. It wouldn't come from some Hindu haiku or Buddhist ballad. He had held this battlefield unchallenged for too long.

"I don't want him to hold that over me any longer. I want the last person I've been with to be kind and funny—someone who cares about me, someone who tries patching all of the holes I feel inside me."

Casper nodded supportively. "I understand. But I don't know who we can find this time of night."

Madison laughed. The last thing she had expected to do. He had the ability to coax laughs out of her as if they were hiccups that came out of nowhere. He smiled but then stared into her eyes with a sad and serious intensity.

"You're an amazing woman, Madison. You have a strength a lot of people miss or don't recognize. I don't think you recognize it. Before we started really talking, I'd see you. And at times, there'd be moments where pain and sadness seemed to take hold of you. But this remarkable thing would happen—you'd have your moment of sadness, and then you just got past it. You think you're weak because these thoughts and feelings ravage you every day. You're wrong.

You're strong because they ravage you every day and you still keep going. You're a scarred woman, Madison. But scars only mean one thing."

"Yeah? What's that?"

"That you're a survivor."

She bit her lip, grinding the inside of her cheek. "You have some pretty good lines."

"Had some inspiration from Destiny's Child."

A laugh escaped her again. He knew exactly how to diffuse her anxiety; he knew when she needed to laugh. Madison asked him for music, and he opened his laptop and played 90s love songs on YouTube. It was corny in the best possible way. Casper wouldn't rush her, and they stood still as statues till halfway through the first song. Then tentatively and trembling, she lifted his shirt. His hands did the same. Goosebumps spread where his fingertips caressed. They moved to the bed—she on top. She had to be. *Control.*

She closed her eyes, but the Man in the Mask waited for her there. She flicked them back open. Casper cupped her face, prompting her to focus on him, into his open eyes.

Madison hoped the Man in the Mask could feel his power disintegrating like a destroyed horcrux.

Afterward, Casper showered. Madison put on her pants and one of his t-shirts, one that displayed the Goonies with Pirate Sloth's face and the immortal words, "Hey, you guys!" She strolled the apartment, glancing about at the few photos on his fridge—nieces and nephews presumably—and the bookshelf full of Blu-rays. His mail was on the kitchen counter. She smiled at the serendipity of it. It'd been the constant mix-up of their mail that eventually led her to where she now stood. But not everything had been great. He'd given her the manila envelope that started it all. Why couldn't he have tossed it by mistake? But that wouldn't have stopped any of it from happening. Andrea Collins would still be dead. So would Kimberly Johnson, Ryla Abrams, and Jasmine Sanders.

Jasmine.

Her eyebrows scrunched inward, anxiety churning in her stomach like battery acid.

"I know you did everything you could to save Jasmine."

A harrowing lightheadedness rushed over her. She'd never told him Jasmine's name, neither in her apartment earlier nor in the brief text she'd sent to him before she left for Philadelphia.

A muffled beep from somewhere in the living room garnered her attention. Madison waited for it to beep again. On the second beep, she recognized it as a dying cell phone. She traced the muffled sound to a black backpack leaning against the wall beside the couch. Not caring if it was right or wrong, she unzipped the backpack. Her mind raced. She was a scientist separating the atom. At any moment, it could all explode. Something in this bag could put her mind at ease. Or… it could confirm the terrible thoughts boiling inside.

She drew a black sweatshirt from the backpack. Then a plane ticket: Philadelphia International to Chicago O'Hare. Her body reacted as if a tiger had leapt from the bag. The third item she drew from the bag caused her hand to go from trembling to paralyzed: a flesh-colored latex mask with black-mesh half-moon eyes and a warped smile.

An instinctive feeling warned her, raising the hair on her neck. The fear made her so lightheaded she thought she'd pass out. She slowly turned around.

Casper was watching her.

Her body wanted to respond in three drastically different ways—it wanted to charge forward and attack; it wanted to leap out the window and hopefully sprout wings and fly away; and quite shamefully, it also wanted to curl up in the fetal position, hoping the predator would find her so pathetic it would leave her alone. Instead, Madison stood there, frozen, as if her feet had grown roots.

"What's wrong?" Casper asked.

Then his eyes caught the sweatshirt and plane ticket on the floor and the mask clinging to her fingertips.

"Oh, God. This is not how I wanted you to find out," he said, stepping toward her.

"Stay back!" she shouted.

Madison readied her base, feet planted shoulder-width apart. Her purse—and more importantly, her Glock inside it—hung off a kitchen chair behind Casper. She was going to die less than five feet from salvation. It was like having a guardian angel apparate beside you but only to get a better look as you died. Casper glanced at her purse, then grabbed it. Maybe she would get lucky, and he would shoot her. What an absolute idiot she'd been. Casper had given her the manila envelope. It wasn't happenstance. It was planned—his deduction of the lyrics to determine the city was New Orleans, his disappearance in New Orleans, his convenient work trips. It all fell in line, but she couldn't figure out how he knew her. Had Casper seen her at a party when he was visiting a friend in UW-Milwaukee or Marquette?

The only solace Madison could take was that the gunshot that kills her would be heard. There was a chance Casper could be arrested before he could escape. But to her utter shock, he didn't take the Glock out; instead, he extended the purse toward her.

"Here," he said.

From Lana's training, Madison knew that this was a way for the attacker to get close. A false sense of security. She weighed the risk. She'd rather die fighting for the gun than be too scared to fight for it. The reward was worth the risk. When she reached for it, she expected him to yank her toward him. But the moment her hand wrapped itself around the leather strap, he let go. She clutched the purse and stepped back, retrieving the Glock from its depths. Casper raised his hands. With her right hand, Madison dug through the purse for her phone. She drew it out. Her purse fell to the floor. Her fingerprint access had been set up with her left thumb, forcing her to use her four-digit pin. She entered it wrong twice and cursed after each mistake, all the while making sure to keep an eye on Casper.

"Come to 5114 right away," Madison spoke into her phone.

It seemed she waited half a century for Atticus to arrive. Finally, a knock on the door. Madison ordered Casper to open it. He did. Atticus stepped inside and made quick work as to what was going on—Madison aiming the gun at Casper and the mask and plane ticket on the floor. It was probably the easiest deduction of his career.

"I can explain," Casper said in response to Atticus's scowl.

"I hope you can," Atticus said.

Before Casper had his moment in kitchen court, they waited for Vasquez. Like Atticus, she put it together instantly.

"You do have the right to remain silent," Vasquez said, not reading Casper his Miranda Rights but reminding him he did have that option. A lawyer would certainly recommend it.

"No, I can explain this," Casper said.

Vasquez waved her hand. "Explain away."

"Can I get dressed first?" Casper asked.

He was still clad only in a bath towel, looking equally cold and embarrassed.

"No, that kilt will do fine," Atticus said.

Casper took a deep breath. "I was in Philadelphia for work last week."

"Plane ticket gave that one away," Atticus said.

"You knew Jasmine's name. I never told you," Madison said.

"The hotel I stayed at had a bar. The news had the story on. They said there was a missing woman named Jasmine Sanders. Madison had told me there was a missing woman in Philly. Once they showed a picture of Jasmine, I knew she had to be the same one. Dark hair. Blue eyes."

"Awfully suspicious you were even there," Vasquez said.

Casper sighed, trying to remain calm. "I was there for work."

"Work bring you to Knoxville and Atlanta too?" Atticus asked.

Casper shook his head, both as a gesture to answer no and to show his disbelief at his current predicament. "No, it did not."

"And the mask? Part of the company uniform?" Atticus pressed.

Casper was going to have to work for that "innocent-until-proven-guilty" status.

"I bought that mask at a costume shop in Philly. I bought it for Madison," Casper said.

Madison's eyebrows scrunched inward. What in God's name was he talking about?

"You bought the mask for Madison?" Atticus repeated slowly so the stupidity of the comment could be fully appreciated. "Philly was all out of postcards?"

"I bought it so she wouldn't be afraid of it anymore," Casper said, ignoring Atticus's jest.

Vasquez was seconds away from calling Chicago P.D. "You better explain and explain real fast."

"I heard Madison's trainer tell her she needed to change the way she reacts to the mask. I thought if she had the mask, she could put it on her punching dummy or... God, I don't know...." Casper said, struggling to find the words to exonerate himself.

"I'll be able to confirm or call out your bullshit on everything you said in five minutes," Vasquez said, delivered in a way that told him it wasn't too late to come clean.

"Yeah, I know. I'm counting on it," Casper said.

Vasquez's phone call was torturous for both Casper and Madison. She tried gauging what Vasquez was told based on her facial expressions. Vasquez uttered phrases like "Are you sure?" "Has that been confirmed?" and the irritating "Really?" Then she pocketed her phone.

"His boss confirmed Casper flew to Philadelphia for work. A coworker named Terri Melcher verified they were at the hotel bar watching TV. She remembered seeing Jasmine Sander's name on the news," Vasquez reported. Her phone vibrated, and she read the text. "Maurice confirmed there's nothing that showed Casper was in Knoxville or Atlanta."

Though Casper knew that *should* be the case, he was nonetheless relieved that it could be proven. Innocent people were imprisoned all the time. Atticus and Vasquez both offered to leave with Madison, but for her to do so would have been cowardly. She stayed, trying to hastily find a way to apologize. Workplaces were breeding grounds for rumors, and soon, everyone would know that the FBI had asked about Casper Jackson. She had tarnished his reputation. How can someone apologize for that? She half-expected him to tell her to get the hell out. But he didn't. He was silent, wrapped in a towel and covered in goosebumps, which only added to the humiliation.

"Casper... I'm so sorry," Madison said.

Inconsequential was a fifteen-letter word whose literal definition was "meaningless." Yet the English word to convey regret, remorse, and a plea for forgiveness was the five-letter word *sorry*. The voice of Martin Brody from *Jaws* echoed in her head: "You're going to need a bigger word." And she sure did. She was on *The Orca* and sinking fast. She considered herself in possession of an extensive vocabulary, but right now, she didn't even know what language she spoke.

"Thanks for letting me explain before I was dragged out in nothing but cuffs and a towel."

"I told you I trusted you—"

"Madison, I understand. You found the mask. You'd be an idiot if you didn't think it was me. I kept flip-flopping on whether to give it to you. One minute, it seemed like a great idea, and the next, completely stupid and cruel."

An awkward silence filled the room. Casper looked into her eyes and tentatively reached for her hands. She didn't pull them away.

"You need to be cautious," Casper said. "Skeptical of everyone. If Atticus and Vasquez are right, it means someone you know is doing this."

Madison nodded, grinding the inside of her cheek. She deserved to bleed. "I think the mask is a good idea."

"You don't have to say that. We'll get rid of it."

"No, you're right. I can't let fear paralyze me. Sooner or later, I'm going to see him again."

She grabbed the latex mask. The price tag was still on it. $29.99. How could something so cheap hold such power over her? She rubbed the mask with her thumb. Smooth yet abrasive, it felt as if a million tiny tentacles grabbed her fingertip and wouldn't let go. Just like the Man in the Mask.

"I thought maybe this could help narrow down where the mask is sold. But it's made in China. I googled the name of the mask—it's sold everywhere," Casper said.

Madison returned to her apartment. Atticus called on the elevator ride up, under the guise of asking how she was doing. His true purpose for calling was to ensure she was still alive. He didn't seem to trust any of the facts of the case, only willing to concede that the Man in the Mask was not himself, Vasquez, or Madison. She cleared her room and then slipped the mask onto Century Bob's head. She punched it. Then punched it again. And again and again.

Thursday night came, and with it, the realization that Friday would bring another chapter. Atticus and Vasquez were back in Wisconsin, but instead of going to Milwaukee, they drove to McFarland, a suburb of Madison. They parked in an old, beaten-down, and rusted playground.

"He knows we're here to talk about Madison, not to buy crack, right?" Atticus asked.

"He didn't want to talk with his wife around," Vasquez said.

"Well, did he have to pick a haunted playground?"

They'd spent hundreds of hours sitting in a parked car—late nights watching buildings and houses, sipping coffee from Styrofoam cups, and snacking on gas station junk food. No energy drinks back then. If you wanted caffeine, you had to learn to love coffee.

Headlights lit the interior of Vasquez's Challenger. A black Chevy Impala parked beside them. Vince Propelli stepped out and sat at an old wooden picnic table. He'd aged tremendously better than Shane Benson and had kept himself in respectable shape. Atticus and Vasquez joined him. It was cold, and the swings shrieked eerily in the night. The table was filled with graffiti— sharpie, pen, and knife carvings—declaring B loves M, then the aggressive crossing out when that proved untrue, the ubiquitous dick drawings, and toll-free numbers to call for a good time.

"I went to grade school here. This is where we had recess," Propelli said.

Atticus blinked slowly to show how riveting he found that fact. Vasquez got the introductory preamble out of the way and discussed the issue at hand.

"It was a lot more serious for me than it was for her," Propelli said when asked about his relationship with Madison.

"You wanted it to be serious? Exclusive?" Atticus asked.

"Definitely… I lied to my wife about her. I didn't want her to know I loved Madison."

"Did you tell Madison you loved her?" Vasquez asked.

Propelli shook his head, remnants of regret visible in his dark eyes. "Writing was on the wall already."

Vasquez mentioned the Halloween party and Shane Benson.

"Shane Benson… Could have gone without hearing his name. He and I almost got into it a few times over Madison."

"How come?" Vasquez asked.

"I didn't care for the way he treated her. We both wanted her, but we did it differently."

"How so?"

"I reached for her hand; he reached for her ass."

"You stayed at the party all night?" Atticus asked.

Propelli ran his hand through his oil-black hair. "Yeah… I… I slept with Madison's friend Jade. I was drunk, but… I wanted to get over Madison… But when… when I found out what'd happened to her…"

His answer corroborated what Jade had said, and his narrative of the party fell in line too.

"Were there other men?" Vasquez asked.

"Listen, it's not my place to discuss her sex life," Propelli said.

"That's admirable, but she's not on trial for premarital sex. We want to know if there were other guys actively trying to be with her."

"Yeah, a list of them. But there was this guy named Rigel Rose. I wanted to hate him because he and Madison really had a connection. I mean, we never talked that way. But he was such a nice guy, super polite. Impossible to hate, you know?"

"He was a T.A. for Grey Moore," Atticus said, not in the mood to hear about Rose again. And he had no trouble hating anybody, Rose included.

"Yeah, that asshole."

"Did you have a class with Moore?" Vasquez asked.

234

"Yeah. Guy was a first-class dick with honors."

"There were rumors that—"

Vasquez couldn't even finish her sentence.

"Slept with students? Yeah, not a rumor. I remember one class, he and this blonde girl got into a heated discussion. And I mean *heated*."

"What about?" Atticus asked.

"Not about the Oxford comma, I can tell you that. It was obvious there was something personal. Apparently, she slept with him to get an A, and he still gave her a C."

"Describe 'heated.' What did Moore look like? What was he doing?" Atticus asked.

"Red-faced, veins bulging. Like Hitler at an anti-Jew rally."

"And nothing came of this? This girl didn't tell the Dean?"

Propelli shook his head. "No. Unless she filmed it, she had no proof. Her C was justified. An A would have been fishy."

A cold wind swept through the decrepit playground. The merry-go-round groaned as it spun. Propelli leaned forward as if he feared that somewhere in the abandoned Chernobyl-like playground a Soviet spy was hiding.

"Can I ask you something?"

Vasquez nodded.

"What if Madison's abduction wasn't a moment of opportunity?"

"What do you mean?" Atticus asked.

"I mean, what if it was planned?"

"Why would you think that?" Vasquez asked.

They'd said nothing about the chapters or the murders, nothing that could've informed Propelli that Madison's abductor and rapist was currently active and had advanced to murder.

"Madison could handle a few beers. At that party... I don't know. The way she looked... how tired she seemed..."

"What is it you're trying to say, Vince?" Atticus asked.

He knew the answer and knew Vasquez knew it too, but they needed to hear him say it.

Propelli hesitated, looked around, giving Atticus the impression that he was about to tell them who had truly killed Kennedy. "What if someone spiked her drink? I know they tested her blood after she escaped, but that wouldn't still be in her bloodstream days later, would it?"

"No, it wouldn't," Vasquez answered.

At college parties, slipping a date-rape drug into a drink was far too easy and far too common.

"Did you see anyone leave when she did?" Atticus asked.

"I mean, people were coming and going all night," Propelli answered.

Vasquez showed Propelli a picture of the mask Casper had purchased in Philadelphia. "Do you remember seeing anyone wearing this mask?"

She knew what she was asking. She was asking him to remember one particular mask from a house party years ago in which he had been drunk, and in which hundreds of people—all dressed in costumes—had been coming and going. But Propelli said he'd gone over the night a hundred times after the story of Madison's abduction and rape broke. Even all these years later, he still thought about that party. He hadn't forgotten the event, and unlike Madison, trauma hadn't buried the details connected to it; in fact, guilt had refined it. So, to the shock of Vasquez, Propelli's eyes bulged in recognition.

"Yeah, I do. I mean, maybe not that exact mask but damn close."

"Where? Outside?" Vasquez asked.

Propelli nodded again. "Yeah, I followed Madison outside for one more embarrassing plea, but she was already on her bike and down the street."

"Where was this person in the mask?"

"Standing under a streetlight. He looked super creepy."

"You're sure?" Atticus asked.

"Yeah, you kind of remember the setting of where your heart gets broken, you know?"

Atticus did know.

"Did he stay there?" Vasquez asked.

"No, he got in his truck."

Atticus and Vasquez leaned forward at the word 'truck'; the rush of excitement bubbled.

Vasquez swiped to a photo of the white Dodge Ram. "Did it look like this?"

"Yeah, it did," Propelli answered, looking back and forth at Vasquez and Atticus.

"Any identifying features? A decal, a bumper sticker..." Atticus asked.

Propelli paused, thinking back. "Yeah, one of those *coexist* bumper stickers."

Vasquez and Atticus looked at one another. It eliminated the possibility of Madison's abduction being a random encounter. The Man in the Mask had stalked Madison, waited for her to leave that party.

"You think that's the guy who took Madison?" Propelli asked.

"We do," Vasquez said.

Propelli nearly started crying. "The police never asked me these questions. Why didn't they ask me? Jesus Christ... I watched him drive away.... Then I got drunk and slept with her best friend while he ran her off the road and raped her."

Vasquez had to stop herself from reaching over and squeezing his hand. Propelli looked as though he would vomit or cry or do both. If he was faking any of the emotions, he deserved an Oscar. He buried his face in his hands, clawing at his head. His grief was gut-wrenching to witness.

"Do you have any photos of that night?" Vasquez asked.

"Yeah, on Facebook. Maybe some on Instagram," Propelli said.

Vasquez asked him to send them to her. Propelli nodded as he sniffed back his runny nose.

Vasquez and Atticus stayed until Propelli got his emotions in check, but there was no doubt Propelli would cry his whole drive home. There'd been much about that night Vince Propelli regretted. Vasquez and Atticus had added more. Long ago, when Vasquez and Atticus had first become partners, Atticus had compared grief to a bomb. When something awful happened, the bomb exploded. Some people get hit with more shrapnel than others. Vince Propelli had been mere feet away from the bomb.

They watched Propelli back up and drive away, then headed to Vasquez's Challenger and left the creepy abandoned playground.

The following morning Atticus drove his dependable truck, Vasquez riding shotgun; both silent so that Springsteen's screams went undiluted. When they reached Grey Moore's residence, Atticus refused to use the lion-head knocker, instead using his bare knuckles. Moore answered. Atticus put his hand on the door in a seemingly innocent fashion, but it was to actually stop Moore from shutting the door in his face.

"This isn't a good time," Moore said.

Vasquez flashed her badge, holding it mere inches from Moore's face. "How about now?"

Moore exhaled deeply, looking like a kid who'd been told he had to go to bed ten minutes before the end of his favorite show. Atticus pushed the door open.

"I'd appreciate it if we could keep this brief," Moore said to his two unwelcome guests.

He was dressed in expensive khakis and a sky-blue Kashmir sweater. A strong dousing of cologne and a subtle hint of scotch clung to the fabric. He checked his thousand-dollar-plus watch, perfectly calibrated with the Earth's axis, so there was no mistaking how little time he had for them.

"Now, if you could get to—" Moore began.

"Your wife have any more of that delicious lemonade?" Atticus interrupted.

"No. Please get to the—"

"His wife makes the best damn lemonade," Atticus told Vasquez. Then he directed his words at Moore. "Is she home? Maybe we can have her make some and join us for our questions."

Moore threw his hands up. "No, that won't be necessary."

He hurried to his kitchen and returned with two glasses of lemonade. Atticus took a sip and sighed with supreme satisfaction. He and Vasquez exchanged compliments about the lemonade to further irritate Moore.

"Now, why are you here?" Moore asked bluntly.

"Peculiarities," Atticus answered vaguely.

"Okay… peculiarities about what?"

"For one, you were in Tennessee recently," Vasquez said.

Moore nodded and shrugged at the insignificance of it. Vasquez handed him scans of his airplane tickets.

"I nodded. I don't need to see a copy of my ticket," Moore said.

Vasquez handed him a copy of his signed and dated rental agreement with Enterprise.

"Yes, I rented a car. How odd of someone to do that."

"No, but when a person rents a car the day *after* they arrive, that *is* odd," Atticus said.

Moore's eyes darted about the room like a pinball. His toes scrunched, creasing his leather loafers; he rubbed his temple. If nervousness had a scent, he'd reek of it. He was silent, obviously trying to buy time for a lie to come.

"Don't know? That's okay. Maybe your wife does," Atticus said, rising from his seat as if he was about to go and search the house.

"Don't! I had a speaking engagement at Georgia State University."

"Why did you have to look about the house for your wife before you answered?" Vasquez asked.

People opened their eyes to escape a nightmare. Moore had to close his to escape it. He cursed under his breath.

"I saw someone there," Moore said.

"Yes, I'm sure you did see people. But who, Moore? Enough bullshit," Atticus said in a warning tone.

"Christ!" Moore cursed again.

"Man or woman?" Atticus asked.

"Woman," Moore answered, offended he had to clarify.

"Her name," Vasquez ordered.

"Victoria Murphy."

"Now you said you *saw someone*. Is she a therapist? Doctor?" Atticus teased, knowing damn well what Moore meant. He wanted Moore to think of him as a mosquito, and he enjoyed buzzing around Moore's ear.

"I slept with her, okay? Jesus Christ..."

"Her number?" Vasquez asked.

"What?" Moore exclaimed, his eyes doubling in size.

"Telephone number. Give it up."

"What are you going to do?" Moore asked.

"Corroborate your story," Vasquez said.

Moore sprung to his feet. "What does this have to do with what happened to the Monroe girl?"

Vasquez glared at him and pointed at his chair. "Sit down."

An innate instinct for self-preservation told him it was in his best interest to do exactly what she said.

"What happened to the Monroe girl was that she was abducted. She was raped. She was humiliated, tormented, and tortured. And she would have been murdered had she not escaped. So, you're going to give me the number for Victoria Murphy, and you're going to sit there and shut up."

"I can make you leave. You have no warrant," Moore threatened.

"True. But I promise you your wife will find out every steamy detail of your affair. Then I'll pay the Dean a visit and tell him about your special attention to the female student body," Vasquez said.

Atticus leaned forward and pointed a finger at Moore's chest. "Let's get one thing clear, Professor. I'm bound by no badge. I'm old. I've got nothing to lose, so trust me when I say if you disrespect Madison and what she went through again, you'll be sipping soup and applesauce through a straw for the next year."

Moore gave Victoria Murphy's number and stayed silent as Atticus dialed it. The phone rang until the call went to voicemail. Moore breathed a sigh of relief. Vasquez cautioned him against forewarning Victoria Murphy and then she and Atticus left.

Short of Atticus's truck, Vasquez's phone rang. She looked at the name, then worriedly informed Atticus, "It's Madison."

Vasquez answered.

"There's another one."

The moment I saw you, *I knew I was going to kill you. Needed to kill you. It was that feeling of jubilation you experienced as a kid seeing the newest toy in an ad on the television. You knew you were going to bug your parents about it every single day. It was an itch impossible to ignore.*

You find your routines reassuring. Routines give people moments of stability in a chaotic world. But routines are dangerous. Predictable. To the predator, routine removes risk, improves the chances of success.

You don't have Madison's eyes. They're close, but they don't tell the same story hers do. But it was the smile you flash as we hurried past each other in a frenzy to get to where we needed to be. It was the same smile she had. I watch you enter a coffee shop and note the time. In exactly twenty-four hours, you'll be in the same exact spot.

The rest of the day is long, you fill my thoughts. I can't sleep. The itch is getting worse. The next day, I'm waiting in line at the coffee shop. I know you're behind me. I can smell your perfume—subtle strawberry and a caress of cream. I loosen the lid on my coffee and turn around, bumping into you and spilling the scalding coffee down my chest. I feel it even through my sky-blue sweater. It's a small price to pay in comparison, for you will the pay the ultimate price, and once more, the city will be home to a massacre.

"I'm so sorry!" You apologize repeatedly.

You rub napkins on my chest, trying to remove the coffee stain from my shirt. Later, I'll be trying to get your blood off it.

"It's entirely my fault. I should mind my surroundings better," I say, looking around helplessly.

You dry my sweater as best you can. "Maybe the fault lies with us both," you say.

You smile organically. A nervous giggle leaves your lips.

I force a smirk. "Maybe."

"We seem to be on the same schedule," you say.

"Yeah, I left a minute early to beat you in line."

"How do you take your coffee?"

"A splash of cream and on my sweater."

We both laugh—one organic, the other the tool of an actor.

"Listen, I hope I'm not being too direct, but would you allow me to take you to dinner tonight?" I ask.

You look at me, reading me. I'm a book. My cover is romance, but I'm all horror inside. You tell me your name is Layla. I tell you mine. We agree to meet at six. You're already there at quarter to. Even with your back to me, I can tell you're nervous. You have a moment of self-doubt about how you look. I tell you you look beautiful. It's not a lie. The attraction between us is magnetic. An undeniable bond.

Our dinner includes the city's staple. I love the sound of the crack. We fill the dinner with the necessary preamble. I love your accent, not romantic like the French but nonetheless historic or iconic. We share a bottle of Merlot. I want you inebriated. A woman from your side of town could put up a fight.

"Easy. It's a marathon, not a sprint," you say when I go to refill your glass.

I laugh, even though I want to slam your head against the table. I pay for the meal, in cash of course. The eyes of all women light up when they see a man fan through hundreds. Is it evolutionary? A sense of survival? Cling to the dominant male.

All species have a relationship. The gold-digger thinks she offers a relationship of mutualism. Where both parties benefit. She gets cash to stock her closets with shoes and clothes and decorate her fingers and neck in precious gems, and the man gets to fill her holes. But it isn't a mutualistic relationship. It's parasitic. You use the man for your own gain like a mosquito constantly sucking blood. If the money ran out, you'd follow it out in a sprint, not like the marathon you claim.

But my relationship to you is predation. You are the prey. I am your predator. Some would call a person like me an animal. But I don't recall a wolf giving a sheep a meal before it killed its prey.

I talk you into one more glass of wine. After all, we can't leave a bottle unfinished.

We stroll the city. At twelve, we take a ride upon a horse and carriage. You hold my hand. I can feel your heat. I can't stand it. Fear makes the skin cold. Death, even colder. Soon enough.

Enjoy the sights filling your sapphire eyes. Soon, they'll see nothing. Enjoy the smells of the city. Soon, your flesh will decay, a miasma wafting through the air. Enjoy the sounds of the clatter of the horse hooves, the honking taxis, and the nightlife. Soon, you shan't hear a thing.

After the carriage ride, we walk toward the river, gazing at it, contemplating the secrets beneath it. I kiss you, and hand-in-hand, we leave.

You ask me where we're going.

"I thought I could sneak a kiss or two away from any prying eyes," I tell you.

I offer my hand. But you're reluctant.

"We should get back," you say. "You can come up to my apartment. We don't have to have sex here. It's not exactly a turn-on."

You turn, but I pull you back. You smile at me, thinking I'm playing and then turn once more. But again, I pull you back. Your smile fades, but you recover well. You don't want to anger me. You still feel you can make it out alive. It's endearing, even if it is pathetic. The fear swelling inside you gives off an aphrodisiac odor. The heat in your hands is gone.

"Come on, this is silly," you say.

"Fine, fine."

I release your hand. You exhale a sigh of relief. You turn your back to me, hurrying back toward the bustling city. I bend down, pick it up in my hand and swing. As much as I loved the snappings and crackings at dinner, the way wood cracks on your skull is a pleasure that pulsates throughout my body. And on the second blow, blood explodes out like a crimson ejaculation.

I hit you too hard. You're out cold. You need to be awake when we make love. I drag you behind cover, double-checking we're still alone. Do you feel betrayed by the city? How you can be surrounded by millions and be utterly alone? Don't worry, the same thoughts must run through the gazelle's mind. While the sick and weak gazelle is devoured alive, its herd grazes less than a hundred yards away.

I watch you, slipping on my mask I had planted here. You wake up slowly, gently holding your head with your hand. I press my hand to your mouth.

"Silly sheep, don't you cry, all God's creatures have to die."

The pain you feel is on you. I offered more wine. Had you been good and drunk, you'd enjoy this so much more. You mumble and scream. But your voice is swallowed up by the roar of industry, the shriek of the steel horses. It's cold down here, the winds more violent than me. But the blood dripping down your head warms my fingertips.

After we both have climaxed and you're satisfied, I climb off. You look so much like her. Except those eyes. Almost time to shut them. On the River's Edge, you'll die.

By the time Atticus and Vasquez returned to Essex on the Park, Madison had read the chapter an unlucky thirteen times. She had sent it to Maurice, but he already knew it had come as he'd been monitoring all her incoming emails.

Casper looked disgusted and disturbed, as if he was going to be sick. It was like reading Ted Bundy's thoughts. Madison knew how he felt all too well. Reading this perverse fiction made you sick to your stomach. Was that how simple it had been for the Man in the Mask? Had he simply seen her somewhere and some deranged voice told him he needed her? Needed to kill her? Since *it* had happened, she had had the fear that the Man in the Mask would return. That he had been keeping tabs on her. Watched her from afar. The terror that any moment could be *the* moment he struck again. Dr. Frett had told her time and again she was paranoid, a "victim of an unhealthy neurosis." But guess what, doc? It's not paranoia if it's real.

She would have rather he'd written vulgarly than to have written as if they were separated lovers. His words were repulsive.

"Well, never too early to guess. Seattle? Mentions coffee," Casper said.

Coffee was too generic, and even Starbucks would have done little to narrow down the seemingly infinite possibilities. There are over 150 Starbucks in Chicago alone. Madison created a grid as she'd done before, a list of cities and clues marked with an X when a criterion is met.

"*I love the sound of the crack,*" Vasquez read.

Madison asked which food items crack.

"Crackers, some cookies, peanut brittle…" Casper, the food aficionado among them, rattled off.

"Pistachios," Atticus added.

A pause.

"Lobster?" Vasquez asked.

"That works. Maine?" Madison asked.

"Loves her accent—*not romantic like French but nonetheless historic or iconic,*" Atticus read.

"Northeasterners have accents. It's not like every word, but certain ones you can definitely pick it up," Casper said.

"New York, Boston, the Midwest, Southern, Texas, California… there's a lot of accents," Vasquez said.

Madison reread as the other three continued talking aloud. Guesses were made and refuted. A certain city came to Madison's mind. She read through the chapter again. Certain words leapt out.

Massacre. Marathon.

"What about Boston?" she asked.

The others fell silent, giving her their attention.

"I missed the significance of this line before. *And once more, the city will be home to a massacre.*"

"Like a shooting?" Casper asked. "There's so many cities that could work for though."

"The Boston Massacre," Atticus said. "Red coats shot and killed British civilians during a riot."

Madison nodded, pleased Atticus was following her train of thought. "And the line—*it's a marathon, not a sprint.*"

"Oh, the Boston Marathon," Casper realized.

Madison scanned the chapter. "And this line, if you read it knowing the answer has to be somewhere in Boston, it fits. *We walk toward the river, gazing at it, contemplating the secrets beneath it.* Secrets. What's another word for secrets? Mysteries."

"The Mystic River," Vasquez said. "Keep looking for clues. I'm calling this in." She rose from the table and made her phone call at the window.

Atticus read, *"The roar of industry, the shriek of the steel horses.* 'The roar of industry' has to be factories."

"What are the steel horses?" Casper asked.

"Trains," Madison answered.

With the flight set, she rushed to her room to throw on a sweatshirt and winter hat. Casper insisted on coming. Even though the evidence and witness testimonies had ruled him out as a suspect, he still felt that he needed to clear his name.

Nerves shrunk her bladder and dried her throat—a vicious combination. She guzzled water even though she knew she shouldn't. Once on the plane, she let the smooth, soulful voice of Sam Cooke soothe her. Vasquez was on her phone, Casper looked out the window, his leg nervously shaking, and Atticus looked as though he was living his nightmare.

When the historic city of Boston came into view, the pilot announced their descent. After they rushed off the plane, they were handed body armor.

"I'd make sure that's tight," Atticus told Casper. "It's your turn to get shot."

"Gee, thanks," Casper said.

Madison helped him tighten his vest. She'd worn body armor more often of late than jeans.

"No separating this time," Vasquez said.

A short and rail-thin FBI agent waited for them. He introduced himself as Agent Wong. He screamed over the shrieking engines. "We're searching the area you gave us, but those tracks stretch all the way from The Neck to South Medford in the west. It crosses the Mystic. Boston P.D is doing all they can."

Vasquez handed a copy of the chapter to him. "Have the locals read through this to look for clues."

"I'll pass it around," Agent Wong said.

Atticus took the issue into his own hands. He approached a middle-aged female officer, wide around the waist.

"From here?" he asked.

"Yes, sir," she replied. Her thick Boston accent was answer enough.

Atticus asked her to read through the chapter, looking for anything that narrowed down a location. She took the folded chapter and read.

"Right here," she said, tapping the page. "*On the River's Edge, you'll die. River's Edge Drive.*"

Atticus thanked her and then called out to Vasquez. He told her what the officer had said. She asked Agent Wong how far away River's Edge Drive was.

"15 minutes."

They hopped into his black SUV. The city of Boston was a blur. Agent Wong coolly drove through red lights, weaving between lanes. His stop at the outset of River's Edge Drive was anything but subtle. It jerked Madison forward, her seat belt tightening around her waist. Hundreds of homes were close by. Hundreds of people. And to Madison that was more heartbreaking of a situation than the secluded cabin in the woods she had been held in. Out there, there had been no one to hear her scream. The desolation and despair had been overwhelming. Layla had been taken less than a football field's length away from a major metropolis. There were thousands of possibilities for someone to save Layla, yet no one had.

Casper kept his hand close to Madison's as they searched on foot. Atticus was on their left, Vasquez to the right. Flashlight beams lit the darkness like a luminous fog. Madison feared what they would see. She wanted to find Layla, not her body. They walked down the train tracks south toward the Mystic River. Fear had caused her to tremble, but the chilly winds gusting off the river made her shiver, ripping through her clothing as easily as through tissue paper. All but two officers stayed to search the massive Wellington station and its even larger parking lot. There were nearly a dozen tracks on the opposite side of the station, and they too needed to be checked. Casper, Vasquez, Atticus, the two police officers, and Madison continued ahead, following the tracks across the Mystic River. Out there, the winds were cruel and violent, shoving them one way and then the other. One second, it was at their back, propelling them forward, and the next, it became an invisible concrete wall.

Madison's flashlight caught something along the tracks in the distance. More detail became visible—a sprawled-out mass... long hair... a woman's face. The wind pushed Madison's shout back into her throat. She swallowed, then tried again.

"It's her!" Madison screamed.

She ran ahead, cautious of where she stepped. Officer Lucy Taylor blew her whistle, but the wind's howl was too loud for it to be heard. Madison crouched beside Layla, telling her everything would be okay. Duct tape, a quarter-inch thick, was wrapped around her mouth. She was naked, her body tinted with a blue hue from the cold. An overpowering stench of bleach attacked and burned Madison's mouth, nose, and eyes. The abrasive chemical had caused bright red burns across Layla's skin, but most severely around her breasts and vaginal area. Despite it all, her chest still rose and fell as air filled her lungs. She was still alive.

There appeared to be no signs of restraint around her wrists or ankles, only metallic bracelets on each wrist. Casper and Officer Logan Wilkes gently grabbed Layla's arms to lift her but couldn't.

"What the hell?" Officer Wilkes exclaimed.

Madison moved her hand toward Layla's. She took her keys from her pocket and moved them closer to Layla. The keys flew from her hand to the bracelet as if a ghost had snatched them away.

"They're magnets..." Madison said.

Casper aimed his flashlight to examine the bracelets. "There's something on the other side of the track. I'm gonna try to break it."

A silver puck-shaped disc was stuck to the railroad track. Atticus, Vasquez, and Officer Taylor arrived. Madison explained about the magnetic bracelets. A single line from the chapter came to her mind.

The attraction between us is magnetic.

A disgusting feeling rumbled in her stomach. The goosebumps on her skin multiplied. Vasquez told the two cops to confirm all trains heading this direction had been stopped while Casper put the flashlight between his teeth

251

and then heaved and tugged on the puck-shaped magnet. It didn't budge even a sixteenth of an inch. Madison examined Layla's wrists in greater detail. They were bruised and bleeding. The magnetism was so powerful it had nearly broken her wrists. Officer Wilkes pushed on the puck-shaped magnet as Casper pulled. It didn't move a nanometer.

Casper stood, nervously rubbing his head. "How do we get her out?" he asked, his voice bleak.

Officer Taylor shouted into her police radio for the officers searching behind them at Wellington Station and those ahead to convene at their location. Atticus's flashlight revealed small black font on the puck-shaped magnet.

ACHTUNG! STARK NEODYMIUM MAGNET!

"What does that mean?" Vasquez asked.

"It's German. It says Danger," Atticus said.

"And Neodymium?'

Madison googled, her trembling fingers causing her to mistype, but Google knew what she wanted to see.

"It's the strongest magnet available commercially," Madison said.

"They can't sell handcuffs like this," Vasquez said.

"They look like something MIT would mess around with," blonde-haired Officer Taylor said.

"See if you can get somebody from there on the phone. See if they know anything about these magnets and how to separate them," Vasquez instructed the two police officers.

"Let's get her covered and the tape off," Atticus said.

He carefully pried at the tape, unraveling and tearing it off to free her mouth, but left the tape stuck to her hair alone. They'd be able to dull the adhesive at the hospital and prevent her the pain of having her hair ripped from her scalp. Vasquez asked Layla if she knew who had attacked her, but Layla was too weak to even move her lips. Her eyes were cold and distant. Officer Wilkes removed his jacket and wrapped it around her. Vasquez rubbed it against Layla's ice-cold skin, in an attempt to create much-needed heat. She examined Layla's head as she did so.

"There's a wound here. Looks like he did bludgeon her," she said.

"Bleach did a number on it," Atticus added.

"Let's keep trying at this," Casper said. "We'll work on the puck; you work on the bracelet."

He and Wilkes heaved while Atticus, Vasquez, Taylor, and Madison tugged on the bracelet. They grunted and groaned, having as much success as pushing a train uphill.

Casper swore through bared teeth. The magnetic puck wouldn't budge.

Something got Madison's attention. She wasn't even sure if she had truly felt it. She rose and walked a few paces away and then stood still. A soft, faint vibration lightly massaged her feet. She cautiously crouched and put her hand to the track. It pulsated and vibrated like an earthquake.

Atticus studied Madison's face. His formed a you-got-to-be-fucking-kidding-me look. He touched the track. "Shit!"

He hobbled down the track toward the middle of the river. Vasquez sprinted after him for a better view. Officer Taylor yelled into her radio, asking if there was any train approaching Wellington Station from the south, while Casper used his flashlight to bludgeon the puck-shaped magnet.

Atticus and Vasquez stood frozen, listening for the unmistakable sound of a speeding locomotive. The fog hindered their sight—nothing but a veil of smoky white was visible. But then two distorted spheres of waning yellow light broke through the fragile veil. Bright and blinding. The tracks vibrated violently. The ground shook as if the mythical Titans at Tartarus had broken free.

"Train!" Vasquez shouted.

Officer Taylor continued yelling into her radio, telling whoever listened to immediately stop all trains heading toward Wellington Station.

Vasquez and Atticus sprinted back toward Layla, waving their flashlights behind them to catch the attention of the train's conductor, but the fog was too thick for their puny beams of light to be seen. Atticus's knees were on fire, threatening to shatter.

Casper attacked the puck-shaped magnet with dire desperation—kicking, pushing, pulling, and hitting. Madison joined Atticus in waving their flashlights. Vasquez drew her Glock and fired into the air. Forget the shriek of the steel horse, it was the sound of a fire-breathing dragon descending upon them. The pebbles along the tracks leapt like Mexican jumping beans.

The train continued at full destruction speed. A shriek of its whistle violated the night air, sounding like a thousand kettles of tea coming to boil, followed by an ear-bleeding squeal of cacophonous sounds. The train struggled to stop, the railway breaks flashing like sparklers.

"It can't stop… Move! Move!" Atticus yelled.

Casper screamed in frustration. Even in Layla's near-death state, she knew what that sound was and what that abhorrent vibration meant. Fear radiated from her eyes.

"Run!" Vasquez shouted.

Officers Taylor and Wilkes sprinted toward land. Atticus's knees wouldn't allow him to make it that far that fast. He and Vasquez leapt from the tracks to the dark water below.

"Madison! We have to go!" Casper yelled, tugging at Madison's arm.

The mechanical tornado blitzed ever forward. Madison's cobalt-blue eyes locked onto Layla's sapphire-blue ones with a magnetism matching the magnetic restraints on Layla's wrists. Madison cried out how sorry she was for what she had to do. She wanted to cry. She wanted to puke. But she couldn't deny she wanted to live. Casper snatched her hand, and together, they sprinted to the edge. Poor Layla was frozen in place. The train shrieked, powering through, eviscerating Layla—squirting blood and spitting chunks of bone.

Casper and Madison looked from the train to the river below and then plummeted into the frigid depths of the Mystic River.

The frigid water stabbed her all over. Madison gasped from how painfully cold it was. The sweatshirt she'd worn to keep her warm absorbed water like a sponge and dragged her under. She kicked and broke through the surface, gasping for the ever-evasive breath. Casper swam to her, his breathing heavy and frantic. Together, they swam to the shore. Atticus and Vasquez pulled them from the water as sirens wailed in the distance. Emergency crews hurried to where Layla had lain. Madison hadn't lost feeling in her fingers and toes but wished she had. They throbbed as if they were on fire. She had zero dexterity. Her shivers were violent spasms. Madison and Casper hurried to an ambulance and sat in the back, the vehicle's heat blasting at them through the vents. The medics wrapped large blankets around their shoulders.

Some minutes later, an officer stopped by to ID the victim. Layla's last name was Kuzick. 33 years old. No children. She had five brothers and was a beloved aunt to twice as many children.

A man in a thick winter jacket and fogged-up oval glasses paced nervously, waiting to be acknowledged by anyone. Madison tried to look away before he saw her, but it was too late. Since she was the only person who seemed aware of his existence, he staggered toward her. He introduced himself as Professor Kozlovsky from MIT. He was beyond eager for an explanation as to why he had been called here late at night. Vasquez gave it to him.

"Let me see if I can help—" he said.

"She's gone," Vasquez interjected.

"Oh, you were able to separate them?"

"No, the train came through."

The sentence registered with him, and his mouth dropped. Vasquez asked him to come with her. He nodded and followed her and Atticus to where Layla had been. They had to put on foot booties and gloves. It was a fool's hope they'd find any evidence, for in the attempt to save Layla's life, the search party had greatly contaminated the scene. The sight was truly gruesome. Professor Kozlovsky dry-heaved. Vasquez told him to take a moment, and Atticus instructed him to breathe through his mouth, not his nose.

The professor kept a clenched fist in front of his mouth to keep his bile at bay. The tracks were covered in blood, giving the air the smell of copper. Kozlovsky took a few deep breaths through his mouth, then stepped forward. Even the tremendous force of the ten-thousand-plus-ton train traveling at 80 miles per hour hadn't broken the magnetism. The Neodymium magnets had been chipped and cracked, but the force bonding them was as strong as ever. Gruesomely, Layla's hands remained in the bracelets while the rest of her was spread out over the tracks like clumpy jelly on toast. Atticus offered Kozlovsky a white handkerchief. He accepted it and pressed it against his mouth and nose. He crouched to examine the magnets. He recognized them immediately. They were from his lab at MIT and had been donated by a German company located in Dachau. His students had designed the bracelets to be the handcuff of the future. Professor Kozlovsky was about to explain further, but Vasquez stopped him. There was no reason to know now that Layla was dead. He could tell the rest to the local police.

"Safe to say these are the only pair?" Vasquez asked.

"I can't definitively say no one else is working on something similar, but these certainly aren't something you buy on Amazon," Kozlovsky said.

The magnets were stored in a locked room, but no other security measures had been taken. No guests had visited the lab, but Professor Kozlovsky had given a lecture about magnets a few days prior. The lecture was open to the public, and neither were tickets necessary nor was the event video recorded. He asked if they could finish the conversation elsewhere. They left the crime scene and headed back toward Wellington Station. Kozlovsky returned the white handkerchief to Atticus, elated to be away from the vile smell and horrible sight.

256

"How many people know about this project?" Vasquez asked.

"Depends on how many people read this month's *Tech*," Kozlovsky answered.

"*Tech*? What's that?" Atticus asked.

"MIT's student newspaper."

When Kozlovsky and his students met on Tuesday, the magnets had been there, and no one had reported them stolen. They thanked him for his time and watched him head back to his Volvo at what someone in his field would call an accelerated rate.

Before joining Atticus, Casper, and Madison in the SUV that would drive them back to the airport, Vasquez met with Agent Wong to ask him to look into the missing MIT magnets. The plane ride was solemn like the others before had been, but this one imparted a visceral pain Madison hadn't felt before. Andrea Collins had been a smiling photograph on the news. She hadn't seen Ryla Abrams. And even though she had seen Jasmine Sanders, dead and sprawled out like da Vinci's Vitruvian Man—a ghastly sight certainly—Jasmine had already been dead when Madison reached her. But with Layla Kuzick, Madison had watched her die. Smell would be the first sense to go. Right now, she could smell the copper-heavy air from the liters of blood spat out and coating the tracks like varnish. That would fade, perhaps months from now. Hearing the roar of the train, the shriek of its whistle, the scream of its breaks, and Layla's agonizing death cry would take years, maybe decades, to die away. But the sight of the powerful train speeding toward her, cutting through the fog like a vengeful ghost, as Layla's beautiful blue eyes widened with unfathomable fear was an image that would never fully leave her. Madison would forever see shards of flesh and bone spat out in bloody projectiles in her nightmares.

Casper blinked once every minute until sheer exhaustion and melancholy made him fall asleep. Vasquez reacted the same way, falling asleep with her phone in her hand. It had been different for her this time too. There had been an opportunity to save Layla, and they had failed.

"How you doing?" Atticus asked Madison.

"Unequivocally shitty," she answered. "You?"

He gave a sorrowful yet supportive look. "Want to talk about it?"

"No, but I could use a good conversation."

"Never my strong suit, but I'll certainly try. What should we talk about?"

She hesitated.

"Ah, that's what's called a caesura, which means, you want to ask me about Allie," he said.

Madison knew that it was none of her business, but she was too tired, too depressed to care. If it would stop the train from speeding down those tracks and stop Layla Kuzick's gruesome transition from a beautiful blue-eyed brunette into bloody chunks of meat from replaying in her mind on loop, she had to ask.

"You want to know why it ended?" he asked.

Madison confirmed by not looking away. Atticus took a deep breath. He was a relic from an age when men didn't express their feelings nor show any perceived weakness. He'd been able to live with this caged inside. Not everyone could. Nobody should.

"We had reached a point where we didn't care to be secretive anymore. The lying, the half-truths… it was exhausting. People in the department had grown suspicious. We decided we'd come clean… to the department, to our friends, to our families. The plan was to tell our spouses and then meet at O'Hare. Go to Europe for a few weeks. Let the shock and gossip subside. I… told Mary… everything. My kids too. It was…" Emotion threatened to overwhelm him. His voice cracked. "It was the hardest thing I'd ever done. Then I grabbed my suitcase and drove to O'Hare."

Madison was an expert in reading pain, and what pain did Atticus's face show hidden within the wrinkles of his weathered flesh. Realization filled her eyes.

"She never showed…"

She didn't require confirmation, and Atticus couldn't give it. Every person has a defining moment in their life. Hers was the Man in the Mask. Atticus had his, standing at O'Hare with a suitcase in one hand and a plane ticket in the other. Different causes. Different pain. Same crucible.

"I'm sorry you chose wrong," Madison said.

"Who said I chose wrong?"

His words brought a smile to her face. Atticus Wallace had never stopped loving Alejandra Vasquez.

"Did she tell you why she didn't show?" Madison asked.

He shook his head. "No, I was too much of a coward to ask. Decided it didn't matter what she would say because, in the end, I still ended up standing in that airport. Alone."

"Did you try to make amends with your wife?"

"No. I had too much respect for her. She was no man's consolation prize."

Bad memories need to be buried. It takes time for them to decay. But eventually, decomposition creates fertile soil that allows new things to grow. Atticus and Madison had never buried theirs.

The following morning, Atticus forced himself to go for a walk. When you keep moving, keep busy, pain needs to work to keep up. His knees ached, the cold only amplifying it. His phone rang. Until recently, he didn't take his phone everywhere. Murder has a way of changing that. He glanced at the number—unknown. It was most likely a telemarketer who he could send on their way with a courteous piss-off.

"Is this Atticus Wallace?" the woman on the phone asked.

"It is…" He waited for this woman to talk about his car's extended warranty or our Lord and Savior Jesus Christ.

"This is Victoria Murphy."

Atticus adjusted the phone and sat on a bench overlooking the Buckingham Fountain. He thanked her for calling him back. "I'd like to ask you about Grey Moore."

"Are you a private investigator? Did his wife hire you?" she asked, panic in her voice.

"No, I'm not a P.I., and his wife didn't hire me."

He explained who he was and his association with the FBI.

"Did Grey do something?"

"That's what we're trying to find out."

A pause. "Okay…"

"When did you last speak with him?"

"A couple of weeks ago."

"Can you be exact?"

"Umm… September 25th or 26th. He called yesterday, but I missed it."

The weasel had tried to give her a heads-up.

"Did you speak with him on the phone or in person?" Atticus asked.

"In person."

"How long have you two been intimate?"

A long, drawn-out pause followed, one in which she was most likely contemplating hanging up on him.

"I know this is awkward, but I need to establish a timeline," Atticus said.

"About two years."

"This isn't going to get any more comfortable. But I have to ask—in the bedroom, is Moore domineering?"

The heat from her blushed cheeks could be felt through the phone.

"… He needs to be in control…"

"Aggressive?"

"He doesn't like to waste time, but he's never violent."

He asked her how the two had met. It'd been at a writer's workshop.

"Who approached who?"

"Neither of us, actually. We were introduced by a mutual friend, Rigel Rose. He's an English professor too."

Rigel Rose. Atticus had grown to hate the name and all the fanfare that came with it.

"He set you two up?" Atticus asked.

"No, it wasn't like that. I don't think he knows about us—"

"Moore stayed the night?"

"No, he leaves as soon as… as soon as we're done."

"Last question. You still have a lifeline if you need it."

Victoria laughed. "I'd rather the audience not know about this."

Atticus chuckled. "What color hair and eyes do you have?"

"Dark brown. Blue."

Dark hair and blue eyes. Vasquez had listened to Atticus recall his conversation with Victoria Murphy. Behind her desk was a map of the United States. Red pins signified where their unsub had killed: Turkey Creek, Tennessee; Atlanta, Georgia; New Orleans, Louisiana; Philadelphia, Pennsylvania; and Boston, Massachusetts. She examined the board. Moore had been in Knoxville, a few miles from Turkey Creek, where Andrea Collins had been killed. He'd also been in Atlanta when Kimberly Johnson was murdered. They spent the next two hours going over crime scene photos, victim profiles, maps, and photographs of the victims—alive and post-mortem. Atticus handed the Kimberly Johnson/Atlanta photos and documents to Vasquez and then opened the Jasmine Sanders/Philadelphia folder. The aerial photos around Hermit's Cave showed mostly wooded areas except for a small road called Hermit Lane, two buildings, the four-lane Henry Avenue, and the 18-hole Walnut Lane Golf Club. Then there was nothing but trees.

Atticus cursed. "How the hell did he get away?"

It was a frustration Vasquez shared. When you were reduced to wondering whether magic had been involved in a sudden disappearance, you knew you had shit to go on. Roadblocks had been set up, the woods searched by men and dogs, and a helicopter had come in later. The Philadelphia police had done everything right.

"Maybe he stayed in the woods until the search was called off," Vasquez said.

"Yeah, then he walked out and golfed 18 holes before going to Boston to kill Layla Kuzick," Atticus muttered.

He passed the folder to Vasquez, too frustrated to be of any use. They hypothesized what could have brought Moore to New Orleans, Philadelphia, and Boston. There could be distant family, but most of Moore's family lived in Wisconsin. Vasquez suggested the possibility of a convention or conference. It had been where he had met Victoria Murphy after all. It was the best idea either of them had had thus far, so they called Victoria Murphy and asked if she knew of any conferences Moore may have attended.

"I don't know about any conferences," Victoria answered.

Vasquez and Atticus shared disappointed looks. More dead ends.

"But I do know he gives lectures around the country. Talks about the origin and evolution of the English language. He had one at Georgia State the weekend he was here."

They thanked Victoria for her time and hung up. Then Vasquez called Maurice into her office and asked if he'd look into any speaking engagements Moore may have had at colleges in or around New Orleans, Philadelphia, and Boston. He was more than willing to, but he reminded her they had no charges or tickets of transportation linking him to any of those cities. When he left, Vasquez sighed in preemptive frustration at another possible dead end.

"I doubt Moore would take a Greyhound," she said.

Considering the way he dressed in his own home, Atticus agreed. He stood, trying to pass off his painful grimace as a sigh. He was damn sick of having his arm in a sling. He approached the map, studying the red pins and the connecting string.

"I think he flew," he said.

"With no ticket?"

Atticus nodded. "With no ticket."

Vasquez considered Atticus's theory. If true, it made everything possible and replaced their dead end with a paved highway.

"A private plane..." she said. "We could find out pretty quickly if he's got a license."

She searched the Pilot Records Database. The last name "Moore" produced a frustratingly large number of results. Adding the first name "Grey" thankfully resulted in less than ten, but when adding "Wisconsin," a big, fat *No Results Found* appeared on the screen.

"Then he hired someone to fly him," Atticus said, undiscouraged.

Vasquez left the task to Maurice while she and Atticus walked over to Ferrara Bakery for lunch. They both ordered sandwiches loaded with fatty Italian meats while continuing to discuss the case. The shoe prints found in Philadelphia had been a size 13. The treads showed the boot was made by Skechers, a make of boot sold everywhere.

"But here's the thing," Vasquez said, pausing to take a sip of her Coke Zero. "Judging by the indentations of the print, most of the pressure was put on the center of the shoe. If he was running, which we know he was, most of the impact should have been on the ball of his foot."

"Meaning 13 isn't his real shoe size? He padded it?" Atticus asked.

"Yup. His true shoe size is smaller."

Their unsub had pulled out all the stops, all the tricks. The bottom of a person's shoe picked up dirt, grime, and stones, all possible clues that could help trace where an unsub had been. People also left these items when they walked. But nothing had been found. The tread showed no wear, which meant the shoe was new. And knowing their unsub, they didn't doubt he bleached and scrubbed his boots before he put them on and periodically after.

"Lysol wipes maybe," Vasquez said.

Casper had been proven innocent, but his shoe size—14—only verified it. When they returned to Vasquez's office, Maurice rushed in like he was on a blitz.

"Grey Moore spoke at Tulane University," Maurice said.

"That's in…" Atticus replied, trailing off so Maurice would finish.

"New Orleans. Look at the date," Maurice said, handing a sheet of paper to Vasquez.

She read: "October 1st."

The same day(s) Ryla Abrams had been taken and killed, Moore had spoken at 6 p.m. for over an hour and a half. Those titillating tingles came back. Another check mark.

"Your smile tells me there's more," Vasquez said.

Maurice grinned. "Moore spoke at Temple University on October 8th, and last week, at MIT."

"Great work," Vasquez said.

Atticus offered his praise too. Then he turned toward Vasquez.

"Let's go visit *too many scarves*," Atticus said.

"Rose?"

"Yeah, the son of a bitch can tell us about Victoria Murphy and Moore. And he may have an idea as to where Moore may be speaking next."

Even in his walking boot, Rose had a strut to his gait. There was an air of superiority about him, but Atticus was too biased to say if it was intentional or not. Either way, Atticus didn't care for it. That said, he respected the way Rose presented himself.

Rose was digging through his leather satchel when Atticus called his name. He turned toward them, removing his glasses to give them a quick polish with a lint-free rag he kept in his pocket.

"Well, hello. I'm afraid I have a class in ten minutes," Rose said.

"We only need a few," Vasquez assured him.

Rose acknowledged with a smile and a nod. Vasquez asked if he knew a woman named Victoria Murphy.

"If you're referring to Victoria Murphy, an English professor at Georgia State University, then yes, I do," Rose answered.

"You introduced her and Grey Moore?" Atticus asked.

"Well, yes and no. Yes in the basic definition of the word. It wasn't something I had planned. We were at a conference. I had been talking with Victoria when Professor Moore saw me and came over. It would have been rude to not introduce them to each other."

"Are you aware the two have been carrying on a romantic relationship?" Vasquez asked.

Remorse filled his gray eyes. "I assumed Moore cheated, but with Victoria… I didn't know that."

Vasquez told him about Moore's flight to Knoxville, his rental car, and his unaccounted-for night in Atlanta. Then she asked Rose if he could guess what Moore's missing night may have entailed.

Rose couldn't—or wouldn't—even offer a speculation.

"Moore was in Atlanta the same day a woman named Kimberly Johnson died," Vasquez said.

"Died? I take it she didn't die peacefully in her sleep?" Rose asked.

Vasquez shook her head, studying his eyes and his mannerisms. "No, she did not."

"She was bludgeoned on the back of the head and tossed into the Chattahoochee," Atticus said bluntly.

Rose's eyes widened in shock. "Oh… that's horrible."

Atticus and Vasquez stayed silent, letting Rose go over what they'd told him. Then the realization hit him.

"Wait, you think Professor Moore is a suspect?"

"Yes, and whoever killed Kimberly Johnson is also responsible for the murders of four other women as well as the abduction and rape of Madison," Vasquez said.

Rose grimaced, and for the first time since they had known him, a curse word escaped his lips.

"Holy shit…" he took a few seconds to process his thoughts. "I can't see Moore murdering someone… The man has his faults, but…"

He looked like he'd either vomit or collapse.

"Do you know if Moore saw Madison shortly before her abduction?" Atticus asked.

"No, I don't. That's not something Moore would have told me," Rose said.

"What about you?" Vasquez asked.

"Did I see her that day?"

Vasquez nodded.

"Yes, we met for coffee and to talk about a book we'd been reading. It was a short get-together. I had a flight to catch."

"You never mentioned this before," Vasquez said.

"Your questions were directed at Professor Moore," Rose replied.

True as that may be, Atticus still glared at him. Rose should have mentioned it. Rose confirmed the coffee shop Madison had said they usually went to. Atticus asked if anyone around that day had stood out, gazed at Madison longer than is normal.

"I honestly don't remember. As far as anyone who looked at Madison longer than a quick glance, most likely. She got a lot of second looks."

"She had her bike?"

"Of course. Rode that everywhere."

He glanced at his watch. Female students strolled by, eyeing him up, blushing as they did. One of them stopped. She had dark-red hair and pale-blue eyes.

"Thanks for the book recommendation, Professor. It was incredible," she said.

"Any time, Julia. I'm glad you liked it. Now go write your own masterpiece," he said.

Julia blushed, then rushed off. Rose apologized to Atticus and Vasquez for the interruption.

"One more question," Atticus said. "When a professor gives a lecture or speaks at an event, who pays?"

"The university bringing in said professor," Rose answered. He said the costs are covered up front, and that housing is near campus, and you mostly never pay for meals.

"What about a rental car?" Vasquez asked.

"Usually your housing is within walking distance of wherever you're speaking. But I'm sure the university would provide transportation if needed."

Rose apologized for having to go, then hurried off.

"Do you know where Moore is speaking next?" Atticus called out.

Rose shook his head, apologizing again. Vasquez and Atticus watched him, his walk slightly awkward due to his walking boot.

"There's our answer as to why we have no transactions from Moore. No hotel. No restaurant. No flight. No record. No trace," Vasquez said.

Atticus kept his eyes on Rose as he nodded. "A ghost. A ghost free to wander among the living."

Bruce Springsteen played on the radio. There was no better driving music. An electronic voice interrupted Big Clarence's solo. "Incoming call from Maurice Gold."

Vasquez answered.

"Big news. Grey Moore has a pilot under his payroll—a man named Alexandros Alexi," came Maurice's deep voice through the car's speakers.

He gave Vasquez the address. She veered into the left-hand lane, away from their normal exit. Back to Brookfield. Vasquez turned down a narrow road that felt like one long, continuous S, the kind of road where you prayed no car was coming toward you, or else, one of you would have to go into the ditch. Siri told her to turn right. Vasquez did, turning onto a gravel road, every proud car owner's greatest bane. Any pebble could be the one that shoots into your car like a bullet. The road looked as though it would be swallowed up by the massive trees. But as the first branch plopped onto the hood of her car, a runway stretched before them.

Vasquez parked. They stepped out and approached the semi-domed hangar. Inside was a sleek, elegant single-engine plane, immaculate-white in color with a red horizontal lightning bolt emblazoned on one side. Atticus looked at the plane, then the runway, dumbfounded as to how that plane could take off on that short of a distance. He checked the bottom of the plane, expecting to see scratches from the forest canopy.

A man walked around the plane, an inspection board in his hand. He had dark olive skin, wavy black hair, and a hooked nose. He jotted on his clipboard, then slipped the pencil behind his ear. He didn't hear Vasquez approach and jumped when she spoke.

"How can I help you?" he asked in a Southern French accent.

Vasquez showed her badge and made the customary introductions, then asked, "Do you have a client named Grey Moore?"

"I do."

"Keep flight records?"

"Of course."

Vasquez asked to see them. Alexi walked to the back office and opened a file cabinet. He returned moments later with a leather-bound logbook.

"Where'd you fly Moore to last?" Atticus asked.

"Boston," Alexi answered.

Those shivers returned.

Vasquez asked Alexi where he had flown Moore starting in September through the present day. Atticus got the impression that Alexi took extra care to retain his French accent on certain words because it was an accent women swooned over. He opened the leather-bound logbook and flipped through it. Listed left to right was: Date, Aircraft type, Aircraft identification, and the Flight route. Vasquez scanned the log.

New Orleans. Philadelphia. Boston.

She gave the log to Atticus. He glanced at it, noticing the same cities.

"Grey Moore was a passenger on your flights to New Orleans, Philadelphia, and Boston?" Vasquez asked.

"*Oui.*"

The French should have irritated Atticus, but it didn't.

"You stay at the same hotel as Moore?" Atticus asked.

"*Oui.*"

"These trips... are you with Moore the whole time? Eat together? Sightsee?"

Alexi shook his head adamantly. "*Non, non, non.* I am to be invisible to Monsieur Moore. I am free to do whatever I like, but of course, I cannot consume *de l'alcool.*"

Did Alexi call Moore Monsieur because he was French or because Moore had requested it? The latter seemed entirely within the wheelhouse of a supremely arrogant prick like Moore.

"What about Mrs. Moore? She tag along?" Atticus asked.

"*Non,* only the Monsieur."

Atticus nodded to Vasquez. Her turn. No more slow pitch. The heater was coming.

"Have you ever seen Moore bring women into his hotel room?" she asked.

Her question flustered Alexi. His words were more French than English. He turned his hands over. "Look, I do not judge."

"Not looking for your judgement, just an answer."

He dropped his head. Rose's words came to her: *Moore had the power to get you a job or make sure you never got one.* The same was probably true about his pilot.

"This is between us. Moore won't know we spoke," Vasquez added.

"On occasion, I have seen women enter his room," Alexi finally answered.

Atticus nodded, encouraging him to say more. "These women, what do they look like? Tall? Short? Stocky? Slim? Blonde, brunette, redhead?"

"*Belle...* Beautiful. Slender figure, average height, I would say."

"And their hair color?" Vasquez asked.

"Black."

"What about their eyes? What color?"

He shook his head. "*Je ne sais pas.* I did not see them very close."

Vasquez drew her iPhone from her back pocket and opened the photo gallery. "I'm going to show you pictures of women. I need you to tell me if you've seen them with Moore. Look hard. This is extremely important. Look at how they appear in the picture and then imagine if their hair was styled differently, if it was shorter or longer, if they wore a hat or sunglasses, more makeup or less makeup. Okay?"

Alexi nodded. He took the offered phone, and picture by picture, he swiped through. Andrea Collins. Kimberly Johnson. Ryla Abrams. Jasmine Sanders. Layla Kuzick.

"I do not believe I have seen these exact women, but I cannot say for sure. But the women I did see looked like these women."

Vasquez took her phone back and stated they would need a copy of his log. He offered to do it, but Vasquez did it herself using Alexi's all-in-one printer in his office. Atticus asked where Alexi and Moore would be flying to next. Alexi answered Brunswick, Maine on Thursday.

Atticus walked the length of the plane, taking in its sleek design. "How long you been flying?"

"Twenty-three years."

"Take it you don't listen to Skynyrd?"

"Sorry, I do not know this name."

The joke was clearly missed.

"Famous band. Anyway, how far can you fly without refueling?"

"With this plane, four to six hours."

"What about miles? I suppose you use the metric system."

Alexi gave a guilty-as-charged smile and then shrugged, saying it all depended on altitude and speed. Atticus said he was looking for an average.

Alexi turned his head as he did quick mental calculations. "Under the right conditions, twenty-four hundred kilometers is possible."

Atticus turned to Vasquez, who had returned from making copies in Alexi's office. "What is that in miles?"

"Roughly fifteen hundred," she answered.

Alexi neither nodded nor shook his head. It appeared his knowledge of the imperial system was as extensive as Atticus's knowledge of the metric.

Atticus pointed to the plane. "And this is a…"

"Stratos 716X."

It was an impressive shape—a hybrid of a space shuttle and a great white shark. Atticus asked him how much it had cost. It was certainly a rude question, but when you're FBI—or rather, working with them—you can get away with it. The answer was three point five million American dollars—Alexi made sure to specify.

Atticus whistled at the astronomically high price. "What's a good starter plane? Something with less zeros."

Alexi tilted his head, thinking on it. Coming up with a reasonable cost for a plane when you yourself had dropped three and a half million on one wasn't an easy task.

"Cessna is a good plane."

Atticus repeated the word as if it brought him a better understanding of the aircraft. "How much runway do you need for takeoff? For a plane like the Cessna?"

As it seemed to be the case with everything, there was no straight answer. With so much math involved, you'd think there would be. Alexi said it was greatly dependent on the pilot. More experienced aviators could take off in roughly 160 meters. Atticus looked to Vasquez, the translator between two people speaking different languages.

"About 525 feet," she said.

They thanked Alexi for his time, then left the hangar and walked back to Vasquez's Challenger.

"Why are you so good at metric? Bureau force you to take a class?" Atticus asked.

"No, my high school did."

Atticus chuckled, granting her the win. "Yeah, well, this is America, not Canada."

"Yeah, yeah, yeah. Why so interested in planes? Going to buy one?"

"Yeah, you know me. Love flying. Plus, what else am I going to do with that three and a half million dollars under my couch cushions?"

Vasquez crept down the gravel road; her car roared, upset it was forced to drive at such an insultingly slow speed.

"All this plane talk makes me think of Buddy Holly. Put him on."

Ugh! Why do I put myself through this? Were four years not enough? While so many of my friends are done with school and have gotten jobs and, more importantly, paychecks, I went to grad school. With the mounds of debt I'm acquiring, I'll be a stressed-out doctor making what will essentially be a glorified minimum wage. I also wonder if I've done permanent damage to my back, carting around a backpack nearly tearing at the seams. My medical book doubles as a kettlebell. But for all my complaining, I can't deny how beautiful the campus is in the fall. I adore it—the way the scarlet and gold leaves float to the ground, the crisp chill invigorating me.

There are house parties on every block with wannabe men shouting the most unoriginal, unflattering pick-up lines. I turn toward the Breeze and drop my anchor of a backpack off at my place. I really should study tonight. But I need a break. I walk a mile. A band plays outside. I order a beer, some Oktoberfest special. I'm bound to know people here.

There's a man in a regal-looking suit. He's looking at me, smiling. He's good looking, reminding me of my ex-boyfriend but not enough for it to be weird. I spend a moment thinking about how he had cheated on me and how much of a stab to the gut that had been. The thought comes and goes, and I bring my attention back to the stranger. He's too old to be a student, unless he was some poor bastard who was still pursuing his career. Dear God, will I be one of those people? A career student? He looks too young to be a professor. Then I wonder, if he's too old to be a student and too young to be a professor, what the hell do wannabe professors do in those in-between years?

I finish my beer, making eye contact with him, so he knows where to find me. I see him finish his. I'm waiting in line. I know he's just stepped behind me. I've always enjoyed this moment. The moment before anything is said. The invisible allure between two strangers. Both bodies producing pheromones. Knowing the euphoria I feel is caused by a flood of dopamine, and the increased heart rate and sudden surge of heat from adrenaline and norepinephrine, doesn't diminish the magic. On the contrary, it only makes it more incredible. This strange man is literally causing a chemical reaction inside of me, and he hasn't even touched me.

"You ought to try the Pilsner," he says.

"How do you know what type of beer I like?" I ask with a flirtatious tone.

He breaks out in a smile, and what a smile it is.

"Because you still don't know what good beer is. You've spent the last five or six years drinking Busch, Hamms' Special Light, or Natty Light. At most, you've splurged with Bud Light."

"Please. I certainly don't drink Bud. I'm a Miller girl."

He smiles, his eyes reflecting the golden lights. "Tough day?" he asks.

"Why do you say that?"

"Your eyes are a bit bloodshot, and you don't strike me as high, so those red eyes are due to extreme fatigue. You've been up until one or two in the morning studying. You should be studying now, but you know you'll just reread the same line because you're falling asleep."

He couldn't be more right if he read my palm. But I'm not going to give him the victory that easy.

"And you're here to what? Keep me out? Show me a good time?" I ask.

He smiles again. "I'm optimistic I can. But I make no guarantees."

I'm up to order, but he steps beside me and orders for us, saying this one's on him. We grab our beers and move a bit away from the band, so we can hear each other speak. I ask him what brought him here. He tells me he's going to the game tomorrow.

"Planning on wearing that suit?" I tease.

He certainly would look better than some shirtless guy in overalls with his face and stomach painted. He says he's not much of a football fan, but he went to school here and his college buddies got him a ticket. They all plan on being completely inebriated before kickoff, but he's graduated into the two-day hangovers and plans on being sober as a pilot. The next few moments are spent sipping our beer, trying to find the next organic topic. To break the silence, he asks me if I'm going to the game.

I shake my head. "I do need to study. But it's so hard. Every time I hear a cheer, I have to look to the TV to see what happened. Then I usually get caught watching until the next commercial."

"Do you want to know a secret for the best place to study?"

"Is it your bedroom?"

I laugh. I'm totally expecting an immature pick-up line. But only because I've been conditioned to expect it. He's anything but immature. He's got the confidence of an actor from the 50's like Paul Newman or Marlon Brando. More of a Carey Grant than a James Dean.

"If you thought that was something I'd say, you wouldn't be standing here."

More chemical reactions explode inside me.

"I'll show it to you," he says. "You don't need Wi-Fi, do you? Because this is old school, B.C. stuff. I studied from a book. You know what that is? It's a collection of pages of written words used to inform the reader about a certain subject. You have to physically turn the page. No scrolling."

I playfully push him. "Jerk. Yes, I do know what a book is."

"It's a bit of a walk. I don't want to take you away from the music."

I try to pick up what song is being played. The band isn't bad by any means, but they're also playing here on a Friday night for a crowd of a hundred or so and not in an arena. It's safe to say they're playing one of the cover band staples—Bon Jovi, REO Speedwagon or Journey.

I have a choice to make. Say no to this good-looking, silver-tongued stranger, finish my beer, hear one more song and head home in hopes of cramming more curriculum into my cranium—a sensation I like to call "blitzing the brain."

Or I say yes. Say yes to the unknown, maybe yes to another great, unexpected experience.

He's waiting for a reply. There's no begging in his eyes. Not like the "men" I'm used to who would sacrifice a goat to get into my pants. He's so indifferent about it. I'm inclined to say yes just to prove to him I'm worthy of his time.

Our eyes meet. His melt me. My body is imploding.

"No, show me this secret point."

We finish our beer, then stroll away. Along the water's edge, the winds are cruel. I tighten my scarf, no longer a decorative accessory but a necessity. A bit of a walk was an understatement. My back was sore before we started this expedition. I'm tired—physically and mentally. I didn't think this would be a legitimate place. He fills the walk with questions. What am I studying, what do I hope to become? He's genuinely listening. It's not part of a seven-step program to getting laid. We merge onto a trail. My hands are painfully cold. I shiver. He takes my hands in his and softly blows on them, his warm breath reviving sensation back in my fingers (and other places). It's a moment that will dictate the night. If I pull away, he'll know I'm only here for a conversation. But let's get real—I didn't walk over a mile for a study hack.

I let him blow on my fingers. I'm curious. He's handsome, experienced. A real man. He's taken the effort to look his best, and God damn did he succeed! We continue on, and soon, emerge through.

"Wow, I've never been here at night before," I say.

"Beautiful, isn't it?"

"Absolutely."

"And you can take my word for it. The roar of the stadium is nothing more than a whisper from here."

"So, all you did here was study?"

I grab the front of his pea coat, staring into his eyes.

He shakes his head. "It's a thrill, isn't it? The forbiddenness of it? Vulnerable to the voyeur? At any moment, you could be caught. But that drives you as much as lust, doesn't it?"

Beneath this well-dressed, well-mannered man is a kinky satyromaniac. But everything he's said is true. More pheromones are released. His body is releasing his own, and they drive me wild.

He tucks my dark hair behind my ear, staring into my eyes, drifting off into their ocean of blue. He leans forward and kisses me. He cups my cheeks, his fingers tracing upward, then grabbing handfuls of my hair. Squeezing. Pulling. Then with a surprising strength, he lifts me off my feet.

I unbuckle his belt, unbutton his pants. He tugs my leggings down, then spins me around. My eyes dart to the entrance, fearful somebody will come through. But there's a part of me throbbing at the thought of being watched.

It's hard to believe I was freezing before, because right now, an atomic bomb is going off inside me as we have sex. When I try to stand, he puts his elbow against my spine just below the neck.

"Too rough," I say.

He ignores me.

"Hey, stop."

I repeat myself again and again, louder each time. My eyes dart to the trees again, now pleading somebody comes. Not because it makes it kinkier, more forbidden, but because I'm terrified.

Am I being raped?

How does that work when it starts off consensual and changes mid-act? Society calls it rape. But do I? He's rough, not violent. And it was mutual up until about ten seconds ago.

But suddenly, it becomes clear. It is rape. I try pushing him off. But this wolf has shed his sheep's clothing. He finishes, emitting his own howl of pleasure.

"I told you to stop," I say.

"You were giving into fear," he tells me.

That pisses me off. He doesn't get to decide what changed my mind. He doesn't know me. But something's changed in him. He's no longer charming. He's frightening. His eyes are wide and psychotic. I turn, ready to leave this picnic with the big bad wolf behind.

"Where do you think you're going?" he asks me.

"If we hurry back, we can catch the end of the band. Maybe get another lager," I add.

He doesn't answer. I turn around. He's inches behind me. I'm beyond startled. I turn to run, but he grabs my arm and drags me back. I scream. But Fall is cruel. The winds off the lake are resounding. The waves crash violently. I claw at his hand, but he drives his fist into my face. A throbbing pain erupts. Blood oozes out of my nose.

"You're never leaving here. You'll be sitting here watching the tides roll away forever."

He pulls a roll of duct tape from his breast pocket and tapes my hands. I start to kick, but he easily grabs my feet and tapes them together.

I scream again. He hushes me with a finger to his mouth, delicately brushing the hair from my eyes with his other hand. He duct tapes my mouth, wrapping it around my head. He brandishes a knife from his pocket.

He lifts my black leggings at the waist and carves a hole. Then he tears them off. He runs the blade along my leg, softly enough not to cut the skin. He slices my gray sweater next.

"Silly Sheep, time for a shear."

He's stripped me down to my bra and underwear. The wind is arctic, carrying a freezing mist. But it's fear that makes me shiver.

He takes a deep breath. "Our little dance has come to an end..."

He thrusts the blade into my stomach, away from my liver but deep. My eyes bulge. He rips the knife out, then strokes my hair.

"It's okay. It'll be over soon. It'll all be over soon."

Because Alexandros Alexi had said he'd be flying Grey Moore to Brunswick, Vasquez alerted both the Brunswick Police and Boston FBI (the closest branch to Brunswick). Though the investigation continued to incriminate Moore, it was too early to arrest him. For Moore had both money and contacts. He'd hire a fantastic defense lawyer, and he'd get off. Because what concrete proof did they truly have? Sure, Moore had been to each of the cities on the same exact dates as the murders, but the word "coincidental" would get used early and often. These weren't small towns in rural America. These were densely populated, tourist-destination cities.

It was time to wait, to be patient, something that went against how Atticus and Vasquez were wired. Waiting for the next chapter to come had been painful. The days were long, and the nights longer.

Atticus was asleep in his recliner when Madison next knocked on his door.

"I just got one," she said when he opened the door blearily.

What she said meant another woman had been abducted, perhaps raped and soon murdered, but Atticus looked elated at the news. To him, the game had entered the fourth quarter. The elevator seemed to know they were in a rush, so it stopped on each floor between Atticus's and Madison's. They had just gotten inside when Vasquez knocked.

"They're not in Brunswick," she said, hanging her coat on the back of a wooden chair. "Alexi didn't fly him anywhere."

Atticus had been hoping for a slow lob, but instead fate had side-armed a vicious curveball.

"What? Why the hell not?" he asked.

"He canceled. Didn't feel like he was getting paid what he deserved."

"Smug bastard," Atticus whispered, chewing the words like it was a gamey piece of meat.

Casper asked who *he* was. Atticus and Vasquez looked like two parents deciding on whether or not to tell their kids the truth about Santa Claus. Madison knew whatever it was, it involved her. If they were trying to protect her, the gesture was appreciated, but it was foolish. Protected was not something she'd felt in a long time.

"Tell me," Madison said, both a request and a plea.

Atticus looked her in the eyes. Her instinct was to look away, but to prove her point, she couldn't. Madison had to embrace the awkwardness and not submit to intimidation.

"Grey Moore was supposed to give a speech at Bowdoin College. We believe he may be the Man in the Mask," Atticus said.

The words took Madison's breath away as if someone had stuck a vacuum hose down her throat. She couldn't say it, but her eyes begged for an explanation. Vasquez explained everything—Moore's visit to his wife's family in Knoxville, his affair in Atlanta, his speaking engagements in New Orleans, Philadelphia, and Boston, and the private pilot on his payroll. Math was a subject Madison had never been drawn to, but even she could appreciate the odds that one person would be in five different cities on the same day(s) as five connected disappearances and murders. She didn't have a gut feeling one way or the other whether she truly thought, truly felt, that Moore was the Man in the Mask. The unrealistic expectation that she would simply know hadn't come. Madison had hoped—pleaded—that something in her gut, her heart, or some inner voice would provide a sudden, profound realization.

Atticus elaborated on what Vasquez had said, telling Madison about dark-haired, blue-eyed Victoria Murphy and Moore's propensity to invite women of that look into his hotel room. Madison listened, only speaking after she had thought over everything she'd been told.

"So then, there are two possible explanations," Madison said. "Either Professor Moore isn't the Man in the Mask, and this"—a quick nod at the chapter on the table in front of them—"could be any college campus in America." A pause. "Or Moore *is* the Man in the Mask, and if he is, that means he didn't fly."

Vasquez nodded, knowing where Madison was going. Alexi hadn't flown Moore, and Moore hadn't flown commercially. "Then it's a university within driving distance of Milwaukee."

Atticus asked if Madison had a map, but before he even finished asking, he realized hardly anyone under the age of seventy had physical maps. He hurried to his apartment and returned with a map of the U.S. that had been folded a thousand and four times. He sprawled it open across her table, using the salt and pepper shakers to secure it. Maurice had confirmed with Marquette University that Moore had been to all his classes this week. On Mondays, Wednesdays, and Fridays, he had classes at 9 and 3, each class scheduled for sixty minutes. On Tuesdays and Thursdays, he had class at 10 and 2:30. These were 90 minutes a piece.

"So if Moore did kidnap this woman, he did so between 3 p.m. and 9 a.m.," Vasquez said.

"So what, that's like 17, 18 hours for him to travel, find a dark-haired, blue-eyed woman matching Madison's build and age, stalk her, abduct her, and…" Casper didn't finish the last part, though he had gone further than he had wanted to.

"So, what do we say the cutoff is to travel? Five hours?" Atticus asked.

It was a tough question to answer. When you didn't have a plane on call, the distance you were willing to drive was much greater. But a round of nods signified it was a good starting point.

"Math quiz here. Grey Moore travels at 70 miles per hour for five hours. How many miles has he traveled?" Atticus asked.

Casper was first to answer. "350."

Atticus drew a compass from his back pocket, calling it a relic from the ancient world. He placed the sharp point on Milwaukee, adjusted and tweaked the compass, then traced a perfect circle. He tapped it with his finger. "That's our search area."

They all leaned forward for a better view. The circle encompassed all of Wisconsin, parts of eastern Minnesota, nearly a third of Illinois, and some of Indiana and Michigan. There was a fortuitous blessing in the fact that Lake Michigan was 118 miles wide and covered much of the search area. Unless there were any island universities they weren't aware of, a huge portion of the search grid could be dismissed.

"Okay, now, let's recap the clues we have," Madison said.

"It's a college town with a football team. They mention a game," Casper said.

"Okay, what colleges have football?" Vasquez asked.

Madison deferred to Atticus or Casper to answer. She did not watch football.

"Oh, man, that depends. We talking just D1? Or D2 and D3 as well?" Casper asked which only elicited further silence from Madison.

"Apart from Turkey Creek, which is close to Knoxville, all of these murders were in highly populated cities. I say we start with D1 or schools in large cities," Vasquez said.

Casper glanced at the map, then listed off colleges as his eyes darted from state to state. Minnesota. Wisconsin. Northwestern. Notre Dame.

"He mentions a lake. I think South Bend is too far away," Madison said.

"Minnesota? The land of 10,000 lakes," Atticus said.

Ten thousand. What a cruel number to even consider in this situation.

"Wisconsin is too far away from Lake Michigan," Vasquez said.

Madison couldn't help but think that the University of Wisconsin was located in a city bearing her name. A cold shiver ran across her body, and a strong desire to vomit crept up her throat.

"What if it's not Lake Michigan? I've been to Madison loads of times. They have a few lakes—Mendota, Monona, Waubesa," Madison said.

Atticus pointed to a line that had stood out to him. *"You'll be sitting here watching the tides roll away forever."*

"What is that?" Casper asked.

"You knew the bacon and beans song, but you don't know this? He's paraphrasing Otis Redding," Atticus said, annoyed.

"Well, my apologies. I didn't know you were getting royalties on it."

"But that song's about San Francisco," Vasquez said, unsure of where Atticus was going with it. He knew his classics and certainly would know this.

"Yes, it is. But Otis Redding died in a plane crash over Lake Monona."

That feeling of disgust again consumed Madison, making her want to shower and shower and shower. The answer was so obvious. A sickening love letter.

"It's Madison," she said.

Vasquez looked at her, nodding with the realization that she was right. Everything that had happened had been because of, and about, her. Why would it be anywhere else? Was it truly Professor Moore who had thrust her into this rat race? All she wanted to do was ponder why, but there was no time for that now.

"Where in Madison?" Vasquez asked.

"Breeze is capitalized," Madison said.

Atticus found the word in the chapter and nodded. "Right. *I turn toward the Breeze.* So, it could be a street name."

"Camp Randall is on *Breese* Terrace. Different spelling," Madison said.

"Let's go with that. Is the final location on *Breese*?" Vasquez asked.

Madison shook her head. Her first thought had been Memorial Union Terrace, known for its colored sunflower-shaped chairs, beer, and music, located on the shore of Lake Mendota. It was a starting point Vasquez ran with. Madison, though large in its own right, was no Atlanta, New Orleans, Philadelphia, or Boston in sheer size and scope. At this point, they could afford to be vague.

Madison put on an extra layer of clothing, considering how last time she had ended up in a freezing river. They piled into Vasquez's Challenger, a challenging task for tall, lanky Casper. Police escorted them to O'Hare. This time, it wasn't a plane but a helicopter waiting for them.

Atticus mumbled under his breath, "You gotta be shitting me."

Buckled in, they waited for the pilot.

"You ever been in one of these?" Casper yelled over the deafening rotors.

"Yeah, last time I was, I got shot down over the Mekong Delta," Atticus said.

Casper stared at him, dumbfounded. "Well... let's hope that doesn't happen."

Chuf. Chuf. Chuf. Chuf. Chuf. The whirling blades sliced the still, cold night. It was an entirely different sensation than flying in an airplane. In a plane, you sped forward and up. In a helicopter, it was up and up and up. Both scary and exhilarating, it offered a view of the Chicago skyline that had never looked more magnificent. The metropolitan skyline soon vanished, replaced with rural Illinois and Wisconsin. With little to no lights, it felt like flying through space, and what few lights they came upon below glittered like stars. A short time later, the Wisconsin State Capitol building shone like a luminescent pearl. The helicopter descended, coming to a rest on a grassy field outside the city. Like in Atticus's tour in Vietnam, it was touch-and-go. Helicopter down, they jumped off, and the chopper was back in the air. Police cars lined the street ahead. A burly man with a thick, Groucho Marx–looking mustache greeted them. His name was Sheriff Lauer.

"We've had the campuses reach out to their students to check in with any female students with dark hair and blue eyes," he said.

"Did you limit the search to medical students?" Vasquez asked.

"No, as you requested. In case he lied about what she was studying."

Vasquez was confident only in that the woman would have dark hair and blue eyes, so she limited the search criteria to only that. The last thing she wanted on her conscience was a young woman's death because she had narrowed a search based on false leads.

"We've got six colleges in the city, and it's still early for college kids. On Friday and Saturday nights, a lot of 'em crash someplace else. We've had a shit ton and some change worth of false alarms," Sheriff Lauer said.

He led them to his Ford Interceptor. Traffic was bumper to bumper and belonged in Chicago or New York. Atticus commented on exactly that. Sheriff Lauer explained that Ohio State was in town—a matchup of two top-5 teams. Lauer took Observatory Drive two miles to Memorial Union Terrace without stopping, thanks to the flashing police lights, steady hands on the horn, and timely tapping of the brake. The Terrace was packed. People laughed, told stories, or listened to the live band all while warming their bodies with cold beer. In another life, Madison would have been one of the girls near the band, belting out and dancing.

"We have to find trees," Casper told her.

Madison loaded Google Maps on her phone, then switched from map to satellite view and scanned the area, hoping something jumped out at her. Finding nothing, she was forced to zoom out. Increasing the search area was the last thing she wanted to do.

But there it was, protruding into the water in the shape of an elephant's trunk.

Secret point… leave this picnic… behind…

"Picnic Point," Madison unknowingly whispered out loud.

"Lots of trees there," Sheriff Lauer said with a shrug. Translation: "It's the best we've got."

They climbed back into the Interceptor, and Sheriff Lauer drove back onto Observatory Drive, speeding past and around other drivers. They pulled into a gravel lot, the path ahead wide enough for only emergency four-wheelers to drive down, but they weren't going to stand around and wait for one. More police cars parked beside them, the gravel crunching under the weight of their wheels.

Guided by flashlights, they ventured down the path. It didn't take long for the trees to cover the sky, giving Madison the feeling of venturing deeper and deeper into a dark cave. Claustrophobia was a fear she didn't have before, but she had it now. The path was nearly three miles long. If she was right, at the end of that three miles, they'd find a woman—a woman still nameless, her absence still undiscovered. The waves of Lake Mendota crashed against the shore, the sound wild and foreboding.

Sheriff Lauer sped up to catch up to Madison and the others. "UW campus security received a call from a concerned roommate. Said her roommate has a big med exam coming up and told her she'd be studying all weekend. Hasn't seen her since yesterday afternoon. She's not the partying type either."

"What's her hair and eye color?" Atticus asked.

Lauer consulted with the voice on the other end of the radio. "Dark hair. Blue eyes. Name's Harper Evans."

Hearing the woman's name brought a new gravity to the situation. She'd moved from being a statistic to being an actual person. No longer a Caucasian female in her early twenties with blue eyes and dark hair, she was Harper Evans, a young woman in med school trying to achieve her dream and struggling with the suffocating weight of balancing school and life.

It seemed the trail would never end, something Madison both appreciated and abhorred—it prolonged what they'd find. The classic case of Schrodinger's cat. Right now, Harper Evans was alive, and as long as the trail continued, she would stay that way. Then, a clearing emerged. A circular mosaic of stones lay ahead, a fire pit in the center and stone blocks surrounding it. It was hardly the time for it, but Madison couldn't help but gawk at the night sky. Its beauty never failed to awe. A bright, pulsating dot of light caught her eye. What she had taken to be Mars or Jupiter flashed and moved in the sky. Must be a plane of some sort. The people on-board heading home or to a vacation destination, oblivious to what was transpiring beneath them. Madison longed to be anywhere but where she now stood. But she needed to think of Harper. Harper would trade places with her in a heartbeat.

They called her name repeatedly, but only the crashing waves answered. For Harper's sake, Madison hoped her roommate was wrong. That Harper had given up on studying all night and gone out for drinks, met someone, and went home with them, or that she had taken an impromptu trip home to see her family. But crippling self-doubt afflicted Madison again. What *if* Harper Evans wasn't their missing woman? What if their missing woman was in a different city? Madison sat on the stone, trying to ignore that treacherous voice susurrating slurs from its forked tongue. Had she been narcissistic in adding up the clues to equal Madison? Her shoulders folded inward. She rubbed her temples. Casper sat beside her, and much to her appreciation, he didn't try to give any pep talk. He massaged her shoulder, then rejoined the search. Madison took a deep breath and opened her eyes, staring at the ground in front of her feet. The flashlight hung limp in her hand, its light revealing a faint smear of blood. She focused the flashlight, following the bloody trail. It continued beyond the flashlight's reach. She rose and followed it toward the northernmost point. The mist hit her face like sleet, the winds howled, and the waves crashed with ship-splitting strength. Madison swung her flashlight left to right, then right to left.

Nothing.

Nothing.

More nothing.

Then a hand rose weakly. Madison gasped, focusing her trembling hand to hold the flashlight steady. Harper Evans lay naked, her hands clutching a bleeding wound on her abdomen. So weak she didn't even react to the light pointed directly into her eyes. Madison ran back toward the others, shouting her discovery. Then she sprinted back to Harper and knelt beside her. Harper's skin was corpse-white, her lips a frostbitten-blue. Goosebumps covered every square inch of skin. Madison softly lifted Harper's hand away from her wound to examine it. Duct tape covered the wound. Bits of adhesive residue clung to her cheeks. Harper had peeled the tape off and sealed the wound the best she could, buying herself precious time. The tape around her legs was varnished with blood. She had tried to free the tape until her strength left her. Casper draped his coat over her, and Vasquez squeezed Harper's hand, asking her to do the same so she could gauge her strength. An emergency four-wheeler sped toward them. Two medics jumped off and examined Harper. They worked on her briefly before sharing solemn looks. They lifted Harper onto a stretcher and covered her with a silver-foil emergency blanket. She was motionless.

Harper Evans was dead.

But as the medics carried her, her eyes opened, fixing themselves on Madison.

Harper Evans was alive.

Harper Evans had done everything she could to survive. Sealing her wound with duct tape had granted her invaluable time. She had been rushed to the University of Wisconsin Hospital, where she was now unconscious but in stable though critical condition—too early to celebrate a victory.

Casper and Madison waited at the hospital. All the victims of the Man in the Mask had looked like Madison, but none more so than Harper. Since Madison and Casper weren't family, or even friends, they had to sit in the waiting room. Nor would the doctor tell them anything, so Madison wasn't sure what she hoped to accomplish. At the minimum, it gave her something to do, and there was plenty of hallway to pace down.

The sliding entrance door opened and two couples rushed in. They checked in with the front desk, and Madison was able to pick up the name, "Harper Evans." Harper's father was tall with a balding head of blond hair. Her mother had dark-blonde hair dyed to keep its color. Where had Harper gotten her dark hair? Maybe she had dyed it. Madison shuddered at the thought of something so innocuous leading to her nearly being murdered. Had Harper chosen red, she would be in her apartment asleep at her desk, head resting on her Med book. Harper's biological parents followed a staff member through the forbidden doors; meanwhile, Harper's stepparents, sat across from Madison and Casper. Madison smiled politely, the sort you gave a stranger in a waiting room.

Madison wanted Harper to pull through for her own sake, but there was also the answer to the urgent, life-or-death mystery of who the Man in the Mask was that she could potentially provide. If the chapter was honest about their interaction, Harper would have the answer. Was it Moore? That's what their evidence and theory suggested. A single confirmation from Harper would seal Moore's arrest.

Casper strolled to the cafeteria and bought a couple of Red Bulls. Madison was exhausted, but she wouldn't be able to sleep unless her body literally shut down.

Harper's stepfather was in his fifties but old enough that he talked into his cell phone like it was a walkie-talkie.

"Tough to tell right now. Shock, you know? I think she feels awful for how things ended," he said.

Indecipherable chatter came in reply from the other end.

"I know. Harper's strong. Bull-headed like her mom."

"And dad," Harper's stepmom chimed in.

"We'll keep you posted," the stepfather said.

He pocketed his phone, and Madison instantly became aware that she had been staring. She diverted her gaze to the information pamphlets strewn on the table in front of her.

The Red Bull had increased her anxiousness, and she paced the waiting room like a tiger that had decided today was the day it would eat the zookeeper. Casper watched an eighties movie on his phone with no sound. Harper's stepparents stared blankly into space, taking periodical sips from their Styrofoam cups of coffee.

Then, the doors leading to the ICU opened, and Harper's parents rushed out.

Atticus and Vasquez had returned to Chicago, waiting for Madison to inform them if Harper had woken or if she wouldn't ever wake. Vasquez cleared emails on her phone. Atticus drank a beer as he stared out of his apartment window.

"I've got those photos Vince Propelli sent over," she said.

She reached into her bag and withdrew her tablet. Atticus sat beside her, and Vasquez swiped through the photos. Dozens and dozens of people clad in costumes, hoisting red Solo cups. Beer pong. A counter full of liquor bottles. Vince Propelli was dressed up as a 1920's gangster. As with photo dumps, not all were worthy of scrapbooks. Many were blurry, appearing as if ghosts had been caught midflight.

"Wait, wait, go back," Atticus said.

Vasquez swiped left. Her eyes saw it too. A man dressed in a Kwik Trip polo shirt, a joint in his mouth, and a red Solo cup in his hand. Westin Pierce at the same party Madison would be arriving at.

"Keep going to see—" Atticus started.

"—If he was there after Madison had left," Vasquez finished.

She called Maurice and told him to get to his computer.

"Okay, ready," he said after a few moments.

"I sent photos from the party on the night Madison was abducted. You'll see Westin Pierce on photo number twenty-one," Vasquez said.

"I see him," Maurice confirmed.

"Can you analyze and tell me if you see him in any other photos and if you can decipher a timeline?"

"I'm on it."

The frenetic sound of clicking keys followed.

"Remember when photos had time stamps on 'em?" Atticus asked Vasquez. What a gift those had been.

"Photos 34, 47, 61, and 93," Maurice said.

There were 107 photos in total. Westin Pierce was in just five of them.

Vasquez swiped to each of them. The program had found Pierce in a Where's Waldo-type image.

"Any photos of Madison *and* Pierce?" Vasquez asked.

A pause.

"Number 34," Maurice answered.

Vasquez swiped to it. A blurry image of Madison and Jade with Propelli sandwiched in between. There were even blurrier faces in the background.

"One of these people in the background is Pierce?" Atticus asked.

"Sending an enhanced image," Maurice said.

Vasquez opened the JPEG. The photo had been cleaned up, worthy of being framed in Madison's apartment. Westin Pierce loomed in the background, standing sideways, mid-drink, but his eyes were fixed on Madison.

"Son of a bitch..." Atticus said.

"Maurice, the last photo of Pierce... can you determine a time?" Vasquez asked.

"I'm looking," he said.

A forever pause. The photo showed four people playing beer pong and the spectators cheering them on. Toward the left-hand side, people danced. Westin Pierce stood in the back. In the lower right-hand corner, a girl dressed up as a Marvel character looked at her phone. Finally, the attachment bearing the photo and possible time stamp came through.

The time it showed would vindicate or incriminate. Would Westin Pierce be the name Harper Evans would mutter if she woke? Someone they hadn't truly considered?

The visible puffs of breath leaving her mouth looked as if Madison had joined those smoking outside. She needed the fresh air and that cold comfort it provided. Harper's mom was among those smoking.

"Are you Madison?" she asked.

Madison nodded, bridging the gap between them but leaving enough distance that the distressed mother's cigarette smoke didn't swarm her.

"The police told us what happened… You saved my daughter. Thank you," she said.

Madison deferred with a meek shake of her head. Harper's mom introduced herself as Paige.

"Can I ask how she's doing?" Madison asked.

"Still out. Doctor said it was the cleanest stab you can hope for," Paige said.

"I'm glad. Did you talk to her before this happened? Did she give any clue of whom she'd met?"

Paige took a final puff and then burst into a gravelly laugh. "We haven't spoken in three years."

"Oh, I'm sorry," Madison said, almost adding *I didn't know*, but of course, she didn't know.

"Because of you, I'll be able to rectify that," Paige said.

She drew her phone to swipe through her photo gallery, then held it up for Madison to see.

"Last photo of us," she said.

Madison couldn't even recognize the girl as Harper. She and Paige were standing in front of a college building, both beaming. Paige looked years younger and a few pounds lighter, but her transformation was nothing compared to Harper's. Her hair was pixie cut and sandy blonde.

"I wouldn't have recognized her," Madison said.

This poor girl wouldn't be in a hospital bed right now if she had kept her hair short and blonde. But because she had grown it out and dyed it, she had been raped and attacked and left for dead.

"Part of our falling out," Paige said, then explained. "I thought, uh, hell, might as well be honest, I *accused* her of being someone she's not. I had the idea she was becoming who other people thought she should be and not remaining true to herself. After her freshman year, she transferred here and gave up her dream."

Giving up on dreams is a cruel but common enough part of adulthood. Sometimes, we realize the person we thought we wanted to be wouldn't happen. A mother should always instill belief, no matter how farfetched. And it sounded like Paige had done that to a fault.

"Is it alright if I speak with her when she wakes up?" Madison asked.

Paige put a hand on Madison's shoulder. "Sweetheart, we'll be taking you to dinner when this is over. Of course you can."

"I'm sorry…"

"Sorry? You had nothing to do with this."

"The police told you about the chapter, about what's been happening?"

"They did. Honey, you can't honestly think you're to blame. As the mother, I know none of this is your fault. None of this happened because of you. Now get inside before you catch a cold."

She smiled. Madison forced one too. But it was a mother's forgiveness she had desperately needed for all the others she had failed.

The image resolution and quality was impeccable. The enhanced and zoomed-in photo of the cell phone captured in photograph number 93 showed the phone had four bars of service, WIFI was in use, and that the girl might want to think of finding a charger. But, most importantly, it displayed the time.

1:37 A.M.

That meant Westin Pierce was still at the party when Madison was in that shack. And judging by the enhanced photos of the guy himself, he was epically high. He very well might not have mentioned his presence at the party simply because he didn't remember ever being there.

"I've got debit transactions galore showing Pierce in Wisconsin during these murders," Maurice added.

Vasquez thanked him and hung up. She and Atticus took a moment to collect their thoughts.

"I don't know, Allie," Atticus said, frustrated.

"About Pierce?" she asked.

Atticus shook his head. "All this. Moore's been in every city. He's a dirt bag, but do you think he's capable of something like this? What was done to these women?"

Vasquez sighed. "I couldn't imagine a single human being capable of committing such acts," she said.

Truer words had never been spoken.

"What's on your mind, Wallace?" she asked.

"Does the evidence lead to Moore, or have we been led to Moore?"

"Who are you thinking?"

"Rigel Rose."

"Rose? Alibis rule him out. He was in Wyoming when Madison was abducted, and in Colorado when Jasmine Sanders was killed."

"I know. It's just…"

"He's arrogant?"

He shrugged. "So is Moore."

Vasquez stole a sip of his beer, then dialed Madison and asked how she was. Madison told her about her conversation with Harper's mom and the update on Harper she had provided. Casper listened in.

"That's great news," Vasquez said.

"Yeah… so, what's up?" Madison asked.

"Grey Moore spoke at the University of Wisconsin-Madison tonight. Well, technically last night," Atticus said, conferring with his watch.

"That puts him in every city on the day of the murders," Vasquez added.

They'd given Madison the formula and waited for her to do the math. To utter the name Grey Moore. But Madison was swimming through too many thoughts, feeling too many emotions to answer. The Man in the Mask had been a myth, more beast than man. She often wondered if there even was a face beneath the mask, like a creature from a Stephen King novel. She couldn't help but think of the *Scooby Doo* cartoon. She felt as stupid as Shaggy, thinking it was an actual ghost only to find out it was a loser draped in a white bedsheet. Putting a mortal's face—Grey Moore's face—was a letdown of epic proportions. Perhaps she just couldn't fathom how much a single human being could hold power over her.

"He can write; he's got a history of inappropriate behavior with women, including you," Atticus said.

"And he's got a type. Dark hair. Blue eyes," Vasquez said.

"What about the pilot?" Casper asked. "If he flew Moore, that means he was in every single city too."

"He was still living in France when Madison was taken. He was in Brookfield when Andrea Collins was murdered. And since the canceled trip to

Brunswick, Alexi flew to San Francisco. There are hotel, credit, and debit card transactions, security camera footage as well," Vasquez said.

Should Madison know if it was Moore? Should some revelation have opened her mind now that each puzzle piece was all laid out before her?

"… I don't know…"

"She's awake."

Words that elicited a frenzy of emotion in Harper's family, and in Madison too. Awake. Alive. Among the living.

The Man in the Mask had failed.

Madison called Atticus right away, and he and Vasquez rushed to the hospital. Their travel distance allowed Harper time to embrace her family. Time for her mom to try to make amends.

Vasquez and Atticus hurried toward Casper and Madison, each with a nervousness and excitement Madison hadn't seen in them before. In a way, it felt like Harper had died and they were communicating with her ghost.

Who murdered you, Harper?

They waited in the lobby, all of them now pacing nervously. The doctors had to meet with Harper and her family. And awake didn't necessarily mean coherent. She'd be overwhelmed with sleep from the pain meds and her body's plea for rest.

Paige stepped out, her face moistened with smeared tears, but she wore a huge smile.

"She's in the clear!" she nearly yelled.

They all smiled. Madison introduced Vasquez and Atticus.

"May we talk to her?" Vasquez asked.

"Of course," Paige answered.

Casper stated he would stay in the lobby and search for "sustenance." Madison's stomach flipped and rolled as they walked down the hallway. It felt like she had been putting a diamond painting together for years. Most of it was complete, but she still couldn't see what it was of. But now she would.

They stopped outside the closed door. A nurse checked on Harper. Atticus rubbed his forehead, and Madison grinded her cheeks, but Vasquez did nothing to betray her apprehension.

The door cracked open, and a middle-aged nurse squeezed past with a smile. They stepped inside. Harper had regained the color in her skin. Her dark hair was disheveled and her lips, chapped. She wore a pair of giant glasses that covered half her face, the sort no one would have dared to wear when Madison was growing up. Vasquez made the introductions, then asked Harper how she was doing.

"Sore," she said, her voice scratchy.

"I imagine. Are you up for a few questions?" Vasquez asked.

Harper nodded yes to Vasquez, but her eyes were trained on Madison. Did she notice the similarities between the two of them? Madison stared back, blue eyes locked onto blue eyes. Only Harper's weren't blue. They were dark brown. She must have worn contacts. Or had Madison projected her own image onto Harper?

"Do you know the man who attacked you?" Vasquez asked.

Harper shook her head.

"You met at the Terrace?" Atticus asked.

"No. I was out for a walk. He grabbed me from behind."

The chapter had lied. Were all the others similarly false? Had he courted none of them? Did he attack them all stealthily from behind? Madison's heart plummeted. If he had attacked her from behind, he must have worn the mask. Harper wasn't alive because they'd saved her. She was alive because it was a cruel joke to him. She'd be able to offer the same description Madison had been able to: flesh-colored mask, black gloves, and black clothing.

This would never end.

"Did he wear a mask?" Vasquez asked.

Please say no. Please say no.

"Yeah," Harper said.

Vasquez held up her tablet, showing a photo. "Was this the mask?"

300

Harper nodded, both excited and scared.

"Were you able to see any markings, tattoos, scars, jewelry, anything that could help identity him?" Vasquez asked.

Harper shook her head. "He wore that mask, but he briefly took it off. I saw his face... at least, I think I did."

Madison's heart started the long climb back into her chest, fueled by hope.

"I'm going to show you a couple of photographs, let me know if you recognize the man who attacked you," Vasquez said.

Harper nodded as she took a sip from her water. Vasquez removed two printed photographs. Madison saw the pictures before they were shown to Harper. The first photograph was one Madison had expected to see: Grey Moore. He appeared slightly older than Madison had remembered him. The second photograph was one she had not expected to see. Atticus nodded his confirmation to Vasquez. It was a photo of a person from Madison's past: Rigel Rose. Madison looked at Atticus, confused.

Vasquez held both photographs up toward Harper. "Is one of these pictures of the man who attacked you?"

Harper's eyes filled with fear as if the man was standing at the foot of the bed. She nodded. A trembling hand pointed to the picture on the left. Who was it? Rose or Moore? Madison stepped forward and turned to look at whom Harper had just pointed.

It would soon be over. It all could be put behind her. A nail in the coffin, the ending of a chapter, whatever cliché you wanted to use. And Madison would use them all. The night *it* happened played on the hospital room walls as if from a movie projector—the Halloween party, the bike ride, *London Bridge*, the shack, the Man in the Mask on top of her, fondling her, caressing her, and raping her. Then the anticlimactic—but quietly torturous—years that followed.

Andrea Collins, Kimberly Johnson, Ryla Abrams, Jasmine Sanders, and Layla Kuzick appeared like a casting call at the end credits. But as Madison stood there, she truly felt like she should be counted among the dead. Sure, her lungs breathed, and her heart beat. But the person she had been before was gone. She may feel differently tomorrow, but at that moment in time, she didn't feel elated or relieved, only disappointed. She had clung to the unrealistic hope that when she found out who had done this to her, the woman she'd been would come back. That one day, all the anxiety, worry, and pain would simply go away. That fragile hope had survived off the barest necessities in the recesses of her mind. Emaciated and feeble, yet alive. But now, it finally had died. She was Madison Monroe in name only. She closed her eyes, battling the tears forming in them. She'd spent hundreds of nights, maybe a thousand, crying herself to sleep. She had put a stop to that. Even if she had to cheat and splash water on her face to disguise the tears, Madison wouldn't let them fall. But a lone tear escaped its prison and trickled down her cheek like a slow-moving river.

Harper had pointed to the photo on the left. Then pointed to it again when Vasquez held it less than a foot away. Her answer didn't change.

Grey Moore.

Vasquez and Atticus excused themselves, leaving Harper and Madison alone.

"You okay?" Harper asked.

Madison wiped the lone tear, passing it off as an itch.

"Yeah…"

Harper continued to study Madison.

"So, what's so special about you?" she asked.

"Nothing." Madison laughed. She explained what had happened to her in the most generic way she could. Harper stated she was sorry and looked guilty for her blunt question.

"I bet you wish you'd kept your hair blonde," Madison said.

Harper looked confused.

"Your mom showed me a picture," Madison added.

Harper rolled her eyes. "Of course she did."

"You wear blue contacts?"

Harper nodded. "I get bored. I should have kept my green ones."

Some people thrive with change. Madison wasn't among those, and though she feared it, she appreciated the carefree lifestyle and all the unexpected adventures change could bring. She wished Harper well and stepped out into the lobby, ready to get the hell out of the hospital, but Harper's mom waved her over.

"You're leaving?" she asked.

"Yes, I have to get home."

"The man who attacked you and Harper, he'll go away for the rest of his life."

Madison nodded.

"I hope Harper finds herself again," Paige said. "Something like this, it changes you. Something happened to her before; nothing like this, but something she changed herself for. I tried changing for her father. You become a different person, trying to become what they want you to be. But be you… oh, heck, I'm sorry, I'm a mumbling wreck."

Madison shook her head, dismissing her apology. "It was nice to meet you."

She turned and left before Paige could wrap her in a hug. Paige called out, "We owe you a dinner, honey!"

Madison, Casper, Atticus, and Vasquez flew back to Chicago, and once home, that sleep which had avoided Madison was swiftly captured. Maurice had called Vasquez and stated that the badge stationed outside Rose's house said that Rose never left his house last night. He also had photographs of Moore lecturing at the University of Wisconsin.

Professor Grey Moore was the Man in the Mask.

Atticus popped off the bottle cap and tossed it, Rick Barry style, into the garbage. He handed the Miller High Life to Vasquez. They both sipped, knowing the reason that had brought them back together was a beer away from being over. Two proud people, fearful of vulnerability. A large part of Atticus's heart had never made it out of O'Hare. It was left there like unclaimed baggage. But the reservoir of beer kept being drained, and soon, there'd be none left to cower behind.

"You going to be able to adjust back to civilian life?" Vasquez asked.

"Never did. What about you? Retirement in your near future?" Atticus asked.

Vasquez hesitated. "I don't know. Sometimes, it feels like the job is the only thing I have left."

Atticus had that feeling every day, but he didn't even have the job anymore. The last month had given his life meaning again. The job had been an addiction for forty-four years, and retirement was his sobriety. The last month had been his fall off the wagon. How great it had felt. His kids, Carter and Jeanette, had no use for him; the high of the job was all he had.

Vasquez bit her lip, forcing herself to look into his eyes. "Atticus... I—"

"Don't. You don't have to say anything," he said, waving it away.

Out of sight, out of mind. He needed to keep it that way.

"Yes, I do. It's something I've known since December 14th, 1996. Something I've known every time I looked over in bed and saw David lying there... I chose wrong, Atticus."

He took a swig of his Miller, hoping the alcohol would numb everything. He pressed his tongue against his bottom lip to stop it from trembling.

"I know I hurt you… hurt you in a way you should never forgive me for, and I'm not asking you to."

He raised his hand, stretching it out to stop her from speaking anymore. "Allie." He looked deep into her olive-green eyes. "I wouldn't change a thing. Even if I knew how it'd end. I'd do it all over…"

They'd shared their own fleeting moment of Camelot. A mist filled her eyes. Atticus wiped them with a brush of his thumb. He wouldn't let those tears fall for him. She breathed deeply, taking in his Brut cologne. Atticus had thought the Peterson boy's murder was the defining moment of his life, and in many ways, it was. But mostly, it had been the defining moment of his professional career. Holding Vasquez in a silent embrace, a slow waltz to silent music, they both understood there was life before December 14th, 1996, and life after.

… You can never turn back…

Atticus stopped by Madison's apartment around noon to tell her Grey Moore would be arrested—Vasquez, along with the Milwaukee Police, was on her way there. Madison poured a glass of whiskey for him and for herself.

"I... I don't know what I'm feeling. Does that make sense?" Madison asked, her hands wrapped around the ice-cold tumbler.

"Of course it does," Atticus said.

"I was raised Catholic, went to Catholic grade school and Catholic high school. I prayed before meals, before bed. Prayed I remember what I studied for, prayed I'd run my best in track... but I had never prayed like I did in that cabin. I pleaded to God. When I made it out onto that road, I saw this twinkling, flashing light. I thought it was God watching over me. And I believed that every day since. In Madison, I saw that same light again and thought God was there too. But it was just a plane. And I realized that's what I had seen that night. You like to think your life being spared is part of a great plan, but it was just... luck. Maybe Andrea Collins or Kimberly Johnson or Ryla Abrams or Jasmine Sanders or Layla Kuzick saw a similar light and thought it was God watching over them. I can't imagine the heartbreak of believing that and it turning out to be nothing more than a fucking airplane."

Atticus leaned forward. "It's time to let it go, Madison. You need not carry the burden of guilt for being alive. Give up the dead. You live. Fully. Freely. Live with reckless abandon. You go and do everything you've ever wanted. You bury the Man in the Mask in an unmarked grave and never return to it."

A more comfortable person would have thanked him for everything, but it was an intimacy that made her uncomfortable. But he knew. They were two people who could read eyes, and hers were a long missive of gratitude. She couldn't imagine getting through the last month without him and Vasquez. Maybe she couldn't imagine it because she wouldn't have.

"What about you? Should I send Jehovah's Witnesses to your door late at night?" Madison teased.

"Sure, I keep my Smith & Wesson loaded," he said.

Atticus gazed at her rows of books. She read anything and everything, old and new.

"You edit any of these?" he asked.

"Some on the top shelf," she replied, pointing to the books.

Atticus read the titles on their spine:

On Rolling Tides
The Ferryman
The Second Death of Madalyn Marie
Last Mission
The Flickering Light
The Death of Antebellum
Sunken at Sea: A Lusitania Novel

Atticus asked if there was one she thought he'd like. *The Flickering Light* was the story of a group of American soldiers during World War II who survive a torpedo attack and make it to an island in the Pacific, except the island is overrun with Japanese. He said he would like that. Madison pulled it from the shelf and placed it in his hands.

"Critique story and character all you want but keep any missing words or missed spelling errors to yourself," she said.

Atticus laughed. "Fine. But misused commas is where I draw the line."

"I wouldn't expect anything else."

Madison moseyed to the kitchen to prepare lunch—turkey and chicken deli meat sandwiches—leaving Atticus to freely look through her book collection. He flipped through *The Flickering Light*, glancing at the front matter of the book, then the book's entirety to see how much blank space was left on most pages, and lastly, checked the final page count. He said he'd been sold on the book as soon as Madison had said World War II, but the only issue was if he could stay awake.

And then, for a reason he couldn't explain, Atticus's eyes shot back to the bookshelf with the gaze of an Alzheimer victim. Something on the bookshelf was of noticeable importance. He just didn't know what and why. Was it because a book he glanced at was something he had read decades ago? A Hemingway or Salinger novel? Or a film or television adaptation he'd seen? He scanned shelf by shelf, hoping the book's spine would return the thought to him. He was certain it was on the top shelf. Looking. Looking. Then, eyes darting back, he grabbed a book from the shelf. The memory came back the moment he saw the cover. A worried feeling seized his stomach. He flipped the book open and scanned the first few pages. In the acknowledgement section, it read:

To my editor, Madison Monroe, for knowing when I've said too much and knowing when I had more to say.

"Hmm," Atticus said.

"What?" Madison asked.

He thought on it, then sighed. "Ah, nothin'. I have to go."

"Where?"

"Tell Rigel Rose about Moore."

"Why did you suspect him? I saw the look you gave Vasquez. You thought Harper was going to identify him."

Atticus sighed. "I'm a skeptical person. Moore fit perfectly. It made a lot of sense, which is why it didn't." He finished his whiskey with a satisfying sigh and left.

How would Grey Moore react? Vasquez chewed on that question on the drive over. Would he take off running like Lawrence Floyd had? Would he resist? Get violent? She wouldn't kid herself; she hoped he'd take off running so he could get clotheslined, maybe even tasered. But that would mean Moore implicitly confessing he was guilty, and Vasquez knew he would never do that. Moore was too arrogant. It'd only be after his lawyer reviewed the case against him and recommended a plea deal that he'd come clean. Her money was on Moore spewing threats. *Do you know who I am? I will end you! You won't get a job working night security!*

Getting an arrest warrant had been easy. The simple mathematical odds of someone being in all six cities, having a history with Madison, being a skilled writer, and most of all, Harper Evan's testimony had been enough. But now, Vasquez wanted more evidence to wrap this case up. His computer could be a gold mine—written chapters, drafts in Microsoft Word, browsing history, emails, and purchases. Serial killers collected trophies from their victims, mementos to remember not the victim but the ultimate rush and pleasure their death had brought them.

Two of Milwaukee's finest, Officer Jackson Weathers and Officer Samantha Edwards, escorted Vasquez. Polar opposites of one another, Weathers was well over six feet tall, a combination of fat and muscle, and he was dark skinned. Edwards was barely over five feet tall, even with a good pair of heels; she was slender and had alabaster-white complexion. The way Officer Weathers instinctively stepped in front of Officer Edwards after she had rung the doorbell made Vasquez think the two had become more than partners. It was the same way Atticus had always stepped in front of her. But now wasn't the time for nostalgia. She forced the thought away from her mind.

Mrs. Moore answered the door. Her Botox-altered face was incapable of showing shock, but her eyes certainly made up for it. Officer Weathers explained why they were there and didn't wait for permission to enter.

"What the hell is going on?" Grey Moore shouted from inside his study.

He came out like a flash fire, bumping his wife out of the way. Officer Edwards listed the charges and then read him his Miranda rights.

Moore shouted over her. "What the hell are you talking about!"

Officer Weathers took out his cuffs and ordered Moore to put his hands behind his back.

"This is bullshit! I've never heard of any of those women!"

Moore's eyes radiated hate. Officer Weathers gave Moore one last chance to willingly submit himself to the arrest. Moore continued shouting until Officer Edwards snatched his wrist and wrenched it behind his back with surprising strength. She kneed the back of his leg, shoving him face-first onto his couch. The cushions temporarily muffled his yells. The handcuffs were locked into place, tighter than needed because of Moore's squirming. They dug into the bony protrusion in his wrists.

Moore's wife looked on in horror. Officer Weathers heaved Moore to his feet and prodded him like cattle toward the door.

"You're having me arrested because of some imagined slight against a former student!" Moore shouted, then spewed vile swear words.

"Keep talking, Moore. This is great stuff for a jury," Vasquez said.

Moore turned to his wife as he was dragged to the front door, screaming at her to call their lawyer. His shouting continued, only drowned out when he was placed in the backseat of the police car and the door slammed shut.

Vasquez turned to Moore's wife. "We have a court order granting us the right to search the premise. I need you to step outside."

More police arrived to search Moore's home. Considering it was nearly double the size of most homes, extra help had been called in. They searched drawers, closets, cupboards, bedrooms, bathrooms, and basement. In Moore's study, they confiscated his desktop PC and his laptop. Vasquez grabbed her phone, debating on whether to call Atticus. She decided against it. She stepped outside, leaving the search to the local police. She let the chilly gusts of wind cool her as she leaned against her car, feeling confident more evidence would be found. She was ashamed the thought even crossed her mind, but a feeling of regret had taken hold. A part of her wished it wasn't Moore, only because that would mean the case was not over, that her time with Atticus was not over. But it was. The reason for seeing Atticus may be gone, but the need hadn't been satiated. It couldn't be satiated.

Vasquez had never believed great things happen unexpectedly. Great things happen because you worked for them. Days, months, even years. You put in the grind. Luck was a word frequented by the lazy and uninspired. But maybe something great could develop without planning, without work. Without scrutinizing the consequences, she drew her cell phone from her left back-pocket, googled a number, and dialed.

"Two tickets, please."

Madison tried not to think of Atticus's rushed exit, so naturally, she thought of nothing but. Had he been waiting all month to rid himself of her? She'd come to consider Atticus her Gandalf. But maybe she wasn't Frodo Baggins, but Gollum, a pathetic creature to take pity on but to be kept at a distance nonetheless.

Casper stopped by shortly after 5:30. Madison was halfway through a comforting pint of Ben & Jerry's.

"Cheating on me? With two men no less?" Casper asked.

"Every Friday and Saturday. Sorry."

Casper scrolled through Amazon Prime, Netflix, and HBO Max, watching previews of movies that sounded promising. After each preview, he turned to her to gauge her interest. But she was too preoccupied with scrolling Instagram on his phone. Jade had an unrestricted account, so Madison was able to view her photos. She stared at one of them. Both Jade and Madison were smiling; a gleam in their eyes showed a decent amount of alcohol had been drunk. Madison hadn't smiled like that in a long time. Kimberly Johnson's pictures had shown her physical degradation. Would Madison's have shown the same decay? A decay caused not by drugs but by depression and anxiety.

The date of the post read October 26, 2013, mere days before the Madison in the photo had died. And so had purity and innocence. Every smile she gave now was forced and masked pain, and her acting only continued to worsen. Casper caught the picture. Knowing she was lost in reverence for the past, he granted her privacy by looking through her fridge and cupboards for a snack. Madison saved the photo and sent it to her cell phone. Then she searched for Harper Evans. No Facebook account, but she did have an Instagram account. Madison could only see a few photographs. A recent photo startled her.

Harper looked so much like her. So drastically different than how she had looked in the photo of her and her mom. That photo was here on Instagram too, one of her oldest posts in fact. The caption read: *Chi St, to the start of something great!*

Chi St. Chicago State.

Casper munched on some blackberries as he studied her books. He certainly wasn't an avid reader, but he had grown up with *Harry Potter* and *Lord of the Rings*. He tallied the number of books on the shelves he'd read and kept the single-digit number to himself.

"I'll have to hand out library cards," she said, to which he cast a quizzical look. "Atticus borrowed one earlier."

"What'd he borrow? *Ten Reasons Not to Shoot the Stranger at the Door?*" he joked.

Madison chuckled. "Do you have a favorite book?"

"Are you borrowing my tried-and-true method of getting to know someone?"

"Yes, it works quite well."

"I'm supposed to answer *The Great Gatsby* or *A Farewell to Arms*. Maybe Homer's *Iliad*."

She smirked. "You answer truthfully… unless your answer is *Spot Goes to the Farm*."

"Of course not, give me a shred of credit here." A beat. "*Spot Goes to the Zoo* was way better."

Another laugh. His ability to make her laugh even when her thoughts went dark never grew old. It was like a flashlight in the dark.

He finally settled on *Harry Potter*. Madison pressed him for his favorite out of the seven. He accused her of being one of those people who couldn't appreciate how the books were all part of one, collective story. She didn't back down, and he did eventually concede, answering *Goblet of Fire*. It was her personal favorite too. She told him about her first edition *Harry Potter and the*

Philosopher's Stone. Casper nerded out, his twelve-year-old self reclaiming his thirty-one-year-old body. *"Philosopher's?* As in the British version?"

Madison nodded, beaming with pride.

"Damn, I may have to steal that one. Have any other first edition or rare books I can steal?"

She told him about her copy of *The Outsiders* signed by S. E. Hinton and a signed copy of her favorite Stephen King book, 11/22/63. Casper sifted through her Shakespeare collection and asked if Shakespeare had signed any of his plays.

"That would be worth millions, but I don't think any signed copy exists. His signature may be in a few museums."

"You read his stuff?"

Madison smirked at his choice of the word *stuff.* "I do."

Casper scanned the collection. The well-known titles were there—*Romeo and Juliet, Hamlet, Macbeth*—but he grabbed the lesser-known *Antony and Cleopatra* from the shelf.

"That was purchased at a gift shop where he was born," she said.

"No shit! I had no idea he was born at a gift shop."

She laughed and shook her head at his lame but effective dad joke. "A friend had gone with a class to England, and he got me that."

Casper opened the book like Robert Langdon would examine scrolls from the Council of Nicaea. Written in the first page was an inscription and signature. *"To My Fair Lady,"* he read. But then said, "Can't make out the signature though."

He continued flipping through, reading a few of the stereotypically Shakespearean lines containing words like *thou* and *shall* and *thy.*

"God, I can't believe this is the same language as what we speak—"

"What did you say?" No smile or smirk on Madison's face now, curdling worry instantly invading her stomach again.

"I said it's hard to believe it's—"

"No, before that."

"I don't know what... oh, you mean the inscription?"

She nodded, swallowing spit thick as corn syrup. Casper flipped back to the first page.

"To My Fair Lady."

A cold shiver slithered across her body. She asked to see the book. Casper handed it to her, a confused look on his face in response to her serious demeanor. She read the words, then flipped through the book. Near the end was a bookmark—a receipt folded into the letter M. A feeling of utter doom had descended into her stomach, so volatile she thought she would vomit. She unfolded the receipt. It was for the book. Printed on it was the total of £21.17, the gift shop name, and the book's title. But it was the date she couldn't take her eyes off.

26/10/13.

His old reliable Chevy had never let Atticus down before, and it didn't now. He drove north and parked alongside an immaculate home in the affluent North Shore. He walked the stepping-stone laden path and knocked on the door. It opened.

"Mr. Wallace," Rose greeted him.

"Can I come in?" Atticus asked.

Rose waved him inside. The calming smell of pumpkin pie, apple cider, and crisp leaves hung in the air. Flames crackled in the fireplace. The design of the house suggested Craftsman, but inside, it looked like a home from the early 1900s. In the back was an expansive bookshelf stretching from floor to ceiling an impressive twelve feet, equipped with a sliding ladder. There was no television in the living room, seemingly making him one of only a dozen in America since 1950 to not have one.

"So, Mr. Wallace, what can I do for you?" Rose asked.

Atticus, hands behind his back, surveyed the bookshelf. It was truly an impressive collection. "Dewey Decimal System?"

Rose smirked. "No, alphabetical order by title. Fiction in the first two shelves, non-fiction in the last two."

Atticus browsed the fiction shelves, keeping a mental list. "Read them all?"

"I have."

Atticus whistled. Normally, he'd call bullshit. For some people, books were no different than rugs or canvas art—they were merely decoration. But this time, he believed it.

"You know what's odd?" Atticus asked. He drew a book and handed it to Rose.

Rose read the title. "*The Death of Antebellum.*"

"Remember this one? White Southern belle. Black slave. Forbidden love," Atticus said.

"Vaguely. But as you can see, I read a lot," Rose said with a guilty shrug.

"Of course, of course. But open that up. This one hooked me. Before even the first chapter. I'm talking the Acknowledgements section."

Rose flipped through to the aforementioned section.

"To my editor, Madison Monroe," Atticus recited.

"Okay…?" Rose said, holding onto the word.

"You had this book on your desk. You said you didn't know Madison was an editor," Atticus said.

"Well, Mr. Wallace, I can't say that I make a habit of reading the front matter of books. Besides, I wouldn't know if the Madison Monroe mentioned in this book is the same Madison Monroe that I knew," Rose said.

"Certainly. But you know what's peculiar is that you have every book she's edited."

"Yet, still just a constellation of stars among a galaxy."

Atticus nodded in concession, a playful smirk on his face.

"So, is that why you're here?" Rose asked. "To scrutinize my library? See if I have any gay erotica?"

Atticus chuckled. "No. On Friday, Madison received a chapter about an abducted woman. We deciphered the city as Madison, Wisconsin. The abducted girl was Harper Evans. We found her, bleeding out, freezing."

"I'm sorry to hear that. But you mustn't blame yourself for her death," Rose said.

"She's not dead. She's recovering nicely. I spoke with her. And guess what? She saw the man who attacked her."

Rose listened, offering Atticus a seat on the leather couch.

"Do you know who I thought she'd say was her abductor?" Atticus asked.

Rose shook his head.

"You."

"Me? Why?"

"We'll get to that."

"Seeing as there are no police vehicles storming down the street, this Harper Evans did not say my name," Rose concluded.

"No, she did not."

"Are you at liberty to say whose name she revealed?"

Atticus both shook his head and nodded with a shrug, meaning he wasn't sure but didn't care. "Grey Moore."

Rose's studious face changed to confusion. "Moore?"

"Arrested today."

Rose removed his glasses and wiped them with a lint-free rag. "I'll reiterate what I said on my campus: I struggle to believe he's capable of something like this."

"Nothing surprises me anymore. In 1994, an 11-year-old boy beat his grandmother to death with a rolling pin because she burnt the chocolate chip cookies. After that…" Atticus shrugged.

Rose grimaced at hearing the story.

"Say, anything to drink? Alcoholic preferably?" Atticus asked.

"Of course, how rude of me not to offer." Rose stood. The right of the fireplace led to a study, and to the left lay the kitchen. When Rose walked into the kitchen, Atticus drew his Smith & Wesson revolver. He grabbed a decorative couch pillow, set it on his lap, and covered the revolver.

My Fair Lady.

My Fair Lady.

Ugh! Where the hell had she heard that before? Think. Think! Something old? From the 1950s or 60s? Marilyn Monroe or Jane Russell? No, Audrey Hepburn. She starred in a movie called *My Fair Lady*. But though it was relatively old, Madison knew the true answer was much older. She paced the length of her apartment, trying to remember where she knew that phrase. She had the ability to recall like a stenographer conversations where she had said something stupid. She could remember movie release dates, chapter titles in books, and useless Snapple-cap trivia, but no, when there was something important, Madison couldn't bring the damn thing to mind. 10-26-13. The date reminded her of 11/22/63, the date of John Kennedy's assassination. She reexamined the conspiracies surrounding it, then thought of Stephen King's book. *Ugh! Stop!*

"What's wrong?" Casper asked.

Madison stopped pacing and faced him. "My fair lady. Have you heard of that saying?"

"Yeah, it's like an English saying or something," Casper said.

She let out a frustrated "ugh." She stared at the receipt, hoping something would jump out at her. Thoughts sprouted like weeds, and most of them were equally as useless and unwanted.

Shakespeare. London. October 26th, 2013. My fair lady.

Something connected them and was vital to what had happened to her. My fair lady... Was it from a Beatles' song? Or the Rolling Stones'? Or one of the dozens of other bands from the British Invasion?

Madison listed off British names, places, and items. The Queen. Big Ben. Tower Bridge. Tower of London. The London Eye. The Spice Girls, for heaven's sake!

Tower Bridge…

Bridge…

London…

A decade of haze lifted, the fog dissipating to reveal a clarity she had so achingly longed for.

"You figured it out?" Casper asked.

Madison met his stare, her eyes large and filled with fear, sadness, and pain.

"London Bridge is falling down, falling down, falling down, my fair lady."

Paper and plastics bags and crates containing Moore's clothes, laptop, PC, hairbrush, toothbrush, and shoes were carted and carried out of Moore's home. Vasquez had inspected a few pairs of his shoes—he wore a size 11.5. Forensics dusted his Audi S5 for fingerprints. As for tokens or mementos taken from the victims, Vasquez hadn't expected to find them in a dresser drawer. Moore was too smart for that. They'd be hidden in the garage in a box labeled "Old Clothes" or in the attic next to a decorative Santa Claus or under a broken floorboard concealed by a chateau rug.

Vasquez entered Moore's study. His desk was mahogany, an unfinished glass of lemonade rested on a coaster. Hand-crafted bookshelves lined the eastern wall, picture frames on the wall across it. A quick glance showed the only photo of Moore's wife and children was a measly 4 x 6 pushed back toward the right-hand corner of his desk. The entire wall was devoted to photos of Moore or frames of his degrees and certifications. There were photos of him giving commencement speeches and lectures, and class photos of international trips he'd taken with his students. These were in chronological order. The first was from 1999. Moore and his students lined along the Great Wall of China—an English teacher with an English class going to China under the ludicrous guise of learning the history of the English language. How had the university approved such an audacious expense? The next photo was dated 2003 from Mexico City; 2006's class had gone to Rome; 2009 to Alaska; 2010 to Paris; 2011 to Madrid; 2012 to Vienna; 2013 to London; 2014 to Berlin; and back to Paris in 2015. Moore had traveled the world on a college's (and by definition, its students') dime.

Vasquez paused, not moving on to see where Moore had gone in 2016 and beyond. She turned back to the early 2010s, scanning the photo of his trip to

London. She snatched the frame from the wall. Moore and his students stood in front of the Palace of Westminster and Big Ben. Moore was front and center. There was no month or day listed on the gold plaque with the year. But given the fact the students wore sweaters, sweatshirts, light jackets, and some hats, gloves, and scarves, it had to be autumn. The photo troubled Vasquez more than a photo of an American class in London should.

Casper scratched his head. "Okay, run this by me again?"

"Rigel Rose. He gave me that book," Madison said.

"Okay." But his face was still warped in confusion. "But, what about… okay, just from the top," he said.

She could hardly blame him for not keeping up. She'd spat out words faster than her tongue could form them.

"He was in London days before I was taken. *London Bridge is falling down.* He must have heard it there. That's why he whistled that song. I don't think he even knows he did it," she said.

"But… you said it was Moore's class, so he was there too. He could have heard that tune and whistled it," Casper said.

"Maybe everything fits with Moore because it's supposed to."

"But, Madison—"

"Hang on. I was most likely drugged, right?"

Casper nodded, thinking. "You met Rose for coffee."

"Right! I never saw Moore that day."

His excitement quickly vanished. "But that was hours before your party?"

"Anyone who knows me knows I can't drink things hot. I didn't drink my coffee until my bike ride to the party."

Casper nodded, hopping onto her train of thought. "And he'd know that. You guys got coffee all the time. He teased you about it."

Rose knew her routines and had gambled on it. Precisely like what he had written in the Layla Kuzick chapter: *Routines are dangerous. Predictable. To the predator, routine removes risk, improves the chances of success.*

"But Harper Evans identified Moore. That's checkmate. No matter how many holes we poke," Casper said.

"I know. Which means she lied."

Harper Evans. The girl who lived and the girl who lied. The first part was unequivocally true. The second part needed to be proven.

"Look at this picture," Madison said, showing Casper the same photo Harper's mom had shown her.

"Yeah, drastic makeover," he said.

"Now, look at this one." She scrolled to the photo where Harper's resemblance to her was most striking.

"Yeah, she looks a lot like you there. I mean the makeup, hair style."

On her phone, she then showed him the picture of her and Jade that she had saved. Madison and Harper's outfits might not be twins but they were definitely close.

"Yeah, kind of eerie. Actually, totally creepy. Almost like she was trying to be you. But wearing a similar top doesn't prove anything."

"She went to Chicago State."

Casper's face furrowed in thought. "That's where Rose teaches…"

She nodded. "Harper's mom thought Harper started changing who she was for something. What if it wasn't for something but *someone*? And what if that someone was Rose?"

Casper ran his hand through his hair. "So that would mean she was willing to get stabbed for him… to stab herself. Rose didn't leave his house when Harper was taken."

"A stab wound the doctor said was the cleanest you could hope for."

Casper scratched his head, then dropped his hands, visibly uneasy. "This is a serious allegation, Madison. How would we prove it?"

"We can't. She will."

Madison dialed Harper's mom. Her greeting was loud and happy and one Madison had to interrupt. "I'm sorry. Can I have Harper's number?"

"Sure. Is everything alright?"

Madison hesitated, not long but long enough for a mother to catch the unspoken tension. "Madison?"

"Forgive me, but I have to ask. You told me you thought Harper had changed herself for something…"

"Yes, I did…" Her confusion was clearly evident.

"Do you think she could have changed herself for someone?"

Paige paused. "That's what I suspected."

"Did she ever mention anybody?"

"No, Harper was very secretive."

"She went to Chicago State before transferring to Wisconsin?"

"Yes."

Madison could tell her questions were making Paige nervous. She didn't have long before Paige asked her what was going on.

"Did she take any English classes?"

"Yes. She wanted to be a writer... Madison, honey, please tell me what's on your mind."

Lie or tell the truth? She still hadn't secured Harper's number. If she told the truth, she may not get it. But lying was wrong. Paige may see through it. Maybe if Madison told the truth, Paige would reward her.

"I don't have an easy way to ask this, so I'll just say it."

"Please do…"

"Do you think Harper could have lied about who she said attacked her?"

A silence filled the call, long enough that Madison checked to see if the call had ended.

"Why would you ask that?" Paige finally responded, delivered with a tone Madison didn't know how to take—somewhat angry, nervous, worried, and inquisitive.

"Because I believe the man who attacked me was Rigel Rose, an English professor at Chicago State University. Is it possible Harper grew her hair out, dyed it dark, and wore blue contacts because he suggested it? And that she listened to those suggestions to gain his attention? Become who he wanted her to be?"

The sound of restrained crying filled the speaker. "Harper isn't the girl I knew. I don't know her anymore..."

"Do you think it's possible?" Madison asked again.

"... Yes..."

The heartbreak in the delivery was painful to hear—the acknowledgement that a mother no longer knew her own daughter. It took two tries to understand the number Paige gave. Madison thanked her, then FaceTimed the number. She set the phone up against the napkin holder. The image connected. Harper was lying in her hospital bed, no longer wearing those oversized glasses but those strikingly blue contacts.

"Hello?" she said.

"Harper, it's Madison Monroe."

"Hi... what's going on?"

Madison studied her, grinding away at the inside of her cheek as she did. "Harper, I know the truth."

"Truth? What truth?"

"I know you lied to the police."

Under the table, Madison squeezed Casper's hand. He squeezed it back.

Harper scowled at her phone. "Fuck you. I didn't lie."

"I know you were seeing Rigel Rose."

Harper only briefly showed surprise. "Screw you. How dare you accuse me of lying! I was stabbed!"

Casper squeezed Madison's hand. It was the support she needed to keep speaking.

"Harper, I don't know what he's told you. If I'm right, Rigel was the man who ran me off the road and kept me prisoner in a shack and raped me… repeatedly. It also means he's killed at least five women."

Harper's face revealed glimpses of emotions. Anger. Confusion. Worry. "I'm hanging up. Quit harassing me, bitch."

Madison had to switch tactics. Appealing to her good nature was not going to work. Rose's claws had sunk too deep into her. She was a crazy woman in love with a psychotic man. In the hospital, Harper had asked Madison what made her so special. The question took on a different meaning. She now realized what Harper had really been asking was what made her so special that Rigel Rose had become fixated on her. Had chosen *her*.

"He'll always love me more," Madison said.

Her words cut Harper like the knife had. Worse because she wasn't prepared for it. She didn't get to decide where that knife struck. Those fake blue eyes reflected morose pain.

"You're a fake," Madison continued. "Your hair color. Your contacts. You changed yourself to look that way because he told you to. You can see why, can't you? He wanted you to look like *me*. You realized that when you saw me in the hospital. He wanted *you* to be *me*."

Harper looked away, biting her trembling lip and holding back her pained rage.

Madison continued on. "You lied. Grey Moore didn't attack you. You knew where to get stabbed to avoid serious harm but leave enough blood for it to be theatrical. You did it yourself."

Even with what Harper had done, Madison wanted to reach through the screen and hug her. The depths Harper had descended. The self-mutilation she had committed.

Tears welled in Harper's eyes. Angry tears. "Grey Moore attacked me."

Madison smiled painfully. She'd never fallen so absurdly in love with someone that it made her psychotic. Rose was a Svengali. Harper had been a sweet, troubled girl begging for acceptance. Someone who was still molding into who she would be. But instead, she forfeited that creation to someone who molded her into what he wanted her to be. Tragic. But Harper had made her choice.

"It was Grey Moore! Grey Moore!" Harper bawled.

She repeated it, crying harder and harder, not like a religious mantra she believed but something she was told to believe. Madison ended the call. Harper had chosen her sword to die on.

Casper looked ill. "She lied…" he said, horrified. "But I don't understand. Rose was in Wyoming when you were abducted…"

"If she lied, he found a way to lie too."

The feeling Madison had prayed for when she found out who was behind the mask had come. An epiphanous relief, a clarity she'd never had. And with that realization and clarity came the broad band of human emotion. Anxiety and sadness were at the forefront; they had staying power, sitting like two immovable boulders. Anger came and went like hurricanes or earthquakes, and like those natural disasters, its effects lasted far longer than the actual disaster.

Why was a question she had asked a million times since *it* had happened. All these emotions were familiar to her. What wasn't familiar was the feeling of betrayal and the ancillary emotions that came with it. The possibility of the Man in the Mask being a stranger, though still horrible, was easily preferred over the alternative. It meant a man had selected a young woman based solely on her desirable looks. It was more animalistic and less personal in that regard. But knowing it'd been Rose—someone who knew her, had been her friend—meant there was more to it than just lecherous lust. It meant he had chosen her, not like some predator scouting for the weak and sick among the herd, but because of who she was—the person, not just the body.

"Madison, we have to tell Vasquez."

Atticus held out the whiskey tumbler as his host poured from the bottle of Jack Daniel's. Rose took a sip of his drink, but Atticus kept his in his hand, listening to the ice crack.

"So, Moore's wife could offer no alibi?" Rose asked.

Atticus explained about Moore's pilot, Alexandros Alexi, and his speaking engagements at universities in or around the same cities the murders had taken place in, and that his wife wasn't with him.

Rose leaned back in his recliner, legs crossed, gently swirling the glass of whiskey in his hand.

"I wish we'd gotten him sooner," Atticus said.

"You can't blame yourself. You got him before he could hurt any more women."

Atticus nodded, his glass of whiskey in his left hand. "You know we almost got the son of a bitch in Philadelphia? He got lucky. He ran right into my path. I thought I had 'em, but the bastard dove out of the way."

"This is… where you were hit by the car?"

"Hatchback," Atticus corrected. "I get shot, hit by the hatchback—not car—and the unsub sprints into the woods and disappears. Pulled a Goddamn Harry Houdini. How in the hell did he do that? Before I passed out, lying on the road, flat on my back, bleeding, rain pelting my face, I saw a bright, twinkling light. Something I didn't think anything of. Not until I spoke with Madison. She mentioned that when she escaped, she saw a bright, flashing light. And yesterday, in Wisconsin, she saw a similar flashing light. You know what it was? A plane."

"For a second, I thought you were going to say UFO. I was going to get my aluminum hat." Rose smiled before taking a cat-like sip of his whiskey, barely enough to wet his tongue.

"In my line of work, coincidences cannot be taken at face value."

Rose took another sip of his whiskey and conceded Atticus's point with a nod.

"I spoke with Moore's pilot," Atticus said, his right hand securely wrapped around his Smith & Wesson under the pillow.

Rose sighed after his sip of whiskey. Atticus didn't trust it and wouldn't drink it.

Atticus continued, thirsty and sober. "My knowledge of planes is limited to ones that crashed with famous musicians on board."

A coy smile spread on the lips of the man across him.

"Moore's pilot shared his knowledge thankfully."

Atticus told him what Alexi had said about the required takeoff space.

"Anyways, back to Philadelphia," Atticus said. "Across Henry Avenue—where I was hit by the hatchback—is a golf course. Walnut Lane. There's a veil of trees separating Henry Avenue and the 15th hole. Hole 15 is a par 4. Over 340 yards. That's over a 1,000 feet."

"I think I know what you're getting at. Moore flew a plane off a golf course. Don't you think a golfer would have complained there was a plane on the fairway?" Rose asked with a derisive laugh.

Atticus smirked, refraining from throwing a strong right hook. "Right. They would have had the course been open. It was closed. Called the owner. They had fertilized the course and closed for winter. No staff. No golfers."

"What about tire marks?" Rose asked.

Atticus waved a finger, smiling. "Great question. They used machines to spread the fertilizer. Big honkin' things. Nobody second guessed there being tire marks."

Rose conceded the possibility. "So Moore—"

"No, not Moore."

"His pilot?"

"No, because whoever killed these women is the same piece of shit who raped Madison. Alexi was still living in France in 2013."

Rose took a sip of his whiskey. His body language showed he had grown tired of this.

"You," Atticus finally said.

"How kind. So, I assume you ran my name to see if I have a pilot's license."

"I did."

"So, you know I do not."

Atticus nodded, but it wasn't a nod of submission. He was simply agreeing to the fact.

"This fanciful story—excuse the pun—doesn't take off," Rose said. "For one, you're forgetting I was in Colorado."

"No, no, I didn't forget."

Atticus's playful agreement caused a shift in Rose's friendly demeanor.

"Alright, Mr. Wallace, I enjoy a good work of fiction. So, spin your yarn."

"Do you know how far a single-engine plane can fly without refueling?"

A lazy, bored nod from Rose. Atticus continued unfazed.

"That value, of course, is dependent on certain variables. Height, speed traveled, the type of plane, etc."

"Naturally… Mr. Wallace, I am deeply confused by your sudden fascination with aviation. I've been most generous in allowing you to come into my home and accuse me of such heinous crimes, ignoring facts, and embracing fiction. There is nothing proving I was in those cities, and do you know why? Because I wasn't. I appreciate you telling me about Professor Moore, but I'm going to have to ask you to leave."

"I haven't finished my whiskey," Atticus said, leaning back against the comfortable couch.

"A person cannot be in two places at once. I flew to Aspen commercially and flew back to Chicago commercially. Flying is the only way the math can come out."

"Right. Which is why you flew."

The man's frustration was on full display. "I. Do. Not. Have—"

"A pilot's license. Yeah, I know. But you do know how to fly. Your father taught you."

The tokens and mementos Vasquez had hoped they'd find hadn't appeared. She wasn't as discouraged as she thought she'd be because this fell in line with the nagging feeling that had set in when she was in Moore's den. She kept thinking back to that photograph of Moore and his class in London. But it wasn't Moore who had claimed her attention; it was Rigel Rose. Vasquez flipped through her notepad. She stopped when she found the notes she'd taken during Madison's interview. Madison's attacker had whistled *London Bridge is Falling Down*. Both Moore and Rose had been in London. They surely had seen Tower Bridge, and surely, some tourist or tour guide had sung that song. Her gut feeling no longer told her Grey Moore was the man behind the mask.

A line from one of the chapters came to her.

His name sounded made-up, like something from a steamy romance novel.

Had he planted that, arrogantly thinking it'd go unseen, unnoticed?

But Rose had been in Wyoming, flying out in the late evening on the day Madison was taken. He was at the Wyoming airport when Madison had been rescued. Movies and books refer to that gut feeling a detective gets as a hunch. Atticus had referred to that feeling as shit. Dry shit. Wet shit. If a thought came and went, fleeting in its life cycle, it was dry shit. The smell didn't follow you and didn't cling to you. But if a thought stuck with you, followed you, came to you in the shower, came to you as you lay in bed, it was wet shit. It clung to you, stuck to the bottom of your shoes, discharging that rancid smell to everyone around wherever you went.

Wet shit. Vasquez was covered in it. Yet Harper Evans had stated that it was Grey Moore who had attacked her. So, why wouldn't this nagging feeling go away? She traced Rose's timeline on that fateful October day. He'd flown out of General Mitchell International Airport in Milwaukee to Chicago, where he'd caught a connecting flight to Jackson Hole, Wyoming. Before his flights, he had met Madison for coffee. What if Rose had spiked her coffee? But even if that was true, Rose was on an airplane to the Old West. Then a thought took hold. Its inception might be new, but the thought was wet shit. Vasquez knew it. What if Rose's timeline was spurious? She reached for her cell phone. She patted an empty pocket, then the other. Of all the times to misplace her phone! She cursed in Spanish, something she reserved for her most frustrating moments.

She stormed outside, her annoyance skyrocketing when she couldn't even remember what the hell she had been looking for.

Cell phone! She rushed to her Challenger. The fingerprint sensor didn't recognize her hand, and the car door stayed locked. Another colorful Spanish curse followed the failed attempt. The door then opened. She grabbed her cell phone. Her home screen showed a list of missed calls. Atticus. Madison. Maurice. Before she had to choose who to call back first, her phone rang.

"Been trying to reach you," Maurice said. "Atticus had a bunch of questions about—"

"Rose?" Vasquez asked. After all these years, were their minds still in sync?

"Yes…" Maurice said. "I don't get it though. We have an eyewitness testimony that it was Grey Moore who attacked her."

Vasquez recapped the photograph and the series of thoughts it'd brought forth. "What if Rose didn't get on the plane to Jackson Hole?"

A confused silence. "He got on the plane though," Maurice said.

"He got on the flight to Chicago. Yes, there's proof of that. But we never checked to see if he boarded the connecting flight to Jackson Hole because why would we? He flew back from Jackson Hole to Milwaukee just days later."

"Atticus wanted to know if Rose had a pilot's license. He doesn't, but his dad flew for over forty years," Maurice said.

The thick, hot rancid smell of metaphorical manure was inescapable.

"That's how the timeline works! He never got on the connecting flight! He went back to Milwaukee!"

"At the time of his death, Rose's father owned three planes. Two were sold. One was not. A Cessna Skylane."

He detailed the specs of the plane. It was capable of taking off in less than 800 feet and travel over 1,000 miles. Rose's father had lived near Spotted Horse, Wyoming, less than 1,000 miles from Chicago. Philadelphia to Aspen was nearly double that distance. But he could have refueled. Maurice relayed Atticus's comments on the Walnut Lane Golf Course in Philadelphia. If Rose had landed his plane on the course, it was the key to his improbable escape. Vasquez hung up and then dialed Madison.

"Madison, is everything alright?" Vasquez asked.

"Harper Evans lied."

Whiskey tastes perfect when it's celebratory. But right now, Atticus would have to celebrate by gazing upon the look of shock Rigel Rose was trying to hide. Rose was silent, neither refuting the claims nor bringing up a dozen counter-arguments. He had his moment of surprise, then sipped his whiskey as if the statement meant nothing. This was no novice liar. He had perfected his craft.

"Rose is your mother's maiden name. Your father's last name was Wexley. Anders Wexley. He was a pilot for over forty years, flying cargo before graduating to flying corporate heads around the world," Atticus said. "What am I telling you for? You obviously know this, but grant me the stage if you will."

Rose raised his whiskey in a toast: Go ahead.

"Your father flew you out to Spotted Horse to visit him."

Rose said nothing, only swirling the whiskey in his glass.

"Your father taught you to fly. You don't have a license, true. You kept your father's Skylane after he died. So, here's what I think happened. You never went to Wyoming that Halloween night."

Rose chuckled. "So, I board a plane at Mitchell, and then I what? Go into the bathroom, remove the toilet, crawl down to the landing gear, leap from the plane, and land in Lake Michigan with a landing not even the East Germans can dock points on. Swim to shore, steal a truck, and then kidnap Madison? Are you sure this isn't a scene from the next Tom Cruise film?"

"No, no. You got on the plane in Milwaukee and landed in Chicago. But you never got on the connecting flight. You returned to Milwaukee. Maybe on a bus or maybe a train. You steal the white Dodge Ram, go to the party, and wait for Madison to leave. I don't have any questions on that. The question I do have is where did you go when Madison escaped? You're supposed to be in Wyoming, so you can't risk being seen."

Rose only listened, his demeanor showing he thought everything Atticus had said to be bullshit, but his eyes revealed a hidden truth: that everything Atticus had said was indeed true.

"Madison escapes, and you give chase, but she's saved. So you hightail it back to the cabin and burn it down, destroying all evidence. Madison saw your plane, flickering in the night sky. The same plane I saw in Philadelphia and Madison saw last night. And then, when the news about what happened to Madison breaks, you're in Wyoming, disqualifying yourself from being a suspect." Atticus set his glass on the coffee table between them. "How'd I do?"

Rose chuckled. "You're forgetting that there is a survivor who stated she was attacked by Grey Moore."

Atticus shrugged. "People lie. Evidence doesn't."

"Mr. Wallace, how do you think the public will respond to an old, straight, white male calling a victim of rape a liar?"

"The truth will come out. They'll dig into every phone conversation and message you ever sent," Atticus said.

Rose smirked. "Mr. Wallace, you really can't get with the times can you? A woman claims she's been raped. It's no longer innocent until proven guilty. Careers are ruined with whispers now. Do you think John Kennedy would be assassinated by a bullet in today's world? No, no, no. You assassinate his character. You think bringing this girl to trial and accusing her of lying will fare well for you? It'll be all over CNN. Another case of society protecting a rich, entitled white man. And then tack on the overwhelming evidence?"

He clicked his tongue like Atticus was a naughty pet then eyed Atticus's glass, then set his own beside it. A silence took hold of the room. Atticus would not back down. And for the first time, Atticus saw the real Rigel Rose. The ultimate chameleon. His gentlemanly demeanor was gone, and so was the kind smile and the human gleam in his eye. His face was stoic, and his eyes emotionless, cold, calculating.

"Well, I must say, Mr. Wallace, I am impressed. I do hope you allow me a moment of candor. I would like to apologize for shooting you. The car… that was outside my control but a fortuitous event nonetheless."

"It was a hatchback, asshole, and apology not accepted. Just like you won't accept mine when you're passed around cell to cell like a basket of breadsticks at Olive Garden. When they're done with you, your ass will look like a baboon's."

Rose smirked—no reservation to his arrogance now. It was on full display. The change in his eyes was horrifying. Now, lifeless eyes stared back at Atticus. The eyes of a great white shark.

"It's poetic, really," Atticus said. "Your mother named you after the brightest star in Orion's Belt. And when you flew over the women you murdered, you were the brightest light in the sky. You lived up to the name."

"As have you. The virtuous man," Rose said.

"Why Moore? Why frame him? I have to say it was masterfully done. He's a good patsy. Cocky. An asshole. I wouldn't have minded if he was the guy."

Rose gave a look that said: *Isn't it obvious?* "He wronged her."

Atticus studied him to see if Rose was serious or not. When it was clear he was, Atticus laughed. "You gotta be shitting me. He wronged her? You raped her!"

Rose nearly leapt at Atticus, looking more like a savage beast than the immaculately domesticated man he presented himself to be. Atticus's first glimpse at the monster lurking behind the curtain of flesh.

"I did no such thing! Rape is violent. Aggressive. Invasive. I was gentle. I listened to her moans telling me when to slow down and when to speed up. I made love to her."

Atticus had been a cop his whole adult life. He'd mastered many skills. But one skill he'd never been able to or willing to master was remaining impassive in the presence of murderers detailing their crimes as if they'd done nothing wrong. He scowled scathingly at Rose, shaking his head at the man's rationale. Listening to him describe his rape of a crying, defenseless bound-and-blindfolded woman as pure romance disgusted him beyond measure. And that disgust gave way to hellacious anger.

"You are one sick son of a bitch."

"I looked at Madison the same way you gaze at Agent Vasquez. Tell me, Mr. Wallace, on those late stakeout nights when it was only you and her in that small confined car, did you imagine taking her in the back seat? Did you smell her perfume, see the way she filled out her blouse? Did that animalistic urge consume you?"

"Shut your mouth."

"Oh, my!" Rose cast a delicious smirk. "Who made the first move? Did you have to force her to realize she wanted it?"

"I've made mistakes in my life, but don't you ever compare yourself to me."

"How different are we? I have broken a commandment, and so have you."

Atticus shook his head. "Jesus Christ. You're a murderer."

"And you take the Lord's name in vain. You've coveted your neighbor's wife, and you committed adultery. You've broken more commandments than I have."

Atticus shook his head in disbelief, laughing at the audacity of the statement. How had this blatant psychopath conformed to the constructs of civility?

"Why the chapters? Why put Madison through this?"

"She was stuck in her own self-sentenced quarantine. I didn't know how to help her until I saw her name in the front of a book. The answer was simple. Save Madison with the thing she loves the most. I made Madison a heroine. She was a scared girl. I gave her the chance to become a brave woman."

"And then what? You randomly reconnect with her?"

"Madison would always be skeptical of people from her past. I knew we could never be together unless that chapter of her life ended. Until she lived a normal life, absent of fear. And for that to happen, her attacker needed to be found."

"Then you two walk into the sunset, is that it?"

"Things are in the works. A funeral for a common friend will bring us together."

Then Rose sighed as if two casual friends had just discussed as many basic topics—sports, job, and weather—as they could and had nothing more to say.

"This chess match has been fun, but it is time for this match to end," Rose said.

"I agree."

Rose smiled arrogantly. "Check, Mr. Wallace?"

"No, not check." Atticus tossed the pillow aside and raised his revolver, aiming the barrel at Rose's chest. "Checkmate."

"You're going to shoot me in my own home? I'm unarmed. You're a civilian. If you kill me, it's murder."

Atticus shrugged. "Maybe. But I don't give a shit."

Rose's pompous smile didn't fade. It grew.

"Not too many people die with a smile on their face," Atticus said.

"You have impressed me, Mr. Wallace. But you're failing to realize you think you have me in checkmate because I wanted you to think you had me in checkmate. You have two choices. One, you kill me. Everything I have confessed to you is lost. Harper Evans was attacked by Grey Moore. You rot in prison for the rest of your life, and judging by your appearance, that will only be ten years, maybe less."

"Deal."

Rose held up his hand. "Hold on. I haven't finished. You kill me, you rot in jail, and an innocent woman dies."

Atticus stared, looking for any sign of deceit. "Bullshit. You framed Moore. Another dark haired, blue-eyed woman goes missing, it'll prove his innocence."

"They'll never find her. There's no chapter, no clues. They'll chalk her up as another runaway. Every time a dark haired, blue-eyed female body is found, you'll wonder if that was the woman I had kidnapped. Or if she is still out there? Unfound? Unknown?"

Atticus kept his gun trained on Rose, fighting the urge to squeeze the trigger.

"So, choice number two," Rose continued. "You set down the gun and your phone, and we take a drive."

"You'll never let her live," Atticus said.

"Why not? She's never seen my face. She was taken before Moore was arrested. You, on the other hand… I'm sorry but your part in the story will have to end."

Rose took a swig of his whiskey to finish it.

"So, what will it be, Mr. Wallace? Shoot me and forsake an innocent woman to death or save her and damn yourself?"

"How do I know you're not lying?"

"May I show you a photo on my phone?" Rose asked.

Atticus nodded. Rose slowly drew his phone from his pocket and scrolled through his deleted photos. He showed the photo to Atticus: a woman's wrist with a gold chain around which hung three birthstones—a ruby, opal, and blue topaz. Atticus recognized it, and who had worn it.

The smile on Rose's face was one that had gotten him out of trouble, invited people in. It was as much a weapon as any knife or gun.

For Atticus, there was no choice to toil over. In a world of wolves and sheep, Atticus had and would always be a sheepdog. He set his gun on the coffee table and then his phone. Rose grabbed both of them. He rose from the chair and retrieved a roll of duct tape from a drawer.

"Hands behind your back," Rose ordered.

Atticus did as ordered. Rose ran the duct tape around his wrists, loop after loop. He reached into Atticus's pocket and took his keys. He kept a hand on Atticus's shoulder as they stepped out into the dark night. Rose opened the passenger door for him, then sat in the driver's seat. The old, reliable Chevy drove out of the suburbs and onto the interstate and to the Man in the Mask's last victim.

The drive back to Chicago had never taken longer. Slow drivers stayed in the fast lane, confused tourists turned their blinkers on, then veered back when they realized it was the wrong exit, and semis and delivery trucks congested the middle lane. Vasquez had Madison and Maurice on speaker phone.

"Wait, did she or did she not tell you she lied?" Vasquez asked.

"She didn't say it, but I could tell," Madison said.

"Yeah, she was super upset. Trying to talk herself into believing," Casper added.

"Maurice, you find anything linking Rose and Harper Evans?" Vasquez asked.

"Phone and text will take a bit, but Harper Evans did attend Chicago State University. She had at least two... no, three classes with Rose," Maurice said.

Vasquez thought back to the first time she had met Rose. The flustered look the girl had had. And then, their most recent visit with Rose outside campus, and the girls who goggled as they strolled by. Imagining a confused, vulnerable girl like Harper falling madly for Rose wasn't a stretch.

"No pictures on her social media with him," Maurice said.

Of course not. These conversations would have been in person or on prepaid phones.

"There's enough for reasonable doubt," Vasquez said.

She explained about the Cessna plane and how it had allowed Rose to manipulate his timeline and craft an airtight alibi.

"Vasquez, Atticus isn't answering his phone," Madison said.

Vasquez glanced at her GPS. "I'm still forty-five minutes from Chicago."

"I'll go by Rose's," Maurice said.

"Maurice, if we're right…"

"I know. Whatever happens is on me."

"Get some uniforms to go in with you."

Maurice said he would and hung up.

"Does Atticus know about Harper lying?" Vasquez asked.

"I'm not sure. I couldn't get a hold of him to tell him," Madison said.

"So, as far as we know, Rose thinks his alibi is holding up." She paused. "How are you… reacting to it being Rose?"

Madison was silent as she gathered her thoughts. "I don't know. I'll process it later. But it feels right, that it's him, you know?"

Wet shit. "I do."

Vasquez hung up and unleashed the Dodge demon, pressing the gas pedal to hell.

God, Madison hated waiting. She clenched her phone in her hand, lighting the screen up any time it went dark. Casper paced beside her. They both knew Maurice had to leave the FBI headquarters here in Chicago and drive to the North Shore. Traffic was always unpredictable. But even five minutes after the call with Vasquez had ended, she thought something terrible had already happened. Now that it was over half an hour, it felt like the world was ending.

Finally, her phone rang. She pecked at the screen to answer it.

"Madison, it's Vasquez and Maurice," Vasquez said.

"What's happening?" Madison asked.

"No one's home," Maurice said. "Atticus's truck isn't here."

"Any signs of struggle?" Vasquez asked.

"Nothing."

"What about his phone? Can you track him?" Madison asked.

"Last ping came from I-94," Maurice said.

"And just stopped?" Madison asked.

Maurice confirmed.

"Then that means his phone was tossed," Vasquez said.

And with that one sentence, the whole situation became so much graver. Something was wrong.

Maurice had to drop off the call and promised to keep them posted.

"Where could they be going?" Madison asked.

"There has to be something that made Atticus go with Rose. Even if threatened at gun-point, I don't imagine him giving in," Vasquez said.

"Then maybe it's not something but *someone*," Casper suggested.

"What do you mean?" Vasquez asked.

"I mean, what if there's another victim," he said.

"No chapters have come through though," Madison said.

"No, if Rose wanted to pin Moore, the murders need to stop. He wouldn't risk it," Vasquez said.

"If Rose found out we know, maybe he's leaving town," Madison said.

"And taking Atticus with him? That doesn't make sense. He would just..." Casper didn't finish the words *kill him*.

"Not necessarily leave town. If he thinks only Atticus knows, he may not be trying to leave," Vasquez said.

"Whether he's escaping or staying, he won't let Atticus live," Madison said.

An uncomfortable silence took hold. Vasquez was too rational to dispel that notion. She knew it was true.

"Rose has a plane, right?" Casper asked. "Can't we use radar to find it?"

"Only once he's in the air," Vasquez said.

"That will be too late," Madison said.

If Rose was in the air, it meant that Atticus was dead on the ground.

"If Rose has another possible victim, it could be how he got Atticus to willingly get in the truck," Madison said. "Rose will have to kill him, but if he does, his gig is up. So he'll hide the body. Some place hidden, far from people."

"But all the murders were in big cities," Casper said.

"Right. He wanted them found, just not in time to save them. But he won't want Atticus to be found."

"He could make it look like an accident," Casper said.

Madison zoned Vasquez and Casper out, retreating to the deep center of her mind where she did her most prolific thinking. Rose had flown to each city. If he was going to escape, he would fly. He needed a long stretch of land to fly his plane. Though he had landed on a golf course in Philadelphia, he'd have to have a privately owned area to store the plane. Rigel was from Northbrook. If he had visited his father on the weekends via flight, his father must have owned land where he housed his plane. She shared her thoughts with them. Vasquez ended the call, so she could find out.

Madison's mouth was sand dry. She guzzled a glass of water, but it offered only temporary relief. Each minute that passed made it all the more likely that Atticus was dead.

Her phone buzzed, startling her so much she almost dropped it.

"Rose's father owned seven acres west of the city of Maple Park," Vasquez said.

Casper was a step ahead of Madison, typing it into Google Maps. He showed her. It was approximately seventy miles away, even further for Vasquez as she had just driven by Six Flags Great America.

"Okay, so Vasquez send the damn SWAT team," Casper said.

"No…" Madison said. "If the police show up, Atticus is dead."

"Madison, he may be anyway," Vasquez said, the break in her voice unmissable. "We can't let Rose get away. Atticus would tell us that."

Madison took a deep breath, gathering her strength to deliver the hardest phrase she'd ever said in her life.

"I need to go."

Casper looked at her as if she had betrayed him. He shook his head, finding the idea inconceivable.

"Madison, it's too dangerous," Vasquez said.

It was. And it was foolish and reckless. But Madison didn't care. She couldn't live the way she had been living anymore. This was her chance to end it.

You can't put the past behind you until you get out in front of it.

"It's about me. It's always been. If something happens to Atticus, I'll never be able to live with that. And if Rose flies away… I can't continue to live in this fear. And don't try to tell me I can. I have to do this."

The truth was she would rather die than continue living the way she had. It was exhausting and terrifying. Madison strongly believed in heaven. She didn't want to die but minutes of pain versus a lifetime of it was an easy choice. Like a terminally ill patient choosing to go out on their own terms. The alpha she-wolf in her snarled. She wouldn't back down. This was her fight. There'd be no surrender. For the first time since *it* happened, the omega wolf was gone, banished forever from the pack, and the alpha had finally taken its place at the front.

Vasquez knew Madison's plan, so Madison hung up before she could attempt to talk her out of it.

"I'm going with you," Casper said.

Madison started to speak, but Casper cut her off. "You won't let me talk you out of it, so don't waste time trying to talk me out of it either."

She grabbed her keys, and they headed for the elevator. A mix of nerves and excitement boiled in her stomach. But those feelings were dulled, replaced by an overwhelming sense of relief. A long journey was nearing its end. She thought of Rigel and a jolt of pain followed. He was a man many of her friends had called odd, strange, or downright weird. She had defended him. To think he was the man responsible for causing her so much pain and hurt. Life can be ironic. She had spent the last several years burrowing away from the world, doing everything she could to prevent an encounter with the Man in the Mask. Now here she was on a cold and dark October night, driving to him.

Darkness is a relative term. Chicago is never truly dark. Skyscrapers, traffic, street lights, all prevented total darkness. But in the rural parts of the country like her hometown in Wisconsin, and on this barren street, it was a level of darkness Madison had forgotten.

Casper's directions off Google Maps led to a small wooded area. A lone gravel road snaked through it. The literal end of the road was ahead. The nerves kicked into overdrive. Madison didn't know how this would end, but it would end, and that was all the encouragement she needed to continue.

The tree branches tapped against her Chevy Impala with the pitter-patter of rain. Madison braked when they came to a long clearing. Atticus's truck was parked ahead. Their suspicions were proven true. Madison killed her headlights. Her Impala crept ahead like the eponymous animal. She put the car in park and shut it off. Fear tried to intimidate her into leaving. She took a few deep breaths to exorcise that fear, then grabbed her Glock. They exited the car as quietly as they could, creeping forward, around the bend. Rose's Cessna Skylane was parked at the start of a paved runway. The runway was completely hidden, surrounded by the forest. A small storage shack was ahead to the left. As they drew closer, the moonlight revealed a figure tethered to the pipes leading into the shack. Atticus. His mouth was duct taped. So were his wrists and ankles. Goosebumps spread on Madison's skin, as if a million insects scampered over her. She raised her Glock and scanned ahead, listening for any sign of Rose, but there was only the sound of wind whistling through the trees, the leaves swirling on the ground, and the chirping crickets.

Casper rushed to Atticus to free him. He picked at the duct tape while Madison kept her eyes peeled for Rose. Her body shook. She kept two hands on her Glock to keep it steady. Casper ripped the tape from Atticus's mouth.

"Where is he?" Madison asked.

"I don't know. He has someone else," Atticus said. "It's Jade."

Jade… her best friend… *was* her best friend. Worry and nervousness blitzed over her, but it was anger that trumped them all. Her eyes caught sight of movement from the east, and her ears caught sound of crinkled leaves and snapping twigs. Rigel Rose, wearing his mask, stepped across the runway. In front of him was a woman whose head was covered by a burlap sack. Her hands and legs were duct taped. Madison recognized the woman's walk. She walked the same way she had those drunken Saturday nights. It was Jade. Rose must have drugged her. Had he raped her? The thought made her trigger finger twitch.

"Stop!" Madison shouted. "Don't fucking move!"

Rose clung to Jade like a shield. Because she was. Casper froze too, stopping his attempt to free Atticus, not wanting to risk Rose hurting Jade.

"I know it's you, Rigel," Madison said. "Take the sack off her head."

Rose obeyed, lifting the bag off Jade's head. Jade's eyes found Madison's for the first time in years. Somehow, even in their current predicament, Jade looked pleased to see her. Rose didn't speak. His face was concealed behind the mask, but it was easy to imagine his face contorting in thought at this new development.

"Let her go," Madison ordered.

Rose peeled off the mask like a snake shedding its skin. His hair was damp with sweat. He looked older than Madison had remembered him. But he had aged gracefully and distinguished. His reaction to seeing her was mixed. There was delight as if they had spontaneously ran into each other at Walmart. There was an apprehension, a nervousness. But there was also sadness in his gray eyes. But in those stone-like eyes lived pain and anger, and below the surface, hate.

"How'd you know? Did he tell you?" Rose asked, thrusting a nod at Atticus.

"No, I found out by myself," Madison said. She told him about *London Bridge*, and how he had whistled it all those years ago, the folded receipt in the copy of *Antony and Cleopatra*, and the inscription written in it. Something so trivial had planted the seed, and she had watered that seed until the truth bloomed.

"You always were brilliant. This isn't how I wanted this to go, Madison. Truly," Rose said.

He lifted his arm around Jade. In his hand was Atticus's Smith & Wesson.

It took a moment for Madison to find her voice. "You were my friend…" she sounded like a five-year-old who had been fooled by a magic trick, but she couldn't help it.

"I know you can't see it right now, but this—" he waved the gun at Atticus and Casper, then Jade and then to the surrounding area as if pointing to all the cities in which he'd committed his murders—"was all for you."

"For me?" Madison spat the words, never feeling more disgusted in her entire life.

"You weren't living life, Madison. I never meant to take that from you. I had to find a way to give it back to you."

"By framing Grey Moore? By getting a vulnerable girl to lie for you? What was your plan for Harper? She would have come clean if you left her."

"Harper was a necessary character in our story, one needed for plot, but she has a tragic accident in her near future. Overdose, car accident, drowning. T.B.D."

Madison nodded emphatically. "And these grand romantic gestures were meant to make me forget that you ran me off the road, restrained me to a bed, and raped me?"

"Don't say that word," Rose said, turning his head away in disgust.

"Rape?"

"Yes."

"You raped me!"

"I made love to you!" Rose shouted, spewing spit like a rabid dog.

Madison's accusation of rape had made Rose as volatile as grease fire. He had his gun pointed at Jade's chest. Madison had hers pointed near him, keeping the barrel away from Jade.

"So you were going to kill Atticus and what, hide his body? The police know, Rigel. You can't hide. You can't make this go away."

Rose scrunched his eyes. For the first time, he no longer looked confident and in control. His web was unspinning.

"Everything had gone to plan. But this decrepit old bastard couldn't stay away." Rose thrust his gun at Atticus.

Madison took a step closer to Atticus. Even though she was directly in its line of fire, she had no fear. Rose wouldn't shoot her. The gun was too cold, too impersonal. Knife was his phallic weapon of choice. Each stab, an orgasmic penetration.

"And you're here… no, this wasn't supposed to happen. It's not my fault," Rose said.

"Why kidnap Jade? Moore was arrested." But the answer came to Madison. "… You were going to kill her, make it look like an accident. You knew I'd go to the funeral. And you would too…"

She shook her head in disgust, that impure feeling as if she wore someone else's skin.

Rose smirked fondly. "Like I said, brilliant."

We steer clear of people based on how they dress, how they smell, how they talk, and how they walk. People whose mugshots fit the crime. We constantly filter people, making them pass these arbitrary tests. But sometimes these tests fail us: grandmothers who have killed twenty infants; doctors who kill their patients; church leaders who bind, torture, and kill; and men like Rose who become so unnaturally infatuated, they commit horrible acts in the name of distorted love.

Rose's expression slithered into a serpent's smile. "You know it was you who told me I should consider writing. As you know, I took you up on that offer." He paused, breathing in the chilled air. "I'm going to need you to toss that gun."

Madison steadied her base. "You first."

Rose smirked again. "I gave Mr. Wallace a choice, and I'll present you with one too. You can choose to not drop your gun, and Jade and I go back into the woods and I kill her. You can try to shoot me, but I'll kill her first."

Jade sobbed, the sound muffled by the duct tape covering her mouth.

"Or you drop the gun and we keep chatting," Rose said.

Madison considered her options. She'd criticized characters in horror movies and books for choices they made in such situations. The choices are always easy from the comfort of your couch. But the choice she had was either watch her best friend get shot mere feet away from her or drop her weapon and postpone Jade's death. Vasquez was on her way. Madison had to keep Rose busy until she arrived. Grinding the inside of her cheek, she tossed the gun, far enough away to please Rose but short of the tall grass that lined the runway.

"Let Jade go. Please," Madison said.

Rose released Jade, but she could hardly run even if she wanted to—her legs were taped together at the ankle. She waddled a few steps, then fell face-first beside Atticus.

"Do you remember all the books you and I discussed, dissected, and disassembled?" Rose asked. "Characters. We loved to talk about characters. Some stories are weighed down by characters who don't serve a purpose. Maybe they're there for blunt exposition, or maybe they're not interesting or necessary. You… well, you're our main character. The protagonist. Our heroine. Agent Vasquez is our link to law enforcement. Mr. Wallace, he's our disgruntled, grizzled sleuth. And Jade here, she's our link to the past you abandoned. Me, I'm the love interest the main character fails to see." Rose paused. "And then, we have him."

No nod. No wave of the gun or pointing of his finger. But Madison knew he was referring to Casper.

"We seem to have a love triangle. But what do all love triangles have in common? They end."

Madison knew what was coming, but it wasn't humanly possible to stop it. A shot ripped through the night, its echo swallowed up by the white oak forest surrounding them. Casper stumbled backward, his gold sweatshirt stained with a rich red blob that spread in a Rorschach pattern. He collapsed to the ground, clutching his stomach. Madison slid down in front of him to prevent a second shot.

"All this because I turned you down?" Madison asked.

"I had to show you what we could have been. A glimpse," Rose said, sounding hurt that she couldn't see that.

"A glimpse? A glimpse of a lifetime of being taped to a bed and raped?"

"I said, don't say that word! Don't use that fucking word!"

Atticus struggled against his restraints, trying to break free.

"Let them go, Rigel. Let them go, and I'll do whatever you want."

"Really?"

"Yes. I'll get on your plane, and we'll go wherever you want."

356

"Whatever I want?"

Madison nodded. His eyes were locked in on hers. She met them. He shook his head in frustration.

"You don't get... you don't get it! I don't want you to do what I want. I want you to realize you *want* to be with me."

Madison bit her lip, suppressing her urge to scream at him.

"Dear Madison, you're forgetting that I'm in control," Rose said.

"You are not in control. I choose what happens," Madison said.

"Right. Just like you chose to sleep with everyone but me. The one guy who'd treated you with respect. You were so blind. So. God. Damn. Blind! Everyone saw it but you."

Casper reached for Madison's leg. His face was pale. "Don't... get... on... plane..."

"Looks like somebody has unfinished business." Rose smiled. "Let's finish it."

Vasquez's Challenger had roared along the interstate, and now it purred as it crept along the road leading to the runway. She pulled over along the main road, stopping short of the gravel path. She took her Glock from her holster, removed the magazine to inspect it, and then slammed it back in and rode the slide to chamber a round. She pressed ahead, light on her feet, aware that any cracking twig or crunching gravel would betray her.

The wind howled eerily. Voices carried through, and she made one out to be Madison's, but the other she could only make out as male. She crouched and gazed through the trees, their leaves swaying in the wind. Atticus's and Madison's Chevys were to the right. Rose's Cessna Skylane was in the background. Atticus had his hands above his head, restrained to a piece of pipe leading into a shack. Jade was on the ground beside him, and so was Casper, flat on his back. Vasquez scanned away from them, finding Rose pointing a gun at Madison.

Vasquez paused, unsure of her next move. Madison stood directly in front of Rose, granting Vasquez no clear shot. She had to flank him, but she knew that if she did, there was a chance he'd see her and an even greater probability of being heard. The dry leaves would crunch, twigs would snap, and leaves would rustle. And the longer she contemplated on what to do, the likelihood of Rose shooting increased.

She crept ahead, choosing to flank him. She needed a better angle in order to shoot. She treaded cautiously, carefully brushing aside leaves and branches. She stopped, digging her boots into the earth and took deep meditative breaths. Knowing she had little room for error, Vasquez wiped every thought from her mind but one: Rigel Rose would kill Atticus. Aiming further left than she would have had Madison not been standing so close to Rose, she aimed for his right shoulder below the collarbone to ensure the bullet didn't strike Madison.

Even if she hit her mark, she knew it wouldn't kill Rose. She took two quick breaths followed by a long, drawn-out one. A shot blasted into the hallowed night.

The shot sounded like a cannon, so loud every bird within a mile took flight. The force of the bullet eviscerated the air around Madison. Vasquez's shot had found its mark, striking Rose above the collarbone. The force of the bullet spun him around and knocked him to the ground. Madison looked to the trees. Vasquez, gun at the ready, rushed out. But to ensure Madison's safety, Vasquez's shot was far from fatal. Rose stumbled to his feet, gun raised. Madison dove to the ground, caught between the potential crossfire. Rose had the advantage. Vasquez delayed her fire until Madison had hit the ground, but Rose was in full survival mode. He fired immediately. Three shots sliced the air above Madison's head. The first zipped over Vasquez's left shoulder, the second mere inches above her head. But the fortuitous misses stopped at two. The third bullet torpedoed into her abdomen. The force was immense, spearing her to the ground. Pain pulsated. Every nerve ending fired. The bullet had struck near her liver. If it had pierced it, she'd be dead in a few measly minutes.

Madison, hands covering her head, gazed upon Vasquez. Atticus shouted, pulling and twisting against his restraints like the demonically possessed when shown a crucifix. Rose advanced, the Smith & Wesson jutting out like a spear. He picked up Vasquez's Glock and threw it as far as he could. Vasquez raised a bloody hand, a puny, useless attempt to stop him. But she was too proud to beg. She wouldn't give Rose that satisfaction. Her eyes weighed a ton, but she forced them to stay open. She would stare into his gray eyes as he killed her.

Madison sprinted in front of Vasquez, her hands wide, blocking Rose from executing her.

"Move," he ordered.

Madison shook her head. "We'll get on the plane. We'll go far away. I want to get on the plane."

Rose tilted his head, scrutinizing her words. "I've longed to hear you say that, Madison." He chuckled to himself as if to say all this could have been avoided had she realized this years ago. "You know, during our little conversation, Mr. Wallace asked me where I had gone when you escaped. Do you know? Did some indescribable gut feeling give you the answer?"

Madison shook her head. It was something she'd always wondered.

"I was digging your grave. Struggling to decide what to do with you. The clichéd good and evil battling for supremacy. There is a part of me that could never hurt you, Madison. But there was this voice telling me you had to die. That there would be no Disney ending to our story. If I revealed myself to you, you could never grow to love me. And I loved you. Not just your body. All those men viewed you as nothing but fuckable meat. But I respected you. Listened to you. I knew the way you thought, the way your nose crinkles when you get to the climax of a novel. The way your cobalt-blue eyes light up when you're excited and darken when you're sad, as if clouds had blocked the sun. But there was this voice telling me you had to die. I struggled back and forth. Neither voice would silence itself. But then you ran away, and fate granted me a do-over. I knew you'd need time to return to normal. And I waited. God, did I wait. But you never called, never texted; you never even friended me on fucking Facebook."

Madison had a role to play. She had to get Rose to calm down, fall into a false sense of security. And that role required her stepping into a disgusting costume.

"I know. I'm sorry, Rigel," Madison said. "I had cut everyone from Milwaukee out of my life. Not just you. I haven't seen Jade in years. I had to put that life behind me. But please don't hurt them for my actions."

Rose studied her. How did her new character hold up? Did it mask her true feelings? The spotlight was on her.

"Get the plane ready," Madison said.

"Don't get on the plane, Madison!" Atticus shouted.

Rose pointed the gun at Atticus. Madison again stepped in front of it. She turned to Atticus and betrayed nothing with her facial expression. But he read her eyes and fell silent. He could do nothing. He was tethered to the pipe. Vasquez was dying, maybe Casper too. Jade could barely hobble with her duct tape restraints, and she looked distant. Whatever drug Rose had used still affected her. It was all on Madison. And there was a poetic justice to that. She'd been alone in her own private prison. She had descended into Hell alone; it was only fitting she ascend out of it alone.

Madison extended her hand. "Put the gun away. We don't have much time. The police will be here shortly."

She stared into Rose's eyes, hiding her hate, suppressing her sadness, and instead conveying compassion. She took his free hand, feeling his cold fingers in hers. His touch revolted her, but she couldn't show that. Rose didn't pull away. He'd been longing for her touch for as long as Madison had recoiled thinking about the Man in the Mask's. She stroked his face. His cheeks flushed with color. She absolutely despised the arousal her touch caused, the bulge in his pants. But lust overrides rational thought. Rose lowered the gun and leaned in. Every instinct, every nerve ending told her to dodge the kiss. Madison ignored her body's plea.

People close their eyes when they kiss, and Rose was no exception. This was her moment to go from victim to victor. She seized it, knocking the gun from his hand and kicking it away. She planted her foot behind his and drove him to the ground. Madison pushed away from him and hurried to her feet. Betrayal took form on Rose's handsome face, then anger.

She could run. But she was done running. She'd been running and hiding for almost a decade.

Fight. Fright. Or flight.

Madison knew her choice. *It's fight and fight and fucking fight.* There would be two possible endings. He would die or she would.

She secured her base, her hands ready to block his strikes. Rose was stronger. But she acknowledged that. Rage had cut off the pain of his gunshot. Rose was now a feral, rabid animal. He punched and kicked, then flung himself at her. Madison telegraphed his strikes, then landed one of her own, driving her fist into his nose. It cracked like a pistachio. Blood gushed out, guzzling down into his mouth. He lunged at her, tackling her to the ground. Madison tried to squirm free, but Rose climbed atop her, pinning her to the ground with his weight. He drove his fist into her ribs. Madison grunted from the virulent pain, her whole body pulsing like a heartbeat.

Atticus shouted at Rose, fighting against his restraints. Jade tried to crawl to him, but she looked as though she'd fall asleep at any moment, like a surgery patient trying to fight off the anesthesia. Casper struggled to stand. He collapsed, then crawled toward Madison, grabbing fistfuls of grass to help him move. Vasquez's color rapidly drained from her face. The thread of her life in grave jeopardy of being sheared.

Rose leaned back and sniffed his bloody nose. Blood ran down his chin and onto Madison' face; its warmth incongruous with the frigid air. Rose punched her ribs again, sucking out the breath in her lungs as if she sucked on a vacuum hose. She gasped for air, her eyes widening when none came in.

Rose pinned her wrists to the ground, steadying his own breathing.

"You know, I told you there were two voices," Rose said, gazing at the trees. "But you know what, Madison?" He looked down at her. "There aren't two voices anymore." His hands lunged at her throat, wrapping around it like pythons. He grew enraged, veins bulging as if worms tunneled under his skin. The air in her lungs had nowhere to go. The constriction of her throat caused a sharp pounding in her head like some painful hellish drum. She scrunched her toes so hard she cramped. Yet a bodily reaction made her legs thrash. Her eyes widened, then bulged. Atticus was shouting, but his words were distant and incoherent. Her peripheral faded. The stars above her lost their luminosity as if they had burned out. The dark borders around her vision encroached ever inward like spilled ink.

Madison was going to die.

People and places filled her mind, a slideshow to offer comfort as she died. Then cruelly, it replayed missed opportunities and declined offers—the years since her attack had been filled with regret. But then she made a pledge.

I will not die a sheep's death. I will die like the wolf. There was only one way the alpha wolf inside her would relinquish her rule—death.

Madison wrapped her legs around Rose in a closed guard and crossed her feet to keep him locked in place. There would be no escape. He was trapped. But the air in her lungs was gone. Sheer panic threatened to overwhelm her. Her head no longer pounded like musical drums but the drums of war— violent and loud.

Focus.

She crossed her arms and grabbed his elbows. Then, mustering every ounce of strength she still possessed, she pressed down on his arms. His grip around her throat slipped. She sucked in a massive breath, then lifted her legs onto his shoulders.

Lana's instructions played in her mind: *Now you blast your hips up, and you break his fuckin' elbows.*

With the power the breath of air had gifted her, and tapping into every sap of strength, Madison shot her hips up, keeping pressure on his arms and forcing them down. Rose screamed as his arms bent. Further and further. He cried out a guttural roar.

Snap!

She could feel the bones break, a disgusting sensation that made her want to let go. But she ignored it, holding on until he had no ability to continue choking her. She squirmed free, then readied herself for an attack, but Rose dashed for Atticus's gun. Madison deliberated: go for her own gun lying somewhere near the grass or charge at Rose and race him to the Smith & Wesson. Her Glock was too far. She sprinted after Rose and tackled him to the ground. His arms were swollen, turning a water-color spectrum of blacks, blues, and purples. He could do nothing with them but flail them around.

Thousands of times Madison had punched Century Bob, every one of those times in preparation for this moment. She sent a hook, a jab, and another hook. Rose stumbled back. Madison lunged for the gun.

Rose dove atop her. Madison squeezed the trigger. The sound startled them both. Rose looked at his chest and the blood spreading across it. Madison pushed him off and climbed to her feet, the gun trained on Rose. He stared into her cobalt-blue eyes, even now, with adoration. Then Rose slumped to the ground, his chest still. Even so, Madison had seen too many movies, read too many books to know that death was temporary in them. She stared at his lifeless body, looking for any subtle twitch, any clue that his apparent death was but a deception.

Somebody called her name, snapping her from her daze. Atticus. She rushed to free him.

"Call 9-1-1," he ordered as he rushed to Vasquez's side.

Madison ignored the throbbing pain in her side and dashed to her car to get her phone. Her hand trembled when she dialed. The emergency operator answered, but she could already hear sirens wailing in the distance. Vasquez had secured backup before she had arrived.

Atticus tore his flannel shirt off and pressed it against Vasquez's wound. She shook her head meekly, a defeated smile on her face.

"It's not... good..." she said in a weak whisper.

Her luminous golden-brown skin had been drained of its glow; the life inside her faded away.

"No, no, you're gonna be fine, Allie. I can hear the sirens. They're almost here," Atticus said.

Her fingers were icicles. Her body was a mighty ship sinking into the abyss.

"More poetic... than dying... from salt..."

A limp smile formed, followed by a violent cough. Blood erupted from her mouth, spraying onto Atticus's white t-shirt. The glossy gleam in her eyes faded away.

Police and emergency vehicles swarmed the runway. Two paramedics loaded Casper onto a stretcher. He reached for Madison's hand as they placed him inside the ambulance.

"Is he going to be okay?" Madison asked.

"Prognosis looks good. Bullet passed right through," one of the EMTs said.

Casper's fatigued face formed a limp smirk; Madison knew he wanted to make a ghost joke. She told him she'd follow him to the hospital.

EMTs worked on Vasquez as they rushed her to her own ambulance. Atticus jogged alongside her, squeezing her hand. Madison didn't even have time to say anything before the ambulance was speeding away. There was one other person Madison needed to check in on: Jade. She was speaking with two uniformed police officers. The restraints had been cut from her wrists and ankles. She now looked like she had on those Sunday mornings during college—crying from how hungover she was. Jade wrapped herself in a plaid-green flannel blanket. Her mascara had left a trail down her face.

What should Madison say? What can you say? Madison stood beside her. Physically, Jade had only minor bruises, and the duct tape had left her skin red. But Madison knew better than most that the longest-lasting wounds were mental.

"Are you okay?" Madison asked, fully aware of how stupid a question it was, but it seemed a necessary preamble of sorts.

Jade shook her head. "I thought I understood the pain you went through… but he never…"

Jade didn't need to finish. Madison knew what the final word was. Rape. Rose had spared her that horror.

"A lot of these tears are for you. I'm so sorry, Maddie. I never should have forced you to go to that party."

Knowing it was Rose, someone close to Madison, meant that had she not gone to that party, he would have only tried again and again. Madison told Jade as much.

"Besides, you didn't force me," Madison said. "Persuaded, maybe."

They both smiled at that.

"He did this because we were best friends," Madison said.

The past tense stung them both. They fell silent as Rose was loaded into a black body bag. It was a visual image Madison needed to see. During dark times, fits of depression, and anxiety attacks, this moment would be the soothing balm. The zipping up of the body bag gave her a feeling of supreme satisfaction and the perfect image to realize and remember that it was finally all over.

Closure.

Jade asked how Madison knew it was Rose. Madison explained as briefly as she could.

"How did he get to you?" Madison asked.

Jade had made a habit of running after supper to help her lose some unwanted weight. On Thursday evening, she parked her Yukon by a running trail.

"I heard footsteps, but before I could even turn around, this white rag was pressed over my mouth."

Routines. Jade had established a new one, and it had not gone unnoticed. Police found Jade's Yukon. Liquor bottles had been strewn around inside the vehicle, the seats damp with whiskey and vodka. Jade adamantly claimed to the police that the liquor was not hers. The bottle of water Rose had given her was mixed with vodka. Both Jade and Madison guessed at what his plan had been: fake a drunk-driving accident. Rose had even known what brands of whiskey and vodka Jade and her husband routinely drank. The toxicology report would have shown Jade was drunk.

What if Rose's plan had worked? If Madison never had figured out it was him? Jade would have died in a tragic drunk-driving accident. Madison would have gone to the funeral. Rose would have been there too. He would have asked her to coffee, and she would have agreed to it. To catch up. Oblivious to the fact that it had been a coldly-calculated fate. The thought made her shiver.

Madison didn't know the exact number of emotions a person could feel, but she experienced every single one of them that night. She wanted to cry, not for anything Rose had done—those tears would come later—but because the woman next to her had once been her best friend. Now, she was a stranger. A woman who had married and mothered children. Children whose names Madison didn't even know.

"I should have been there for you, Jade. I'm sorry I cut you out of my life. Everything... everyone... reminded me of him."

Jade grabbed her hand like she used to do when she had something important to say. Back in college, it was usually about a guy or a major cliffhanger of a TV show she had binge-watched over the weekend.

"Ditto."

The opulent Eiffel Tower shimmered in the high sun. Atticus sat outside the café called *The Givre Strudel,* sipping black coffee, his eyes fixed on the historical Parisian landmark. The indoor and outdoor café was filled to capacity inside and out with Frenchmen and tourists alike, dining on baguettes, croissants, macarons, and strudels, and drinking from doll-sized cups of espresso. Atticus sat alone, left to his coffee and thoughts, a half-eaten croissant glistening with melted butter on the plate in front of him. He'd enjoyed the city, and the people were nice, but they were too slow-moving for him. *Move with purpose,* he thought. But there was no urgency, something he'd been told to enjoy on his vacation.

Over two decades ago, he and Allie had planned a European getaway. Here he was now. The flight had been an ordeal. It did a number on him mentally, flying over the ocean and looking out the window and seeing nothing but water. The language barrier proved difficult; not only did Atticus speak English, he spoke American English. The damn English people, with their affinity to not finishing a word before moving onto the next, had been harder to understand than the French. Christmas was six days away, and Paris had lived up to its billing as one of the most beautiful cities in the world. The trip had begun in London, then on to Rome and Venice, then Vienna and the Alps to Bavaria and Berlin.

Atticus scanned the café entrance, then stood. He couldn't help but smile. Alejandra Vasquez, still moving gingerly, headed toward him. The bullet had indeed struck her liver and ruptured her gall bladder. Peritonitis had set in and required emergency surgery followed with a hefty dose of antibiotics. She was on a mix of medical leave and vacation, but it was doubtful she would return to duty.

"Maurice says hi," she said. She had stepped away from the café's chatter to give Maurice a quick call.

"And Moore? Has he passed along any greetings?" Atticus asked.

"Oh, threatening to sue. Saying it cost him his marriage."

"I think the infidelity did that."

Vasquez grabbed the last of his croissant.

"And the Evans girl?" Atticus asked.

Vasquez's expression saddened. "She didn't help commit any of the murders. She says she had no idea they happened. She's facing jail time for lying to the police. Moore's suing her. She's a very troubled girl."

It was a situation Atticus didn't know how he truly felt. Everyone is responsible for their own actions. Yet, it never failed to amaze him what some person could get someone else to do.

"So, what's the plan for today?" Vasquez asked.

"We could go visit the battlefield of Verdun."

"Atticus Wallace, do you plan on doing nothing but visiting World War I battlefields?"

"Don't be ridiculous. Of course not. I plan on seeing the Second World War's battlefields too. Why else come to Europe?"

"For the culture."

"I get culture in my yogurt."

In Greek mythology, there are three Fates who assigned the destiny of all mortals. Clotho spun the thread of life, Lachesis measured the length, and Atropos cut the thread with her shears. We never know how long our thread is, when it will be cut. But for Atticus and Vasquez, their threads were finally woven together.

Vasquez smiled, then reached for his hand. "We made it."

Atticus held it and squeezed. "Yes, we did."

Casper stood in front of the bathroom mirror, switching between a red-and-black-striped tie and a black tie with marble swirls of green, reminding Madison of a 90's rom-com montage where a character tries on every item in twenty-three seconds of screen time with an accompanying catchy song.

"Which one do you think I should go with?" he asked her.

"Neither. You're going to The Cheesecake Factory."

"Okay, I don't like your cavalier attitude toward cheesecake. Do you know how many wars throughout history could have been avoided had both sides had the opportunity to sit down and negotiate over cheesecake?"

"Fair point. I rescind my slander."

Madison tossed a maroon sweater at him. Then she buttoned her black pea coat and grabbed her purse. She pushed aside her wallet, phone, and two packs of gum to find her Chapstick. It was so much easier to find things now without her Glock taking up space. The purse was lighter. She was lighter not having to carry its weight—real and metaphorical. She applied a layer of the glossy, waxy resin to her lips, enjoying the taste of peppermint.

Snow fell in thick flakes, pure and white, yet to be tainted by the city. Christmas wreaths hung from city lampposts. Santa Clauses waved bells in front of red Salvation Army buckets for both donations and to regain feeling in their frostbitten fingertips. Street musicians played commercial Christmas music while street choirs sang traditional Christmas songs. Christmas in Chicago drew a large number of tourists, two of whom Casper and Madison were on their way to meet. Numbness spread in her thighs, and her nostrils froze on their walk to The Cheesecake Factory.

The hostess greeted them. Madison pointed to a booth occupied by a man with short-cropped, dark-blonde hair and a woman waving frantically like she had just eaten something extremely hot. Jade rose to greet her. She introduced her husband Grant and slid a glass of sweet red wine and a domestic beer in front of Casper and Madison's spots. Jade and Madison hugged; Casper and Grant shook hands.

"It's nice to meet you, Madison," Grant said. "Though I know every single thing the two of you have ever done, seen, heard, or talked about."

"Oh, please," Jade said, giving him a gentle, teasing push. "He doesn't know *everything*."

Jade looked great, her face full of color, with the same infectious laugh. She was the sort of person people were drawn to. A positive, bright light that human moths flew toward.

They stayed at The Cheesecake Factory for nearly three hours, talking about their time in college, the years between then and now, Jade's children, their jobs, where life had taken them, and where they hoped it would take them now. There were laughs, and there were tears.

Madison was an editor of fiction. The Man in the Mask had been the hidden, domineering antagonist for many chapters of her life. Her story had been a coming-of-age narrative. There was teen melodrama, there were laughs, and there were poignant moments. But then one fateful, snow-covered Halloween night, the genre of her life had transformed to horror. And it had stayed horror for years. But a new chapter was now upon her, and with it, the limitless possibilities a blank page offered. Her life would be a blend of genres—some romance, some comedy, and drama; there may even be more horror lurking behind a tree or in a dark alley. But the Man in the Mask had left her story for good. For a long time, he had been the story of her life. Dr. Frett had constantly stated, "You can't put the past behind you until you get out in front it." And for the first time, it truly felt like she had gotten out in front of it. As time goes by—months turning into years and, God willing, years into decades—the Man in the Mask would go from the entire story to an act to a chapter to a paragraph, and finally, to nothing but a singular sentence in a long-lived life.

Author Bio

The Final Edit is the third novel by author Bret Kissinger. His first two novels are also available on Amazon. He lives in Wisconsin.

Scan the QR Code to join our mailing list:

www.ingramcontent.com/pod-product-compliance
Lightning Source LLC
Chambersburg PA
CBHW051319250626
47155CB00007B/2386